Honor Edgeworth
Or, Ottawa's Present Tense

By

Vera

Double 9
BOOKS

Honor Edgeworth
Or, Ottawa's Present Tense
by Vera

ISBN: 978-93-62760-57-9

Published by

DOUBLE 9 BOOKS

2/13-B, Ansari Road
Daryaganj, New Delhi – 110002
info@double9books.com
www.double9books.com
Tel. 011-40042856

ABOUT THE AUTHOR

Vera, an accomplished author, is renowned for her masterpiece "Honor Edgeworth: Or, Ottawa's Present Tense," a captivating exploration of political intrigue and personal struggles set against the backdrop of Ottawa's tumultuous landscape. In this compelling narrative, Vera intricately weaves together the lives of diverse characters, each grappling with their own ambitions, loyalties, and desires. Through vivid prose and meticulous attention to detail, she paints a vivid portrait of Ottawa's political scene, exposing the complexities and contradictions inherent in the pursuit of power and honor. As the story unfolds, readers are drawn into a world of clandestine meetings, backroom deals, and moral dilemmas, where the line between right and wrong becomes increasingly blurred. Against this backdrop, Vera delves into themes of loyalty, betrayal, and the quest for redemption, offering readers a thought-provoking exploration of human nature and the pursuit of justice in the face of adversity. "Honor Edgeworth: Or, Ottawa's Present Tense" stands as a testament to Vera's skill as a storyteller and her ability to captivate audiences with her intricate plots and richly drawn characters.

CONTENTS

PREFACE.. 7

CHAPTER I 10

CHAPTER II... 23

CHAPTER III.. 30

CHAPTER IV 36

CHAPTER V... 46

CHAPTER VI 55

CHAPTER VII.. 59

CHAPTER VIII... 64

CHAPTER IX.. 69

CHAPTER X 74

CHAPTER XI.. 80

CHAPTER XII 90

CHAPTER XIII 96

CHAPTER XIV.. 104

CHAPTER XV 108

CHAPTER XVI.. 112

CHAPTER XVII 116

CHAPTER XVIII 124

CHAPTER XIX.. 133

CHAPTER XX 138

CHAPTER XXI.. 144

CHAPTER XXII... 153

CHAPTER XXIII 157

CHAPTER XXIV 162

CHAPTER XXV 168

CHAPTER XXVI 171

CHAPTER XXVII 178

CHAPTER XXVIII 186

CHAPTER XXIX 193

CHAPTER XXX 203

CHAPTER XXXI 212

CHAPTER XXXII 221

CHAPTER XXXIII 228

CHAPTER XXXIV 238

CHAPTER XXXV 249

CHAPTER XXXVI 254

CHAPTER XXXVII 267

CHAPTER XXXVIII 270

CHAPTER XXXIX 281

CHAPTER XL 292

PREFACE

In these days of plenty, when books of every subject and nature have become as commonly familiar to men as the blades of grass by the roadside, it seems superfluous to say any word of introduction or explanation on ushering a volume into the world of letters; but, lest the question arise as regards the direct intention or motive of an author, it is always safer that he make a plain statement of his object, in the preface page of his work, thus making sure that he will be rightly interpreted by his readers.

In the unpretending volume entitled "Honor Edgeworth," or "Ottawa's Present Tense," the writer has not proposed to make any display of the learning she has acquired by a few years' study, and she would therefore seek to remove, in anticipation, any impression the reader may be inclined to harbor, of her motives having been either selfish or uncharitable.

The world of art and science is already aglow with the dazzling beauty of the genius of her many patrons,—the world of letters has in our day a population as thick as the stars in the heavens, or the grains of sand on the beach—and hence it is that rivalry is almost a *passé* stimulant in this sphere; the heroes and heroines of the pen aim at individual, independent and not comparative, merit. In nine cases out of ten, the author of a work, apart from the gratification it gives himself to indulge his faculties, and whatever influence for better or worse his opinions may have, in the political social or religious world, knows no other aim.

In "Honor Edgeworth" the sole and sincere motive of the authoress has been to hold up to the mass the little picture of society, in one of its most marked phases, that she has sketched, as she watched its freaks and caprices from behind the scenes.

Ottawa, in this work, is taken merely as a representative of all other fashionable cities, for the simple reason that it is better known to the writer than any other city of social repute. Her object in publishing the volume at all, if not clearly defined throughout the work, may be discovered here: it is primarily, to attract the attention of those who, if they wished, could exercise a beneficial influence over the sphere in which they live, to the moral depravities that at present are allowed so passively to float on the surface of the social tide. It would with the same word appeal to the minds and hearts of those women who are satisfied to remain slaves to the exactions of an unscrupulous society, at the sacrifice of their most womanly impulses, and their noblest energies; and would also remind some reckless sons of Ottawa, of how miserably they are contributing towards the future prosperity of their country, by adopting, as the only aim of their lives, the paltry ambition of an unworthy self-indulgence.

The predominant feeling throughout the entire composition has been one of pure philanthropy, as the authoress desires to benefit her fellow-creatures, in as far as it lies in her very limited power. The book has not been composed with any other ambition than the one mentioned; it aspires to no position on the scroll as a literary work of merit; it is going forth clad in its humble garment of deficiencies and faults, to perform, if possible, the little mission appointed it. When it falls into the hands of an impartial reader, it asks only the reception and appreciation it merits, in proportion to that given by one another to society's patrons,—in other words, it would ask to be dealt with as generously as the world's sycophants deal with the faults and foibles of their fashionable friends.

Any imaginative person, choosing to use his pen, knows full well that the sensational department of letters, in our day, affords a freer and fuller scope than has ever been tolerated before; it is therefore left to the author's own choice to secure his favorites, numerously and easily, if he but pay attention to give his work the exact tinge of the *"couleur locale"* which predominates in the spot where his plot is laid; but because the eye of the critic has become familiar with such unworthy productions as these, it must scan with more eager justice any pages which are a happy exception to this miserable reality; it must not hesitate to discern whether the motive has been merely to arouse emotional tendencies, by clothing life's dangerous forms in unreal fascinations, or (where the author's hand, guided by his unsullied heart, has taken up the quill as a mighty weapon) to preserve or defend the morals of his country.

Let not the over-sinister reader censure the writer of "Honor Edgeworth" because she has appeared to him to subject to a merciless criticism, society in several of her moods; her object has not been to dwell upon the good points of her subject, for she knows too well that they will never be neglected; it is the drawbacks and the failings of the pampered goddess, Society, that need to be borne in mind and carefully dealt with, and unfortunately, in our day, her enamored victims voluntarily blindfold themselves to her evil influence, and extravagantly magnify the extent of her good.

Without another word of justification, therefore, does the authoress of this little work, send out her simple, humble donation towards the social refornation that is so sorely needed in our day.

Whether the seed be sown on fertile or on barren ground, time alone, the unraveler of all hidden truths, will tell; coming years will break the secret to the authoress as she would want to know it, in the meantime she makes her most respectful curtsey to the world of readers, wishing her humble effort a *bon voyage.*

CHAPTER I

"His life was gentle, and the elements
So mixed in him, that nature might stand up
And say to all the world, THIS WAS A MAN"
—Shakespeare.

It is night! Not the cold, wet, chilly night, that is settling down on the forlorn-looking city outside; not the cheerless night, that makes the news-boy gather his rags more closely about him, and stand under the projecting doorway of some dilapidated, tenantless building, as he cries "*Free Press,* only two cents:" not the awful night on which the gaunt haggard children, who thrive on starvation, crouch shiveringly around the last hissing fagot on the fire-place, with big, hungry eyes wandering over the low ceiling and the mouldy walls, or resting perchance on the wet, dirty panes, with their stuffings of tattered clothing, or gazing in a wilder longing still, on the bare shelves and the empty bread-box: Oh no! There are no such nights as these in reality; such a scene never existed out of the imaginations of men; there are no cries rending the very heavens this night for bread while handfuls are being flung to pet poodles or terriers. There are no benumbed limbs aching in the dingy corners of half-tumbled down houses, no wrinkled, aged jaws chattering, no infants moaning at their mother's breasts with cold, while many a pampered lady grows peevish and irritated, if Dobbs forgets the jars of warm water for the end of her cosy bed. Merciful God! and *this* is to live! But no! *this* is to dream!

I said it was night, so it was, but the heavy curtains were drawn, the gas was lighted, the grate-fire roared up the chimney, the lounge was supplied with its cushions, the *fauteuil* was drawn up to the fender-stool, the decanter and glass stood on the silver salver and in his velvet slippers and embroidered cap, Henry Rayne smoked the "pipe of peace" before his cheerful fire. As we intrude upon him in his sanctuary, he lays down his meerschaum, stretches his toasted limbs, and extending his hand touches the little silver bell on the table beside him; simultaneously, good old Mrs. Potts' slippers clap up the basement stairs, and her head popping in at the door, betrays her face full of broad smiles as she utters her well learned words of announcement.

"Is't annything ye'd be wantin sur?"

"Yes Potts," Rayne answers, still lying back among his crimson cushions, "Go and ask Fitts if he called for the mail at my office to-day. He knows what his duty is when I am not well enough to be stirring"

"Och, doan't fret Misther Rayne sur, shure he did bring the little bundles, ivery wan o' them, an' it's meself jest knows whare to lay the palm o' me hand on 'em this very minit 'idout troubln Mr. Fitts at all, at all," and away she darted again on a clatter down the inlaid passage to the letter box, and gathering up the contents, brought them back to her master's sitting-room. She was eyeing them closely as she laid them down beside him, exclaiming half audibly as she did so "Well now thin: that I may niver die iv it isn't jest the quarest thing in life!"

"What is that, Potts?" Henry Rayne asked good naturedly. "Well, yer honor," began his confiding old servant shyly, "I larned to do many's the nate job in me day, but if gettin' th' inside o' these in, 'ithout tearin' th' outsides don't bang all iver I larnt, my name's not Johanna Potts," and as she spoke she looked curiously at the bundle of letters before her. Potts' good sayings were never lost on her generous master, and this was no exception; he leaned back on his chair and fairly shook with laughter. "Why Potts:" he said at last, "You don't mean to say you never saw envelopes before they were sealed, do you?"

"Faith it's not the only thing I've lived to this 'ithout seein" Potts answered resignedly.

"Well, I must show you Potts," her master said kindly, and there and then he took the trouble to explain to good ignorant Mrs. Potts how "th' insides were got in 'ithout tearin' th' outsides," and greatly satisfied with her new information, she clattered off down stairs, shaking her head all the while, and repeating absently to herself "Well now, there's nothin' can bate 'em, nothin' at all, at all."

As soon as Henry Rayne was alone again, he poked the now smouldering fire into a bright blaze, drew his chair close to the table and began in a business-like way to break the seals of his letters and packages and as he sits in his cosy room, with the gas light falling on his pleasing face, we will take the liberty to sketch his form and features in their most natural state. They are those of a stout, well built, good humored sort of man, of about fifty, with just enough of the "silver threads" among his curly black locks to show that he had met with a little of the tear and wear of life—just a few lines of sadness on his clean shaved face, but for all that, looking the jolly, good sort of fellow that everyone acknowledged him to be, with a tender heart and a ready hand for the unfortunate, always honest and upright, yet thoroughly practical and business-like in all his undertakings. Henry

Rayne was descended from a good old English family, whose name he bore proudly and honorably, and many an interesting anecdote he was wont to tell at his dinner table of the "Stephens," "Edwards," and "Henrys," of the bygone generations of "Raynes."

With his private life was connected a sad little secret. He had been a young man in his day, and the charms of the weaker sex had not fallen vainly on his susceptible soul, oh dear no! Henry Rayne had loved once, earnestly and well, and had offered his proud name and comfortable fortune to the object of his devotion, but though he, to day, was the same hale hearty Henry Rayne of the past, the young bud he had cherished so fondly, lay withered in the churchyard far away in old England. Death had come between them, and in the grief that followed, Rayne outlived his susceptibilities, preferring to dwell fondly on the memory of the old tie, than to reopen his heart to any new appeal. But a day came when Henry Rayne had to incline his ear again to the winning voice of a woman, when his forced indifference had to give place to the old warmth and the old enthusiasm, when the withering heart revived and bloomed afresh under the tender influence of a woman's smile, a woman's care and a woman's sympathy. Of the causes of this happy revival we will have to deal in the course of our narrative. Let us return to the scene by the fireside where Henry Rayne sits opening his letters.

Three or four dry-as-dust laconic productions, of no earthly interest to anyone but the unromantic writers, one formal note soliciting a generous subscription to an hospital fund, two postal cards, one begging his patronage towards the tailoring department of an up-town dry goods store, and the other notifying him of a meeting of prominent citizens to be held in the City Hall, a couple of newspapers and legal documents, and there remained still two letters, less formidable looking, less business-like than the rest.

As he tore open one of these he chuckled a low laugh to himself, saying —

"It's Guy, the rascal, I suppose he has just been dunned for some little account that requires immediate payment, it must be some mercenary cloud that hangs over him." He was right, it was only another of these little periodicals that Guy Elersley was accustomed to "drop" his uncle, mainly to ask after his health and welfare, generally sliding in a P. S. which explained the last difficulty in his balance account with the tailor or boarding-house keeper; but Mr. Rayne made no objection, he never tired of indulging this handsome nephew of his, for besides being of an upright and affectionate disposition, his uncle loved him as the only child of a favorite deceased sister, since whose death, which happened when Guy was a mere child, Henry Rayne had been at once a kind, indulgent uncle and a just solicitous father to the boy.

But this particular letter which Mr. Rayne now glanced over, had another object besides the post-script and the uncle's health.

"I write so soon after my last," he says, "to tell you that I met a gentleman in the Windsor House the other night who interested me for a full hour in an account of an old friend of yours, this fellow's name is Orbury, it appears he was in Europe some years ago and was one of a company of card players one evening in a hotel at Dublin, when, out of a conversation of miscellaneous details, came a very jeering remark, made by some one present, relative to some rascally act under discussion. 'It is worthy' said the speaker 'of a man named Rayne, whom I blush to own was once a school-fellow of mine.'—But the words were scarcely uttered when some one beside the speaker brought the back of a sinewy hand a little forcibly across his face, telling him at the same time to measure the words he dealt out on an honorable man's name. Of course a scene ensued, everybody present was of respectable standing and the thing assumed a serious look. Not to interrupt the game, the two antagonists left the room to settle their difference elsewhere, and everyone wondered who the ardent defender of the man 'Rayne' could be.

"After a while the interesting unknown returned holding his handkerchief to a wound in his temple which bled profusely, and having apologized to those present for the interruption he had caused, he proceeded to inform them that Henry Rayne stood in such a relation with him, as justified him in silencing any man who took his name in jest; the little wound he had just received, he thought was well earned, when he knew he had the satisfaction of horse-whipping the meanest man in creation, 'for any other offence, gentlemen' said the stranger 'I could not lay hands on him, for "he that toucheth pitch shall be defiled" but to pronounce my friend's name in a slanderous lie, I could not endure. Perhaps,' he continued, 'it is like kicking a man when he's down, to tell you now, gentlemen, that the fellow who had just maligned an honest man was once thrashed within an inch of his life by this same Henry Rayne at college, for a cowardly, disrespectful deed of his towards some lady friends of ours. The hatred born of the moment that he lay in the dust of the college yard, with the finger of scorn raised at him from every hand, has never flickered in its steadiness. As you see, he thought to gratify himself somewhat by abusing this gentleman when he saw no friend of the absent one near, but he will likely look the next time before he speaks, and now,' said he, taking his hat, 'once more I apologize and express my regret at having been forced to disturb you, but I feel that you will easily forgive me under the circumstances,' and dear uncle, what do you think, but every man there shook him by the hand and stroked him on the shoulder, speaking his praises loudly and all they knew of the chivalrous stranger was that he was a transient guest at the house, who was passing through Dublin on his way farther south, and that his name was 'Edgeworth.' So is this not an exciting piece of news, dear uncle; think while you are living placidly in America, your wrongs are being enthusiastically righted in the old world."

Henry Rayne laid down the letter and looked steadily into the fire. What a torrent memory had let loose upon him! he lived the old years all over again, he saw the dear familiar scenes buried in the half-burned coals, the smiling associations of the past. "Poor Bob" he said, "and I have never seen him once in all these years, to think he should have stood by me now as he did that day at college when I punished that rascal Tremaine. How I wish I could find him out! good honest friend that he is, can I ever repay him, I wonder, for this noble action done me?" Here Rayne lost himself in a long reverie, he went over the days of his boyhood again, and as he thought, a smile half sad stole over his face, and in the end a tear was actually glistening in each eye. It was the old old story over again, memory weeping over dead joys, experience sighing for the happy long ago. The same influence was upon him now as guided the pen of Blair when it wrote "How painful the remembrance of joys departed never to return," and as inspired Byron when he sighed "Ah, happy years! once more who would not be a boy?"

We may wonder how long Henry Rayne would have sat motionless in his chair by the fireside, with his inclined head resting on his hand, while he brooded over the years of his life and clasped anew in their old warmth, hands that had long grown cold, either in the gloominess of death, or for need of the responsive touch, from those that were extended to them in far-off climes; but as the clock struck eleven Fitts appeared in the doorway, breaking the spell by asking his master if he "need replenish the grate before retiring?" "Yes—No," replied Mr. Rayne, "you may go Fitts, I want nothing else to-night."

Drawing a long sigh, he gathered up the scattered letters and was about to consign them to the flames but in turning to do so, he knocked his arm violently against the back of his chair, dropping them all again at his feet. Stooping to gather them, he noticed for the first time the heavy letter with the foreign post-marks and large legible hand-writing which, had it not been for this timely accident, would have been thrust unconsciously into the fire, thus forcing our narrative to close here, but instead he raised it hurriedly, throwing the rest back on the floor, and scrutinized it with a searching, confused look, but the more he saw it the more it puzzled him, he was evidently in the dark: finally he tore it open and readjusting his gold spectacles, straightened out its creases and began to read.

It was a very long time afterwards, when the paper dropped from the cold, trembling hands of Henry Rayne; a sort of stupor had been creeping slowly over him while he read; now he had finished the last word but he did not move, the coals had fallen to ashes, the wind had risen and howled around the house, the room had grown chilly and damp, the rain lashed in huge drops against the panes, but Henry Rayne saw not, felt not, heeded not, he was far far away by the side of an esteemed friend, he was swearing a vow of eternal friendship, and was accepting gladly, gratefully from his hands a precious charge, a weighty responsibility— how could he hesitate? he was pouring out all the consolation and sympathy of his ardent soul to the man he had loved as a boy, and he never felt the chill that was stiffening all his joints, he never heeded the ceaseless patter of the dreary rain. The clock had stopped and the fire had gone out, and still he sat crouched in his chair, with the strange letter lying listlessly between his fingers.

What a queer phase of life was dawning upon him! what a strange mission was coming to him from over the seas! what freak had destiny taken to send him his nephew's letter with its interesting detail, and this other one, on the same night! Guy's letter brought back an old friend in the freshness and vigor of his youth, with hand uplifted to defend *him*, this other one revealed the same dear friend, but worn and wasted from premature age, with the daring hand laid quietly on his breast, sleeping the last long sleep—yes; this puzzling letter had been traced by the feeble hand of Robert Edgeworth and had been forwarded to Henry Rayne at his death. It contained an anxious, serious request. It asked of Henry Rayne to open his heart and home, to the only child of an old friend, to father an orphan girl for the sake of "old times," and the happy "long ago." It would not have meant much for some others, but it seemed the greatest of all responsibilities to Henry Rayne, who had become an utter stranger to the female sex, and who had settled down in an old bachelor's home for the rest of his life. He tried to think it all out, but the fragile form of a young, beautiful girl, glided between him and his thought, and he saw upon her face the sweet, sad smile, of a parentless child pleading for protection. He was lost—he was dreaming; he never stirred for hours, until the dawn streaked in between the drawn curtains, giving the room an unnatural look, with its glare of gas-light and the straggling rays of the misty morning's sun crossing one another, until "Potts" stole down with her slippers under her arm, and in her bewilderment at the sight of the gas-light, put her head in at the door.

When she saw her master's firm, set face and vacant eyes, and the letters laying around the floor, her heart gave a bound, and she screamed outright.

Henry Rayne raised his head, rubbed his eyes, and tried to stretch his limbs, now numb with the damp dullness of the night. Potts had run to him and was asking the "matter," with dilated eyes and anxious voice.

"Don't be afraid, Potts," he said at last, "I have been reading a very very strange letter, and I forgot the hours, I will go and lie down now; don't make any fuss about it, and I'll tell you the important news after breakfast."

Poor Potts went off to the kitchen shaking her head as usual, and murmuring to herself all the while, such exclamations as "Well, well now." "That's quare now." "Well to be sure." It was with her brain quite in a whirl that she went about her morning duties, wondering very much what could have come over her master, to make him forget to go to bed. When Fitts came in at the back door, with an armful of wood, Mrs. Potts could not conceal her gratification at having been the first to discover the secret, and she rattled on (to herself, as it were) with her back turned to Fitts, "Well shure 'tis the quarest thing in life—all through the night, too; dear, oh dear! Such a life's enough to turn one gray in no time."

"What have you there all to yourself now, dear Mrs. Potts," came from Fitts as he flung the wood into the box, "come now, I heard you, what's throublin', what's inside your purty border this time, your mind I mane?"

"Be off with you now mister Fitts; 'tis other people's minds that's bothered, an' I'm only sorry for it: but y'ell know soon enough; the master 'ill tell ye when he sees fit, and ye can be preparin' for it till then."

"Well now, that's funny," says he. "How did *you* come to know anything since last night?" and there was a suspicion of jealousy in his voice, "I left the master meself the last thing, last night, an' he's not up this mornin' yet, so what are ye dhrivin' at?"

"I know what I know," said the irritating Potts, "and I'm sorry I can't tell ye but its a saycret yet awhile; be patient."

"Who wants to know it anyway?" said Fitts, who was quite vexed now, "I'm sure *I* don't," and he went out with a slight intimation that he had securely closed the door behind him.

At nine o'clock Henry Rayne came downstairs, looking tired and pale, and instead of his usual hearty breakfast, he merely drank a cup of warm coffee. He had just finished this, and was balancing his spoon on the edge of his cup, as he cogitated upon the strange mission that had been thrust upon him, when Potts came in to serve his "second cup," but instead of this, he bade her summons Fitts, that he had something to tell them both. When a few moments later Henry Rayne turned to confront his servants, who stood expectant before him, his troubled face and serious air made them start perceptibly; in an earnest tone he said,

"I have received an important letter from a friend of mine, who has died since the writing thereof; he has entrusted me with the care of his only child, and to comply with his dying request I must make immediate preparations to leave home, for I have a long way to travel before I can accomplish his desire; I therefore want you to understand that I may be a very long or a very short while away from home, but I wish you both to serve me as faithfully on this occasion as you have on all others. Don't talk about my absence more than you can help; I can give all the necessary explanation on my return." "Potts," he said, addressing the solemn looking old woman separately, "you must renovate the house a little, I think; those spare bedrooms must be well aired and touched up somewhat, for we will need them henceforth. My little charge happens to be a girl, and unless you can contribute towards making things to her liking, I am lost. Spare no expense to make the house comfortable in every respect, for the *protégée* of mine is a lady, I know. And you, Fitts," he continued, turning to the dignified male servant, "will, I am sure, lend a hand towards the general improvement. See that the phaeton and sleighs be in good order, and, in fact, I think you will each do your duties well, without my enumerating them. You know I have full confidence in both of you, and I think you will not abuse of it." The two devoted attendants answered sincerely, each with a suspicion of moisture in their eyes that answered Mr. Rayne more than anything else.

On the following afternoon Mr. Rayne left Ottawa, on his extended trip, much to the surprise of his friends, and according to promise, his servants displayed the greatest discretion possible. Within the week, Mr. Fitts was delighted to receive news from his master, informing him that in a few days he would sail for Liverpool.

The voyage across the majestic ocean, was a fair and enjoyable one, and Mr. Rayne spent the days out on the deck of the splendid "Parisian," smoking and thinking, and wondering at the unusual turn things had taken for him, since last he crossed that same Atlantic. He was anxious to know how it would all end, and whether he would be able for this new responsibility brought to him so suddenly. Heaven had not willed him the experience of a wedded life, and so he resolved to devote himself to this little charge as though she were his own flesh and blood; he would teach her to give him a father's love, and if he could help it, she would never know the want of a father's care.

The first duty of Henry Rayne, on landing at Liverpool, was to consult the letter of his deceased friend, and write to the address given therein, to inform the parties alluded to, of his arrival. Special mention was made of one, "Anne Palmer," who was spoken of highly, as a faithful and trustworthy woman, who had nursed the child from her infancy. This gratified Henry Rayne immensely, for he resolved, at any cost, to secure her, knowing how necessary her long and untiring attendance must have made her to the girl's existence.

A reply to his kind letter reached Henry Rayne some days before he had expected it, informing him that Honor Edgeworth and her maid had left on the day following the receipt of his letter, and would shortly join him at Liverpool. Such indeed was the case, for even as Henry Rayne read the words over to himself, as fast as steam and water could carry her, Honor Edgeworth was travelling away from her native home. She saw not, heeded not, the passengers, the scenery, the bustle, and confusion that surrounded her; she only leant her head on the shoulder of her old nurse, and wept silent, bitter tears all the while. Poor Nanette strove hard to console her in her woe, but the swelling never left the pretty eyes, and the sighs never ceased escaping from the dainty lips during the whole voyage.

"It is such a queer destiny, Nanette," she said repeatedly, "this man may hate me. He was only a boy when papa knew him; perhaps he has grown up a wicked man that will detest me, you know Nanette, people change a great deal sometimes."

"Don't fret, my beauty," was all the disconsolate woman could say. "You may be sure your father did not act in the dark, where his little girl was concerned. He had great trouble in finding the gentleman's address at all, so you may be sure he looked for other information at the same time."

"Yes, I suppose he did," Honor sighed, half resignedly. "What the end will be, time will tell."

From London they telegraphed to Mr. Rayne, telling him of their safe arrival thus far, and seized with an insuperable impatience to become known to his little *protégée*, he answered them immediately, that he would meet them in Manchester. The night was wet and dark and cheerless, as Nanette and her pretty charge rolled into this large manufacturing city of England. All the other passengers had hurried out, they alone remained, careless whether they went or stayed, sadly and listlessly, they proceeded to gather up their little belongings, dashing away as they did so, scalding tears that welled into their eyes.

"Are you ready, love?" Nanette asked plaintively, turning towards Honor.

"Yes I am," the girl answered with a sigh, "ready for the battle of life — come along, Nanette."

Just as she uttered the words, and before she had stepped from the railway carriage, the guard, accompanied by a gentleman, thrust his head in, and hurriedly announcing "Mr. Rayne, ladies," darted off again, leaving them together. The long looked for moment had arrived: the first meeting, upon which so many thoughts were spent by all three, was already over. Honor Edgeworth raised her eyes to the gentleman announced, and a smile of infinite relief broke over her face; Mr Rayne raised his hat to the younger lady, and a mysterious smile of infinite admiration stole over his face. He broke the silence by addressing Nanette.

"I presume, madam," he began, "you are the person in charge of Miss Edgeworth, the young lady recommended to my future care?" and before she had time to answer, he had extended both hands to Honor.

"Yes, sir," said Nanette, a little nervously, "I give into your hands all that I hold dearest in life;" and then, lowering her voice, she continued, almost to herself, "I can go back again to my poor old home, but the sunshine is gone out of it forever."

Henry Rayne looked quickly up at her: he was assisting Honor out, as she spoke.

"Is it possible that you are not coming to Canada with us?"' he asked in a confounded tone.

"Ah, sir!" answered the poor creature, "I will go in heart, indeed, but there was no provision made to send me all the way with the child."

"Oh this can never be," Henry Rayne interrupted, hurriedly, "I have intended from the first, that you should not be left. Come, come, we will manage everything smoothly by and by. Do not leave one another now, unnecessarily, when you have been together all your lives." There was a shout of delight from both, and clasped in each other's arms, never to part again, they thanked God sincerely for His goodness to them, so far.

"The dear child, sir, I'd have died without her." Nanette sobbed through the tears of joy.

"Of course you would," Henry Rayne answered, handing them into the carriage that awaited them. He cast an admiring glance on "the child" in question, as he sat himself opposite to her on the leather buttoned seat of the hack. If "child" she must be, she would undoubtedly prove an interesting one, for she was now, to all appearances, in her seventeenth year, and showed promises of future development into a splendid woman. For the first few moments Nanette never ceased her protestations of gratitude, and when at last she finished them in a great sob behind her handkerchief, Honor looked sweetly up in Mr. Rayne's face and said.

"Your first act, dear guardian, was one of unsolicited kindness. What will after years bring, when we have learned to respect and love you, and do you good turns as well? The future seems so bright, now that Nanette is coming, for," she explained "you must know, Mr. Rayne, she is the only mother I have ever known, and when dear papa lived he treated Nanette just as he would a member of his own family."

"And I will never be the one to make the first difference," answered Mr. Rayne. "My house is large; I am a crusty old bachelor, with no other tie binding me to the world, except this new link that has just filled me with a desire to live anew from this out. All I have is at your disposal: you must make yourself perfectly at home with me. I don't know much about winning the confidence and hearts of young girls now, but I shall expect you to come to me with yours, because henceforth you are going to be all my own."

"I do not wish to dispute it, Mr. Rayne," Honor answered sweetly, "but I have a presentiment that you are going to spoil me."

"Oh I won't be *very* cross with you, unless you steal my spectacles or court my footman, or do anything like that," Henry Rayne answered playfully.

Thus, in the pleasantest manner possible, were the first hours of their *rencontre* spent. When their drive ended, they alighted before a handsome hotel, ablaze with light, where a tempting supper awaited them. Henry Rayne, fancying that it was the right thing to do to young girls who had been travelling a great deal, told Honor she must retire immediately. "We have our lives long to chat," he said, "so rest yourselves well to night"

When they had reached their rooms, Honor turned with a bright smile on her face, and said to Nanette,

"Don't you think he will be just lovely and kind, dear Nanette? He is a perfect gentleman."

"God bless him," answered Nanette, "he is a good man and has a good heart, and we must never have him regret what he has done for us."

"Well, it is a great weight off my mind anyhow," said Honor, with a sigh of relief, "I am full of hopes now for the future, and I know we cannot help loving dear kind Mr. Rayne;" and over such enthusiastic words Honor and Nanette fell into their deep calm sleep.

All this time Henry Rayne was smoking quietly in the parlor below, and thinking of the lovely face that was going to shed its radiance henceforth on his silent home. Already he longed for the morning to come, that he might look on it again. In the course of his meditation, a thought came to him, which had not suggested itself before, and it was this:

"If the world should choose to attach its own interpretation to this new relationship, if a word was cast afloat which could scatter the germs of a suspicion, what then? If those venomous tongues that keep the world buzzing with scandal chose to attack *her*, how was he to prevent it?" A cloud overshadowed his face, there was a momentary pang in his heart, but he consoled himself that he had thought of it in time—he would defy the world, his manner towards her would dare gossiping tongues, he was nearly three times her age now, and had his life not been such as could defy the babbling of the whole world?

But it was only the old tale, a woman's name is a tempting bit to society, in one of its particular phases, though, of course, even society in this, its calumniated epoch yet retains its discrimination, its rules are not so arbitrary as its enemies declare them, and its heart is *at times* susceptible to the pleadings of misfortune for mercy. Woman, alas! has her fallen sister on every rung of the social ladder, though from general appearances one would be led to judge, that wealth and position and fame, claim virtue as all their own, it seems, that vice and error thrive only where poverty and ignorance and destitution abide, is this so? Ye who know the secrets of a fashionable world, ye, who have seen laid bare, the hearts full of secrets of pampered ladies, and pretentious dames, say, are they so guileless, so spotless, so blameless as society would have them? Is it only the poor seamstress, or the working-girl that is human enough to err? Is it only the breast which heaves under tatters and rags, that bears the impress of the trembling hand that has struck the *"mea culpa"* in its woe? O, I doubt it, I for one deny it. True it is, painfully, shamefully true it is, that the "nobodies" of the world who meet misfortune are mercilessly forced to stand in the corridors of time, that those, who domineer in virtue, may ostentatiously compassionate them, but will such a paltry show of charity as this, blind the world, as it tries to do? Let us hope not. Let the pampered daughter of wealth and social fame, who goes astray, share the pitiless fate of the beggar who does likewise, or, better still, let the beggar be shown such mercy, and justification and pardon as is granted her sister in high life. In the sight of God crime is the one color, why not so with men? If anything, vice repels far more forcibly, when attired in its velvets and silks, than when it looks out from scanty rags, which after all, may be turned more easily to sack cloth. Who can doubt that there are hundreds of outcasts, living in persistent wrong doing, on account of this lack of humanity, this total abstinence of Christian charity, whose exercise could redeem just as many as its scarcity ruins. Poor foolish souls! Why need they thirst for mercy or sympathy that is human, know they not, that they are as justified in spurning the world's great ones, as those great ones are in spurning them. What can human mercy avail them, after all, is there not a Good Shepherd, so eager, so ready, so anxious to grant forgiveness for the asking? Why do ye not seek Him, ye whom a rigorous society has cast out of its pale? be not content to live on as drudges and slaves to such a heartless world when there is a harvest for you to gather so near, and you have only to learn the words of Him who spoke truth and wisdom themselves to encourage you onward, that "there is more joy in heaven over the conversion of one sinner than at the perseverance of *ninety-nine just.*"

CHAPTER II

"Ah poor child, with heart of woman
  Solitary, quiet, grave;
  Strong of will and firm of purpose
  Self absorbed in silence brave"

A page or two, of the record of time, turned over unnoticed, will not be missed out of the careers of our characters, it will include the days that have elapsed since that night that Honor Edgeworth lay wide awake on her pillow, playing with the shadowy visions of a possible future, as they danced around her bed, since that night in Manchester, when Nanette slept so contentedly and Henry Rayne smoked in moody silence by the fire-place in the hotel parlor. When we become interested again, it is a clear, bright day, blue and white threads of filmy loveliness flit along the sky, a soft, gentle breeze is blowing, and over the restless waves of the broad Atlantic the "Parisian" is skipping gracefully. She is nearing the port, and many are the anxious, weary faces that turn landward with a sigh upon their lips.

Among the others that are gathered here and there on her broad decks, on this lovely glorious afternoon, we are compelled to notice the graceful, slender form, of a young girl, who sits a little away from the others, with her head leaning on her folded hands, and her sad eyes resting on the troubled waters in a fixed, but vacant stare, she is thinking, it is evident, and thinking deeply, there is not a muscle moving in her handsome face, her lips are set, her chin is slightly raised, the loose locks are blowing with the wind now and then from off her brow, but her eyes ever seek the deepest depth of the green blue sea. She might be a perfect statue, only for the gentle heaving of her breast, that rises and falls in little sighs.

Every one has noticed her, but none would intrude upon her in this reverie, that seems to be her normal state, her face has assumed that expression of intense emotion that could fascinate the most unwilling victim, and indeed they are very few who are not willing to pay a tribute at that shrine, while she in her unconsciousness, is living the long sunny hours, down in the bottomless sea, trying to penetrate it with the eyes of her soul, trying to fathom the fathomless, to understand the mysterious, and to shape into existence the uncreated, these are the strange things that rivet the gaze of Honor Edgeworth on the spray of the billows below. At last she starts up, as if in broken slumber, and turns suddenly 'round.

Two heavy hands have been laid on her slender shoulders, two eyes full of glowing admiration are turned upon her, and Henry Rayne, in a low, loving voice says in her ear:

"Come back to the deck of the 'Parisian' Honor for a little while, you have been down with the 'whales and little fishes' long enough now."

Her eyes filled with tenderness as she looked up to the good face bending over her.

"Oh Mr. Rayne, is it you?" she said "I was wondering where you were, is Nanette sleeping yet?"

"Yes, my dear," he answered, drawing a seat near hers, "and I've been amused by the little window there for fifteen minutes, wondering what there was existing capable of making any one strike such a thoughtful attitude as yours."

"Why, Mr. Rayne, all I could condense into my poor little brain at once, is not worth attracting your grand attention. But, I love to think: I have so many little ethereal friends that flock around me when I sit down to think, they are all my ideals, you know." She continued, clasping her hands enthusiastically, "In that little world of thought, where I drift so often in the day, there is none of that coldness nor selfishness that characterizes your material world. We are all equal, and we love one another so much! I don't know when it fascinated me first, but it seems so natural to me now to steal away there from the din of active life. But how is it *you* always catch me just when I've forgotten that there is any reality at all?"

"Because, I suppose," laughed Mr. Rayne "you are always in that state of blissful forgetfulness, and if you don't mind yourself you'll fall into a chronic state of dreaming, and then be no more to us than a veritable somnambulist, now, you wouldn't like that, would you?"

"Oh, there is no fear of that, I am not spiritual enough yet to abandon stern reality altogether, but I fancy you will often tire of me before you grow quite accustomed to my strange caprices?"

"Why my dear little Honor, is that the color you would have me paint your future? surely not. If Destiny has raised my hand to blend the colors in the fair scenery of your life, I will stain the canvas a '*couleur de rose,*' and make it a lovely thing to contemplate, if I possibly can, so do not ever sigh to-day for to-morrow, know beforehand that it will be just as you will have it."

"Ah, ha! Mr. Rayne, who is waxing romantic now," the girl cried playfully, "I'm so glad to have caught you once. But do you know, I sometimes wonder, if all these days have not really been spent in my fairy land, for things have happened as harmoniously as though life were not a series of discords at its best, Nanette was not forced to leave me, and you did not get bored at my eccentricities, and I liked you so much right away, and our safe journey, and everything together."

"Well, I hope it will convince you my child," said Rayne earnestly, "that life in its common-place acceptation is not so dreadful as you have pronounced it—wait a while—a little practical experience will serve to persuade you, that there are a few redeeming traits in the big, nasty world after all, and will force you to give up these wild theories of idealism that are strangely out of place in a young girl of our period."

"So many tell me that," said Honor distractedly, "but I can't know of course, just yet, what difference all the complicated circumstances that wind themselves around other girl's lives, will make in mine, if they change me at all, they must make an entirely different person of me, and if they are baffled, I will only be stronger and more obstinate than ever in my own views. Either of these must be my destiny, as yet I know no partiality towards either one, but I think it is because I feel so safe in myself that I defy other influences to do their worst."

"Well, dear," said Mr. Rayne, rising, "You won't blame me for the consequences, when you really want my opinion I'll give it to you, I'll try to show you fairly and honestly both sides of the picture of life, I would like to see you stand by its colossal works of art, you may perhaps care to imitate the artists. All that is great and good within my reach, you will see, and yet, I think it wise that you should turn from the luxury of wealth and self-indulgence now and then, to look unshrinkingly upon the squalid misery and wantonness that haunt the greater half of the world. But, come, we will go inside, the air is somewhat chilly, and if Nanette intends to wake at all, she must be looking for us now."

Leaning on the arm of her guardian, Honor slowly walked towards the door of the entrance, followed by many an admiring glance from the other passengers. They found Nanette rubbing her tell-tale eyes, and avowing that she had not "slept a wink" all day.

Under the roof of Henry Rayne's comfortable house everything has undergone a change, there is a primness and a fitness about the rooms that used not to be there, a cosy look peeps out from every turn and corner of the well-furnished apartments. The pantry shelves are whole rows of temptations. Very tame lions looking meekly out with their "jelly" eyes, and rare birds perched in trembling dignity on some pudding that has come "beautifully" out of the mould. In fact it seems that good Mrs. Potts has converted her whole "receipt book" into shelves of substantial and dainty representatives, but such fruitful contemplations as these will surely rouse one to action, and appropriate "action" in a well-filled pantry forebodes merciless slaughter for these culinary imitations of animal life.

Upstairs appeals less dangerously to the material element. It is neat and enticing everywhere. There is the sitting room where Mr. Rayne spent his long, thoughtful night under the gaslight with Robert Edgeworth's letter lying between his numbed fingers. The fire burns there cheerfully now — there is no other light than that cast by the fitful flames which leap and dwindle in shadows through the twilight that lingers still, huge fanciful phantoms skipping over the walls and the ceiling and floor, a little flickering subdued light that trembles on the great arm chairs. "Flo" is curled up, with both ends saluting one another, on the velvet rug before the fender, and at a civil distance away is a purring bundle of gray and white pussy, with her paws doubled in and her eyes blinking at the half-burned coals. There is a bird cage in each window, and an odd little lullaby chirp or the grating of the little iron swings is the only sound besides the loosening and falling of the embers every now and then.

Opposite to this is the large drawing room with its deep bay window, its rich carpet and massive furnishings. Not the stiff formal looking parlor of a lone bachelor, but the comfortable, tastily arranged room of a man who had confided such things to the better judgment and defter hands of a woman. There are fine statues and splendid paintings, and *bric-a-brac* enough to deceive anyone into believing it to be the home of a bevy of girls. There is a grand piano in the end of the room, and a violin in its case in the corner — this latter had been the faithful companion of Henry Rayne through many years of his life, and held as conspicuous a place in his drawing room as it did in his esteem. Upstairs again, we find the strangest little room of all. A girl's bedroom, richly, handsomely furnished, a heavy carpet of dark colored pattern covers the floor, a massive walnut set is also there, a cosy lounge is crossways in the corner, near the bay window, which is a perfect little conservatory of blooming flowers. A handsome pair of brackets adorn the tinted walls, holding on one side a fine statue of the "Blessed Virgin and Child," and on the other that of a "Guardian Angel." Hanging opposite the bed is an oil painting of "Mater Dolorosa," besides sundry little chromos and photographs that destroy the monotony of bare walls. There is nothing left to wish for—beauty, utility, grandeur have been harmoniously blended here, and this is the nook that Henry Rayne offers Honor Edgeworth, one worthy of a princess, indeed. Mrs. Potts had promised herself that nothing should be left undone on the arrival of the travellers, and very well she kept her word too. When the violent ring of the bell that announced their coming echoed through the house, Mrs. Potts had only to roll down the sleeves of her best wincey and button them at her wrists. The clattering slippers had been superannuated, and a neat pair of prunella gaiters showed their patent toes from under the hem of her cleanest gown. A broad grin of unmistakeable joy lights up the old creature's face as she hastens to welcome her master, and this changes to a solemn look of profound admiration as Henry Rayne presents her to Honor Edgeworth, and asks her to show the young lady to her room.

"You must make yourself at home, Honor, for the present, with things as they are. After a while we can make things more comfortable, may be, but this is my little home as it was intended for the last days of an old bachelor, to be spent all by himself," and as he spoke, Henry laughed out right, and beckoned her to follow Mrs. Potts.

When Honor stood upon the rich red rug at the threshold of her door, she uttered a low exclamation of wonder.

"This can't be for me, Mrs. Potts" she said, folding her hands and looking in dismay around her.

"Indeed it is, miss, and not a bit too good is it aither, for yer jewel ov a face to smile on. Och, shure it'll be doin' me old eyes good from this out to be lookin' at yer purty face. But come now, miss, you must be bate out entirely wid the joultin 'o the cars. Let me onfasten them things for ye."

Mrs. Potts was quite at home with the "dear young lady" all at once. As she helped to undo the girl's wrappings she grew less shy and reserved, and prattled on, "Shure it'll be the life o' the master altogether, to have ye around the big house that was allays so lonesome like for the wont ov a lady like yerself is, to cheer it up."

"I hope I may do that," said Honor earnestly, "for Mr. Rayne deserves all the comfort it is in our power to give him."

"Oh, troth! yer right there, missy, an' its only half what he desarves the whole of us together could give him, but shure, if we give him all we're able, an' our good intinshions along wid that, he won't be the man to grumble at that same."

Honor began to understand the character of this old servant immediately. She recognized all those traits that invariably betray the Irish nationality. Such whole-souled creatures are of too universal a type ever to be mistaken.

"Well, then, ye'r ready now, miss, are you?" Mrs. Potts queried when all was over. "Well, if ye like, ye can go an' wait for the ould lady, for she's not fixed up yet, an' I'll jist run and throw an eye over the table, ye know, I'm Jack of all thrades for a while."

"Go, my good woman, by all means," Honor answered, "we will be down directly; don't wait for us."

Potts, who rather suspected an odor of over-done victuals, bounded down to the kitchen, leaving Honor in Nanette's care. Nanette's room was next to Honor's, and had been used as a sort of spare room up to the present time. It was now intensely comfortable and neat, without anything costly or expensive which could make poor Nanette feel out of her element.

"Is Mr. Rayne not the very impersonation of goodness itself, Nanny dear?" said Honor. She was standing with her back to the door, watching her old nurse undoing their valises, when she uttered this exclamation.

"Come now, Honor, spare a fellow when he's right behind you," said the good-natured voice of the person thus eulogized. Honor started around, looking very pretty in her confusion.

"I thought 'listeners never heard well of themselves,'" said she in a pout, "but this time it seems to be reversed."

"And you won't take it back for all that," said he, "the oldest of us likes a little praise now and then, you may as well let me keep it."

"Oh yes indeed, Mr. Rayne, you may have that little bit, for you know how good you are and how kind to me."

"Well, that will do after tea, but just now we will give our attention to something more substantial; come Honor—come Nanette."

"Don't wait for me sir," the old nurse answered respectfully, "I'll find Mrs. Potts in the kitchen and we'll sip our tea together there."

Henry Rayne looked quickly at Honor and detected the slightest shadow of a disappointment flitting across her face, this decided him.

"It is my intention that you and Potts will not be quite such good friends," he said, "I am sure that Honor would rather you made the tea at our table."

"Don't appeal to me," Honor answered as she met his enquiring glance, "it is superfluous, you always anticipate my wishes. I've never drunk another cup but the tea Nanette made."

"Nor shall you, so long as we are spared a happy trinity," cried Henry Rayne, "so let's be off, I cry—to tea—to tea—to tea."

CHAPTER III

The Autumn clouds are flying,
Homeless over me,
The homeless birds are crying,
In the naked tree.
—*George Macdonald*

It was a very pleasant, little *tableau* that followed, those three happy souls, gathered around a well-spread table laughing and chatting merrily. Honor no longer felt any timidity or reserve before Mr. Rayne, his advanced years commanded a confidence and trust that she would have otherwise perhaps been slow to give, and the unlimited generosity he betrayed in even anticipating her every wish, gave her no opportunity to feel that she was under the patronage of a perfect stranger. He had shown himself as a kind, indulgent father from the first, and was as solicitous about her as though she had been his very own, or that he had been accustomed to administer to the wants and wishes of a young unripened girl all his life. But this is no mystery to the interpreter of the human heart. Henry Rayne could hardly act otherwise to any lone helpless creature without sacrificing the impulses of his own generous, noble soul, and trampling upon the desire that continually influenced him towards being the direct cause of happiness and comfort to others. Taking away any supernatural motive that might lead him to such generous action, yet leaves the deed a worthy one, and the heart a Christian one, for, to gratify others was to gratify himself, and this alone is characteristic of a great soul. As the orphan child of a friend of his youth, I doubt not that Henry Rayne would protect her at his life's peril. We all know what a firm knot it is that binds the sympathetic souls of rollicking college "chums" which, tied once, is tied forever. It has always been so; it is one of those strictly conservative principles that grows with mankind in every generation, and is yet never found extravagant, if not because of the noble character of the sentiment itself, at least because our forefathers never condemned it, and the world generally continues to favor such an alliance. Such was the nature of the staunch friendship that existed between Henry Rayne and Bob Edgeworth, a friendship that had only strengthened itself by pledges and vows, as the youths shook hands in a fond farewell over the threshold of their college home.

From the day on which Honor Edgeworth settled in her new home, life began to assume its most indulgent phase. Everything around her met her eye for the first time, no sorrowful associations hung in misty veils over anything that entered into the charms of her new life. Nanette was the only breathing, living testimony of the years that had gone, and the home of her childhood that she had left forever. A few old books of literature and of music, a few little trifling souvenirs from her dead mother's jewel box, an inlaid mahogany writing-desk and a miniature likeness of her proud handsome father, were all the visible reminders she now held of the fair, sunny home, under the far foreign skies.

Mr Rayne resumed his duties immediately on his return, and lost no time in propagating among his most intimate and influential friends, the story of the odd legacy left him by a "distant relation." At first Mr. Rayne feared greatly that Honor would find the days long and tedious, while he was absent and unable to ferret out distraction for her, but he grew resigned very soon when she assured him how much more to her taste it was to have the quiet hours of the day to herself, and "in fact," she said, "as the occasion presented itself, she would beg of Mr. Rayne not to expect her to share in any amusement, at least for some time, for besides the mourning she wore for her father, her knowledge of the country and its customs was not yet sufficient to satisfy her with herself," and putting it to him as a request, she knew it would be acceded to on the spot.

The light of the summer days had begun to wane. The leaves had begun to turn. Out door pleasures were being forsaken for the seat by the fireside The world looked as if 'twere waiting. The autumn months had a particular effect on Honor Edgeworth, she would stand at the window, and look sadly through the panes at the red and yellow leaves falling softly, noiselessly down to the cold wet ground, and a shiver would pass through her as she realized even in this the mortality that hangs like an unseen pall over all things below. Just a moment ago, a pretty golden leaf danced on the bough, but the cold wind, surrounding it, bore it away on its fated pinions down into the cold stiff gutter, where it was either trampled heedlessly down by the reckless passer-by, or wafted farther away out of sight, left to wither and die by the roadside. But, perhaps not, either, maybe the slender, delicate hand of an admirer of nature stooped to gather the fallen leaf, to wipe the dust from its golden front, and lay it tenderly by as a souvenir of the dead year, to lie among the gathered blossoms of some dear one's grave, with bitter tears of sad remembrance and grief to bathe it, as its evening dew. And is not this life! How many golden leaves are hurled into the mire of sin, and upon how much marvellous beauty the heavy foot of worldly scorn is stamped forever! How many pretty little amber leaves drift on through the cold wide world, until their beauty is spent, and until wrecked and faded they lay themselves down by the withered blades to die. But oh! there are again those stainless leaves that glide into the fingers of the Great Gatherer of Beauty, to find in His compassion and His mercy a refuge from the coldest blasts. The pity is that these last are, like the leaves of the Autumn trees, the scarcest in number; or, after all is the happy life of one summer month, price enough for a "forever" of withered beauty and faded grace?

Poor Honor turned away with a heavy sigh; she could not learn a cheerful lesson from nature's gigantic book, she had stood by the window for nearly an hour in silent communion with the dumb eloquent world: there was a strange empty feeling in her heart, that she longed to stifle, somehow her reverie had made her feel a little lonesome, for whom she knew not. She was now tasting a little of Life's bitter sweet, and like every other girl of eighteen, was madly wishing for the *dénouement* to come. Poor foolish eighteen! Why will you extract from Destiny the pain that will be yours soon enough: not contented to be free, unfettered, and all your own? You want a sad change, you make an unwise bargain. Do not envy the future its darkness, nor the "to be" its mystery, it is painful enough that in time your poor weary eyes must weep salt bitter tears as they view the unravelling of each. The love that you long for to-day is coming to you, slowly but surely, out of the iron heart of Destiny, but beware! Were it not for Love there would be no hatred, were it not for Fidelity there would be no deception, were it not for Happiness there would be no misery. "'Tis Heaven to love," as love-sick poets have sung. But 'tis Hell to love as well, as love duped wretches have wailed......

Turning from the window, Honor Edgeworth sighed as deep a sigh as if a pain had dwelt within her heart—she was telling herself that she must wait and hope, hope and realize, and so when it did not come to-day, she only sighed again as she laid her weary head upon its pillow, and whispered "To-morrow." When she turned towards the firelight to shut out the cheerless vision of the dreary world from her tired eyes, she started to notice how quickly the shadows had crept over the room. She could see them chasing one another by the quivering light of the grate, and as the silent voices of the gloaming whispered to her heart, her eyes lit up with an unusual brightness and her lips broke apart in a slow dreamy smile. It was nearly six by the marble clock on the mantel, Mr. Rayne would be home in another little while, and with this thought she turned languidly to the *étagère* in the corner, in her search for distraction, and drew from a shelf a small volume which attracted her eye. She then poked a large black coal until it sent a bright lurid flame up the chimney, and filled the room with a cheerful light: slowly, almost tastelessly, she proceeded to turn the pages over, scanning here and there a line or two; at length, smiling, she said to herself, "I used to know these verses long ago. I wonder if I have forgotten them."

She stood up as she spoke, and glancing at the first word, folded her hands behind her back still holding the volume, with one finger inserted on this particular part. She leaned one shoulder gently against the mantel-corner and looked into the fire. Why did she not look towards the window? A moment before, the garden gate had closed noiselessly behind the tall, well-built figure of a man, who before entering the house, had turned to look aimlessly in at the large square window from which was reflected the warm light of the grate. But how soon his eyes became riveted to the spot standing in front of the fire was the fairest creature he had ever looked on before, the fitful flames were casting their light upon her handsome face, her eyes looked almost wild to-night in their sadness, and her cheeks had an unusual glow. Standing with her hands behind her back, she showed to advantage the perfect *contour* of her figure, and while he feasted his eyes on her physical loveliness he caught a little word in a sweet sad voice, that recalled lines he was fond of repeating himself; he strained every nerve to catch the tones within. Knowing the verses himself enabled him to understand her readily as she quoted—

"I have said my life is a beautiful thing,"
"I will crown me with its flowers;
I will sing of its glory all day long,
For my harp is young and sweet and strong,
And the passionate power within my song
Shall thrill all the golden hours;
And over the sand and over the stone
Forever and ever the waves rolled on."

She paused a moment, and puckering her brow slightly as if in an effort to remember, she continued,

"For under the sky there is not for me,
A kindred soul or sympathy,
Must I stand alone in Life's busy crowd
A living heart in a death-like shroud,
And the voice of my wailing o'er sand and stone,
Must it die on the waves as they e'er roll on."

"That verse is her own," said the still watcher at the window.

The girl's voice faded to a sigh, she drew her hands apart and opened the book again, the face outside pressed more eagerly still against the cold pane.

"Why!" she suddenly exclaimed, "the words are all marked in pencil! underlined, just where I have been accustomed to emphasize them, does Mr. Rayne?—Oh impossible.—Whose can it be?" She turned impatiently to the fly-leaf and there in a clear masculine hand she saw, "G. E. from the only true friend and bitter enemy he has in the world—himself."

The book fell from her fingers. She looked earnestly into the fire, and a sad expression stole over her face.

"G. E.! Who was G. E.? Who was it that seemed to sympathise with her already? Who else in the world considered one's self a friend and an enemy, except herself?" She was beginning to long for him, to feel a loneliness for this kindred soul, as if he had come into her life and then had gone suddenly out of it again, leaving her in a melancholy despair. And as she sat there, lost in a long, tangled reverie, the eager face vanished from the window, for another figure strode up the little avenue, and quietly opening the door, passed in. Then the tall young stranger emerged from his hiding place, and noiselessly went out through the rustic gateway, trampling beneath his feet, the fallen leaves, over whose inevitable fate, Honor had spent so many sighs; but his heart was beating quickly, and his face was aglow with a new-lit flame. A strange transformation had apparently settled over all his surroundings. The moon was mounting over the house-tops and shedding a pale, soft light on his way. The world looked fairer and brighter far, than it did a little while ago. The tall trees swaying their naked boughs on the chill night air of mid-autumn, only gave out a responsive sigh to the new longing within his breast, and the crisp rustling of the withered leaves only chimed in harmoniously with the echo of the love lay that was lingering on the chords of his heart; and where the moon in her silent loveliness cast shadows here and there on his way, he saw a vision of the loveliest face that ever haunted a mortal; and wherever quietude reigned profound, he heard the echo of the grave sweet voice saying:

"Must I stand alone in life's busy crowd,
A living heart in a death-like shroud?"

And then his heart burst out its passionate "No." He had not recognized those responsive emotions in that lovely girl to forget them so soon again, he had been searching for them too long not to prize them now. He had thought he was anchoring at despair, and now that a star broke through the clouded heavens, beckoning him on, was he mad to scorn the hope that lay within his grasp? No, indeed, and that very night, under the immediate impulse of his new-born emotions, Guy Elersley made up his mind.

We cannot be surprised at this sudden change in Guy, although it was the most unexpected and unlooked for circumstance that could possibly have come to him. Falling in and out of love is almost so certain a portion of our destiny, that we should never be surprised by it. We know of love as we do of death, that it is to come some day, if not now, by and by. We wait for it without expecting it, we recognize the symptoms that foretell its approach, but of its real bearing on our future lives, we can tell nothing. Time alone, as it unravels the strange mysteries, shows us in what way our love can prove a blessing or a curse. If we were so constituted, in general, as to make up our minds coolly and calculatingly, to fall in love sensibly, but no, with most of us, a look, a word, a pressure of the hand, a sigh, a flower or some such trifling thing, has sufficed to plunge us hoplessly into the delirium of "love." Dreamy eyes that fascinate us, pretty words that gratify us, little signs of preference, have been the prices of human hearts from time immemorial. The pity is, that love so often dies of its own excess, making the dreamy eyes fiery with anger and hatred, turning the pretty words into violent reproaches, and substituting the deeds of preference by coldness and neglect. 'Tis better to have hated all our lives, than to learn the lesson from a blighted love. Life is never bitter, but for those whose misplaced love has caused their faith in men to wither, filling their hearts with that hopelessness of regret, by which misery is recognised in any of its disguises. But these are inconsistent reflections, when proceeding from such suggestive sources as "first love," "moonlight quietude," etc. Let us draw a veil across them for the present. If there must be bitter drops in the deep chalice, let us not spoil the taste of the sweeter ones, by anticipating the loathsomeness of the rest. In another sense we may cry "let us live to-day, for to-morrow we die."

CHAPTER IV

"We talked with open heart and tongue,
Affectionate and true,
A pair of friends though I was young"
—Wordsworth.

The morning following Guy's visit to his uncle's window panes, as Henry Rayne was sipping his rich brown chocolate, with Honor and Nanette, at breakfast, Fitts brought in a note and laid it before his master. The usual broad smile came over Rayne's face, as he recognized his nephew's handwriting.

"So he's in town," he soliloquized, as he opened the folds of the crisp paper and read:

"Dear Uncle,
I came to town last evening, and wish to see you when you
will be quite alone.
Guy."

"There's an ansur wanted, sur," Fitts said timidly.

"Oh, say this afternoon at five, Fitts, that will do."

Evidently, it was not Mr. Rayne's intention to mention the existence of his nephew yet, to his new comers, for he quietly slipped the little note into his pocket and said no more of it. The day wore on, and at five o'clock Fitts brought around the "ponies" to take "Miss Honor" for a drive. They had scarcely gone a block away, before Guy Elersley opened the gate leading up to his uncle's house, and admitted himself. He went into the sitting-room, but it was empty, that is, his uncle was not there, or any other living intruder; but there arose between him and the gloomy coals, the same sweet face and graceful figure that had kept a ceaseless vigil over his slumber last night. The same sad voice filled the room with its wailing echo, and as he listened again to its appealing pathos, he strode idly towards the little *étagère* and took up his little volume from which he had seen her read. A strong impulse rose within him. He imagined himself under the same spell as the romantic hero of "Led Astray," and taking out his pencil, he traced at the bottom of the page, under the words she had recited, this little verse:

"There is another life I long to meet,
Without which life *my* life is incomplete.
Oh sweeter self! like me, thou art astray,
Trying with all thy heart to find the way
To mine. Straying, like mine, to find the breast,
On which alone can weary heart find rest."

He had scarcely closed and replaced the book, when the door opened and his uncle bustled in.

"Hallo, Guy! dear old boy, welcome! welcome!" and Henry Rayne extended both hands to his nephew as he spoke. "And so here you are in Ottawa, eh? What's the trouble now?" and before seating himself to chat, Henry Rayne poked the fire into a roaring blaze.

"No trouble this time, uncle, at least no 'yellow envelopes' trouble, but I've been promised an appointment in the Civil Service, and I've come to you for the 'slap on the back' that makes a fellow stiff when he's in there. Now you know it's all right for a petty clerk in those solemn Parliament Buildings, when he has an uncle that is precious to the government, for the thousands he owns and that he can scarce count. This is why I ask you to come forward, for your assistance is all I want, to make a neat little job of the whole thing. Just snap *your* fingers over my head, and none will dare oppose me. It is not the career I had planned, you know, uncle, but 'half a loaf is better than a whole loafer,' and that is what I threatened to be, if I remained a student in Montreal any longer. The boys are too jolly there in proportion to their means, and I pride myself I escaped in time. I'd just as soon live on the bounty of the people for a while, and eat my lunch perched on an office stool, with plenty of good ice water at hand, and a chance of a cosy 'smoke' now and then, if I don't burn out my pockets hiding the pipe when the dignified 'Boss' approaches."

"Well, well, well, Guy, you are a reckless boy, you know I could have secured you a position in the Civil Service long ago, but you aimed still higher and—missed the mark. I thought you had chosen a profession exacting too much labor for a lover of self-indulgence such as you are; however, I suppose you don't want me to say a single word of rebuke now, and I have grown so accustomed to spoiling you, that I must only give in. You can make yourself easy as far as I am concerned, I will make matters all right."

"You're the best old uncle that ever had a sister married to the father of a fellow like me," Guy said, shaking the hand of his benefactor warmly, "and by and by, when I'm a clever cabinet minister, I'll show you what gratitude is."

"I am afraid such a 'by and by' as that is as far in the past as it is in the future," Henry Rayne said, laughing.

"Oh well, if I am not clever enough to be a solemn minister, they'll make a Lieutenant-Governor of me, or a Judge, Lieutenant-Governor Elersley! By Jove the name was intended to be worn with a title!"

"Well, when you're done all these nonsensical licenses, you are giving your common sense, I will tell you something nice," Mr. Rayne interrupted, as Guy rattled off his idle chat. In a moment Guy's limbs that had been lying carelessly around in the vicinity of his chair, were jerked into a respectable sitting posture, as leaning his face eagerly towards his uncle he asked:

"Something to tell me? Now that is a surprise; I generally do all the talking when I come here."

"Well," Henry Rayne began slowly, and with a look of unusual merriment twinkling in his eyes, "It has taken a long time you see for this surprise to come, but it was worth the trouble of waiting. May be you think that at fifty years all the romance has died out of a man's life, but I am going to show you that such is not the case." (Great Heavens! Guy thought, has the dear old man fallen in love?) "A new life has begun of late for me; henceforth, my love, that has been all yours, must be divided I have assumed a series of new and trying duties—"

"Pardon me, uncle; but you don't mean—you can't possibly be insinuating that you have—have—have done such a desperate thing as to—"

"I have indeed, Guy. I suppose you thought I had no soft corner left in my heart that would be a ready victim to a woman's wiles? but I had, you see." There was a mischevious twinkle in the old man's eye as he spoke. This joke on his clever nephew amused him immensely, while poor Guy was feeling the tight clutch of despair upon his heart Of all the horrors conceivable, Guy had never dreamt of such a thing as his uncle's marriage, and now it was quite evident that his words implied this terrible catastrophe. He saw the long cherished project of his insured welfare passing away so noiselessly from him, dropping through a wedding ring into the clutching fingers of a new-born heir. And when it struck him that the beautiful vision he had feasted his eyes upon last evening was, undoubtedly, the fair destroyer of his every hope, a conflict of violent feelings began to gnaw at his poor heart, making a genuine picture of woeful misery out of the laughing face of a moment before, but he battled against his moral foes, at least—he must not show his uncle that any selfishness of his could mar the sincerity of his felicitations.

"I suppose I am justified in congratulating you?" Guy said in a tone something like that in which one says "'Tis nothing," when three hundred pounds of fashionable humanity apologises for having left its foot print on our toes.

"I know that you do congratulate me warmly," Guy's uncle said, emphatically, "and indeed it is as much for your sake, nearly, as for my own that I rejoice, the benefit will be divided between us." Guy didn't see how— unless his uncle fell into the ordinary routine of wedded life, and grew regretful by degrees—he could share those sentiments very plentifully, but his better nature still revolted against such selfishness, and obeying a generous impulse, he stood up and shook his uncle warmly by the hand.

"I am glad indeed, uncle," he said sincerely, "that at last your earthly happiness is complete. It was poor gratification to you, to trust to me for an ample return for all your unmerited kindness. You deserved some one more faithful and more demonstrative than I. This new tie you have formed will, of course, exclude me from a great portion if not from all of your heart, but, at least, I can still continue to appreciate and love you as though there had been no change. After all, it is the most natural thing in the world for a man to marry."

"Who's married?" Henry Rayne exclaimed in astonishment.

"Why, yourself, to be sure," Guy answered, "I was alluding to you."

Henry Rayne threw back his curly head and laughed heartily and loud; Guy looked on in open-mouthed astonishment, suspecting a temporary aberration of mind in his uncle.

"Oh! that is a splendid one," Mr. Rayne cried slapping his knees violently, and blinking away the tears that were gathering in his eyes from excessive laughter. "You had just better circulate such a piece of slander about me, and see how it would be received, why, the dogs on the road would laugh at your simple credulity." Then assuming a becoming air of mock gravity the old man continued, "This is terrible, Guy, that you should openly accuse me of such a serious piece of forgetfulness is, I fear, more than I can readily forgive—I dare say I do a great many surprising things now and then—but to get married—Oh no, Guy, you wrong me—wrong me terribly."

Guy had to laugh at this, though still lost in the mystery.

"Perhaps now that you have laughed quite enough at rue, you will kindly explain all," he said in an anxious tone.

"Well, the truth is, Guy," his uncle began in earnest, "there is a woman at the bottom of it, of course, and though I have pledged myself at the altar of friendship to love and protect her, there is no such thing as 'till death do us part' in the transaction. I have been left the odd legacy of an only daughter by an old school-friend of mine," Guy blushed inwardly, and felt guilty, "she is a dear, lovely little creature, and will, I am sure, make my home a different one altogether, from what solitary bachelordom has brought it to. I hope you will agree, both of you, I know you will like her just as soon as you see her, you have no idea how lovely she is." (Oh fie! Elersley! how innocent you look).

"Well, really uncle, you are a little more demonstrative over female superiority than I would expect," Guy said lazily, as if he had made up his mind that he would not be so enthusiastic.

"Because she deserves it," Mr. Rayne said, earnestly. "Don't think, my boy," he continued, "that I am a perfect old ogre with regard to women, for I am not, I have travelled over and seen more of the world than you, and I know the difference, vast and mysterious as it is, that lies between woman and *woman*. The word, has, of all words, two meanings, the most antithetical and contradictory, one is the limit of the Beautiful, the other the limit of the Repulsive; one is synonymous with purity, truth and excellence, and the other with vice and diplomacy. The world is often imposed upon when the latter counterfeits the former. Men are dazzled by the glitter and gaudy show of the pretended, and pass by, unnoticed, the less flashy attractions of the real, but I pride myself that I have never been deceived in this way. The girl that I have brought to my home is as genuine a sample of noble, good, pure and honorable women, as could exist, if you had known her father I would tell you, she is Bob Edgeworth's child and you could not then doubt the truth of all I say."

"Edgeworth?" Guy queried, "It seems to me I have heard that name before."

"It was you who revived all my precious memories of him," Henry Rayne said thoughtfully. "That letter you wrote me before leaving Montreal, telling me of an interview you had with a traveller who had seen Edgeworth defend me so bravely and gallantly abroad, was the first I had heard of my dear old friend for many many years."

"Oh yes, I remember now!" Guy exclaimed, "but how in the world did he trace you up after all these years?"

"That was easy enough, I am happy to say. I am pretty well known now, and Edgeworth took the most direct way to me, by applying to our family solicitors at home, but I blame him for not having sought me while he had his health and strength—he is dead now, poor fellow, and all he had prized in this world he has left to me. When I wrote you, that important business called me to Europe, I was starting to execute the first part of my friend's dying request. I did not talk about it much beforehand, but now that we are safely back, the whole world is free to know that I am in charge of the sweetest girl under the sun, let who can, deny it, if you are as anxious to meet her as I was, stay and drink tea with us this evening—they are out driving now, but they wont be much longer—do stay."

"Not this evening," Guy said hastily, as he rose, "I am not prepared, uncle, besides, she is strange yet, and it is as well not to thrust too many new faces on her at once, you can mention my name to her if you will, she will feel more at home when we meet." There was a pause of a moment, and then Guy, as he appropriated a cigar from a china stand that tempted him close by, resumed, "this certainly is a strange, unlooked- for incident in your hum-drum life, but it is also a very fortunate one, since she is such a comfort to you and such an acquisition to your home—I fancy, from your description she could scarcely be otherwise. I hope we will all be an agreeable and sociable family yet, and now, if I don't want to be caught, I had better be off at once," saying which, Henry Rayne's handsome nephew shook himself out of comfort's wrinkles, lighted his cheroot, put on his becoming hat, bade his uncle a temporary "good bye," and departed.

I would undertake too common-place a theme, were I to try and interpret the feelings that struggled for ascendancy in the breast of Guy Elersley. How many pens have been stowed away rusty and old from having told no other tale than that of new-born love? How many gray-haired bards have tuned their lay to the sighs from the human breast under the "first loves" influence? How many eyes, even among those that rest upon this very page, have wept the overflowing of their hearts away, at the moment that love's first whispers stole into their souls? How many tired and weary hands are folded on the laps of those who are sitting in the twilight of their years dreaming all over again in bitter joy their "Loves young dream?" Ah! they are many indeed! and so it is superfluous almost to tell the world what it is to love for the first time. That trembling existence that is balancing on Hope and Despair, is an experience so well learned that no one thinks of telling it. It is a strange part of destiny, that even those who have never heard what it is to love, are not surprised when called to teach it to themselves. Instinctively, we hide our emotion, we steady our hand, we check our words. There is the pity; there are grand unspoken thoughts, burning in the souls of many to-day, that may never reach the threshold of the lips. Men are gliding through the world disinterestedly, day by day, and they know not, often care not to know, that there are devoted hearts existing on their memories alone. There are pretty blue eyes weeping over the "garden gate" where "some one" is "waiting" and "wishing in vain." Let them weep. There are miseries in life, that can be learned only by many repetitions. If they don't break the heart at first they perseveringly "try again."

If my belief be not a popular one, I hardly like to be the first to preach it, but it seems to me that few can study society as it is to-day, without concluding very disagreable things; one of these is the deplorable fact that, in our day, the purest selfishness seems to have established itself as the source and promoter of, not only the indifferent, but the apparently best impulses of the human heart. It is a pity indeed, that our analysing tendency has been so strengthened by cultivation, for most often, by prying into the very remotest origin and causes of things we learn a lesson that for ourselves or the world would have been infinitely better unlearned. Hence it is trait in our own day we are not satisfied that certain lavish displays of generosity pass for Christian charity, simply, and without more ado. We will not look upon the givers, with an admiring eye, and spend our enthusiasm, on a religion which teaches the love of our neighbor so effectively, oh no! we must "open the drum to find where the noise is kept," and how, unfortunately, often, do we find, that practical virtues, or at least, what are so called by the world, have nothing more solid at base than the hollow drum. It sounds deplorable, to say that nineteenth century charity is a Dead Sea apple, even the guilty ones will not like to hear that they have subscribed to this fund, or built that asylum, through policy, or as an advertisement, or for the less harmful but still unworthy reason that they like to give something, when there is plenty around them. Nevertheless, is it not true that in all countries, in our own little city, there are men, who drive the starving beggar from their doors, and who yet head a public charity list handsomely. There are people, who, under their parson's eye, wear down-cast look and thump their breasts, but, who behind his back, would much sooner thump any one else's breast, or cast down any other person's eyes. There are members of high society, who feel it their duty to set good example for their social inferiors, and so they feast and dance and gratify themselves all through the hours of the night, and then in half spoiled frizzes and sleepy looks repair to church in the early morning. This may all be right enough, but if so, there is more than one version of right and wrong, and that is impossible. This omnipotent selfishness has even crept into our loves. Men kiss the dainty finger tips of their lady-loves, to-day, with a passionate fondness that is proportionate to the bulk of lucre that dainty hand can hold. The words "be mine" so sweetly answered by fair trusting damsels, are addressed to them, because estates and dowries cannot speak of themselves, and must consequently be wooed and won by proxy. The divine institution as marriage was wont to be considered, is better understood in our day as a "linking transaction", a "speculation in the matrimonial market," or for the man alone, he is either "spliced" or "fleeced."

At least our century has succeeded in one thing: it is the grandest parody on all that is lofty, or elevated or holy, it is an unparalleled burlesque on any exalted sentiment or practical good. Every ennobling tendency, every redeeming trait is cunningly caricatured, and so cleverly ridiculed that is impossible to respect them afterwards. It is hard to tell what another era may bring forth of good, but it is certain that ours has killed, to the very possibility of a future regeneration, every germ and atom of solid morality, that sustained it. Perhaps that is what was wanted, the end may be achieved now. It has been clearly and undeniably proved to the world, that there is no longer any God, there is no eternity, no atonement, no recompense. We are left to wonder whose business it was to call some of us into this miserable existence, to take us out of it again before we have culled any real happiness, and send us back to—Well, we are not allowed to say where, because there is some inconsistency mixed up with it, but we are sure to go there at all events.

This may seem a most exaggerated deviation from the smooth course of the narrative, but in reality it is not so. The little reflections made may serve to remind the reader, that those great universal movements, social, political and religious, floating as they are at random in the atmosphere, cannot fail, when breathed by our youth to develop into substance with their growth, and to manifest their poisonous influences later, in the lives of their wretched victims. After pondering over such reminders for a moment or more, there will be no call for surprise, when our young men are pictured in their true colors. The mind need not hesitate to enquire, when it views youth and manhood, beautiful and *blasé*, attractive and cynical, credulous to simplicity in many things, and infidels in the one great act of faith that alone merits anything.

From the taint of this evil, and all its sorrowful consequences I am tempted to exempt Guy Elersley, so handsome, so young, so winning; but I cannot give the lie to obstinate reality. Of course, Guy Elersley was not a bad man, he was exactly what most young men of to-day are—what you, my reader, know them to be, what all the world, but themselves, know them to be. Guy thought he "wasn't such a bad sort of fellow at all," and yet in every movement of his, one could detect him—the victim of the age. He had never professed any direct code of belief. He would have been very much offended if any one called him an "atheist." He knew there was some reason why a fellow should go to church now and then, and not be everlastingly doing mischief. He confided to himself in strict secret that "to die" was about the very last thing he'd like to do; but, somehow, such serious considerations as these never lingered long, a good cigar or "half-a-glass" easily sufficing to turn the current of his thought into a more pleasant course. He had all the "might-have-beens" in the collection of qualities that he possessed, to make any one sorry, but as fast as a new trait developed itself in him, he put it to the worst possible advantage, and made those who took an interest in him intensely sorry for his grave mistakes.

He had early fallen in with the tide, and learned to love *himself* before and above all else.

One hardly likes to say that this new born enthusiasm of his was a selfish gratification, and yet in its radical sense it was thoroughly so. He delighted in it because of the benefit it brought himself. He had long felt a void within his heart, a want or craving for something, something indefinite, intangible certainly—something that no sensual indulgence could appease, that no light pleasure could distract, and now all at once it seemed to him that long-felt vacuum was filling up. A something, just as ethereal as his craving had been, was creeping into his heart. It felt like the liquid music of a low, serious voice, or it may have been a passion, such as he had seen in the depths of two large, sad, gray eyes, or it might have been the soft soothing influence of a sweet, dreamy smile. It was just as abstract as any of these, and yet just as fascinating and just as exquisite. This was Love for him, a beautiful but a dreadful thing! feeding his hungry soul and quenching his heart's awful thirst, yet swaying him with a merciless tyranny, for love caresses with one hand and smites with the other. If it can be the exponent of certain delicate phases in our spiritual nature, it can also, alas! almost smother the good it does by the pain it so cruelly inflicts. It has a double mission, for in the cry of joy that escapes the lips under its influence there is an echo of pain and despair, and hence it is that love is so violent a passion. If it were a pleasure only to love, we could never prize the object of our wild affection as when it has cost us sighs and tears, and anxiety untold.

It was thus Guy Elersley ruminated as he sauntered through the streets this sear October day, whistling silently to himself, and knocking the clotted leaves recklessly from side to side with his slender cane. He was persuading himself that at last his destiny was beginning to accomplish itself. She would surely see the lines he had traced for her eye in the book he had been reading, and if she were what he supposed her to be, they would be an eloquent appeal in his behalf—but. Here the misery came in—

> "Love was never yet without
> The pang, the agony, the doubt."

What if she never reciprocated?—if there did not linger in her breast a single responsive sigh? But he dared not ask. What then? Not until hope had quite faded away and left the bare, truthful reality to confront him by itself.

CHAPTER V

"And then I met with one who was my fate, he saw
me and I knew
'Twas Love, like swift lightning darted through
My spirit 'ere I thought, my heart was won—
Spell-bound to his, forever and forever!"

In this interesting meanwhile, life was unfolding its strange mysteries just as unexpectedly to Honor Edgeworth as to Guy Elersley. After she had returned from her pleasant drive, a half hour after Guy's departure from his uncle's house, dinner was announced, immediately after which Mr. Rayne had to excuse himself, having had an engagement "up town." Honor, left to her own resources for distractions, repaired, as usual, to the sitting room, and seated herself on the floor before the grate. Her eyes assumed their old hazy look, she clasped her hands over her knees and looked vacantly into the fire. What a strange girl this was! So dreamy, so pensive. She was reasoning with herself now as she often did, trying to feel thankful for all the good things with which her life was blest, but though she acknowledged to herself that youth and health, and comfort and kind friends were grand gifts of Providence, she could not stifle the dissatisfaction that filled her as she yearned for "something else." She could not say what it was, only she knew that she yearned for a gratification that is not found in any of those things that she enjoyed so profusely.

Oh, that "something else!" Why do we not stop and gather it by the roadside we are passing now? We will not find it farther on. That which is enticing us onward is only the illusionary flicker of a will o'-the-wisp! We will stretch out our hands too late—when we have been caught in its fatal snares, and then in the darkness and misery that will surround us, we will feel how foolish we have been, and our cries of despair and distress will be echoed back to our own ears in sounds of mockery and scorn. Let us not build upon that "something else" that is always buried in the to-morrows, for we are losing the present and risking the future thereby.

Poor Honor, after thinking until her head sank wearily upon her shoulder, sighed and rose up, pacing the room with her hands behind her back. As she passed by the little *etagere* she smiled curiously, and stretching out her hand drew towards her Guy's book of poetic selections. As she slid the pages through her delicate fingers, she murmured slowly—

"I have said that my life is a terrible thing,
All ruined and-"

She stopped suddenly, for her eyes had fallen on the pencil marks traced under these little verses she was accustomed to recite—her heart gave a sudden bound—

"Oh, sweeter self, like me art thou astray"

She quoted the words in bewilderment. What did it mean? There was no one in the house to write such meaning words there! That pretty, legible penmanship did not correspond with anyone's she had ever known—except— where was it she had noticed something just the same? Suddenly she remembered. On the fly-leaf of the book were words traced in the same hand. She turned over the leaves and compared them. There was no doubting their identity. It was, then, G. E. who had written this passionate little quotation. "G. E. How strange" she muttered. Was it her "fairy prince" had come to visit her while she was away? She could not fathom it—some hidden meaning lay stowed away under those pretty words. "They were not there when last I had the book, of that I am sure," Honor said meditatively. "Some one has been in here since, and that 'some one' sympathises with me, that 'some one,' I feel, is my long-sought ideal. Has destiny changed its frown into a smile at last for this lone, eccentric girl, I wonder?" She dropped her hands negligently, still clasping the mysterious volume, and looked wistfully into the space before her. She was undergoing the change that comes over each of us as soon as we yield our hearts to the strange influence that fascinates them. We have been told that "Love is a great transformer," and if we had never heard it we would have found it out for ourselves.

Honor Edgeworth, sitting alone in the cosy enclosures of a cushioned *fauteuil*, thought out the queer circumstance that had visited her to-night; never noticing how fast time flitted by, never heeding the stillness of advancing night, until Mr. Rayne's late arrival roused her from her reverie, and brought her suddenly back from the sunlight of her dreams to the grim darkness of the reality. Kissing him a sleepy good- night, Honor left the room, henceforth haunted by the spirits of her earliest conceptions of love, and went silently, almost gloomily, up to her own handsome little room, bringing to her friendly pillow all the hazardous hopes and fears, and interesting experiences of a love unborn but well conceived.

In the gray of the following morning, the angels of slumber on their upward flight must have borne one another an interesting message, for Honor's guardian spirit had noted the happy smile creeping over her face, as in her dreams she saw the noble hero of her waking reverie—and Guy, as he tossed restlessly on his pillow, betrayed to his "silent watcher" a heart overflowing with a new-born love for a creature to whom he had yet spoken no word. And how those angels must have smiled, knowing, as they did, that 'ere another day had passed those two would have met, to recognize in one another the destiny of each!

"It will soon be four o'clock," Honor said to herself on the afternoon of this same day, looking, as she spoke, towards the delicately tinted window-sill. She had whiled away so many afternoons in this little *boudoir*, or family sitting room, that she could tell by the progress of the sun on the broad sill when to expect Mr. Rayne home from his office. "He will be here in half-an-hour," she soliloquized, then looking aimlessly around for distraction, Honor spied a half-knitted stocking and a ponderous looking pair of gold-mounted spectacles lying carefully on a side table. Smiling mischievously, she adjusted the glasses, very low down on her nose, for of course she can see much better *over* than through them, and unwinding a yard or two of the wool, tucked the ball professionally under her arm, and began slowly to penetrate the intricate mysteries of "narrowing the gore." She had just seated herself in the great rocking chair, when a very familiar sort of tap at the door caused her to look up. She thought to make a joke for Fitts, and feigned "Nanette" accordingly—she dropped her head on her shoulder, slowly moving her needles all the while—and with closed lids, and mouth half-way open, she considered the *tableau* perfect. The knock was not repeated, but she knew that the door had been opened. For a few seconds longer she remained in her interesting attitude, and then considering that Fitts was rather slow to appreciate a joke, she opened her eyes, and was about to close her mouth, but the exclamation of surprise that rose to her lips, kept it wide open for a second or two longer. The blankest of blank stupid wonder looked out from her eyes over the old-fashioned, gold-rimmed spectacles.

"I hope you won't think I am intruding," said the person at the door, "but being quite at home in the house, and having received no answer when I announced myself, I thought I might admit myself here as usual."

Honor detected an effort in the speaker's voice to refrain from laughing outright, and did not feel too comfortable at the success of her joke.

"Did you—did you wish to see Mr. Rayne?" she stammered, dragging the unsightly spectacles off her nose, and throwing them back on the table.

"I certainly expected he was here," the stranger answered mischievously, "but I had mistaken you for him on coming suddenly in."

Honor felt mortified, while her companion evidently was very much amused. She looked at him suddenly, her pretty face suffused with blushes, but on raising her eyes they met his in a quick glance—the large, passionate gray and the deep, dreamy blue penetrated each other's depths in an instant—only during one short breath, and then Honor's fell. She had been about to speak, but the mischief in his look reminded her of the absurdity of this *recontre*, and she could only turn aside, and show him by her shaking shoulders that she was forced to laugh.

At last the situation became too ridiculous, and Honor, between smothered fits of laughter, said,

"If you have made any appointment with Mr. Rayne, he will not detain you, I know. Be seated; I will enquire if he has yet arrived"

"Do not trouble yourself," her companion answered. "My uncle, Mr. Rayne makes no ceremony for me, I assure I you. I must only await his pleasure. But lest I have disturbed you—"

"Not at all," Honor interrupted, "I was only amusing myself."

"We may as well not be strangers," Guy said, courteously advancing towards Honor, "for we are likely to meet very often henceforward. I am Mr. Rayne's nephew, his sister's son, and I was the only toy in the big nursery of his heart until Miss Edgeworth appeared, which young lady I think I have at present the honor to address."

Honor bowed, and, extending her hand, said in her sweetest voice—

"For Mr. Rayne's sake we must certainly be friends,"—then feeling a little more at home with her visitor, she continued, "As no one comes in here unannounced, I ventured to attempt a little disguise this afternoon. I mistook your knock for some one's of the household, and had just struck the last attitude of my assumed character when you caught me—I hope the effect on your nerves was nothing serious," and as she spoke this in her bewitching confusion Guy felt like taking her up in his arms, little bundle of blushes and smiles as she looked, and devouring her, but before he had time for word or action, the door opened again, and this time Henry Rayne bustled in, glaring in bewilderment upon them—

"Why! You two young rascals, how did you come together? Here you've cheated me out of anticipated pleasure by finding one another out behind my back—this is too bad!" and Mr. Rayne as he spoke looked suspiciously at each of them.

"Oh, Mr. Rayne," and "Really, uncle," broke simultaneously from their lips, and then Guy, advancing, explained the interesting circumstances of their premature introduction.

"Well, it's just as well," Henry Rayne said, laughing, "we are all to be the one family henceforth, and the sooner it began the better—sit down Honor—sit down my boy," continued he, drawing chairs towards the fire, "come Guy, tell us the news, you have nothing else to do but gather it."

It was all over and done, those hands that had been groping in the darkness for so long, had met at length in one another's clasp. True it was, that no word had yet betrayed the feeling of either heart, no action, no sign had been made, and yet each knew full well that they had met at a threshold which they were both destined to cross, hand in hand. It was not presumption on either side, but each felt so truly that it would be easy now to love, that they had met. It seemed as though one had sought the other for a long tune, and that now they had met never, never to part.

It will avail us nothing to dwell upon the details that made up the happy days of Honor Edgeworth's life after her meeting with Guy Elersley. To those who know what it is to breathe, live, and act under the soothing influence of a first love, the page would be a superfluous one, and to those for whom such a blessed phase of life is yet among the things to be, mine must not be the pen that will spoil the luxury thereof by anticipating its joy—and again, to the wrinkled brows and aching hearts for which such a thing lies among the "might have beens," oh, I will not surely speak—I see their blinding tears—I hear a long, mournful sigh—somebody's fate is cursed, somebody's hope is trampled, somebody's heart is withered and dead! There remain only those who live their love-days in a holy remembrance, those who, in going backward through time go

"—hand in hand With spirits from the shadowland,"

and to those I whisper the words of our poet, and say—

"'Tis better to have loved and lost,
Than never to have loved at all."

All I will say is, that the sun which set upon the world on the day when, for the first time, Guy and Honor linked hands, never, since nor before, went down upon any two creatures who were more thoroughly satisfied with themselves than were these two.

When Guy left Mr. Rayne's house, the evening was far spent—and such an evening! If an exclamation point cannot imply its happiness it must remain a mystery. Long after he had bade his earnest "good-night," Honor and her guardian sat together over the dying coals and chatted pleasantly. It was their custom to hold this nightly gossip no matter at how late an hour their visitors left them.

"And so that is my brave nephew for you," Henry Rayne said, as Honor stood up and placed her chair against the wall, "How do you like him?"

Like him? If he could have seen her averted face—her eyes—her mouth!

"Don't you ask an opinion a little soon?" she replied, so carelessly, that the shrewdest observer would be baffled.

"Well, I don't mean to ask you if you're crazy about him, or anything like that," Mr. Rayne said, half-laughing, "but do you take to him, do you think you will be *friends*? That's what I'd like to know."

"Oh," she exclaimed, disguising her excitement in a smile of surprise, "I do not doubt that, at least so far as *I* am concerned, I have been friends with more—with less—I mean with more—no, with *less* interesting people."

"Gracious! it seems to have puzzled you if you have," Henry Rayne said, mischievously, as he saw her color and grow impatient with herself, "you seem at a loss to know on what equality you would put poor Guy's interest"

"Now, you needn't teaze, just because I'm dreadfully sleepy and can't talk right; I won't say another word, only—Good-night," and kissing him brusquely on the cheek, she skipped out of the room.

But the subject had not dropped through with these remarks.

The following day as Honor sat in the library alone, Mr. Rayne bustled in, and sat down beside her, as he said, to read her some interesting item from the morning *Citizen*, but instead of leaving her again, Honor saw that he was lingering in the room purposely. (I wonder if anyone ever yet loitered around a place pretendingly to no purpose without immediately betraying that he was full of purpose.) After Henry Rayne had looked at the titles of several books, and gazed vacantly at the paintings that decorated the walls, and raised the cover of a massive ink-stand just to drop it again, he made a bold stroke and began his subject as though it had only entered his head at that very moment.

"Honor," he said somewhat timidly, "I was going to ask you to do something, last night, but you left me so suddenly that I had to put it off."

"Oh, I am so sorry," Honor answered, raising her lace frame to her mouth, not to hide her face, but only to bite off an obstinate knot of thread that provoked her. "Is it too late, now?" she queried anxiously, looking at him.

"Oh, no; it's not too late. It's about Guy."

"Guy?"

"Yes."

"Why, what can I have to do with Guy?"

"Well, I just want you to promise me you will do all you are able. If you do that, I can almost promise you I will never ask you to do me a favor again."

The puzzled, asking look in her gray eyes deepened, a curious smile stole round her lips.

"I need not tell you how strange this is to me," she said slowly, "you must know that you proposed an enigma which I cannot solve."

"Come here, Honor," Mr. Rayne said seriously. She laid down her work and went towards him. He was sitting in a velvet arm-chair, and she knelt beside him, with her white, delicate hands clasped on the ruby upholstering. He put one arm gently around her, and as he smoothed her wavy hair with one hand, he asked her earnestly,

"Honor, you know how much good is done in the world by mere contact, do you not?"

"Of course I do, Mr. Rayne; good and evil alike have been kept circulating from the beginning by individuals."

"That is so. Well, now, don't you think it is a pity when there is a very susceptible person, one who would be good if he was led, or who would be wicked if he was led—don't you think it a pity, I ask, that such a person as that should go to ruin because there is no good influence open to him in his life?"

"Undoubtedly," the girl answered seriously. "But Mr. Rayne, no one need be wicked if he wishes to be good, evil is not forced on us you know."

"I know that, my child, but we are not always as strong as our inclinations—the spirit is one thing and the flesh another. Now, I want to appoint you a mission—you are a good girl, and your pleasure is in doing good. Supposing you would favor me by doing good at my request?"

Honor started a little, and looked enquiringly into his face.

"You know you have only to tell me your wish, dear Mr. Rayne. I wish I could have anticipated it; but as that could not be, I pray you tell me immediately. What can I do for you worth the asking?"

"I want you to promise me that you will begin right away to work your influence over Guy." The color rose to her cheeks, and the smile faded out of her eyes and mouth. "This, mind, is a profound secret, Guy has neither father nor mother—he has no home, nor no real friends. I, like the rest, have spoiled him but God has sent me you in time. I know that my dead sister would rebuke me severely were she to see her boy, my charge, so reckless and so dissipated. But I fancy it is not so much my fault—my influence could never change him much.—I want you, for my sake, to try yours. You have only to meet him often, and talk with him. If he has eyes at all he must see in our practical life all the theories he has heard preached to him so often. Show him in all the indirect ways you can, how foolish and frivolous are the ways of society to-day. He is a clever boy, and susceptible, and your trouble will not be lost. Come, now, will you promise me only to try, for my sake?"

"How you exaggerate the capacity of a weak woman," she said a little sadly, then, after a moment's pause, she continued—"It is no trifling mission you appoint to me, Mr. Rayne; it is full of responsibilities. But there!" and she clapped her little hand firmly into his, "That means my strongest resolution—I will do my best You can ask no more."

"God bless you" the old man murmured slowly, squeezing the slender fingers tenderly between both his hands, "I am sure you will never regret it."

No other word was spoken. Henry Rayne had left the room, and Honor stood there alone—stood with folded hands and dreamy eyes—thinking. What a strange request this had been! How was she going to fulfil her promise without betraying the real impulse that had spurred her to make it? How was she going to work her way into his confidence, and yet guard her own? Oh, if this were a task for Mr. Rayne's sake only, how easily she would convert it into a pleasure—but she had promised, that cancelled all her misgivings. She would do it now, if it were in woman's power, she would make it her duty, and with a resolute will and an anxious heart, surely the accomplishment would not prove too hard—"Only—if I had not seen my want supplied in him—if I had not recognized in him the hero of my life's dream. Oh, Guy! What a joy it will be to me if I can teach you to come to me, turning your back upon gaiety, and pleasure, and temptation, to sit by my side, when the voice of a more powerful tempter is stifling mine. What joy for me then!—but no, I am wrong!—it is not my gratification I have been sent to seek; this is a mere duty. If I had loathed you at this moment, my duty is still the same. Just now, it is not *your* sake nor *mine*—it is Henry Rayne's."

The door opened slowly and the croaky voice of the old male servant broke upon her reverie.

"Beg pardon Miss, but dinner is served."

Heroically she stowed away her emotions, the old pleasant smile stole back into its home, and with a beaming face and cheerful step she passed into the dining-room.

CHAPTER VI

"Oh the snow, the beautiful snow
Filling the sky and the earth below.'

"It will be a stormy night I think," Honor says, shrugging her pretty shoulders behind the window-blind she is just lowering, "I wish I had the stout brawny arms of a man to-night...."

"Around your waist?" says a voice from behind her, and, suiting the action to the word, some one encircles her slender waist with "stout brawny arms."

"Guy! I have told you in plain English that I will not allow you to take such freedom with me. *This* time, I say, '*Je vous difends sirieusementde mettre vos bras....*'"

"Oh! that's enough, by Jove, you'd drive a fellow crazy if he'd listen to you long enough, with your recitals on maidenly propriety. Now, there's Miss Bella Dash—many a season's belle—just chuckles with delight when I get this broad cloth sleeve fairly around her blue satin basque"

"Oh! I dare say! but society gives 'poetical licences' to her adopted children, which outside of her pale would be simply atrocious. If Bella Dash saw your coat sleeve around Betsy, the house-maid's basque, it would mean another thing altogether, though Betsy's eyes are as fine as Miss Bella's any day. Besides, you must have learned by now that the 'Bella Dash's' of Ottawa society to-day are *nothing* to me. My sympathy for *my* sex goes out to the whole species and when I offer it to individuals, I exclude the 'Miss Dash's' that make the '*tableaux vivants*' of the modern drawing-room."

"By Jove! that is a fine speech Honor; now see here between you and me (I might also add the only two sensible people in Ottawa) what do you think would become of us young enthusiastic fellows if all the 'girls' stood on their high-heeled dignity like you? Why of course the monasteries and lunatic asylums would have more to do, and by and by, the lunatic asylum would have it all; but destiny is not so cruel a tyrant as you, so she makes your haughty kind the exception and not the rule."

Honor laughed, a low curious laugh, and said "Then she is very kind to *me* to have made me realize soon enough how much too worthy I am to be any man's pastime, a toy for him to play with until the paint is rubbed off — then to be flung aside for something new. If that is all Bella Dash and her prototypes, are worth in your estimation, it is no wonder they are proud, and no wonder they hold their heads high enough to sniff the air over the heads of girls, who, were you to use their names as you do Miss Dash's, would level you to the ground."

"My most supreme stand-offish friend, I hope sincerely you won't preach any of these theories around our gay little city. Why, the young ladies here are just a jolly crowd, who don't transmogrify their whole faces because a fellow likes to spoon now and then to kill time. By Jove! you'd spoil the fun for the winter, and as soon as spring came the whole male element of Ottawa City would 'make' for the fresh pastures of the North-West."

"That is a worthy declaration Mr. Elersly, I must say. I hope you are aware that in speaking thus, you risk the good opinion of your respectable sensible friends — if you have any — outside of this house. It is cold so near the window, let me pass please. I prefer a seat by the fire to this stupid argument here in the window recess."

The mischievous smile died out of Guy's handsome face, as he looked earnestly into the beautiful eyes of the girl standing by him.

"Oh yes, of course" said he, with a sigh, "anything is stupid in *my* company, although I come to you when I'm in good spirits for sympathy, as well as when I'm 'blue' for consolation: you always find it dull and stupid, and you don't hesitate to tell me either. If I bore you so dreadfully, I'll be off."

Honor looked up suddenly; she stretched out her hand and laid it on his shoulder; her voice was changed and earnest as she said. "Stay Guy, and we'll talk it over in a friendly way. There are two seats by the grate, and I will be very amiable — I promise you."

There was a moment of hesitation — temptation — both ways for Guy. At last he looked up, saying: "I'm really sorry, Honor, but I made an engagement for eight o'clock, and I've only ten minutes to walk over half a mile; so we'll have to postpone our little '*veillée.*'"

She turned from him and looked into the fire "Very well," she answered quietly, "the night is stormy, but I suppose you don't mind that."

"Not much," a fellow has to humour the weather for the weather won't humour him.

"But by Jove! its eight o'clock," said Guy, looking at his watch, "and I'll be puckering my patrician brow to invent an excuse for this delay. So 'ta-ta.'"

"Good night," Honor said in a low voice, extending her hand as Guy approached the fire to light his cigar. Another moment, and the young girl was alone with her thoughts.

We might stop here and wonder at the mysterious conventionality that is influencing all our lives now-a-days. It is not a deception, and yet its consequences are often the same. Here was a striking instance of its existence. It might have been noticed from the beginning of the last interview that Honor and Guy had grown somewhat more familiar with one another. It was Mr. Rayne's doings, for had he not interfered, the same cold mysterious distance would still have been between them; but there was no sacrifice too great where he was concerned, and it was purely for his sake the young people dispensed with the formality of their early acquaintance. And yet, how superficial this familiarity was on both sides! Just now, look at them— read their thoughts—see their hearts.

Guy closed the front door with a heavy bang and went out into the street troubled. He was talking to himself: "Such a farce, by Jove! one would think she was a little sister, by the way I try to speak, and if she only knew how I struggle to suffocate the passion that rises within me, when she looks up so earnestly out of her big dreaming eyes; it is sheer folly and I'll go mad if it must continue—and yet—if uncle ever suspected my love he would separate us then and there. But it is dangerous dust I am flinging in his eyes by being free and easy with her in this way. In a little while more I won't be able to trust myself, and God help me then. Confound those Teazle girls, only for their invitation I would have stayed with Honor to-night, but a fellow belongs to every one in this city before himself, and I can't expect to escape"

"Alas! for the rarity
Of Christian charity
Under the sun."

By this time he was mounting the steps of his boarding-house, and he flung the butt of his cigar violently at a gaunt spare cat that just ventured its pinched countenance from under the verandah. As he turned the latch-key, he was indulging in a strain of "In the gloaming, oh! my darling" as though he were the happiest of living creatures.

For some moments after Guy left his uncle's house Honor sat motionless reading the coals. She was troubled: Mr. Rayne expected her to be able to entice his nephew away from these never ending parties of pleasure, and she could not. If she did not care for him quite so much, her task would indeed be easier, indifference spurs on so to a task that is mere duty. How miserable she was, here, all alone, on his account, while he, where was he spending these moments fraught with so much anxiety for her?

At this juncture Mr. Rayne bustled in and, somewhat surprised to find his little girl alone, he took the seat Honor had placed for Guy, and settled himself for a comfortable fireside chat.

CHAPTER VII

"The lamps shone o'er fair women and brave men:
A thousand hearts beat happily: and when
Music arose with its voluptuous swell,
Soft eyes looked love to eyes which spake again,
And all went merry as a marriage-bell."
—*Byron.*

Let us now contrast the two pictures which present themselves to the imagination on this stormy winter evening. One is quiet, usual, familiar; the other is noisy, glittering, but also familiar. One is the drawing-room in Mr. Rayne's comfortable house, with the gaslight falling gently over the silent room—it is not turned very high. Mr. Rayne is dozing in an arm-chair. His hands are folded across his breast, and his limbs are extended at full length—he is dreaming. Honor is seated at the piano, stealing her slender fingers over the ivory keys. It is a low, rippling strain—*Valse des Soupirs*—such as fairies might bring from their magic touch. 'Tis the music of her own heart—the sound of her sighs, and she plays on softly, heedlessly. She is lost in the ecstacy of her own reverie.

We turn to the other side of the picture. Noisy strains of dance music, merry peals of laughter, little snatches of society gossip, beaming faces, silk and lace and flimsy loveliness, bouquets and gloves, trains, handkerchiefs, fans and flirtation, all in a sweet confusion. This is Ottawa at its best, as every one allows when the Misses Teazle throw aside their family portals for their annual ball. Every one is there— married and single, young and old, homely and pretty, rich and—(no! not rich and poor), the rich only, the powerful only, the most influential papas and the best-dressed mammas that Ottawa can afford, and the "juveniles" get in on pa's and ma's qualifications. It is the first private ball since the opening of Parliament, and every one feels very fresh for pleasure. The Misses Teazle themselves look charming (what hostesses ever did not in Ottawa?) and the rest vie with one another.

We are somewhat confused on our entrance into the brilliant room, but some glaring objects attract our attention, thereby kindly taking that look of vacant bewilderment out of our eyes. We have often wondered what the scene was like inside those closed shutters, and here we are now, transported all at once to the very midst of the interesting proceedings.

There is a group near the door that we readily take in, in our first sweeping glance round the room. Mrs. Mountainhead, a lady prodigiously inclined to embonpoint, looking exceedingly warm and uncomfortable, is the central figure. Her two daughters and their attendant cavaliers are also there. But it is plain to see that Mrs. Mountainhead does not enjoy the ball. She stands in holy awe of her aristocratic daughters, who are just "fresh" from a very modern boarding-school. Every word she utters has an accompanying look thrown either to the short-sighted full- complexioned eldest daughter or to the slim, unprepossessing younger one, seeking approval from their responsive glances. And, after all, poor Mamma Mountainhead, in her ruby velvet and Chantilly lace, has, by far, more brains of her own—if she could get a license to use them— than either of her daughters have ever admitted within the limits of their well-frizzed heads. But who is the apparently devoted admirer of Miss Gerty Mountainhead, who is leaning over her chair from behind, with the top of his aquiline nose in ridiculous proximity to her very red face? Who but Mr. Guy Elersley? There he is, whispering all kinds of nothings into the blushing, susceptible ear of dear Miss Gerty, never heeding the thought of the lonely girl at the piano in the quiet home of his uncle.

Then there is a silvery laugh, and you hear the words—"Well, between the Racquet court and the skating rink, and calls, and going out, what do you think I could ever do? Why, the day is not half long enough as it is."

"Surely not, Miss Dash," a deep voice makes answer in a tone of quiet amusement, "you must be dreadfully worried in trying to make things harmonize. You are so tired at night that half the morning must go for repose, and then—"

Here the speakers moved on and it was seen that Bella Dash was happy on the arm of a wealthy bachelor who was fast becoming interesting to all female friends, mamas and daughters. It is easy to see at a glance that every one is fooling every one else, and the male element in the room is absorbing all the real fun.

With the exception of a few newly-appointed civil servants who have "made their calls" and run an account at the tailors, the other gentlemen are mostly well-versed in the drawing-room slang and will certainly not bore their fair partners by discussing anything outside of Rideau Hall, or the other fashionable and interesting haunts of gay winter festivities. These gallant knights are easily distinguished looking around the ball room with half-closed eyes (they are mostly short-sighted), or parading their audible element through the room with such a lazy drawl—beautifully substituting the r's with a perfectly Italianized "aw."

Among these indispensables, were Jack Fairmay, Willie Airey and a great many more of our "Sparks Street" elegants. How much better they look on a freezing afternoon with their noses blue and their fur caps pulled comfortably down over their ears, than in the painfully proper looking long-tailed broad cloth and white kids, exactions of society's absolute laws.

All the blondes and brunettes of Centre Town and Upper Town and Sandy Hill, all the "tony" Post Office clerks, all the young, flourishing, embryo and genuine lawyers, doctors, engineers, rich lumber merchants, and civil servants, *ad infinitum* were there.

What a gay picture! What an interesting sight! Who would not love Ottawa for its self-made gouty papas and its fat, airy, comfortable mamas? Think of the wonderful influence of these thoroughly Christian women on the sphere in which they shine. Even in this one gathering can we not realize how the improvements and customs of the day cast their benign influence over a mighty world, through the rising generation. Those dear pretty pink and white dimpled darlings done up in "illusion" and silks, how happy it makes one feel only to look at them! This must be the nature of the remarks, Guy and another male friend exchange in the bay window. Let us draw nearer.

"You're wrong, Bob my dear," Guy is saying, "I agree with you they do look like fish-hooks strung in a row, but I heard Miss Nellie Teazle tell Mrs. John Prim, that that was the 'Montagu' style; so excuse me for contradicting you."

"Oh! don't mention it, the name almost redeems the folly of the thing. By the way Elersley, you have been 'going it' in rather a pronounced way with Miss Mountainhead to-night. Is it too soon to be the first to congratulate?"

"Oh Lord!" Guy smothers the exclamation under his heavy moustache. "You might try the names of all the dear ones in succession on me. They're just immensely jolly, you know, but I never heard of a young Ottawaite in his sane sober senses, go choose his future wife in a ballroom."

Just here, Miss Dash comes up and throws a coquettish look at Guy through the opening in the curtains. He nods a temporary good-bye to his companion and goes off to claim the next waltz which Miss Dash has promised him, and, oh Guy! naughty boy! if he is not saying over the identical pretty nothings to Miss Bella, that are yet filling the heart of Miss Mountainhead. with a delicious souvenir of him.

In another corner of the room Bob Apley is "spooning" most suggestively with the same Miss MacArgent whose "fish-hooks" he has just been ridiculing so mercilessly. This of course is pardonable according to the world's wise indulgent maxims, especially when we consider that Miss MacArgent's father's income, daily, is almost identical with the amount of dollars and cents that find their way to the pockets of the impecunious Bob in a whole year.

Besides Emily is rather a good-looking specimen of the "foreign" belles that winter in Ottawa, and some one even said last winter that one of the Governor-General's Aides-de Camp and she—oh! we all know how the green-eyed monster tortured the hearts of the poor belles of countless seasons, when they saw their indisputable rights usurped by a comparative stranger. The two Misses Begg, for instance, who have been twenty-five and twenty-six respectively for the last eight years, waiting for the turn in their lives, that will never come, have cause for bitter complaint. The same faces are here that are ever on exhibition as the champion tennis player, the champion skater, another an unrivalled waltzer, and some more distinguished vocalists and instrumental performers. These grow wearisome once the novelty wears off. There is nothing in them besides the foam that blows away after a little and leaves no trace of its once august presence.

We will make our adieus gladly to the affected civil servants, the young embryo professionals, the rich independent bachelors, the corpulent papas and mamas, the famous tennis, skating, singing, dancing and playing heroines, and go joyfully back to the snug little parlor of Henry Rayne, where sits the only one sensible girl we have seen to-night.

She has ceased playing, and is now sitting by a low table with her lovely head bent earnestly over a lap full of wool-work. The little clock goes ticking on through the noiseless moments that come and go and still her busy fingers ply hurriedly through the stitches. At last it is ten o'clock and instinctively she rises, puts away her wools and needle, and goes over to the chair which yet supports the sleeping figure of Henry Rayne.

"Good night, Grandpapa," she says softly in his ear.

He hears the low sweet whisper. Her voice would penetrate the depth of death itself for him, he fancies. She said "Grandpapa." She only calls him that when she is sad, whenever a sense of bitter loneliness fills her heart, making her miss a kind mother and her dear handsome father most.

He opens his eyes instantly and raises his hand to draw the pretty bowed head closer still to his.

"Good-night, my dear little child. How stupid of me to have dozed here all night leaving you by yourself."

"Don't fret, Grandpa dear, I love your company, and all that, but remember I am never less alone than when alone, and an evening by myself is never lost to me."

"No, my pretty one, but you must grow tired some day thinking so incessantly, I must try and distract you; it is dreadful of me to keep you housed up, so secluded, when there is so much for your youth and beauty to enjoy outside. May be I'm responsible for many a sigh you've heaved lately, but it never struck me you see, my pretty darling, that our sentiments and sympathies run so widely apart, it is not very surprising if an old prosy bachelor should forget to ferret out the pleasures of youth, to bestow them on a fair young beautiful thing like you,"

"Oh-ho, now dear old Grandpa, you have been sleeping and dreaming of somebody you are mistaking for me. Don't fret for not spoiling me more than you do. I am pampered enough dear knows. Good-night, I am sleepy too, and I think a night's rest would not be detrimental to either of us, eh grandfather?" and kissing him tenderly on both cheeks, she skipped out through the open doorway and ran up to her own little room.

CHAPTER VIII

Grace was in all her steps
Heaven in her eye
In every gesture, dignity and love.
      —*Milton.*

There was no nonsense about Honor Edgeworth. Anyone should like her. There may have been traits in her character that would elicit no sympathy from some, but they either forget the extraordinary circumstances that influenced her young life, or else they are prejudiced against such individuals as she, whose eyes are widely opened to all the existing follies and extravagances of her species.

Honor would have grown up and bloomed to ornament a far fairer land than Canada, her too enthusiastic nature would have been infinitely better developed in another world, but it is useless to sit down and mourn over the "might have beens" that are always such a loss to us, because we see them, devoid of all the disadvantages realization brings to bear on our own sad experience.

Honor was not even one of those exceptionable women created, not out of the slime of the earth, but conceived in the romantic mind of some extravagant novelist, and brought into the world by his magic pen. No indeed, she had certainly a beautiful face, almost a faultless face, but how many have cursed the day when first they knew their own beauty! How many look back over pages and pages of awful crimes and shameful deeds, and the index page, the starting point, is their beautiful face. So do not be too hasty in envying the physical perfection or loveliness of others. Rejoice that you have it not; the want of it must be your salvation. Know well that if it is not yours, it is because the possession and consciousness thereof would lead you to evil, and it is one of those things for which God has his own wise ends.

Perhaps if Honor had mixed with the feminine world more intimately she would not be the standard of maidenly modesty and reserve that she was in her nineteenth year; but in her there was an utter absence of that self-sufficiency and loudness that is painfully prominent now-a-days in the very city we inhabit. And yet in all her meekness and mildness if you by look or word injured the extreme sense of delicacy that was the under current of all her movements, then—she reared her aristocratic chin high in the air and looked down upon you in such scorn and anger, as wounded innocence alone can assume. One curl of that splendid lip, one flash from that cold grey eye and you did not take long to feel how basely you had lowered yourself, and that a pardon craved on your knees could scarce half atone for the offence.

What a loss to the social world that women of her stamp are not more plentiful! What on earth else can redress social evils if not the redeeming influence of good Christian determined women? Why should they not hold the key to the good impulses, the moral treasures of mankind as well as they wind themselves into the evil nature by enticing the susceptible, dealing out gratification to the willing, and dragging souls blindfolded into an irremediable eternity?

Physiognomists tell us, if we can not observe it for ourselves, that there exists not only that universal difference among things, which makes genus, species, classes, etc., but that even among individuals there is no perfect resemblance found. There are the general prominent traits that serve to classify them, but perhaps there is more difference among the individuals of a species, when examined minutely, than there would be between individuals of a different genus.

This is so true of the human species, which is difficult to judge individually on account of the incessant mysterious hidden workings of that ever active faculty of the soul, which manifests itself so differently to other eyes through actions and words of greater or less import.

This is a digression, but, it came from contemplating the singular beauty of one woman's soul, among the tarnished multitude of victims to that social levity and those superficial virtues that society honors, and with which our modern fashionable women persuade themselves they are doing marvels in the world of good.

If I make a paragon of Honor Edgeworth, it is because I can defy any broad-minded, unprejudiced critic to find a single grievous fault in her character.

Besides the ordinary cultivation of her mind in all its faculties, Honor had another and a nobler ambition. She had acquired all the requisite knowledge to fit her for any station in life, from that of a nursery governess to that of the highest lady in the land. Her learning was not a smattering of this and that—a few words of German, a great deal too many of her own tongue, a well-studied enthusiasm for Tennyson and Longfellow, and may be now and then a word for the "Lake" school poets. Who has not met in their long or short run of experience with the modern graduate who "perfectly idolized" Tennyson or Byron, who "raved" about Shelley's poetical mysticism, or who was "fairly enchanted" with Goethe's deep romanticism. In some of her peculiar phases she even reckons as items of her illimitable knowledge selections from her "favorites" among the French romantics, or the realistic school may be more to her taste. She rolls up her eyes for Mozart and Beethoven and Gottschalk, but her heart thumps for Offenbach, Lamothe or Strauss. To make herself "interesting" in society she has "burned the midnight oil" over "David Copperfield," "Dombey and Son," "Jane Eyre," "East Lynne," "Endymion" and other popular volumes as they gain fame. She can sing snatches from all the finest operas, in Italian, German or French. She can dance the Boston and Rush Polka with unrivalled grace, she can flirt and affect the most becoming airs, she never misses a *matinee* or evening performance at the Grand Opera House; she can do the "grape-vine" exquisitely on her silver-plated skates, and can toss the tennis ball with wonderful dexterity.

All this relates to the effects of the superficial cultivation that our women are getting in this century. A mind polished so that the "rough" cannot manifest itself, a little veneering of knowledge and showy accomplishments, but a heart, alas!—ignored and neglected; the source of all womanly perfection blocked up and destroyed—that is the sacrifice that will alone appease the world in its most sensual phase of to-day, the sacrifice complete and universal of women's hearts. Ah! how soon they nourish the briers and thistles of cold indifference and unchristian feeling. In opposition to this sad spectacle I come back to Honor Edgeworth by her bedside, on her knees, at her evening prayer. Here is a woman who has moulded her heart according to the law of Christ. "Be ye perfect, as your Heavenly Father is perfect." Here is a woman who is learned, wise and simple, gay, light-hearted and pious, confiding and discreet, one who can redeem the loss of many because temptation assailed her and left her the victor.

Long after Honor lay sleeping peacefully, her pink cheeks buried in the soft pillows, Mr. Rayne sat thinking in the armchair below. It was growing painfully evident to him that his darling *protégée* was now budding into all the fullness and maturity of womanhood, and had she been his own daughter he would have introduced her formally into society by now. This was what troubled him. He did not relish the idea of sending this fair delicate morsel out among the chills and dangers of a cold world. And yet, if influenced by this good intention, he deprived her of the seeming advantages that active life in society affords, and if in later years she would reproach him as the cause of some misfortune or other, what would these probably groundless fears avail him in his defence? She was old enough to know danger, and she had spoken to him already of the world as though her experience of it was great and sufficient. Perhaps all she needed for a final confirmation of her opinions of the degradation of that same world was a trial of it. And should he wrong her by depriving her of it through a false motive?

Whatever way he turned the argument it looked like a dilemma. He should either send her "out" or not. If he pursued the former course, the advantages were six, the disadvantages half-a-dozen. If the latter, the advantages were twelve, the disadvantages a dozen, so that he found himself almost unequal to the solution of the problem.

Bye-and-bye however, he resolved to come to some conclusion, and thus by getting angry with himself, he narrowed the two inclinations into one, and that assumed the shape of a final decision to give her the same chances as Ottawa's other comfortable daughters.

Once his resolution was made, matters grew easy. He would write to a widowed cousin who was living a seceded life in Western Ontario, inducing her to share his home, and the responsibility that weighed upon him of giving his adopted child her due.

This lady had mourned her departed husband in solitary seclusion for nigh eight years, and it struck Mr. Rayne on this eventful evening that may be she would find pleasure in a change.

Thus was Honor's destiny slowly deciding itself in the troubled mind of her benefactor while she lay blissfully unconcious, fast asleep among a heap of downy pillows, with one fair hand thrown carelessly over her head and a little stray curl or two nestling on her warm flushed brow.

Satisfied with his final judgment, Mr. Rayne called for a light and escorted himself to the downy arms of his comfortable bed, and when we next take a peep—for of course we've not intruded for the few moments he was saying his prayers—he is snoring the snore of the truly heavy sleeper, and his big good-natured face scarcely discernible among night-cap, pillows and sheets, easily convinces one of the indisputable quiescence of the mind's consciousness in slumber.

Is it not almost equivalent to the acomplishment of the deed itself when we have fallen asleep the night before with the resolution of performing it on the morrow? Is not the wrong almost redressed when we have promised our selves to right it at any cost on the morrow? Is not the thought itself equal to the vow if we know that with the morning's sun we shall rise to make it in reality? One feels all the satisfaction of a deed accomplished in anticipation, and God be thanked for this, for how many weary souls must have made their last night on earth endurable, by the peace of mind that such resolutions infallibly bring.

This explains the comfort and utter heedlessness of Mr Rayne's slumber after such a miserable time as he passed arguing against himself in his drawing-room. He had vowed that he would broach the tender subject to Honor the very next day, and thus free himself from any more hours of self-reproach.

CHAPTER IX

"They say the maxim is not new,
That good and evil mixed must be
In every thing this world can show."

—*Patty*

The next morning dawned a calm, mild day. The snow was knee-deep on the ground and covered the housetops with a thick soft mantle. On how many utterly different scenes the stray sunbeams rested that winter morning. Nearly all the heroines of Miss Teazle's ball were sunk in heavy, tired slumber, in rooms strewn with laces and flowers and other fragments of last night's dissipation. The poor over-exerted mammas are neither able to rise nor to sleep, and their pitiably puckered brows and sour looking faces would excite the sympathy of the most cynical misanthrope.

And yet, perhaps if not reminded, some readers would be tasteless enough to overlook the noble sacrifice these mothers were making of the comfort of their lives in order to "chaperone" their stylish daughters to all the haunts of pleasure. These poor fashionable women must indeed drain life's cup of bitterness to the dregs, if we can judge from the worldly girl's soliloquy.

Who rigs herself in satins light,
And goes to parties every night,
To chaperone her daughters bright?
My mother

Who eats late suppers to her grief,
Of jellied turkeys and roast beef,
And finds no dyspeptic relief
My mother

Who tries to talk with pompous air,
And saturates with dye her hair,
To gratify her daughters fair?
My mother

Who snubs our neighbor Mrs. Bell,
In poorer days we knew so well,

And tales of woe did often tell?
My mother

Who calls at Ridleau and all round,
Where rank and titles do abound,
And boasts of cousins newly found?
My mother

Who fears to bow to poorer kin,
For fear her daughters will begin
To growl and scold as though 'twere sin!
My mother.

I give the intelligent reader ten minutes to pause and moralize after digestion.

I anticipate the look of stupid wonder that must necessarily envelope the face. If there is so much in individual influence in the lower circle, what can one expect from the multitude that must submit to a thousand other decrees coming imperatively from the infallible (?) lips of society herself? How can we do otherwise than substitute for truth and simplicity, deception and affectation? What else can we do but fail to recognise one another in the characters we are forced to assume? Is it surprising that good and wise men from their corners of seclusion call the world degenerate, and wonder at the persistent wrong-doing of those who are the work of such merciful hands? Strange to say, most of us know, or pretend to know, that life is all deception; that the world itself, and those who belong to it are essentially, almost necessarily, selfish; that the goodness and charity which circulate at rare intervals are only the superfluidities of comfort, proceeding from no generous impulse whatever. It is not dealt out at the sacrifice of a crust of bread. It is given so that it may not be left.

Oh, the weakness of humanity after nineteen centuries
of fortification! Oh, the despicable degradation of a race
conceived in an Eternal Mind, created by an Infinite
Hand, redeemed by the voluntary sacrifice of a God, and
sanctified by the Spirit that pervades the universe!

Knowing this, realizing this, as most of us do, why do we not make a move towards independence? Not the independence of the State, that gratifies the paltry ambition of thousands, not that social independence whose meaning has of late been so shamefully misapplied, not even the individual independence that satisfies many. These are but names. I mean that independence that leaves one unfettered by one's self, that makes one victor over one's own evil tendencies and impulses—for man has no enemy so cunning as himself. If he cannot conquer his own inclinations to error, how is he going to subdue them in others?

If we are slaves, mentally and morally to our sensual selves—if we raise the material element above the spiritual within us, we then lose the right of opinion on good or evil, for a man that is passion's slave is the mouth-piece of evil, and an active agent of the enemy of mankind! If we open our volumes of literature, every page bears a reflection of some kind on these things.

For instance, see what a great writer says, speaking of the deception in life:

> "I am weary
> Of the bewildering masquerade of life—
> Where strangers walk as friends and friends as strangers,
> Where whispers overhead betray false hearts;
> And through the mazes of the crowd we chase
> Some form of loveliness that smiles and beckons.
> And cheats us with fair words, to leave us
> A mockery and a jest, maddened, confused—
> Not knowing friend from foe."

Every one who chooses to think at all has a thought in common on the question. In a biography of George Eliot, Hutton speaks of the manners of good society as "a kind of social costume or disguise which is in fact much more effective in concealing how much of depth ordinary characters have, and in restraining the expression of universal human instincts and feelings, than in hiding individualities the distinguishing inclinations, talents, bias and tastes of those who assume them. After all, what we care chiefly to know of men and women is not so much their special bias or tastes as the general depths and mass of the human nature that is in them—the breadth and power of their life, its comprehensiveness of grasp, its tenacity of instinct, its capacity for love and its need for trust."

I fear we will never find this among the leading men and women of our day. Great minds, like George Eliot's, when they wish to spend their genius in written books, will leave the lighted hall where refinement and *bon-ton* hold their nightly revels, and will descend to the huts of laborers and mechanics that form one distinct phase of English life. Like Charlotte Bronte, and some others, she seeks substance for her work in a true, open character, and that is rarely found among the educated classes, who learn from books to unlearn the lessons of nature.

We will now leave the "lollipop" darlings of material nature and pass on out of their dishevelled untidy rooms, leaving their painted faces and powdered heads to spin out the late morning among the blankets,—and seek gratification elsewhere. It is breakfast-time in Henry Rayne's house and the curling steam rises in graceful clouds from the hot tasty dishes that Mrs. Potts concocts with so much art. Honor, Nanette and Mr. Rayne are as usual the only participants of the wholesome things. Honor has just come in, fresh and rosy, all smiles as she steps up to Mr. Rayne's chair with a cheery good-morning. Then kneeling beside her guardian, and looking into his kindly face, she says shyly:

"I have something to tell you all, a surprise, and don't begin breakfast before you know it. If I were not a little orphan this morning, I would let it pass likely, but having only you and Nanette I must tell you, that you may not spare your kind wishes for me. To-day is my twentieth birthday!"

Mr. Rayne rose instantly to his feet and his eyes looked suspiciously moist as he kissed her tenderly on the brow. Then Honor turned to Nanette, but the poor woman was weeping mournfully in her blue handkerchief.

"I'll never forgive myself," she was saying, "to have forgotten your birthday above everything else, and your dear kind father when he gave you to me, a tiny thing in my arms, said, 'she will be a year the 24th February, don't ever forget the day,' and there it slipped from me this time and I never thought of it."

Honor flung her arms round the old creature's neck and drowned her reproaches in a volley of kisses.

"Don't mind that Nanny dear, say you wish me a good Christian life for the next year and you will have done your duty."

"God grant it you, my pretty child."

"Amen," answered Mr. Rayne's deep voice as he left the room.

Honor looked up surprised, but in a few moments her guardian returned with a morocco jewel case in his hands. He placed it in hers, saying, "My you live to wear it out in goodness and virtue, and may God spare you from the snares of this wicked world."

With trembling fingers Honor opened the little box which revealed to view a spangling collection of diamonds. It was an oval locket, profusely set with diamonds with her initials turned artfully on the surface. Inside were the miniature pictures of her father and mother. She laid down the costly gift and went over to her benefactor with tear-dimmed eyes. She put both her slender arms around his neck and pressed one long fervent kiss upon the old man's brow.

"Are you determined, dear Mr. Rayne, to put me under an everlasting obligation to you? Are you not satisfied with bestowing those tokens that I might in time repay by constant love and care, without forcing such a splendid gift as this on me? Really your kindness begins to make me uncomfortable, for it is amounting to a debt I can never repay. And where did you get these dear, dear pictures, and how did you have it ready and all for my birthday?"

"Well, my dear, say we sit down and I'll answer all your questions to the music of knives and forks. I have had a miniature likeness of your father in my possession for many years, and it had often struck me, if I could but procure one of your mother's too, how it would please me to have them set together in a locket for you. The other day I was taken nicely out of my dilemma by finding an old-fashioned locket of yours by the fire in the library. I borrowed it for the short space of a few days until I had copies taken from it, and then Nanette kindly slipped it back into your jewel-case for me. I then ordered the little receptacle that you have admired so much and I only received the whole last night. Strangely enough too, that it should have come just in time. I would have given it to you immediately anyway, because of something I am going to discuss with you in the library after breakfast."

Honor was still looking intently down at the open case beside her plate when he finished the last sentence, but she looked up suddenly as he ceased, with a glance of eager inquiry in her eyes.

"It may startle you, Honor, or may not, but we'll see to that."

A little more rattling of plates and cutlery, a few more clouds of steam from the rich coffee, a series of disconnected gay sentences and ejaculations and the meal was over. The grave tones of Mr. Rayne's voice filled the room in a prayer of thanksgiving, and with the last echo of the "Amen," Honor and her guardian came out from the dining-room into the library arm in arm.

CHAPTER X

"Her life, I said
Will be a volume wherein I have read
But the first chapters, and no longer see
To read the rest of the dear history."
— *Longfellow*

Honor had just taken up her crocheting and was plying her needle busily when Mr Rayne drew his heavy leathern chair opposite to the fire and began:

"Well, my dear little girl, here you are a young woman all at once on my hands, and to me you are yet the childish little thing you were three years ago in the railway carriage at the Manchester Depot. But the world won't see things to suit a short-sighted old bachelor like me, and according to that omnipotent, omniscient world, it is now my duty to introduce you into society, to bring you 'out' into Ottawa life, that you may make a display of all the accomplishments which fortune has bestowed upon you. I will introduce you to a world that will not hesitate in appreciating all the physical, mental, and moral beauty, you may choose to display in it. My duty will then be completed for another while. Now what is your opinion on it? You will have Mrs. D'Alberg, my widowed cousin from Guelph, to chaperone you, you have 'carte blanche' as regards toilet expenditure, and my house is open and at your service henceforth."

All along a smile of slow astonishment had been creeping over Honor's beautiful face, but instead of any showy enthusiasm either way, as Mr. Rayne had certainly expected, she straightened out the rosette of lace work on her knee and clapped it with her little palm. Then drawing a long breath she said:

"So! it has come to this. Well, my dear Mr. Rayne, if my position in your house exacts an *entree* into society, I most willingly go forth to it, though had you never spoken of it, it had never entered my mind. I am prejudiced, it is true, against society, but I defy its influence over me. Every woman owes her mite to the social world, and consequently I owe mine, so as soon as you wish it Mr. Rayne, I am yours to command."

She had scarcely finished the words when the door was flung open and the words and air of "I'll live for love or die" filled the room. He was just continuing "I'll live for lo—"

"O pardon, a hundred thousand times, Miss Edgeworth and uncle, I didn't really think the room was inhabited at such an early hour in the morning, but the fact that it is, only enchants me all the more, I assure you."

"Well, well, Guy, you are a 'case.' How are you this morning? Have you breakfasted?"

"Well, uncle, I thank you; and to your second kind query, I respectfully beg to inform you that I helped to clear away Mrs. Best's table this morning very perceptibly. Not that I had any particular relish for her compositions—which were yesterday's lunch and last night's dinner done over *a la Francay*—Rooshan-hash-up! but then a fellow by natural instinct owes himself the indispensable duty of eating his breakfast, and as a slave to duty, I, this morning, about an hour ago, ate my breakfast."

"Well, for goodness sake! as a duty to your fellow-creatures talk sense. Here, sit down," Mr. Rayne continued, rising himself, "I must excuse myself for half-an-hour. I've not had a look at the *Citizen* yet, and I must be off soon to official duties."

Guy Elersley was well satisfied to be a substitute in Mr. Rayne's vacant chair. He had not laid himself out for such good luck when he turned into his uncle's on this eventful morning, so his appreciation was consequently all the more vivid.

"You're bright and early, Honor, for a young lady on a winter morning," he said, as he drew his chair towards the fire.

"Not unusually so for Honor Edgeworth—and that means a young lady, doesn't it?"

"That's right; snub a fellow right and left when he forgets to isolate you from the whole living, breathing creation. Then you are not bright and early—will that do?"

"My dear Mr. Elersley," said Honor, in a provokingly placid way, "don't exert yourself so violently in contradicting your own free, unextracted observations. You can amuse me in a dozen other different ways as well."

"Oh, bother! Come now, Honor, leave off that ice water business, and give a fellow a word of welcome after being out in the cold. Put away that bundle of thread you're fooling with there this half-hour. You have not taken your eyes from off it yet, nor spoken a decent word since I came in."

"Oh, dear!" said Honor, drawing a feigned sigh, "I suppose when a child's spoiled it's spoiled, that's all, and you must humor it." "Now," folding up her work, "what have you to say worth the trouble you've given me?"

"Oh nothing I could tell you would be that in your opinion. I was at a big 'shine' last night at Miss Teazle's, and feasted my eyes on all Ottawa has to show in the way of female loveliness."

"And you have come to spend the gush of your emotions consequent to such a feast on me, have you?"

"No, Honor, I have not. I did see deuced pretty girls, but the emotion, as you call it, vanished as I handed the last fair bundle of shawls into her carriage. While the light burns, you know, the moth hangs around it, but when the flame goes out, spent in a weary flicker, after 'braving it' for a whole night, the moth goes to roost, when he has not been singed, or otherwise personally damaged without insurance. Well, what are you thinking of now? when you cross your arms, bury your gaze in the fire and strike your slipper with such measured beat on the fender, I know you're not paying much attention to what I am saying."

She drew a long breath as though no answer were required, and then in a quiet, low tone she said,

"Guy, do not talk in that light way of any woman. I know what you men have long accustomed yourselves to believe—that woman was made purposely for your pleasure; 'Man for God only, *she* for God in him,'—but, all the same that does not exact the ratification of Heaven. If my sisters of Ottawa society, with whom you one moment amuse yourself, and the next amuse your listeners with a recital of their follies, are weak enough to seek to gratify you and your kind, 'tis not that such a weakness is a natural inheritance, for every woman who realizes her true worth, knows what a grand mission is before her, and consequently crushes such an absurd theory as fashionable women are brought up to believe from their infancy. Perhaps I am too sensitive on this point, if such a thing could be, but it is the awful wrong which is being done to our sex that fires my indignation thus. And then there are those poor deluded 'ornamental women' who sanction that outrage on their own dignity by sitting with folded hands, taking in all the nonsense which is dealt out to them when they should gather up their skirts and shrink away from you as their inveterate enemies. False faces lead them astray, but there are others who see behind them."

"Yes, by Jove! And you are one who can see through the hair of a fellow's head. Well, Honor, it's plain to see, that you and I cannot agree. There's an involuntary performance of 'rhyme' for you, excuse me for so doing, but I could not withhold it. I said that we don't agree, and it is true. You are quite too tremendously proper for me, and I am just too 'galoptiously' awful for you. So begin to maul that wool over again, and I'll go to my respectable office in the respectable Eastern Block, and there I am sure of finding half-a-dozen eager friends with their pens behind their ears wheeled around on their office stools, quite ready to hear all the 'news' that you reject with such dignity."

"Then go. Sow your seed in fertile ground; but if you speak so lightly of any woman in presence of an office full of men, as you do to me, I cry,—shame on you and your listeners."

She had taken the soft bundle of crochet work in her lap again, and as she bent her indignant face over its intricate stitches, Guy could not help acknowledging to himself, that this was the fairest vision man had ever beheld. How was it that her name never crossed his lips in fun? He would have torn the tongue from its roots before uttering hers in jest. He stood at the door, with the knob in his hand, trying to extract one word of earnest friendship from her, but the serious frown never relaxed itself on her brow, and her mouth was set and stern. He could not stand this. He thought if it was only any other girl—any of Miss Teazle's heroines, he could pooh-pooh it so easily, but Honor was not one of them at all—his heart told him that. He left his place at the door and was at her side instantly. She looked quietly up and said nothing. He felt as though the words would not come, and the wee small voice said "another time," so he merely reassumed his old way, and said:

"Good morning, Honor. Don't send a fellow off in the blues. Come now, smile just the least little bit and speed me away with a charitable word." Then the sweet red lips parted, and looking up from her work, she said:

"I absolve you, Guy. Good morning."

"Well, I'll make hay while the sun shines, and be off, for if I delay a minute I shall have a dozen more pardons to ask. By, bye!"

He closed the door and was gone, but though his hurried steps brought him further and further away from the form he loved, yet his thoughts were of her, his heart beat for her, and his memory dwelt upon each little word she had spoken.

Honor sat as most of us do very often in our lives, with the same smile on her face which had absolved Guy at parting. If we meet a friend and are pleased, the smile of recognition lingers on our faces long after he has passed. If we have heard a pleasant word, the gratification is evident on our countenances, long after the words have died; and the same with unpleasant or sorrowful things. I suppose our memory is necessarily a slow faculty, and only revives the expression of our emotion just as that caused by the first experience is dying away. Any one could tell by Honor's face, that she was thinking of pleasant things. Thence we may know it was no 'clairvoyant' tendency on the part of Mr. Rayne, that on entering the room the ne moment, he exclaimed:

"So you're spinning your threads in the sunlight, my pet, are you?"

Honor started—"Sunlight? Yes, I think the sun will be up presently."

"Oh, you distracted child! I am talking of the sunlight of your thoughts." Here both joined in a hearty laugh, and Mr. Rayne having thrown aside the well dissected *Citizen*, re-deposited himself in the arm-chair by Honor's side. He came too to make hay while the sun shone, and the smile on Honor's face indicated that much.

"You see, that fellow Guy interrupted us just in the beginning of our discourse—but perhaps it was just as well, for something has since happened that throws a new light on the subject. With this morning's mail came a document from Turin to me, from your father's bankers, Honor. It seems from the copy of an original letter written by your father, that he wished to test my friendship by holding me responsible for his daughter's welfare and comfort, and he therefore apparently represented you to me as entirely dependent on my bounty. Even as such, it was an immense gratification to me to take you, and at the risk of all I own nou I could not let you go, but it seems your diplomatic father—and my best friend—had arranged it so, that if, after a short period, I had performed the duties of a true friend towards you, supplying you with the necessary comforts and wants out of my own pocket, that on your birthday at the end of that time, which is to-day, this document should be forarded to me. The surprising and intensely gratifying news concerns only you, it makes not the slightest matter to me," and so speaking, he handed her the least formidable looking letter of a pile of correspondence. She read it with dilated eyes and confused look generally, and laid it down only with this difference actually to her, that she had in her own realization, in one short moment been suddenly transformed from Mr. Rayne's dependent waif into a richly endowed heiress, independent and free. A small change indeed for Honor Edgeworth. It had not power to chisel in finer style the features of her handsome face, nor the power to direct into her heart a purer, holier or more worthy sense of duty than already reigned there. No, it could make her no better. Hers was not a nature susceptible to the ready influences of evil, and so she experienced none of that material delight which generally is the result of such a change for the world's ordinary ones. The only gratification it afforded her was, that now she could repay Mr. Rayne for his untiring kindness, she could deck Nanette in "decent" attire, and give such little alms as she longed to distribute with Mr. Rayne's money. She folded the letter carefully back into its primitive creases and handed it to Mr. Rayne, saying,

"I thought I should have had to repay your unlimited kindness to me by love, sincerity and gratitude alone; and though this would have been an easy debt to liquidate, so far as my sentiments went, yet, it seems Providence has not tired of heaping favors upon my head, and I can add to my other offering this new found treasure. But I think, Mr Rayne, had this gold mine never opened beneath our feet, we would still be the same to one another, I know"—and as she spoke she rose and threw herself into the old man's arms—"you, who have been both parents to me when I was alone and penniless, who surrounded me with comforts and luxuries, cannot now be cold to me because I no longer need to be dependent. You have made your home and your kind watchfulness a necessity to me, now will you not let us be the same as ever with one another? I do not want to be a rich heiress if I must thereby cease to be 'your own Honor,' and 'your own favorite.'"

The old man's eyes were wet with tears. He pressed the girlish figure close to him and kissed the fair, flushed cheek.

"We will speak no more of it, darling," he said, "let it be as though nothing had happened, only you must no longer hesitate to accept the many little favors that, up to this, you persistently refused— henceforth *I* am *yours* to command when you want something. But, about your *début* child, I want you to consult some one else on that matter, for you must be as fine to look at as all the rest. You can be ready as soon as you please, for Mrs D'Alberg will be here shortly, I requested an immediate answer."

Honor looked thoughtfully into the fire. "This is all so strange," she said, "but Destiny is Destiny, I suppose, and Fate is Fate."

CHAPTER XI

"A sadder and a wiser man
He rose the morrow—morn."
—Coleridge

"Well, I did not think this at the very worst," Mr. Rayne said over a newly received letter to Honor. "Here's the long expected news from Guelph, and my cousin says she would find it so convenient for you to go up, just for a week and she would come back with you. There are so many things for her to settle, and besides you would see a little bit of life in the meantime. Now, how in the world are we going to live without sunshine or daylight for a week, eh?"

"Oh, Mr. Rayne, you spoil me! But, does Mrs. D'Alberg really want me to go to her? If it is not very far away, and you have no particular objection, I think I'd rather like to go."

"Of course you would," echoed the generous words of Henry Rayne, "and why would'nt you? I am too selfish to live. It will make a nice little trip and you'll feel all the more refreshed when you get back. But, think of how soon you must go—to-morrow morning at the latest, I tell you. So, now be active, my dear. Run and tell Nanette to get your things ready, and I'll drop a note to Guy to come and make himself useful."

Honor bounded off under the influence of the first experience of a new anticipation—that of shifting the scenes, for no matter how short an act. She was going among new faces for a little while. What a break in the monotony of her present quiet life.

When the hastily written note reached Guy's boarding-house, he was absent. It was as a rule rather hard to find Guy when he was wanting; but, I doubt if he ever regretted his absence more than be did on this particular night. I would not care to shock my innocent readers unnecessarily by telling the hours that brought Guy Elersley to his room that night, nor the circumstances that caused him to dream such frightful things through his broken slumber. Some of them either from having been there before or from close observation could suspect one of Guy's worst failings at the sight of his dim sleepy eyes, his straggling cravat and half-buttoned coat, as well as by the thick utterances he hummed to himself, intended no doubt for the familiar strains of his favorite "Warrior Bold" or "In the Gloaming," but, nevertheless differing from them as much as they resembled them.

Oh, Guy! who, among your high-toned lady friends on Sparks Street to-morrow will recognize in you the fast midnight rambler, that the pale winter moon and the cold silent stars see in you to-night? You, the brilliant one of Ottawa's best drawing-rooms, ejaculating all the hard words you know, because you can't open the door with a lead pencil, nor find the handle on the wrong side. How well you have learned the art of veneering your character! Is it then such a breach of Christian charity to discuss on open pages, Guy Elersley by daylight, and Guy Elersley by lamplight? Any one given to moralizing, may surely ask the ladies of Ottawa, if they have ever stopped to think those simple things over. If all their acknowledged purity, dignity and womanly attraction were worth no more than to lay them within the ready grasp of the sons of this century of materialism! Do they never realize how infinitely superior they are to the men of their own days, and do they ever treat them with the contempt and indifference that are at best their due? If such were indeed the case, woman would be more independent in her social standing than she is to-day, but, I blush to say it—there are those among Ottawa's fair ones, who are flattered by the attentions and compliments of such as live these two lives of daylight and lamp-light;—flattered that an arm should encircle their waists in the dance, which is unworthy of cleaning the shoes they wear, or sweeping the ground they tread,—flattered by the attentions and flighty words falling from lips across whose threshold comes the foul breath of sin and dissipation. Such is the dignity of the youth of our century; such is the brazen insolence which causes them to establish themselves as the social equals of well bred women.

Oh, for the long sought day of woman's emancipation, when she will be free, in her own right, to scorn from the pedestal of her superiority, the audacity of the man who shows himself by daylight to the world to be that high society exacts from him, but whose superficial virtues set with the evening sun, leaving in their temporary dwelling place, the craving of material nature to be gratified. Such are the heroes of our popular novels, such are the heroes of our actual society, such are our male relatives, and yet women seem to be satisfied that things should remain thus. If every woman would determine within herself to accomplish the whole or part of the grand mission that is at the mercy of her own hands, how soon would we have cause to rejoice and thank Providence for the great reformation in morals which must be a necessary consequence of such a determination?

Perhaps it is wandering too far away from a simple recital, and giving more than its real depth to the tenor of our Ottawa society, to indulge in this strain. If it be just as pleasant, we will return to Guy who has gained admission by this time. He goes over to the table that stands opposite his bedroom door. He has left matches and lamp convenient, and proceeds to light them. The first thing which attracted his stupid glance was the note in his uncle's handwriting, lying conspicuously on the white linen cover. But this was, after Guy's nightly carousing—the most usual thing in the world, and with a word that signified how secondary his uncle's note was, beside the attempt to reach the bed, he pushed it carelessly aside and proceeded to get himself out of his clothes as well as his nervous limbs permitted him. We may be a "little hard" on Guy's species *selon* the current ideas of justice. We know that many are addressed through Guy Elersley, and this indirect way is adopted of telling them how far below the mark of feminine appreciation they fall in attempting to throw dust in our eyes. As if every circumstance of the times was not calculated to impress more firmly upon us how unworthy the world is becoming of us. We may hold out our hands one to another, for there is none else worthy to give the responsive grasp. Young men of the nineteenth century, be assured that because you are tolerated in society, and because ladies deign to blend their lives in a measure with yours, it does not follow that they approve of the masques you are wearing, and which deceive yourselves far more than they do others. On the contrary, it foretells the advent of the day of our freedom, for, in the performance of our respective social duties towards you, we make the last acts of humiliation to complete the sacrifice before the reward is given us. Of course, if we met Guy Elersley to-morrow morning, the fetters of society would force us to feign an utter ignorance of such a mode of living among our gentlemen friends. We must take it for granted that from sunset till sunrise, Guy was not "sleeping the sleep of the Bacchanal," and we need not fear that *he* will betray himself.

With aching head and parched lips, Guy Elersley opened his eyes on the tell-tale surroundings of his room the morning after "the night before." With the first break of sleep in the quivering of his lashes memory was at work. So long as she remains a faithful servant at all, her mission is waylaying us early and late. From the confused state of things around him, Guy gathered that he must have reached his resting place under difficulties, his feet reposed luxuriantly on the downy pillows, while his poor head was resting on the spare end of Mrs Best's second worst mattress. That his vest lay in an unpretending heap on the floor, from which his watch had rolled resignedly into an old slipper, did not disconcert him so much as his having left his new gaiters where the household puppy conveniently got at them destroying any possibility of a future reunion of their parts.

If a man ever wishes to repent of his yesterdays, let him contemplate them all over during his waking hours in the morning. Then, indeed, is his time. He becomes ashamed before the monotonous rose-bushes that speck the wall, and as his wandering orbs scan the picture-nails and the cobwebs in search of distraction, he will realize the necessity of amendment more fully than the eloquence of a multitude could paint it. It was the weariness of this new realization that caused Guy to stretch out his hand for his uncle's neglected note of last night, seeking as he thought, something therein that need not remind a fellow of what he knew "deuced" well already. As his glance fell on the page, his brow contracted into a slow puzzled look, and as he finished the last word he started up. It was now after nine o'clock and Honor was far on her journey. The note was dated 5 p.m. He would have received it time enough if he had not squandered away his hours from his room, but now she was gone and there was no excuse he could offer to satisfy himself.

It is necessary that we should part from some friends to know how much we love them, and this necessity visited Guy in its most cruel phase. Poor fellow!—After all, he was so much the victim of circumstances. The consciousness of his own weakness only made him weaker, and his knowledge of the infidelity and inconsistency in his character only caused him to resist, as useless, impulses towards stability and firmness. Now he regretted with his whole soul that he had not come home like any christian, at a proper bed-time, then he would have learned the news soon enough to have bade her good-bye. Even if he had read it when he saw it for the first time, the news it bore would have dispelled the mist that other influences had gathered around his senses. What could he do now? He must make the best of a very bad case and go immediately to his uncle's house where he expected to hear some tidings of the girl he loved.

If any man ever looked thoroughly disgusted with himself in his life, Guy Elersley surely did, on this eventful morning, as he sauntered along from his boarding-house to Mr. Rayne's. His sentiments were most likely those that form an item of the very smallest experience, when its victim is forced to realize that he has made a very unwilling sacrifice voluntarily; that he himself is the remote, proximate, direct and indirect cause of his own misfortune. Still, this was the only room for hope left in Guy. So long as a man condemns himself before his own tribunal, making of his inner self the truthful witness and impartial judge, those interested in his spiritual welfare may know that there is yet a lingering susceptibility, to a better influence than that which caused him to do wrong. That such a susceptibility does yet flicker in the hearts of Ottawa's young sons, I have reason to hope; for there is an impulse in some of us that leads us into the minds and souls of one another, there to deposit a judgment or a sympathy, or whatever our nature suggests at sight of our neighbor's failings. In obeying such an impulse one can easily peer through the conventional veil which screens such phases of human character under the meaningless appellations of "Blues," or "Indisposition." They are truly the visible effect of a secret hidden cause, which is sometimes brought to the surface by the magnetic power of one who has studied human faces and characters. So, *en passant*, it may be as well to kindly suggest to such "blue" friends that it were often better to lay bare the veritable cause of such a gloomy feeling, for those before whom they wear the veil are surely persons whose opinion they esteem or whose judgment they fear, and if so they are not so easily blinded as one would think, their deception only serves to render them still more odious. Yet there is no blame to Guy for having gone on his way this morning in such a mood. When he met Miss Dash at the first crossing it was the most natural thing in the world for him to say, "this 'dyspeptic' feeling causes it all," when she stared in open-eyed wonder at his worn out face and variegated eyes. It was breakfast-time when he closed his uncle's door after him, and he was sure to obtain *tête-à-tête* alone with the old man, now that Honor was gone, but he did not think the picture would have changed, into such a sad one as presented itself to his eyes when he opened the door of the breakfast-room. Mr. Rayne was sitting moodily in his chair, staring vacantly at his untasted meal, with his hands folded listlessly before him. At the sound of a voice he smiled and started, but on seeing the intruder the brightness died out again, and he only said, "Good-morning, my boy," in a very quiet tone.

"So you are all alone once more, uncle," said Guy, trying to make the best attempt he could under the circumstances, "Honor's flight was rather sudden, wasn't it?"

"Too sudden to secure your services when they were needed, I think."

"Well, yes, uncle, I was not in when your note came, and only saw it this morning for the first time, when it was too late to do anything, but I am really sorry. Will she not be back in a day or two?"

"I hope so. I hope so," Mr. Rayne answered, more to himself than to Guy. "I had grown quite accustomed to the darling."

"Yes, so had I," said Guy, under his moustache, "but" (aloud) "the little trip will make quite a change for her, and the time won't be long until her return."

A few more very laconic remarks followed, and then Guy began to think it was rather stupid, and in consequence made a move towards the door. This made matters a little brighter, for Mr. Rayne became more animated, and turning his chair towards the receding figure of his nephew, said,

"Hold on a minute, Guy, I want you before you go," and to lessen the moments of waiting, he raised his cup and drank it at one long draught, then he rose and led Guy into the cosy library opposite.

Whenever Mr. Rayne was about to impose any new duty on his nephew, he assumed a stern air that showed a tendency towards the imperative, rather than the interrogative. He had never said, "Guy, will you do this or that," it was always, "Guy, I wish you to do this—you must do such a thing for me," and accustomed to the like from his early youth, Guy never sought to hesitate, or dispute his uncle's will in anything. Whenever Mr. Rayne pushed his glasses up on his forehead and began by saying, "I am getting old and work is no longer light," Guy recognised the *avant-coureur* of some new duty devolving upon him, and this was a phase of this morning's experience.

"I wish copies made of all these documents, Guy," said his uncle in a business tone, while one hand rested on a prosy looking heap of legal forms, "and as it is serious work I cannot leave it out of my possession, so you must come in during your spare hours, now that Honor is away, and help me to write them over; it will keep us both busy during her absence, and leave us free on her return. I will expect you this evening before tea, and to make matters more convenient for all hands, I wish you to remain here until Honor's return. You may occupy the spare room, and time will not be quite so dull as otherwise."

"Very well, uncle," said Guy; but oh! what a hornble misery crept into his heart at the mention of such a thing. Visions of all the most outrageous difficulties possible, in the career of a fast young man, rose before his mind, and the consciousness of his lack of courage caused a shudder to pass through his frame. It must have been apparent, that Mr. Rayne entertained suspicions of this "boy," and resolved to stand between him and immediate danger if he could. This might have been Guy's salvation, if his eyes had not been blinded by the delusive flattery of the world to which he belonged. He only bowed under it as the most weighty of his crosses, and trusted to that fate that often shields the wrong-doer from observation, to turn the tables in his favor.

It was painfully evident to Guy this morning, that his uncle was in very stern humor, and that nothing but square dealing on his own part could sustain even the trembling balance that existed between them. One word, one little wrong deed now, and Guy fancied the fertile looking future realizing itself to him in that awful destitution which haunts the average civil servant, who has no pillar of pedigree to sustain him. It was the hardest policy of his life, to gather all his visible deeds under the approval of his good uncle, and yet he tried to bear these things patiently as one might a kick from the King. He saw a fair vision among the "to be's," if he behaved himself, and is not such an aim as that, the only one in the sunset of the nineteenth century?

Feeling "all over," as he thought, he left his uncle's house that morning filled with a firmer conviction than ever, that he was one of the world's unfortunates. Try as hard as we will, it is tough work living up to other people's principles, for now and then the most clever of us fail to interpret them aright and accordingly commit a fault.

It seemed rather cruel to poor Guy, as he sauntered along towards his office, that the plans he had so easily made for the next fortnight's distraction, should be frustrated thus in a moment. It is so "deuced" hard for a conceited sensitive fellow to bear the taunts of his more free and independent companions, when he is forced to decline their invitation to "come along." It is not natural that a man, able to stand his ground against evil counsellors, showing himself morally superior to them, should then fear their insolent remarks, or their unchristian judgment. We know it, each one for himself, that when we jibe or ridicule a good impulse in another, it is evidence of our weakness and incapacity to experience the same feeling ourselves, and it is the momentary hatred of envy that suggests a taunt or a mocking word on the firm resolution of our companion. But unless the conscience of youth be not obliterated now while it is so weak, the world fears there can be no other such chance again, and what else can hush its "wee small voice," like the ring of sarcasm or the jeering of brave cowards?

Guy's was one of those pliable souls that bent under every influence alike. How then, could he endure the scorn of "the boys" when he must tell them that his spare moments were already occupied? He began to miss Honor already, because one word from her would have spurred him on to duty; but, like his fate, she must be away when he needed her most. What must she have thought of his absence at the hour of her departure? She would, no doubt, accept it as an indisputable proof of his indifference to her, and this scalded his sensitive nature more than anything.

Accompanied by these refreshing cogitations, Guy reached his comfortable office, but oh "how painfully plain an index to his troubled soul was his worried face." All day he stumbled over office stools, spilt ink, made countless mistakes in his calculations, and, as a consequence, smashed pens and used unsparingly all those little monosyllables that seem to grow spontaneously on the tongue's end of an enraged man. His difficulties were beginning in earnest; he had consented to join a party of merry-makers to drive to Aylmer that night, and he could see no possible outlet through which he might escape. He had thought of seeing some of the "fellows" at four o'clock, and of telling them in some off-hand way of his change of determination; but even this little gratification was denied him, for emerging from his office door, the first one he came across was Mr. Rayne. There was that hopeless resignation, which dire necessity forces, in the very tone of Guy's voice as he addressed his uncle, but now, whether he would or not he must yield. Every circumstance showed him plainly how fettered he really was, although his spirit yearned to belong in gain as well as m name, to that band of "Acephah" that walked the streets of Ottawa, free men under their unpaid-for ulsters and seal caps. No wonder the conversation between Guy and his uncle consisted of a series of laconic monosyllables. The one was drinking the bitter dregs of life's awful difficulties; the other absent-minded and sad, thinking of the dear absent one who held within her hands the happiness of his life.

Who would have interpreted these things on this bright sunny afternoon as Mr. Rayne and his nephew walked side by side along Sparks Street, through the gay, bustling crowd of pedestrians and sleighs? The young ladies went home and told one another that they had met Guy Elersley, and that he looked "just splendid," whilst all the time his brain was on fire from trying to solve his dilemma.

They were reaching Mr. Rayne's house, and Guy, accumulating all the moral courage of his soul, resolved to do the worst. He would go willingly to work and try to find a pleasure in honest labor for Honor's sake. He was realizing, in spite of himself, the truth that had dawned on "Adam Bede," that "all passion becomes strength when it has an outlet from the narrow limits of our personal lot, in the labor of our right arm, the cunning of our right hand, or the still creative activity of our thought." Had he only but had the whisper of encouragement from any one he esteemed while in this vacillating mood, that would indeed have been a turning point in his career, but it seemed that a good impulse for Guy Elersley vaticinated infallibly an evil action. The fact that he had tried to vanquish himself by going willingly and deliberately to work, only waylaid him with numberless enticing temptations, alluring him on to the forbidden pleasures upon which he had turned his back. What is there so resistless and so fatally fascinating in those pastimes which are indulged in after nightfall by our young men? Is it the staunch proof that it seems to be, of the entire annihilation of conscience? Is it so certainly the spiritual death that it seems to be?—and if so, what sad, sad wreck! Is there no one whose influence can lead those stray sheep back to the fold? No mother, no sister, no lady love to plead as a woman's eloquence alone can plead, in behalf of that fair young soul exposed to every danger? Is there no volume among that superb collection of books open to all Ottawaites, that would not satisfy you, young foolish souls, by your midnight coals, burning your midnight oils, if you must needs burn both? What advantage is there in facing every peril of the material and spiritual darkness, that you must make a daily habit thereof? Is not this the case, that you never entered upon such a course of life alone? Some one was there who beckoned you on his way. Some one pooh-poohed your scruples, and smoothed down with false words the obstacles that your conscience raised. You never left your father's house alone to squander the hours of midnight's sacred silence in wrong doing Then I hope you will never forget the debt of gratitude you must owe to such a counsellor and friend.

Then comes

> "The tangled web we weave
>   When first we practice to deceive."

At first you were a little unfortunate, may be. If you could not reach home without elbowing some one's pane of glass, or getting into a scrape of a more or less serious nature, you were helped out of all trouble by those steadfast allies who contributed gladly towards making your deception a masterpiece of its kind.

After such reflections one is inclined to pity rather than condemn the weakness to which Guy Elersley resigned himself such a voluntary victim.

When he entered the library in his uncle's house, he began to be comforted by his luxurious surroundings, the same bright fire burned that Honor loved to see and the easy chairs and soft rich carpet suggested satisfaction to the most discontented. A few minutes of fussy preparations and the gloomy twain were immersed in dry business. Apart from the monotonous scratching of their hurried pens there was but an occassional short remark uttered until the welcome sound of the tea-bell broke the spell of sullenness that had fallen on both.

After a short but comparatively lively intermission they returned to their papers and re-attacked them diligently. Poor Guy's heart was beginning to thump. It would soon be eight o'clock, and it seemed to him in spite of all good arguments to the contrary that "a promise was a promise," and that by staying in to-night he was breaking one almost unnecessarily. The minute hand on the electro-plated clock was fast wending its way towards the half hour after seven, and as his eyes followed its quick movement he felt a hurried palpitation accompany every second on its flight to eternity.

Suddenly Mr. Rayne laid down his pen and rested his bald head in his hands. Guy looked up surprised, and as he did so, his uncle rose from his seat saying. "I have another attack of neuralgia to-night, Guy, and cannot continue this work as I expected. Try, however, to finish these single copies for me to-night. I must retire; I am really unable to endure these pains any longer without rest."

"Indeed uncle, I am very sorry for that," Guy said, but I fear that though it was "*malgré lui,*" still there lurked the faintest sense of intense gratification in his heart on hearing these words. "You certainly will be better in bed uncle, will I help you upstairs."

"Thank you, I'm not so weak as that. Remain here and finish those for me, they will be needed to-morrow and must be ready."

With these words he turned to leave the room, but just as though through inspiration, he stood with the half-open door behind him and said in a stern imperative tone, —

"Guy, mind you do not go out this evening; when you are tired writing you will find plenty of distraction indoors, do you hear?"

"I do, sir," Guy answered coldly, and then the old man closed the door and went up-stairs leaving his distracted nephew in the wildest of moods.

CHAPTER XII

For a sweet voice had whispered hope to me.
  Had through my darkness shed a kindly ray:
  It said "The past is fixed immutably,
  Yet there is comfort in the coming day."
  —*Household Words*

It was a cold stormy blustering day. The fierce north wind was moaning and wailing in piteous shrieks around the corners, and through the bare swaying branches of the tall elms. It was a dreary scene to look upon from a car window, and yet it was rather a cheerful face that peered through the tiny panes into the stormy surroundings outside. Honor was thinking deeply, a medley of sad and pleasant things, and she smiled and grew pensive alternately. She had thought of Guy, and of how pleasant it would be after all to have him there beside her, but she did not trust herself far into the subject. The doubtful halo that encircled all Guy's latest actions towards her was not the sweetest of memories, and yet this lovely girl would not whisper even to her own most secret soul, the words, "I love him." It was so girl-like for her to cherish that secret, and yet not acknowledge it to herself as a secret. She loved to rehearse to herself in silence every look and word and action of Guy's. She pondered wearily over the *ennui* of the hours, when he was not by her, and she longed so much to question herself about the sudden blushes and heart-beatings, when she recognized his step in the hall, or heard his deep voice greet her at the door. She knew that his little book with the scribbled verse from "Led Astray" was very often in her hands when he was not there, and yet when the "little voice" asked "Is it love?" She hid her face in her hands and said, "Oh no."

All these things she reviewed at leisure on this cold wintry morning, as she was being borne swiftly on to her destination. She could scarcely get accustomed to the idea that she was the same Honor Edgeworth, that had come a short time ago, alone and friendless to Mr. Rayne's house. And as she sped on leaving each dancing drifting snow-flake far behind, she became tangled up again in the web of fanciful reflections that had so often led her far far away into those transcendental regions of thought where Venus, and Cupid, and Calliope, and other sister muses bask in filmy clouds of golden maze. Here she realized among her ideal heroes and heroines, life as she wished it to be. Perhaps this was why her inclinations were just a little skeptical when she viewed life in its matter-of-fact phases.

Honor was started from her reverie by a loud long shriek from the engine, and seeing the other passengers gather up their fragments of baggage she followed suit. A few moments more and they were ushered into the depot at Guelph. All the usual bustle, talk and confusion characteristic of railway stations were noticeable here. Omnibus drivers shouted in *crescendo* the names of their respective hotels. Poor Honor scarcely knew what to do. Cries of "Royal Hotel," "Windsor House," "Sleigh Miss," deafened her ears on all sides, but great was her relief when a prim middle-aged lady accompanied by a half bashful youth stepped up to her smilingly and said:

"My dear I think you are my guest. Miss Edgeworth?"

"That is my name," Honor said, and then the prim lady handed Honor a card inscribed "Mde. Jean d'Alberg."

They became friends immediately and no wonder under the circumstances. Circumstances have so much to do with the turn and tide of our busy lives. We can make a friend of the most hideous creature in an hour of dire necessity.

Honor was just thinking she might have fared so much worse than come across a lady such as Madame d'Alberg proved to be. To look at her one could read the evidences of worldliness in her face. This woman had graced many a drawing-room as Senator d'Alberg's wife, and when the session time called her to the capital many a fair-haired damsel of eighteen summers had envied the fine face and faultless figure, that had captivated even the fastidious nature of the dignified Senator.

To-day, although somewhat older, the ordinary critic and observer could still detect no flaw of age or tendency to fade in the sparkling black eyes and fair delicate complexion. As Honor saw almost at a first glance, this woman's theory of life began and ended in "self." Not so much as to exclude any impulse towards sympathy or generosity. By no means—if there remained anything, after one had satisfied one's own wants, then let that surplus go to the less fortunate, according to the owners impulse whether limited or great.

In matters less material Madame d'Alberg took as director the great authority of Shakspeare, and none can tell how many countless times she justified herself by repeating in the most suasory tone this little extract from Hamlet:

"This above all to thine own self be true
And it must follow as the night the day
Thou cans't not then be false to any man."

This was an end worth attaining surely, and so easily won as by being fair with one's self.

Honor and her new friend chatted gaily all the way. The awkward youth had received instructions about the baggage. Thus freed from all inconvenience and responsibility, these two became as conversant and as communicative as if they had known each other for years.

Let it not shock the scrupulous reader to know that, in point of fact, Madame d'Alberg did not really care a straw for either Henry Rayne or his beautiful *protégée*, only insomuch as their existence was conducive to her own personal welfare. It was no effort whatever for her, to love in that subdued sort of way in which we are expected by the Church to "love our neighbor as ourselves." To be amiable and agreeable to all was by far more convenient to her than to play the *role* of a grumbler, and so long as she could count on her smiles being worth their representatives in substance to her, her countenance was fairly suffused therewith and her purse or her mouth open for the proceeds. Such women generally live easily—die easily enough too, and scarcely ever leave a memory of any sort behind them.

The first points of criticism that suggested themselves to this world-bred woman on seeing Honor were such as never entered the head of any other acquaintance the girl made before or after Madame d'Alberg's. This lady, physiognomist from tact and experience, sought to learn from the expression and features of Honor's countenance, whether their hidden depths held any of that diplomacy and finesse that are the inevitable characteristics of society's most brilliant graduates. Not that it would have mattered one iota to this indifferent creature, for she never interested herself particularly in anyone, but if certain latent tendencies in this girl could actually be brought to the surface so as to sympathize with her own, would it not be as well for them to join hands and share the spoils? As yet, however, she thought there was no telling, she must wait and see.

The drive from the depot was short, and to Honor's great delight the merry sleigh-bells stopped jingling as they drew up to the neatest and cosiest looking cottage imaginable. The first greeting on entering was the sight of a roaring fire and the next the intensely gratifying welcome of cups steaming at the end of a neat but well-spread table.

Honor's own room reminded her somewhat of the one in Ottawa, except that the idea of exquisite comfort was more pronounced in everything here. In this respect Honor found Madame d'Alberg different from that other class of society women whose ideas of self-gratification are far subservient to the requisites of *bon-ton* and fashion, and who endure heroically the discomfort of the latest absurdities in articles of toilet and street wear.

This was the only point in which Jean d'Alberg did not acknowledge the tyrannical yoke of society. Anything that tended to exclude the supreme ease and comfort of her home was discarded by her, and no one ever dared to find any fault therein.

After a hearty luncheon by the grate fire, Honor and Madame d'Alberg drew up their chairs closer to the fender and began to talk familiarly. The wind still whistled and shrieked around the street corners; little blinding atoms of snow drifted violently in the air, and it made one freeze just to watch the muffled pedestrians as they sped along with their heads bowed against the sleet and wind, holding their half-frozen ears, stamping their feet or pinching the ends of their blue noses.

"The day is too stormy for outdoor amusements, my dear," said Jean d'Alberg, as she poked the fire, "so I must try to distract you as much as possible in the house."

"That will be an easy matter if you like," said Honor, "do but leave me lost in these spacious cushions, before that cheerful fire, and I can prophesy the treat that is in store for me."

Mde. d'Alberg smiled slowly. She turned and took from a small wicker basket near her a bundle of misty looking thread and lace, and with her needle in one hand and the end of her thread between her teeth, she said,

"Whether you know it or not, my dear, you have given me a big peep into your character by that much of an assertion."

Honor looked suddenly up. She was beginning to feel a little nervous with this cool, calculating, all-seeing woman. But not to show what she felt, she sank back imperceptibly among the cushions, and answered, with an effort at in difference,

"I hope I betray my good symptoms first, at least to strangers who are inclined to judge from appearances."

The elder lady looked interested. Her face wore a half-pleasing, half-teasing expression, but like Honor she was seeking to veneer the real truth under assumed veils at the same time that she was dying to draw out the latent phases of her companion's nature.

"The word 'good,'" she said, stitching rapidly, "is such a mysterious one, and has in these days of general improvement, secured for itself a relative meaning which benefits as many as it injures, and particularly, as regards one's personal virtues or defects, which are many or few according to the disposition of the speaker towards the one spoken of. Nevertheless I must tell you that your tendency to dreaminess, and your exalted ideas of sentiment, are what mostly constitute the modern young lady. Take those elements out of human life, and one-third of our fiction volumes crumble on the shelf. Society limps into retirement, for her most prominent limbs have been amputated. The curtain must drop for good on the stage, for there is no other part for actors to play in the nineteenth century. Our streets would be almost desolate, except for fussy businessmen and market women, and those dear few privileged ones, who have the priceless reputation of being *sans coeur*."

Honor grew deeply interested. She had not expected to find such a woman as this. Mr. Rayne had spoken of her as one does of any superannuated person or thing that is always on hand if wanted. It was such a long time since she had indulged in any such abstract conversations, that it was with renewed delight she hailed her turn to speak.

"I think it only fair," said she, looking straight into the fire, "that I should take my turn at interpreting you."

"By all means, my dear; what have you found worth finding?"

"Well, I think," said Honor, speaking slowly and emphatically, "that fifteen or twenty years ago you could not have spoken those words, for I recognize, as far as a limited observation and a small experience allow me, the ruin of a heart full of sentiment, under the new structure that you present to the world to-day, and I also think that at that time you must have felt a superfluity of emotion. Your craving was for trust, for confidence and love, and the cynicism of your words now means something like sour grapes. Don't be offended, dear Madame d'Alberg, the thoughts suggest themselves. If you do not despise sentiment and romance, because they did not yield you what you sought from them, then I throw up my perception as faulty, and my judgment as something worse."

She had not moved her eyes from their fixed gaze on the coals, but as no answer came from her companion, she looked across in expectation. The work lay still in her lap, but her face had grown dreamy and sad. The sudden silence woke her, and she turned to meet Honor's steadfast gaze. The thin compressed lips parted slightly in a nervous motion, and Honor thought she could see a struggle for ascendancy in the workings of the usually calm face. Suddenly, a tear dropped from each downcast lid, and then the die was cast. Jean d'Alberg drew her chair closer to the young girl, and clasped her hands over her pile of work; then, looking straight at the fire, she began—

"Whatever power has inspired you, you have touched a spring over which the cobwebs of wilful neglect have lain during twenty years. It must be because you are so good and pure, that the truth, such as I am striving to hide, is so plain to you. You have uttered the secret of my life in the simple words you spoke. Twenty years ago, I was a young and beautiful girl, with a heart as full of susceptibilities and a mind as full of ambition as any one of you to-day. My face was beautiful, and I knew it; my figure was faultless, I knew that too. But vanity never entered into my heart for a moment. I had a dream that kept such trifling thoughts away. I wanted to endear myself to some one. I wanted to make some one so utterly dependent on me, that a separation should be almost death to him. Where I got this crazy longing I could not tell exactly, but it seized me like a mania. I felt that such must be my fate, or a lifelong of misery instead. While I was in the heat of this emotion my father told me to prepare myself, that I was to appear with him at the grand military ball of the season. This was the great event of the year in our town, for a detachment of British troops always stayed over for the occasion. The girls of the old country, at that time, were different from what they are now on this continent. Most of us had, as a rule, those conservative fathers, whose ideas of maidenly propriety had been handed down to them from unknown ages, and from constant preaching on the subject, I, like most others, grew into their way of thinking, but I did not, all the same, ever censure an impulsive girl who, by gratifying her own caprice, violated these stern views of her father's."

It was getting dark in the little sitting room. At this point of her story Jean d'Alberg rose, and going over towards the window that faced the west she rolled up the blind to let in the last wintry rays of the setting sun. Then, coming back, she rang for the maid to bring more coals, for the fire was dying out.

CHAPTER XIII

"Alas, how easily things go wrong,
A sigh too much or a kiss too long,
And there comes a mist and a blinding rain,
And life is never the same again."
                    —*George McDonald*

When all was comfortably arranged once more, Jean d'Alberg resumed her seat and her story:

"The eventful night of the ball came at last, and I know not what nervous presentiment caused me to fasten my palest crush roses in my hair, and to take from their old resting place the diamonds set in heavy gold, that my maternal grandmother had worn ages before. I knew full well, as I leaned on the arm of my tall, dignified father that night, that he recognized in me more strongly than ever, the likeness to his dead wife, my mother. The only feeling of pride that visited me was when I knew that my father was proud of me as his daughter and his dead wife's living image. My father was an officer in the —th regiment and, as a matter of course, I was to be treated with more than ordinary courtesy. When we entered the ballroom at the lower end I could hear suppressed whispers on all sides. It was my first appearance in any public place, and even if I had not been there, all eyes would have been riveted on my handsome father, who looked the embodiment of manliness and nobility in his regimentals. Perhaps it was the haughty tone of his voice, when he introduced his 'daughter' to the hostess of the evening, that caused them to look upon me with no little wonder. Any way I became painfully conscious that we were isolated, as it were, from all the others, and the blush of confusion and excitement that suffused my face, was, as they told me afterwards, my finest feature. I had scarcely finished paying my respects to the hostess, when my father was surrounded by friends who greeted him earnestly, yet distantly. To each of these I was presented in turn, and agreed to dance once with each of them.

"But I had not yet ceased to feel that nervous presentiment that had haunted me all the evening. Suddenly, the low, sweet strains of a waltz vibrated through the room, and gay, laughing couples wheeled off into its dizzy maze. Among my many partners, none had secured the first waltz and I was beginning to congratulate myself that I could take a good view of everything and everybody before commencing my first dance. While I was scanning the room —'

Here a large coal fell into the ashes causing both ladies to start. Madame d'Alberg poked the glowing embers into a cheerful blaze, and moved closer to the work-table, and as her fingers traced imaginary patterns on its surface, she resumed her story in the same sad monotonous voice.

"I said I raised my eyes to scan the room, but as I did so the blush faded quickly out of my face, and a cold shiver crept through me. I felt for the first time the sensation which all persons experience at some interval in their lives. It was the same as when we know without looking, that someone is watching our movements, the same that causes us to *feel* the approach of someone, though we may have been persuaded that such a one was far away. I felt that I was being stared at, and following a sudden impulse, I looked towards the shaded recess of a large window, and there I saw the tall figure of a man dressed in uniform, with medals and stars upon his breast; his eyes, the largest, deepest, and most passionate blue I have ever seen, were riveted upon me. As soon as he perceived that I was conscious of his attention he left the recess, and though my eyes did not follow him, I felt that his every step brought him closer to where we stood. At last my heart seemed to give one great leap, for I heard him address my father in a low sad voice full of meaning and pathos. The next instant I was bowing at the sound of both our names, to the handsome stranger. The first glances we exchanged must have told a tale, for I read in the limitless depths of his sad blue eyes, all that mysterious, silent pain that entreats and commands a woman's sympathy; he in his turn must have seen in mine the ready response to the calm pleading of his own.

"I cannot remember the first words that passed between us. It was the mute language of soul speaking unto soul that had charmed me, and the next thing I realized was, that we had glided in with the laughing throng of merry dancers, among them, but not of them.

"Our steps suited exactly, and as fate would have it, the music was the dreamiest and most suggestive I had ever heard. We never spoke a word, but he must have felt my heart throbbing against his breast, like a captive bird, struggling for its freedom. For once, when all was excitement and pleasure, he pressed my hand ever so little, and I felt his warm breath very near my flushed cheek. All the emotion that had ever rested latent within me, struggled through the fetters that moment, and I felt that now I loved, madly and hopelessly, and that as it had all been born of a second, so might one other second break my heart.

"While such reflections chased one another through my confused brain, my partner led me mechanically into the long narrow conservatory to the left. Outlines of rich and delicately fragrant plants were visible in the soft hazy light that pervaded the spot, and we were near enough to the ball room to hear the subdued strains of orchestra music that yet filled the air. I dared not trust myself to silence, so I said, trying to assume the most indifferent tone.

"'How pleasant it is in here!'

"I'll never forget the distracted far-away look in his eyes as he answered in that dangerously, low, sweet voice.

"'Pleasant? Yes, when the heart is young and untried, all that is beautiful touches it with pleasure, but the heart that is withered and dead, gets its sweetest pain from the very same source.'

"To say I did not understand him would not be quite true. We English girls, who have lived with stern fathers, and with no mother for the best part of our lives, seem to learn by intuition, the saddest phases of a life's experience. We personify the heroes of our old books, until the worst of written fates, become as natural to us as though such had been items of our own existence. And so I knew immediately, that this man's life had been blighted bitterly. Some awful storm cloud had shaded the sunniest portion of his life, and the memory of that affliction would cast an immortal gloom over the rest.

"After he had uttered those strange words he looked calmly into my face. What could I do? I had too often persuaded myself that a woman is the weakest of all things, under the influence of a first love I could summon no moral courage now to my assistance, and, childlike, I thought this great, sad looking man would never betray to another how efficaciously he had worked his influence over me. Yielding to these resistless impulses, I drew a little closer to his stalwart form, and then he took my hand in both of his, and I could not help showing what all the passion of a lifetime was, when concentrated into one awful moment of existence. I only looked up into those full dreamy eyes, and said, 'Why are you so sad?'

"There must have been in those few words, eloquence enough to teach even his heart the truth, for he rose, and stooping over me, he said in a voice that sounded like a sigh, 'I am sad for the same reason that you will cause others to be some day, if not more careful and land. Do not sadden and ruin as worthy a heart as mine.' Then before I realized my position, there was but the memory in my heart of his lips having touched mine, followed by the feeling of secret dread and horror, that sprung from the awe in which I stood, of my father. I woke suddenly from the listless apathy that came over me. I looked up with all the emotion of fear, excitement and love visible in my face, looked to find the pale angry countenance of my father before me, with all the insulted dignity and slighted authority he felt, pictured therein.

"He did not say much just then. He trusted to the power of his look to wither the heart within me. He told me sternly, to procure my wraps, that I must leave immediately, we could pass out unnoticed by the side door. In a few moments we were in our carriage, rolling in solemn silence along the road that led to our homestead. My father spoke not a word, and I could not imagine any fate ill enough to befall me, before his wrath would subside. I planned no excuses; I promised myself not to vacillate in any way when accused, I knew that neither attempt would blind my rigid parent for an instant. When we reached our home, my father with all his usual courtesy, helped me to dismount, and gathering my superfluous wraps himself, he gave me his arm and led me into the house. But all this only foreboded the determination, changeless and cruel, that comes from the cold deliberate anger of a just, stern man. When I reached my room, I heard the bell rung for Donnelly, our old housekeeper, and then my heart quaked in earnest with its fearful presentiment. I could not stand it any longer, so I stole down stairs, dressed as I was in my white brocaded ball-dress, and hid myself behind the folding-doors that stood half open between the drawing-room, which was in darkness, and my father's study, where a single gas-jet was lighting. I had scarcely gathered in my skirts in breathless terror, when I heard the cold, sonorous voice of my father speaking in low grave tones. Our faithful old housekeeper standing by him, looked scared and white. I strained my ears to overhear the conversation, but failed to do so. Only as the old servant passed out I heard her say, 'It is not for me to dictate sir, but I hope you'll think better of this before it is too late—for her dead mother's sake.'

"I was mortified beyond expression. A servant was pleading for me, before my own father, and he refusing to listen! No wonder I felt the blood rushing hotly to my face. No wonder that I was too proud to wait quietly there for him to punish me at will. He had been severe and exacting all his life, but there was a limit to his authority. The very worst possible anticipations crowded into my brain, when I saw the tears falling unrestrained from poor Donnelly's eyes, as she turned to leave the man with whom all remonstrance was vain. I stole out from my hiding-place again, and on reaching the hall I saw the bundle of shawls my father had carried in for me. A sudden impulse inspired me, I wrapped myself in their woollen folds as best I could, I turned the great bolts of the front door noiselessly, and went out into the cold, chilly starlight, without a friend or a home, shivering, and not having where to lay my head."

Here she paused, and the intense malice and scorn that sparkled in her fine black eyes almost frightened Honor Edgeworth. When she resumed her story, her tone was more calm and subdued.

"I walked on," she continued, "until my feet and hands were numb with cold. The north-east wind pierced its bitterness through my bared breast; I pulled the shawl tighter around me, clutching as I did so, a circlet of diamonds, that would have purchased all the comforts in the land for me, and yet I was alone and freezing. He was comfortable and warm, whose cruelty had driven me into the street, and yet I was his own flesh and blood. He could listen to the wailing of the winter wind, and know that it was the pitiful cry of his child—his daughter, and yet remain unmoved. It was then I missed the tender solicitude of a mother, and I looked up into the cold silence of the stars, seeking in their still, watchful expression, some stimulus, for I thought I must go mad, or lie down to die on the earth's frozen bosom. I did not rashly censure anyone for my misfortune, but that night the coldness and cruelty of life, as it unravelled itself to me, blighted every womanly sentiment within my heart. From that moment dates the cynicism that marked my after life. My old self died out, and the flickering flame that started afresh into existence, was no longer the quiet subdued one of older days I had passed from a gay happy girl, into a hardened reckless woman, and I have never regretted it.

"Cold, and miserable, and friendless, I went in search of a refuge, to an old nurse of mine, who lived at a short distance from the spot to which I had wandered. I reached the house and looked in the narrow window. A greasy looking candle burned on the rough table, casting flickering shadows around the low ceiling and walls, over the pewter dishes and shining delf. It was a kind of comfort to my poor heart, when I saw old Nanny herself, seated on a rocking chair before the fire. I can never forget the expression of genuine horror that covered the old creature's face, as she saw me at the door of her little cottage, shivering in my ball dress.

"'Is it Miss Jean?' she said, with both hands up in consternation, 'sure I declare its more like the ghost of our dead sweet mother comin' to me this blessed night, as I just sat thinkin of her.'

"In silence I entered and crouched by Nanny's cheerful fire. Great Heavens! as I review the agony and pain of those moments of my existence, I wonder that I ever survived it. I did all that was left me under the circumstances. I made a truthful declaration to Nanny and then left it to her to do what she wished with me—but I weary you child, with these details," Mde. d'Albert said, hesitating slightly. But Honor, with the flush of excitement on her cheek, begged of her companion to continue. Thus pressed, she proceeded "Whether it was Nanny's intention to befriend me or not, I was thrust upon her, for a slow fever followed the chills and shivering that had seized me, and for seven long weeks I lay between life and death on Nanny's neat old bed. On the third morning of the seventh week I regained consciousness, experiencing all that vacant wonder at the strange surroundings of Nanny's little room. My memory was struggling with the confusion and exhaustion, brought on by my illness, but I did not care to think. I turned my head peevishly away, and closed my eyes again. When next I opened them it was growing dusk, large grey shadows were trooping out over the little room, leaving but the outlines of Nanny's old-fashioned furniture, visible through their mist. A small, broad clock was ticking out its monotonous notes from the mantle-piece, and the crackling noise of the fire somewhat relieved the great stillness.

"While I was thinking, Nanny's stooped figure cast a shadow across the doorway, and came stealthily over to my bed. I can yet see the look of relief and thanksgiving that came into her dear old face, when she saw that I recognized her. She bent over me smiling, and I stretched out my arms and clasped them around her neck. That night she sat at the foot of my bed, and we talked matters over. Despite all her arguments and entreaties to the contrary, I was determined to leave her as soon as my health allowed me. In the course of our conversation, Nanny alluded to the night of my separation from my father, to see how it would affect me. As I never changed nor moved a muscle, she came nearer and knelt before me. I knew by the strange look on her kind old face, that there were words on her tongue's end, awaiting utterance.

"'What is it, Nanny?' I said, 'speak it out, there is nothing now that can wound my heart—it is free to the worst treatment of fate. It is like the deserted nest in the tall pine tree. The summer of its life is over, now the wind may howl around it and the cold snowflakes fill it up. The birds it once cherished have deserted it, and left it to its fate alone.'

"Poor Nanny's eyes were overflowing, as with a faltering voice she said,

"'O, my poor child, to think your mother's daughter should ever come to this! But, there now, like a good girl, don't talk like that; it'll all blow over some day, and ye'll go back to the old house where I nursed you in my arms a tiny thing, and your mother before you, Now the big, tall man is gone far away, the troubles will cease, please God, and all will be right.'

"I looked sharply up 'What big tall man, Nanny?' I asked, and my heart beat violently as I waited for an answer.

"'Oh, sure,' said she, rising up, 'ye were too weak to tell ye of it, but wait a bit, an' I'll show ye now.'

"She went over to the old mantle-piece and pulled from behind a curious looking box, a small envelope. Then, bringing the candle nearer my bed, she handed me the letter and left the room.

"Its contents were only what helped me towards action. I had not expected this, and yet it had not surprised me in the least. It informed me that my hero had left for the continent; that owing to a series of unfortunate events in his early life he had vowed solemnly never to marry. The worst troubles that had ever befallen him had been on account of a woman he had loved, and he had voluntarily cast the sex out of his life for evermore. In that letter he bade me a strange and last farewell."

When Jean d'Alberg finished speaking her face wore an expression of half indifference and half regret, as though the very last flicker of an old smouldering flame had suddenly darted up, and then died out in the ashes and the darkness. As the sound of the last echo of her voice ceased vibrating in the silent room, she awoke from the revival of memory's lethargy, and her face resumed all its wonted coldness and calmness. She looked at Honor almost suspiciously, and said in a low breath,

"I cannot explain how I have been coaxed into this confiding mood with you, child as you are."

She seemed to be awakening from a stupid dream, and she was tangled in a strange mystery. Honor recognized the feeling as a very common one. It is the doubt that often interrupts us in our confidences, lest the depository of our secret be not a safe one. It is generally a proof of the importance, greater or less, of what we confide.

Honor sat upright, and womanlike, took both Jean's hands in hers, saying—

"Do not be uneasy; I know your heart. I have not a great experience such as yours, but the experience of thought and emotion are not unknown to me. You have been miserable, and even to-day it is not too late to sympathize with you."

Jean d'Alberg laughed—a low, incredulous, skeptical laugh, that half-frightened Honor.

"Do not talk of sympathy any more," she said, "such things are soap bubbles, beautiful to look at from a little distance, but stretch your hand out to grasp them, and what remains? No, no, Honor, give up that foolish game. You see by my tale that I have gone through the fire. I need scarcely tell you with what result. I rose from my bed of sickness with a heart of flint and a will of iron. I worked honorably and honestly to bring myself to this country, where there is true encouragement for industry and perseverance, to this Canada, which is the pride and glory of England, and whose arms are extended in an admirable hospitality to the homeless exiles and fugitives of the world. Here there is labor for all honest hands, and gratification for all honest hearts, and God cannot but bless and cause to prosper, a country so just, so encouraging and so kind.

"I was not long here when I first met Mr d'Alberg. He seemed taken with me, but my heart felt not the slightest passing emotion towards him. In the end he became satisfied to accept me as I was, and though I never wore out my sleeves caressing him, still I made him a tolerably good wife, until death wooed and won him from me, leaving me to live on the plenty he had accumulated in a lifetime. I am now neither happy nor miserable, I neither despair nor hope, I am waiting for time to do its best or worst, I am prepared for either. Life or death offer me equal fascinations, I seek nothing but what chance sends me, I have comforts, and in my way I enjoy them, that is all I want. Let me give you now one word of advice; live, act, and die, independently of every other person and circumstance but yourself and your own immediate concerns, for the mask of life is very deceptive, and we are not always strong enough to bear the stroke when it falls."

A heavy sigh followed these last words and then all was over. The long, intricate story of a lifetime, had been breathed out. The shadows of the wintry evening were trooping noiselessly from the corners of the room, and to the quiet observer there was nothing extraordinary to be read from the surroundings. Honor looked serious, but this was nothing new with her. Jean d'Alberg looked sadder than usual, though not with such a bitter sadness as one finds in the face of an ordinary heroine, who reviews the mockeries of her past for another woman. Were the verdict just, it should call them both sensible women.

It seemed such an unnatural and inconsistent sound when the demure old woman-servant appeared in the doorway and announced supper.

But these two women rose and went to the dining-room as mechanically as though they had just been discussing the last "poke" bonnet or Mother Hubbard mantle, in the most usual way imaginable. However, a new tie bound them together now, and though no direct allusion, was afterwards made by either party to the strange narrative, yet their sympathy so strong, though new-born, manifested itself in the look and actions of each, and they became what the world called "staunch friends."

CHAPTER XIV

"Would you had thought twice,
Ah! if you had but follow'd my advice."
— *Byron.*

We left Guy in Mr. Rayne's study, in sore trouble as to how he could evade the task set him, and join his rioting friends in their proposed amusement. He scratched his head and made countless agonizing grimaces; he walked the room in long strides, until his patience had reached an almost impossible limit. Then he thought better of it, and decided to hold a calm, cool and collected council with himself. It was plain to his one-sided judgment that he was called upon to act, and to act immediately. But this was easier said than done. It is simple enough for a fellow to strike splendid chords on the piano, merely by ear, or in a moment of impromptu genius he may construct some wonderful little piece of mechanism; Guy felt that he could achieve countless feats such as these, but he'd be blessed if he could master a double-locked window, or door, through any innate talent, on a dark night, when every one is just asleep sound enough to start at the slightest noise. He had persuaded himself, by means of such fallacies, as come unbidden to the susceptible heart in the hour of temptation, that he must go out to-night by fair means or foul. Once decided, he did not hesitate to act, every one had retired, and surely he might steal out unobserved. The chances were he could get back the same way, and there would be nothing more about his little escapade. Noiselessly, stealthily, he collected the articles of his street wear, and rolling them up in a bundle, laid them by the window. Then nervously, and fearfully, he began the work of undoing the fierce looking bolt over the window. Every one of those queer little noises, the voices of the night, seemed to Guy the words of his uncle reproaching him with his disobedience. Once as he was just about to raise the lower part of the window, a coal gave away in the grate, and the rattle that followed its fall made him quake with fear.

Finally all was silent as Guy held his breath in eager listening, and making a desperate attempt he lifted the ponderous frame slowly and secured it above. Directly under it was the roof of a small balcony that shaded the side of the house. In the summer time it was covered with green vines, which climbed to the very top, but now the stiff withered leaves and dry branches, rustled and cracked in a horrible way as Guy threw down first his bundle, and then proceeded to follow it himself "the devils' children, have the devils' luck," it is said, and it certainly often looks as if that luck was the luckiest of all.

Without scratch, or hindrance of any kind, Elersley reached the ground, and as he buttoned up his overcoat, matters commenced to look beautifully smooth and easy. He half-expected that the jolly dogs had started on their trip without him, but he was sure of finding company in a great many other places besides, if the first failed him. He was emerging in all possible haste from the gate-way of his uncle's house when he was accosted by the police-man on beat in that vicinity. Here was a "fix." Guy was almost in despair, and it was only on producing cards, and letters, and other substantial proofs of his identity that he was left go. He made a quiet determination to have a good time after such hardships as he had endured, and indeed his determination did not fall too short of the mark. It would scarcely interest the readers to follow Guy Elersley any farther than the gloomy street corner to-night; though perhaps many of them may have often followed his prototype in spirit to such haunts as midnight revellers frequent. Did we accompany him we would have to tear away that opaque barrier, that many young polished gentlemen, have built up before the eyes of their *day* acquaintances; we would have to call forth tears of bitter bitter anguish, from trusting sorrowing mothers, who are at this same moment praying God on bended knees, to save their wild wayward boys. We would pierce the hearts of many pure confiding girls, who are buried in dreams of future happiness, and who would not dare suspect the awful truths that are born of the midnight hours. There are, therefore, too many innocent ones interested; too many mothers to wail; too many sisters to bow their heads in shame; too many young loving hearts that would burst were one to spell out the truth in legible characters. "They have eyes and they see not," let us mercifully leave them in their blindness.

Think of all that Guy had encountered to gratify the paltry ambition born of a moment s passionate desire; a soul so young, almost fresh from the hands of the Creator, and yet to be so covered with iniquities! How soon he had learned to jest and laugh at good, and to make his religion the worship of the senses. Saying with Byron,

> "Man being reasonable, must get drunk,
> The best of lift is but intoxication,"

and striving to find in the wine-cup, the satisfaction that our inner nature craves, trying to feed a soul, hungry for the beauties and perfections of the invisible world, with the poisonous food of sensuality. Let us say to it with Shakspeare,

"O thou invisible spirit of wine,
If thou hast no name to be known by
Let us call thee 'devil.'"

And lest these words betray any of the personal indignation that suggests itself at the moment the reflections upon such lives are indulged in, the voice of this same great poet ran be heard again telling in his emphatic terms,

"I could a tale unfold whose lightest word
Would harrow up thy soul, freeze thy young blood,
Make thy two eyes like stars start from their spheres,
The knotted and combined locks to part,
And each particular hair to stand on end
Like quills upon the fretful porcupine."

But we have only to look around us intelligently to find the secret out ourselves. Society is at the acme of sensuality; it has reached the strangest antithetical condition. It is degraded in its excessive refinement; it is coarse and repulsive in its cultivation, it is ignorant in its enlightenment. Necessarily all this is the effect of a cause, but such a pitiful cause! The total wreck of man's best element. The once individual corruption has spread its fearful contagion until it has become universal; falsehood is disguised in truth, vice in virtue, and fraud and diplomacy in honesty. If women are expected to live in blissful ignorance of this movement, that expectation is a crowning audacity, for woman's life is destined to be one of action, and she will not sacrifice her noble mission through purely human motives. She means to save her brother, her lover, her husband, her son, even if the effort includes the forfeiture of her title of woman in the eyes of society.

Thus it is, we have been persuaded into an unpremeditated leniency towards the sterner sex, blotting out the pictures of their vicious lives, not indeed to spare them in the very least, but only to save the blush, the sigh, the tear of many a woman whose heart is nigh enough to breaking without a stronger hand striking the last blow in the cruel work of laying bare the awful, the contemptible reality which fills their lives with bitterness and heart-burnings.

We will, then, caution and advise without explaining, and call on our co-laborers to make a grand effort towards reformation, telling them that from the heart of the great cities there rises a wail of sorrow and desolation, that must fall on their ears like a cry of distress from the poor suffering stricken ones, that they must rise bravely, spontaneously, and joining hands they must come nobly to the rescue. It is their lawful, binding duty to reclaim. We must save from the wreck at least those "little ones" that are growing up around us, "for of such is the Kingdom of Heaven." Why need they ever know the experience that is drunk in the wine cup? Why must they, too, walk in the well-printed footsteps of vice that their elders are treading before them? They must not; they shall not; they dare not! if they have noble women to direct them, to inspire them with great and holy and generous thoughts, to draw them round the family fireside, to gratify their eager hearts with innocent amusements that elevate the mind and bring the soul nearer to God. Where are the mothers now, who, like Blanche of Castile, can say to their sons, "My child, I would rather see thee dead at my feet than that thou shouldst offend God mortally." Alas! if in our city alone, mothers were to re-echo that wish and have it granted, many a strong youth would be laid in his coffin before night!

Mothers and sisters will ask, "What can one woman do by herself?" What good? If every mother sends a St. Louis to eternity before her, is not that a magnificent influence on society, and who denies it? Be not discouraged then—withdraw the misplaced sympathies that have been enlisted by thrilling manuscripts or exciting anecdotes in the cause of missions and religious undertakings abroad. At home, within your own most intimate circle you have a mighty field for your labors. Hearts to which you are closely attached are sadly in need of your attention, and while you are so solicitous in providing for corporal necessities and comforts, forget not the poverty, the destitution of the moral nature. Wrap the robe of innocence and repentance round the heart that is naked and susceptible to all the influences of foul weather. Go bravely forth in the bark of divine charity and save the soul that is tossing helplessly on an angry sea, without food or support or safety, plunging into irremediable debauchery, as Guy Elersley is to-night.

CHAPTER XV

"Praising what is lost
Makes the remembrance dear."

The cold, cloudy night was just at us period of transition when the misty grey of a foggy morning was slowly extending over the quiet city. A light fall of snow covered the rough fences and the bare branches, and a chilly, freezing atmosphere weighed heavily down upon the earth. There was scarcely a sound to be heard. Now and then the still measured tread of a solitary policeman, or the pitiful chirp of some homeless sparrow under the eaves of a neighboring house broke the monotonous silence of the early dawn. But suddenly another sound burst out upon the great stillness, it was the clock from the Parliament Tower striking the hour of three. The last vibrations had scarcely died out when the figures of two men, arm-in-arm, came round the corner. There is a well-known little *on dit* which says "when two men walk arm-in-arm it is more than probable that one is sober," but it was the exception and not the rule that applied this morning. Both were seemingly under the same influence and to the same degree. Though the sight had its revolting side, still one was also inclined to laugh at the ridiculous appearance they presented. One was short, but had all the disadvantages of his failing compensated in his breadth. The other was, as I have often described him before—tall and slim, our brave Guy Elersley. His features were barely visible, owing to the manner in which he wore his hat, which would willingly repose on his shoulders only for an occasional jerk upwards from the owner. His affectionate friend with the pronounced tendency to *embonpoint*, tried to persuade himself that his head was really covered, although Guy's hat, to do its most generous, could never shield more than the extreme top of his hair. Snatches of their conversation only reassure the looker-on of the absurdity of the situation. The good-natured looking companion, whose name was Morrison Jones, said in the most usual tone in the world—

"I think we're getting home kind of late, Guy," at which Guy laughed unreasonably long, and then added,

"Ye-s, he'l (l-ate) me up, by Jove!" and then Jones clapped Guy, saying,

"Here now! no more of this," and both went off into a ridiculous duet of laughter, that sounded harshly on the stilly air of the peaceful night.

Arrived at the gate of Mr. Rayne's house both young men stood, and Morrison Jones who seemed a little bit the wiser of the two addressed Guy in fatherly terms.

"Here now, Elersley, this is twice I've seen you home to night and I won't do it any more. It's time for honest people to be in bed, and I think I'll go to mine."

"Mine-(d) you do," said Guy slamming the gate after him, forgetting his usual precautions in the unseemly mirth caused by his vulgar attempt at wit. Thus unceremoniously he left his friend to wander back alone through the dismal street.

Guy was just in that delightful state when a fellow is at peace with all the world, when he feels ready to share his last shilling with his brother, and thus in perfect good humor, he was making a drunken attempt to render the "Tar's Farewell." He wandered on blissfully until he reached the balcony beneath the library window. Here he paused and looked up, but to his dismay found that the window had been closed since his departure. The muddled state of his brain prevented him from suspecting that he had been discovered. He only knew that he felt the cold chills of the dawn all through his frame and he could not help longing for the pillows and warm blankets above. He walked around to the back of the house and there began to deliberate. "First—second—yes third" was his window, but he must do it noiselessly for there was danger in the attempt. By degrees he mounted as far as the window sill in tolerable good humor, singing "Pull away my boys," and then making another firm clutch on to some other projection he would squeeze out in a constrained voice, "Pull away." Finally the window was tried and yielded—happy lot. He resumed his song mixing it up with "Nancy Lee," "And every day," here the window went up another little bit, for it was very stiff, "when I'm away," and he rested it on his shoulder, "she'll," here his uncertain balance gave way, and as—"pray for me" escaped his lips in frightened tones, he stumbled head foremost into the room.

He remained there motionless for a few minutes, wondering what he was doing all in a heap on the floor, but suddenly the whole appalling nature of his misfortune burst upon him in its most dreadful aspect There before him, standing erect with a lamp in his hand, was Mr. Rayne, viewing him with all the withering contempt of a cold stern man. Dazzled at first by the light he started up from his recumbent position, and as he did so, the reflection of his frightful appearance greeted him from the mirror opposite.

It would not do to spoil by an attempt at description the conflict of emotions that rent his breast at that moment. It is far better imagined. He, there on the floor, after failing miserably in an attempt to steal in, when he had promised his uncle not to go out, his uncle standing now, petrified, before him, having caught him in the disgraceful act of stealing an entry. Mr. Rayne looked down upon him with all the bitter contempt an honorable man can show to dishonesty; he spoke but a few words in a harsh grating tone—

"I see you have contrived to preserve your bones unbroken in this attempt, although you have shattered your word and my future trust in you beyond reparation."

Then he closed the door and went back to his own room, his face still wearing that painfully serious expression it had scarcely ever worn before.

Guy began the disagreeable act of gathering himself up as soon as the unpleasant novelty of his uncle's apparition had died away, and as each succeeding moment forced on him, with his returning consciousness, the awful reality of his condition, he began to feel that unenviable sensation of distraction, which is almost akin to despair. He tried to shape things so as they might form some excuse, but it was miserably vain. Matters were decidedly against him. He had told his uncle that he would not go out, and the next thing, he is found stumbling in a back window at three o'clock in the morning. As Guy reviewed the situation over and over in his perplexed thought, he found how mistaken he had been indeed, thus to fool with the man on whom he depended for his future welfare. A hearty, though half selfish regret, seized him, and the broad day broke into the room before he closed his eyes in sleep.

At eight o'clock he woke with a start from very unpleasant dreams, just to face more terrible and more unpleasant things in reality. Guy showed more moral courage on this occasion than he had ever before shown in his life. He rose with a fixed determination as to his plan of action. He dressed with his usual care, and was downstairs before his uncle. Sitting by the fire in the dining-room, he took up the morning *Citizen* and began to read. Suddenly the door opened and the room seemed to fill with the chilly presence of Mr. Rayne. Guy never moved, yet he felt that the cold piercing glance of his angry relative was upon him. At last, unable to bear it any longer, he flung the unread paper from him and confronted his uncle. The latter looked fully ten years older, so serious and stern an expression did his face wear on this gloomy morning. Guy began to feel sorrier than ever, but the old man merely raised his hand, and pointing to the doer, said—

"Go, sir, it was not worth your while to spurn me thus, at this period of my years; but you knew that my principle is 'an eye for an eye and a tooth for a tooth,' and so, sir, I give you your reward. Go from my house, for I withdraw all relationship between us; and remember, I will never forgive this insult to my authority, from one on whom I had lavished all my heart's affections."

A flush rose to the young man's forehead, and he burned to say something in self-justification, but his uncle's wrath was great and so he merely answered in a quiet tone,

"As you say, uncle," then before he left the room he turned again, adding, "you have been young yourself, uncle, and you may regret this precipitation when the memory of your own follies comes back to you. As I have been the wrong-doer, I accept your sentence, which all the same cannot cancel in me the remembrance of your many kindnesses." And thus, without a word of farewell from either, these two parted, that a little while before had been all the world to one another.

CHAPTER XVI

"O absence! what a torment wouldst thou prove,
Wer't not that thy sour leisure gives sweet leave
To entertain the time with thoughts of love."
—Shakespeare.

"And so you think of going back to Ottawa so soon? Well, I suppose the magnet is hidden somewhere, that draws you towards it," and Jean d'Alberg laughed playfully as she turned to address her words to Honor, who was yet buried in the snowy linen of her comfortable bed.

Honor clasped her hands over her head and smiled a little sadly, saying:

"Yes, I like Ottawa—more than I thought I did, and if it is just the same to you I think we need make no longer delay here."

"My dear child," Mrs. d'Alberg said as she brushed a long switch of auburn hair very briskly, "I thought I explained to you sufficiently that all things are perfectly alike to me. I will certainly go as soon as you wish, so don't wait for my decision."

"I suppose you will think me capricious and hard to please dear Jean, but somehow I feel a little lonely for Ottawa."

Jean smiled meaningly as she answered "Well I suppose it is a case of reciprocity at its best and what you miss most must be what misses you most, therefore it becomes your duty as well as your pleasure to restore matters to their former equilibrium without further delay."

This was most pleasant encouragement for Honor who could scarcely reconcile herself to pass another single day away, once she had secured the consent of her hostess. And so for the remainder of the week these two good friends made all necessary preparations for their proposed journey on next Monday morning.

It was not with the slightest inclination to regret that Honor watched the scenes, familiar since the last few weeks, fade rapidly now from their view, and yet as each station brought them closer still to Ottawa, she began to fear that sharp eyes like Madame d'Alberg's would guess the real reason of such a premature return. However, it was better thus than that she should be solicitous about Guy, for she knew of what he was capable when the reins of safe guidance were not drawn in by a sure and steady hand. She understood so easily the nature of the temptations that assailed him. She cannot be described better than in the words of the poet Lowell, who says

> "She was a woman; one in whom
> The spring-time of her childish years
> Hath never lost its fresh perfume
> Tho' knowing well that life hath room
> For many blights and many tears."

The two lady travellers spoke little during the journey. Each was sunk in an interesting reverie, cogitating and moralising according to their capacities, and the circumstances so entirely different that caused their thoughts to take the courses they did.

Is it not a gift from God that we are in ourselves a multitude of beings, able to gather ourselves in from the eyes of the world and mix with a whole host of ideal characters of our imagination. Perhaps it sounds a selfish thing when spoken, but the writer speaks from personal experience, having spent many happy hours in self-communion, tasting the full sweetness thereof.

It was a great relief to Honor when she recognized Fitts at the depot awaiting their arrival with Mr. Rayne's own comfortable sleigh. After all, even in the little events of a life-time, we can learn how prone we are to cling to old familiar things, that fill our memories with fondest associations and nestle the closest to our heart's core, and we say with Walter Scott: "The eye may wish a change, but the heart never."

Honor strove hard to conceal her emotion, almost as much from her own self as from those around her. Here was one of those little deceptions, which make up the human life. How can we complain if we are led astray by others when we are so ready to lead ourselves astray?

The meeting between Honor and Mr. Rayne was such as amused Jean d'Alberg considerably. It was "no wonder," she said, "that some people had to give up all their sentiment when there was so much wasted by others." As for herself, she was quite content to thrust three of her gloved fingers into her male cousin's broad palm, greeting him with the coolest "How d'ye do," after a separation of years.

Honor looked the perfect embodiment of happiness, but though her face beamed with smiles and her voice laughed out its gayest accents, she was not nearly so free from pain as one might be led to think. She had expected to find another form among those who had welcomed her back, her eyes hungered for a smile she could not see, and her poor heart thirsted for a word from that voice she could not hear. Only to nestle her hand lovingly within his, only to look up into his big dreamy eyes, only to hear him say, even in his old jesting way, "How we've missed you," and the dull, sick feeling of disappointment that now filled her heart would melt quickly away. Maybe he was hiding in some convenient spot waiting to be missed. But why did not some one speak of him? She dared not trust herself to pronounce his name, and so she went up to her room without having solved the mystery of his non-appearance.

The reader who has not had the experience, can, without being too imaginative, readily understand the sentiment that so completely controlled Honor Edgeworth. All the bright, happy illusions in which she had basked of late had rested on the doubtful, yet hopeful hypothesis that Guy loved her. How many times she argued against herself, striving to find occasions on which he had shown any indifference towards her, but in the end, a sweet smile em eloped her face, and the pleasantest conviction of a young life seemed to thrust itself upon her. She was forced to tell herself that his eyes never turned from her, until they had looked into hers with that deep penetrative glance that makes us feel that a soul is looking into another soul. His hand had never been drawn away from hers until she had detected that slight, almost unwilling pressure that has only one meaning. When the tongue will not be the outlet of our thought, may we not have recourse to those inarticulate words that await utterance in the eye's fond depths, and in the hand's warm pressure?

So Honor asked herself from day to day, and she read her little story in the lines:

> "We spoke not of our love,
> But in our mutual silence it was felt
> In its intense, absorbing happiness."

And after all those days when she had been building up her fairy castle, there came the crisis of to-day, which shook the faith on which her edifice was built, and laid it in shattered ruins at her feet. Yet, with this new-born grief at her heart she must go down among those who cared not, to laugh and be merry, although her voice in her own ears sounded like a long lonely sigh.

She left her room half-an-hour afterwards to repair to the drawing-room, but even as she walked along the corridors, now half shrouded in the shadows of evening, she expected to be surprised at every turning by the sudden appearance of Guy. She felt lonelier now though back among the scenes for which she had longed with a mighty longing, when hundreds of railroad miles had separated her from them. And then she grew impatient with herself for giving in to appearances. She who had prided herself so much on her courage to give up so easily now. Stirred by this new reflection, she ran lightly down the broad oaken stairway and entered the drawing-room, her face suffused with smiles.

CHAPTER XVII

"It is one thing to be tempted,
Another thing to fall."
—Shakespeare.

The clock of the Parliament Tower was pealing out the last stroke of four, and almost simultaneously there emerged from all three Buildings, young men, old men and middle-aged men, all looking as weary and hard-worked as civil servants ought to look.

They did not turn back once to gaze on the spot where the long, dreary hours had been spent, outside that office door life assumed another and an entirely different phase for the government clerk. Even the memory of the lawyer's clerks and "duns" from various parts of the city were left buried within these sacred precincts until the next day, and one and all with a light step wended their way down the Square towards Sparks street.

Among the crowd might be noticed a group of young men that are loitering down the broad steps of the Eastern Block, most of them carry light canes and all of them are smoking good cigars. As I have said they are young men every one of them, and they are fast young men every one of them, and they are likewise inconveniently short of money are these good-looking fast young men. In fact they are a great many things that are too numerous and too uninteresting to mention.

But to Miss Dash and her friend Miss McArgent, who are walking up Wellington street at this moment, they are the most important group of individuals in the whole human menagerie.

Emily McArgent wants to pretend she does not see them, but Miss Dash would not willingly sacrifice all those bows for worlds, and so she gives her plush bonnet a graceful toss upwards and brings it back to its place as her face becomes wreathed with smiles.

"I had to bow, Emily," Bella Dash says, persuasively, "for they saw us, but if I meet Walter Burnett alone I'll cut him sure. The idea of asking me for the fourth dance last night, and then spooning it off with that made-up thing that's stopping at the Bramwell's!"

"You mean Miss Elliott," says Emily a little spitefully, "why I find her rather a pretty girl, and it certainly looks as if Mr Burnett meant to deposit all his wealth at her feet."

"Well, I'm sure," rejoined Miss Bella, in genuine indignation, "she'll soon find out whether he's in earnest or not. It isn't the first nor the fiftieth time that Walter Burnett has made girls believe he was in love with them, but anyway," continued Bella, in supreme disgust, "it is just killing, the way the fellows act in Ottawa, they must always fall in love with strange girls that visit here, and when the scrape up enough pluck and money to venture on a proposal they go right off to Montreal or Toronto or somewhere, just as if there were not good enough for them here."

"Well, my dear, you can't force a man's taste," Emily says in a satisfied tone, and no wonder that it affects her so little, because there are proposals on all sides of a girl who has money, is good-looking, and the daughter of an Hon. gentlemen besides.

Miss Dash is beginning to grow a little cynical. She has walked Sparks Street for the last eight or ten years, not missed a ball or party, or other entertainment during that period, that could bring her under public notice. She has played Lawn Tennis times and again, and has even won a Governor-General's prize, she has gone on expeditions of pleasure with Canada's most distinguished aristocrats and somehow, she is still in "maiden meditation, fancy free."

Occasionally her indignation rises to the surface, and at such times she reveals her sentiments rather recklessly. She is in this complaining mood to-day, but she half suspects that Miss McArgent, is inwardly enjoying her discomfiture, and so quickly changes the subject.

"I wonder what has become of Guy Elersley; Emily. do you know?" she asks in a puzzled tone. "He was not at any of the parties these three weeks. Perhaps he is ill or out of town."

"Couldn't tell you," Emily answers, "but they say he is particularly interested in that young girl that lives at his uncle's. I daresay she knows something about his non-appearance among other young ladies. They say she is exceedingly pretty, Bella have you seen her?"

"Yes, I saw her face in church under the ugliest bonnet you ever saw, and I met her on the Richmond Road the other day, driving Mr Rayne's ponies. She looked reserved, but perhaps she is a nice girl. Hardly the kind that Guy Elersley would like though, he's such a flirt, he flirted with me once till mamma thought—"

"How d'ye do," here the talkative young lady interrupted herself to smile on Bob Apley and Jack Fairmay who were sauntering past them, and for awhile the subject of her interesting flirtation fell through.

They had walked on as far as the Montreal Bank during this conversation, and here they met Willie Airey who was talking to a handsome young stranger in military uniform.

The two ladies bowed and passed on.

"Did you see the new arrival," asked Miss Dash, looking questioningly at her friend, "who is he, I wonder?"

"He looks like some of the Military College fellows," said Emily McArgent, a little more composedly, "I wish Willie Airey would bring him along."

"Let's pass them again," Bella suggested, "and perhaps he will."

Both young ladies deliberately stood, looked for a minute into the nearest shop window, and then retraced their steps to pass the handsome stranger again. As soon as they were within view, Bella cast such admiring eyes on the face that had attracted her so, that the owner of it, drawing his well scented cigar from his lips, asked his friend.

"I say, Airey, who are those young ladies just passed?"

"Those two, right here," said Airey, following his friend's glance, "are Miss McArgent and Miss Dash."

"Aw they pretty girls?" pursued Vivian Standish, replacing his Havana in his handsome mouth.

"Well," Airey answered, laughing, "*entre nous,* you know, Standish, when girls are well off and help to keep up the whole sport of the season, it is no harm to swear they are lovely, when you're sure they'll hear it again."

"Oh, of course not! That's a serious duty sometimes. And are those two of your hospitable entertainers?"

"Yes, by Jove they don't let the fun run down. They are jolly to kill time with, but upon my word, I find the greater number of girls in society here are very insipid. If you can't talk nonsense to them, they can't talk anything else to you. And though we fellows knock a good deal of fun out of their parties, etc., still, we've earned it by the time we've talked over all the little gossip of the day with them, flirted a little, escorted them to some opera or other, and minded ourselves to say nothing but what was most flattering, when speaking of them."

"Well I should think you had," answered his friend, with a low laugh, "you can get something more than that, with less trouble, elsewhere."

"Yes, but half a loaf is better than none," rejoined Airey, "and these young ladies are not so bad when one is in the humor to be amused."

Just as he finished speaking, he noticed a familiar form walking steadily on in front. He clapped his hand heavily down on the shoulder of him he recognized, and shouted.

"Hallo, Elersley," in genuine surprise.

Guy started and looked around. Poor fellow! Already the traits of sadness were visible in his handsome face. He only parted his lips slightly as he turned to greet his friend.

"What, in the name of all that's nice, have you been doing with yourself, Guy? We've missed you awfully."

"I dare say, I have been a little quiet lately," Guy answered. "I am busy at present, but I don't think I need complain of it. I am feeling better than if I were living more on the streets."

Vivian Standish laughed the laziest sort of drawl.

"Now Elersley, don't take to moralizing—you were never made for it, your face would get so deuced eloquent looking, that the rest of us would lose all our present chances."

But Guy neither smiled nor spoke, and this set his friends wondering.

On reaching the corner, Will Airey took an arm of each of his companions, and said:

"Come along boys to see the tumblers. Come Elersley."

"Thank you, no," said Guy, releasing his arm, "I am very busy and must get back to my room. *Au plaisir!* Good afternoon!" and he was gone.

Willie Airey looked after him and then at Vivian Standish, and gave a long, low whistle.

"There's something up there, by Jove," he said, tossing his head in the direction Guy had taken. "If Elersley has started a reform, it is time for the retail dealers in 'gratifications' to close up, for it is a sure sign we must all follow him."

Vivian Standish looked thoughtful for a moment, saying, as he drew a long breath, "I wish to Heaven we could, for upon my word I'm sick of my own life. Anything would be better than the existence we fellows try to drag out. I think we are all fools who do not do as Elersley has done to-night, and I for another refuse the treat with thanks."

So instead of repairing to the familiar marble counter inside a familiar glass door, these two spoilt darlings of sensuality joined Miss Bella Dash and her friend, and escorted them home, much to the intense gratification of the first-named young lady.

Without complimenting himself at all on the moral victory he had achieved, Guy Elersley walked along, sunk in deep reflection. His long strides brought him over many crossings and round many corners, till at length he stopped before a demure, respectable looking hall door. Thrusting a key into the lock, he opened it and stepped into the hall, from which place he admitted himself into a small and silent apartment. Guy's room presented a strange spectacle. Suits of clothes, shirt boxes, silk handkerchiefs, slippers, boots, ties, books, cigars and a host of other male appendages, were lying around on the bed, and chairs, and floor, in fact, every available resting place had been taken advantage of. In the midst of this confusion stood a large Saratoga, wide open. Guy was evidently "packing up" this time, not because he had been "dunned" for half-a-year's board, though that would have been no new item in his well-patched-up experience. He was going away, and I doubt if ever a man felt half so sorry for being "naughty" as Guy Elersley felt on this particular evening.

One by one he folded away all his possessions into the depths of his trunk, and when at last the chaotic mass of belongings had crept into a tidy space, he looked around—that last surveying glance one gives to see that nothing has been left out. Nothing had been left out, so he took down his overcoat, that was hanging on a peg behind the door, and he began to turn out the pockets.

As he did so the most melancholy of smiles crept over his sad face, and drawing out his hand, his eyes fell on a small, narrow band of chestnut hair, fastened with a gold clasp, on which were engraved in large characters the initials, "H. E."

A struggle ensued. The memories he had buried forever, as he thought, surged upon him now in all their force, and almost overwhelmed him. He took the little bracelet in both his hands and looked at it tenderly, longingly. He had not thought it possible that any woman could ever have filled his heart with so much bitterness—the bitterness of remorse and repentance. He who had flirted and fooled with almost every girl he had met, now felt what it was to have met with one who was the embodiment of goodness and purity and truth. Her sweet face haunted him through all his misery. He knew she would be wondering about him, they had been such good *friends*.

After all, must he go away? Perhaps never to see her again, without knowing whether she would miss him or not. Oh! at least, pain and sorrow and suffering are not so crushing when one is loved. It is something when the head is weary with its thoughts of anguish to pillow it on the sympathizing bosom of one who loves us; it is in the deep, imploring gaze of the eyes that watch us with a tender solicitude, that one learns an easy lesson of resignation, it is in the warm pressure of the hand whose power it is to make our pulses throb, that one gathers the courage for action in the moment of distress, and the who have never been loved are they who suffer indeed.

Guy felt that he loved Honor Edgeworth in a way which involved his own future happiness, and yet how could he ascertain whether he might hope or not? Reader, do you know that it is a dreadful thing to love in silence and in doubt? The victim of such a cruel fate wonders at the mysterious Providence which dooms him to spend his most violent emotions in a fruitless combat with himself, gaining no returns for the lavishness of his soul's affection, for if God is love, love is surely mystery.

Still holding the precious little bracelet in his trembling hands, Guy stood thinking and wondering. We are too prone, in our cool and passionless moments, to judge harshly of the deeds that are done under the influence of strong emotion, and for this reason many would condemn Guy for his weakness on this occasion, for as he stood, the large, round, tears rose to his eyes, and he tasted for the first time, the over-flowing bitterness of a heart that is tried. At last he seemed to have learned from this little talisman the proper thing to do, for going over to the table that stood by the window, he sat down, and drawing a sheet of paper to him, took his pen between his nervous fingers, and began to write.

"Honor darling, there are a few little words waiting to be said that you must be good enough to hear. If I spoke them, they would sound like choking sobs, as I write them, know that they are written with tears. Honor, you cannot but feel what it is that I am longing to say. You who understand the human heart so well, will not exact that I should break the iron bonds of a cruel discretion, to let you know that which is often best understood unsaid. By my own folly, I have placed the barrier of distance between us. I go from this place in a few hours more—where? God knows. And for what? He likewise alone can tell. But there is a determination in my heart that was never there before—a stimulant causing it to beat in heavy throbs, and each throb echoes your name. Maybe you call mine a worthless love, I cannot tell, I wish I could. There is one little word, my guardian angel, that will fill me with courage if your lips will but pronounce it. It is "Hope." Remember in any case, that whatever I shall do of right or good will be on account of your redeeming influence, and that the day on which I first met you is in my memory, the day of my salvation. If you have any little word of encouragement for me, my friend, the bearer of this message, will kindly have it sent me. You have taught me to hope once, Honor, do not crush the passion you have awakened, for though it be vainly—wildly—madly, I do hope now. I hope and wait.

Anxiously and lovingly yours,

GUY."

It was done. Only a few scratches of his pen to interpret the misery of his soul, but how stiff it sounded! He has scarcely been able to restrain the gusts of emotions that lay in ready words on the threshold of his lips. But first he must know whether it was all despair for him in the doubtful future before pouring out all the fullness of his heart. He had scarcely finished the last stroke of his letter when a tap was heard at the door, followed by the appearance of a familiar face, the owner of which entered the room and approached Guy without waiting for an invitation.

"Hallo! Elersley, what in the name of all that's wonderful are you at now?"

Guy looked suddenly up, but he could not hide the worn and pained expression that covered his face. His voice assumed a cheerfulness, he was far from feeling as he bade his friend be seated.

"The room is in a queer state," he said, "but you wont mind that."

"Well I mind it a good deal, if it means what it looks like—are you off?

"Yes," answered Guy in a steady tone, "I am leaving Ottawa to-morrow, it's a cursed hole for a fellow to live in, and I'm sorry I did not find it out before."

"Well, upon my word," said Standish, throwing one leg over the end of Guy's trunk, "you *are* a queer fellow. What's going wrong that you are so blue about matters? I thought you were an enviable sort of fellow, with a snug little prospect before you, and here you are, as down in the mouth as if you hadn't a hope in the world. What's up old boy?"

Guy turned his back to the window, and leaned against the writing table with both hands.

"Oh! things have gone a little roughly that's all, and I prefer new pastures when there are troubles in the old ones. I have been a little foolish, I suppose, and now I am reaping my reward."

His face grew pitiably serious as he turned to Vivian saying:

"There's only one little matter I am leaving unsettled, Standish, and will you manage it for me? I cannot do it myself."

"By all means Elersley. Who is he? The tailor or—"

"Oh nonsense!" interrupted Guy impatiently, "it is nothing of that kind. I have a note here to be carefully delivered, and I would ask you to see to it for me."

"A young lady eh?" Standish replied good-humoredly, as he took the offered letter. "I thought there was surely a woman at the bottom of it. Egad!" he continued under his moustache, "we owe them a long debt of revenge, as the cause of all our grievous and petty wrongs. However," this more cheerfully, "you can trust this to me. But talking business, Guy are you actually going away?"

"And why need it surprise you so," asked Guy, peevishly, "what are the railroads for, if not to take us miles away from the scenes we love or hate? I certainly am going, and I have never realized until this moment what I owe to the kind friends I have met during my sojourn here. If I have solved the bitter mysteries of hidden sinful life, I owe a word of gratitude to some worthy companions."

Here the memory of all he had lost through his own recklessness, rushed upon him and before his emotion subsided, he had cursed in bitter terms the false deceitful friends, who had lured him from his innocence into vice and depravity.

CHAPTER XVIII

"With goddess-like demeanour forth she went
Not unattended, for on her as queen,
A pomp of winning graces waited still.
And from about her shot darts of desire
Into all eyes to wish her still in sight."

"Are the ladies at home?"

"Yes. Will you come inside?" said Fitts, with his politest bow, as he extended an exquisite little card receiver towards his visitors.

Then came a few moments of great bustle and confusion, and an accumulation of seal-skins and brocaded silks was ushered into the drawing-room of Mr. Rayne's house.

It was reception day for Aunt Jean and Honor, and both were looking remarkably well in their most becoming costumes, amid their rich surroundings.

Aunt Jean advanced slightly to meet two ladies as they entered the room, and "How d'ye do?" passed from one to another, as they deposited their expensive habiliments and precious humanity into comfortable "*fauteuils.*" Then, while Mrs. d'Alberg tried to sustain a conversation with the elder and more substantial of the two, the younger lady, though not exceedingly childish, drew herself towards Honor, and addressed her patronizingly.

Here were people who were actual exclamation points in the social grammar. Their imposing appearance forced one to hold one's breath, and yet Dame Rumor, who deals in wholesale whispering at Ottawa, told one, with her hand to her mouth, that not so many years ago, Mr. Atkinson Reid was solving the mysteries of existence, inside a scarlet shirt, antique trousers, high boots and a conical straw hat. Only lately, comparatively speaking, had he discarded the one-storey frame house, in a decidedly un-aristrocratic and objectionable neighborhood, where, nevertheless, fortune was first pleased to smile benignly on his efforts to keep the old leathern purse well filled, and where his now precious, airy, nervous, affected daughters first saw their porridge and potatoes. Things went well in the unpretentious little abode, and by and by Johnny Reid was able to indulge in sundry luxuries of life, that naturally belonged to a more advanced stage of civilization than is assumed in the hut of the ordinary shanty-man or wood-cutter. Years were stealing on, and Ottawa was growing up into a respectable size, and at last one day Johnny Reid made up his mind to abandon his rough work, since his accumulated wealth now allowed him to employ substitutes. With these glittering coins, that represented so many strokes of a heavy axe from a strong arm, and so many drops of sweat from an overheated brow, he would go into the heart of the city and buy finery and style and accomplishments for Maria, and Nellie, and Sarah, and the old woman herself as well, and life would bear fruit at last to him, after all his hard toil and bitter experience.

And this is the origin of one of Ottawa's stateliest mansions of to-day, of some of society's most dashing heroines, of John Peter's fine livery and cosy seat behind the best team of gilt-harnessed horses that trot the streets of the Capital, of the best and most sumptuous entertainments that are given in our hospitable City, and of the honest old gentleman himself who from this period must be recognized as John Atkinson Reid Esq., with a decade of distinguished antecedents that every one knows without even hearing their names.

Poor Mrs. Reid dreaded the new responsibilities with which her sudden acquirement of means threatened her, but her daughters fresh from the most fashionable of Canadian educational establishments, undertook to supply for maternal deficiencies by checking their untutored mother, the very many times they deem it necessary, thus making the last epoch of this ill-fated lady's life, a grand piece of misery and terror.

Just now Miss Sadie Reid is fidgeting nervously with a gold and pearl card case held within her primrose kids, that are peeping through the outlets of her brocaded Mother Hubbard dolman. She feels a little ill at ease beside Miss Edgeworth, who is so self-possessed and unapproachable to the stylish Miss Reid. The conversation is the same immortal collection of exclamations and enquiries that one hears everywhere in fashionable circles in Ottawa.

Miss Reid remarks in an almost flattering tone: "Why you don't look at all tired, Miss Edgeworth, after the MacArgent's ball."

"I do not tire myself ever when I can help it," Honor says, "and this occasion came under my rule. I left early and rested well."

"Did you really?" is the reply. "Well, you see, I couldn't have done that. I was engaged for every single dance and it would have been 'dreadfully atrocious' if I left before the end. We dined at Government House last night again and to-night there is an 'at Home' at the Bellemare's, but I suppose I will meet you there. Really it is 'dreadfully distressing' for one to be obliged to go out so much. I am sure you are to be envied, Miss Edgeworth, to be able to keep so quiet."

"I wonder that you realize how fortunate I am," said Honor calmly, "I thought our spheres lay so widely apart that you considered my lot as unfortunate as I do yours."

"Oh! dear no'" said Miss Saidie, "It is 'positively agonizing' to live as we do in such constant demand; I suppose you will feel it soon though, now you've come out. You have no idea of what is before you."

"Excuse me, Miss Reid," interrupted Honor, "but I think I have a very fair one. I have learned already that when a girl creeps into her first ball-dress she is like a cabinet minister getting into power, she has a great many troubles worse than trains to drag after her."

Miss Reid found this remark exceedingly funny, and laughed rather immoderately, Honor thought; but just then Nanette came in with the dainty cups of tea, and so created a slight diversion in the conversation.

As Miss Reid has told the reader Honor Edgeworth had really "come out," with Madame d'Alberg and Mr. Rayne as *chaperones*, and had made a great sensation. She was the same calm, beautiful, composed girl as ever, though a remarkable unseen change had come over her. If anything, it had only given more dignity and grace to her bearing, more music and pathos to her voice, and a more sympathetic and attractive expression to her face. Jean d'Alberg had not failed to notice it, and with her usual keen instinct had readily divined the cause, but she never spoke of it. She grew kinder, if possible, to the silent girl, and was satisfied for the present to hope for better things.

This bright afternoon, Honor felt more cynical than usual, and the conversation with her frivolous guests did not at all tend to improve her humor.

The Reids had just left the door, tucked into their comfortable conveyance, when two gentlemen were announced. Honor recognized them as some of those whom she had met since her *entree* into society, but she neither knew of, nor cared for the admiration that was so freely bestowed on her by them.

When they were seated, Honor found that Mr. Standish was nearest her, and therefore she addressed herself to him. He could be the most nonsensical soul in the world when he felt like it or he could talk the dryest common sense that ever found its way into the wisest of heads, and thus he made his society pleasant to feather-brains, and *savants* alike.

He was well up in almost every accomplishment. According to the girls, he could dance—oh his dancing was heavenly, his singing was equally good, and as for flirting, why he could kill a dozen female hearts with one of those pleading, dreamy, distracted looks, that he sometimes made use of among his lady friends. He knew all the genus and species of small-talk, and when it came to compliments and pretty little nothings, he was without a rival. He could take his turn at tennis and come off favorably. He could ride splendidly and skate admirably, in fact, he had made merciless havoc with the girls' hearts, with all his accomplishments and attractions, and such a fever of envy and jealousy and eager gossip as he created among his fair friends was something so "desperately horrid" (as they would put it) that one could almost hate him for it, and to tell the truth, many of his rivals, who were quite in the shade beside him, did hate him most cordially.

This manner and bearing of his, he looked upon as a *passe-partout*, and there was certainly one item in his character that outshadowed all the rest, namely his conceit, or self-sufficiency which was constantly asserting itself in his every look and action.

Vivian Standish was a thorough man of the world—I use the word in its most literal acceptation. He was one of those cool, keen, calculating, diplomatic men, who never lose their presence of mind, who never hesitate, and yet are never precipitate, who always say the right thing in the right time, and to the right people. No one knew anything of his antecedents, but somehow, he carried an acceptable sort of reputation on his face.

Guy Elersley had done many foolish things, but foremost among them all was, his having made a friend of a man who was as obscure and incomprehensible to him as the most profound ethical mystery.

They got on very well together, however. Guy found Vivian all that one fellow expects another to be, consequently they soon became fast "chums." Now this is no light word at least in Ottawa. If you give a fellow to understand that you are his friend, it means, "thro' fire and water," if anything ever meant it. Ottawa is one of the most unfortunate places in the world for some people to live in. It is pregnant with snares and scrapes for budding manhood, and there is redemption in nothing, if not in the steady arm or well filled pocket of a friend. According to these notions, Guy and Vivian had played saviour to one another on sundry occasions. The last confidence reposed was the note that Guy had given Standish to deliver in, "Honor Edgeworth's own hands," before his departure on that eventful night when we left the two friends chatting over Guy's new troubles and plans for the future.

Vivian Standish had drawn in the comfort of his cigar in rather anxious breaths, as he walked back alone in the starlight after leaving his friend. He detested things that puzzled and crossed him, and nothing under the sun could have puzzled him more than the sudden change that had come over

Guy Elersley. He had been such a happy, careless, daring sort of fellow all his life; and now, all at once, a gloom of skepticism seemed to settle down on him, extinguishing the light of hope and energy which had previously marked his character. This, Standish concluded, was no meaningless nor ordinary effect, there must be a cause for this newer, more thoughtful mood. Had he forfeited his claim to the long- expected legacy of Henry Rayne's wealth? Had Honor Edgworth any thing to do with it? Perhaps he never answered these questions even to himself on this silent night. He walked on quietly till he came to a streetlamp, whose yellow radiance threw fitful gleams around the lonely street. Here he stopped and deliberately unbuttoning his overcoat, took out the note that Guy had confided to his care, tore it open and coolly read, word for word, the passionate declaration held therein. He laughed a low little chuckle, with his cigar between his teeth, and muttered to himself, "not so bad by Jove, not a bad game at all." Then without a trace of shame or compunction on his face, he calmly tore the precious paper into little pieces which he carefully placed in his vest pocket. Then he buttoned up his coat, and putting both hands in his pockets he walked steadily on, still scenting the air with his expensive cigar, and wearing all the while such a look of lazy amusement as betrayed nothing whatever of what might be going on inside of those handsome features.

Vivian Standish was a man of impulse and inspiration; but, strange to say, his impulse or inspiration invariably moved him the right way. I use right, as meaning personal advantages or victory for himself. His latest "inspiration" led him to reflect on the possible and very gratifying advantages he might secure for himself by marrying well. "But then," thought he, "girls are such diabolical ninnies that everything which does not come under the shadow of some big church or fat parson is vicious in their eyes." In spite of this conviction, he had weighed his chances and possessions against every possible drawback, and, with his usual conceit, he fancied the road was beautifully clear.

Here we have him then with the self-appointed mission of choosing a wife. No man had ever held within his soul such volumes of deep sentiment as he could call into his eyes when the occasion required it, and no knight of the age of chivalry ever wooed a fair lady with such winning words and courteous deeds as Vivian Standish could bring to his aid, when he so wished it.

This is an age replete with valuable opportunities for cunning people, and they are the losers who cannot take advantage of the world's susceptibility and weakness, by turning its folly to their own personal advantage and especial benefit.

Vivian Standish had not a genius for everything alike. He never in the world could have created himself an apostle of aestheticism, though he found out later that there was more money than exalted enthusiasm in the business He never could have bothered about a flying machine, or spent his time discovering hair renewers or cures for rheumatism, but he could speculate with the wealth that nature and a little art had given him, in the gold mines of the comfortable houses that were open to him. With a little tinge of communism and a great deal of egotism in his nature he concluded that he had as good a right to the gold and silver of those gouty fathers and mothers as they had, and he was going to prove it too.

With this insight into his character, which is rather a long parenthesis than a direct deviation from my story, we can see Vivian Standish in his true colors, and we can, therefore, easily guess the object of his visit to Mr. Rayne's house on this particular afternoon. No ordinary observer could have detected any other than a purely conventional motive in this call.

He had met Miss Edgeworth, and had solicited the favor from her of allowing him to call at her residence. Every other young fellow had done nearly the same thing, and he himself had acted in the same manner towards many other young ladies. But we, who are permitted to look behind the screens while this little drama is going on, can say more about his true motives. His clever way of reasoning had led Vivian Standish to believe that Guy Elersley had forfeited every right to his uncle's wealth, and without knowing anything of Honor's own fortune, he concluded that it was worth a fellow's while to secure her, as the most indirect, but about the most truly lawful way of getting the "old fellow's" money.

It was this determination that had caused him to cast the fractions of Guy's love letter into the fire when he reached his room on that eventful night. He excused himself very easily on the plea that there was no earthly use in encouraging this love affair, when there were neither hard cash nor good prospects to wind it up with. Elersley had had his chance and missed it. Now, why wouldn't some less fortunate dog take his rejected luck and put it to better account? There is no verdict so prompt as the one a man pronounces over a case of "my own good or another fellow's." And Vivian Standish made up his mind, in plain English, to I do "square business."

"Square business" to him meant something very delightful to the average society girl. Courteous manners, marked attentions, openly expressed admiration, and slavery almost if she proved exacting. But Standish had an idea, and not a too comfortable one about the character of the girl he had to deal with. And so this afternoon, he presented himself before her with all the charm of a studied negligence which attracts in spite of one's self. He was very careful about all that passed, as yet he was only groping in the dark. If he once knew whether she loved Guy or not, his game would be an easy one, and this was the first problem he set himself to solve. He spoke to her of a great many things before he ventured on the subject that interested him most. When he did finally broach it, he merely asked in a simple sort of way:

"Have you heard any news of—a—our mutual friend, Mr. Elersley?"

The die was cast. He had only this instrument with which to apply his skill, and had he used it well or not? The sound of this name was the "Open Sesame" to Honor's heartful of secrets, and Standish scanned her face with a look of penetrating inquiry as he pronounced it. But men are fools. Honor Edgeworth was a woman and a woman's face is not an index to woman's soul. Truly her slender fingers clutched each other nervously until the golden circlets around them nigh entered the tender flesh. But who felt that besides herself? It is a woman's own fault if she is not appreciated to-day, for men will never know from her lips of the hundred moral victories she achieves daily. Even those ordinary common-place females who make the dresses and trim the hats of the creatures our men adore, even these do their inner selves more violence in one short day than a man endures for a life time. Give me a man for courage, if you will, for power of action, if you will, but give me a woman with a heart for an unrivalled endurance and fortitude.

Vivian Standish cool, keen, deliberating, could read nothing in his companion's face, and thus baffled, he began inwardly to wonder what would be his next course.

Honor looked at him in the most provokingly composed way and said dryly:

"You may give the word 'friend' a rather extensive meaning for aught I know. Things have grown into such an exaggerated state, now-a-days, that a commonly sensible person is lost towards understanding them."

Standish winced.

"Which may infer that I am not on intimate terms with my common sense," he thought, and aloud:

"I will retract the word if you please, and consider you and Mr. Elersley as strangers."

Strangers! that was true, deep down in her heart, but with her lips she said:

"By no means, Guy Elersley and I have ceased to be strangers from the first moment we met. But this can not interest you. Let us talk of something else. Do you enjoy the last of the season here?"

"Very much indeed," he replied, but without the slightest warmth, as he was inwardly wondering at this girl's conduct, so different from the others. At this stage of his critical distraction, his friend rose and shook hands with Madame d'Alberg, then advanced to make his adieux to Honor. This necessitated Vivian's doing so likewise, and if ever Vivian Standish's hand clasped another's emphatically, it did on this occasion. He just gathered the soft white fingers of this strange haughty girl within his own, and held them for an instant in that trusting longing way that had done him good service many a time before, then he laid them quietly away, with a look of eloquent pleading in his eyes and a simple "Good-bye" on his handsome lips.

It was six o'clock at last. The gas was lit, the curtains drawn, and the familiar and just now welcome sound of dishes was coming from the dining-room across the hall. Mr. Rayne was expected every minute, and Mrs. d'Alberg and Honor were loitering the moments of waiting around the drawing-room.

"Well, aunt Jean," said Honor, lazily placing her hand on the back of the arm-chair in which the lady addressed was seated, (she had chosen to call her "aunt" since she was to appear in society as her charge), "what do you propose doing to-night? Do you care at all to go to the Bellemare's?"

"Oh, I don't know," Mrs. d'Alberg replied, "one place is as attractive as another for me. You will see plenty of people and nonsense, and you may as well be wearied all at once with these things as to foster the spirit by degrees. You will meet Miss Mountainhead or Miss Dash, or Miss Reid some of these days, and if you can't talk about this one's 'kettledrum' and that one's 'at home' you will be bored to death by hearing their version of it, so you might as well do one thing as the other. You'll see that Mr. Standish too, by-the-way! Do you know, I like him, Honor, it is a stamp you seldom see."

"Really, aunt Jean," Honor was smiling, "this looks suspicious. You should be blind to your favorite stamps by now. But about this other thing, since we've accepted we had better go, as you say, boring one's self to death, or being bored by other people is much the same thing, so we may as well resign ourselves and make the best of it."

*

Vivian Standish was puzzled more than ever when he left Mr. Rayne's house. He had counted on meeting an ordinary society girl, but had been greatly, though not at all unpleasantly disappointed.

He did not dislike Honor Edgeworth in any way. He felt rather attracted towards her than otherwise, but he felt uneasy about the little plans he had cherished and encouraged for so long.

An hour or so after leaving her, he was in his own room, comfortably installed in an easy chair drawn up to the window, with his velvet slippers resting on the sill and the graceful clouds of smoke curling upwards from his handsome mouth and surrounding his languid form. There is not very much to look at from the window of a Bank street boarding house, and yet a passer-by at this moment would have thought this elegant young man was deeply interested either in the dilapidated representations of "Hazel Kirke" that adorned a straggling fence opposite, or in the music (?) which a classic looking organ-grinder was trying to eke out of his instrument to the time of the "Marseillaise," to the great delight of the customary crowd of youngsters who surrounded him.

But Vivian Standish rarely wasted his faculties on such matter-of-fact things, while there were other projects of a more personal advantage awaiting his consideration. He was wishing heartily at that moment that some girls had not one-quarter of the brains that nature had improvidently endowed them with, but this being a hopeless hope, he occupied himself in trying to discover the best way in which to deal with a person so gifted.

A fellow in a boarding-house is a most unfortunate creature, being never quite free from the intrusion of a host of friends. Vivian felt this unpleasant truth in all its intensity. His interesting cogitation was cut short in a little while by the entrance of a bevy of comrades, and he had to come down and stand at the front door, to flirt and "carry on" with the girls that passed, and otherwise contribute towards the amusement of the crowd.

CHAPTER XIX

"Come now; what masks, what dances shall we have
To wear away this long age of three hours
Between our after-supper and bed-time."

Perhaps it was owing to Honor's apparent indifference that Henry Rayne refrained from giving a full account of Guy Elersley's disappearance from among them. He had insinuated something about the misunderstanding that had arisen between his nephew and himself, but the subject was a painful one, and unless pressed for further information, he preferred to remain silent altogether about it.

Honor had taken counsel with herself and had acted very wisely in consequence. She assured herself that it was presumption to suppose that Guy loved her. She had no direct proof of such a sentiment existing. Their whole period of acquaintance and companionship had been tinged with romance, but it would have been the same, had she been any one else. It was almost the certain fate of two young people thrown together as they had been to "fall in love." Yet he had given her no definable cause to count on him as an admirer or lover. He had not even gone to the depôt on the morning of her departure, or shown himself in any marked way, concerned about her; so she resolved to quietly stow away the items of her past that wound themselves around his name or memory, and to begin another life strengthened by this new experience. There is something of a Spartan endurance in a heroic woman. She can carry inside the fairest face, the battered wreck of the fondest heart, and even if we must call this deception, surely it is a virtue. She adopts her sad misfortune as a responsibility akin to duty, and it is a gratification and a solace to herself to know that she suffers alone and in silence.

Honor did not allow this strange turn of things to influence her life visibly. She had learned a new chapter of that mysterious volume that destiny holds open to all men, but it did not seem new to her. She was one of those people who, from acute observation on those who have gathered the fruit of a long experience, or from a study of those authors whom we know as direct interpreters of the human heart, had acquired that inner knowledge and experience of things which, in its moral effect on the system, is equivalent to the actual tasting of the same phases of life. She had prepared herself to meet trials and disappointments in the very heart of her comforts. What other fruit can be born of a selfish, scheming world? But she thought she had discovered a sympathetic bond between her own and this other young soul. Guy did not seem to her as the rest of his kind. At times, when his better nature was aroused, he gave expression to the noblest and most exalted feeling. He had the one failing, however, of being easily led—and there are so many persons to lead astray in Ottawa city, and so many places to lead to, that it takes a very strong arm or a very eloquent voice or a very subtle influence to counteract the effect of evil company on one we love. Honor could not encourage thoughts of distrust towards Guy. The memory of their happy friendship always stood between her and her censure of him, but still she could not cancel the thoughts of all he might have done and did not do. No word, no sign, no message to assure her that he had clung to her memory as a bright spot in his misfortune; and she would lay back in her bed at night, thinking, wondering and puzzling herself about the strange, mysterious things that could transpire while this big, revolving machine of ours turned once around.

There was a kind of subdued excitement in the upper front rooms of Henry Rayne's house to-night. It had been decided to go to the Bellemare's, and all this extra confusion was only about the toilets. Nanette was showering ejaculations of the profoundest admiration on Honor, who, robed in black satin, stood before a tall mirror adjusting her skirt.

It was almost provoking to see the cool, calm way in which she went through the different stages of "dressing." Her brocaded satin fitted exquisitely to her slender waist, and ended over her shoulders in a sqnare cut, whose gatherings of such Spanish lace lay in dazzling contrast to her snowy neck and arms.

A pair of diamond screws were fastened in her ears, but apart from these she wore no other jewel. Before leaving her room, however, she plucked the bursting bud of a white rose that grew in a dainty pot on the window sill, and with a spray of its leaves fastened it at her breast. She was ready before aunt Jean or Mr. Rayne, so she stole down to the dimly- lighted drawing-room to while away the waiting moments in playing dreamy chords and half-remembered snatches of pensive airs.

Aunt Jean was a most fastidious woman, and dressed according to certain rules and regulations, any aberration from which was a gross mistake not to be tolerated. Henry Rayne, for an old man, was also uncommonly exacting. He spoiled, on an average, a dozen white ties nightly when he decided on going out, and it was a task to insert his shirt studs in a way that would satisfy him. When Honor had time to arrange things in the afternoon, all went smoothly enough; but for him to dress on a short notice meant a good deal of trouble to his household.

The brilliant light of a dozen chandeliers is flooding the ball-room at Elmhurst. The walls of the spacious apartment are decked with festive decorations. The air is heavy with rich perfumes, soft, sweet strains of dance music float through the crowded rooms, and women, the fairest, richest and noblest are gliding by on the arms of their interested partners. Every face is smiling, some are perfectly happy, some are perfectly wretched, some are perfectly indifferent—but all are smiling, all look pleased. Even Miss Dash and a few other friends, who look suspiciously like wall-flowers, smile broadly at the least amusing remark, just as though they were not being consumed with jealousy and disappointment. They talk eagerly and gladly to deaf old members of Parliament and stuffy bachelors, whom they hate more intensely than ever after the evening is over. Fans are waving in every direction, the great, broad, heavy "coolers" of the fat mammas, who are just dying from heat and exhaustion; and the pretty, feathery, spangled things, behind which is whispered many a coquettish word by the pretty lips of gay young girls; and the poor, ill-used one's of the wall-flowers, that are either being bitten viciously at the safest end, or that fly impatiently through the air, cooling the puckered brows of disappointed belles.

Everyone is there who is "anything." The Bellemares are very well known in Ottawa. Strangers point to their splendid mansion, situate a little way outside the city limits, and ask, "Who can live there?" And the resident of Ottawa tells all he knows. Mr Joseph Bellemare, one of our great lumber merchants, is the proprietor of that grand residence. He has plenty of money and comfort, a small family—a marriageable daughter and two sons—who help to diminish very considerably the family treasure. The house is finely adapted for large entertainments, having immense rooms for reception, and dancing and refreshments. Then there was the handsome library, the conservatory and billiard room, all with little *tête-a-tête* nooks and corners in which spoony lovers might take refuge for hours, without being noticed.

There were lawns and groves, and boats and fishing for the delightful summer-time. In fact, nature and art had both contributed largely towards rendering this superb dwelling-place one of the finest, and most attractive in the whole country around.

Nature however, with characteristic inconsistency, had never intended Miss Louise Bellemare, for a beauty. But nature proposes, and art disposes.

There are those among that crowd of beauty and *éclat* to-night, who would not attempt to dispute the omnipotence of Belladonna, or *blanc-de-perle*, or any other item of the homely girl's toilet repertoire, for it would have gladdened the eyes of the inventors of these cosmetics, if they could have beheld for an instant the charming effect produced, by the skilful use of their Helps to Beauty.

It is now quite on the late side of nine o'clock, and the night's sport has fairly begun. Young men, pencils in hands are standing before their favorite acquaintances, soliciting the favor of "at least one 'dance,' for me, you know." The first waltz is in full progress. The inviting strains of the "Loved and Lost," are floating through the air, and the room is alive with the "poetry of motion." Just at this moment Honor Edgeworth passes from the Reception Room, across the Hall, leaning on Mr. Rayne's arm, and into the Ball-room. No one makes any pronounced interruption to their occupation as she enters, but somehow the buzz seems to abate considerably, and the voices seem to dwindle into a whisper.

There are different reasons for this proceeding. The girls' reason is a natural one. She is new in society, very attractive, and her presence thrusts itself on them as a warning. They don't see what she wants among Ottawa *coteries*, born and bred, no one knows where. But the men's reason is also a very natural one. They are a little tired of continually meeting the same fair faces wherever they go. A woman is to them like a good thing that won't wear out. They do not wish to give up either altogether, but they weary at the sight of them, and so long as they can substitute them for any other—whether inferior in merit, or not so provokingly durable, they are happy, with the knowledge of course, that the other is always on hand when they require it. This flattering opinion that fashionable men entertain of most fashionable women is what is richly deserved by them, for women who flatter and spoil men as they are flattered, and spoiled in Ottawa, can expect nothing else. A suit of clothes of respectable tweed, or broadcloth, is the object of more spare enthusiasm than a whole collection of moral qualities in a rival woman.

This explains why the male element of Ottawa society is extremely gratified to hail such an interesting acquisition to their circle as Honor Edgeworth. The other girls are "dreadfully disgusted" to note the sensation she creates, and instead of looking at her openly, they pretend to be a million times better occupied while they are peeping at her behind each others' backs, and over each others' heads. There is something to look at after all. Honor is surrounded immediately and those who have not met her before, flock around the hostess, and Mr. Rayne, in the hope of obtaining an introduction. But Honor displays no more sign of gratification at this lavish display of admiration, than if it had been an every day occurrence of her life. She gives each anxious solicitor a dance without any of the condescending airs of other ladies, and her programme is almost full when some one brushes through the crowd and addresses her hastily.

"Miss Edgeworth, not too late am I?"

She looks up and sees Vivian Standish before her, as handsome a picture as ever riveted any one's gaze. She smiles a bewitching smile of assumed despair.

"What am I to do," she asks in perplexity, "I have only one dance to divide between two of you," and she turns to another importunate claimant, a diminutive man, very well inclined to *embonpoint* who wears red whiskers and spectacles, "I think you were first Mr Vernon" she says, smiling graciously, as she confronts his homely face.

Vivian's face was clouding perceptibly when some one laid his hand on Vernon's arm, and drew him aside, apparently not noticing that he was engaged, Vivian had a friend around that time.

"Mr. Vernon does not evidently appreciate my partiality for him," Honor says laughingly, looking straight into Vivian's eyes.

"And yet you would throw away on him, the favors I crave to obtain."

He said this half reproachfully, half eagerly. She placed her dainty little programme in his hand, and smiled when he returned it, to find he had written, "Lucky Vivian S." opposite the promised waltz.

I wonder if any realization in life thrusts itself so forcibly upon us, as that of the flight of time. Our dearest and most precious moments do not dare to linger with us an added instant, but hasten on with ceaseless flow to lose themselves in eternity's gulf. Only the hours of sorrow seem to halt in their flight. The clock never ticks so slow and measured a stroke as during the night of waiting, or watching. Then the rules of time become reversed, and in a lonely vigil one counts by heart-throbs, sixty hours in every slow, slow minute. The very moments, laden with gaiety and pleasure, that are dropping so quickly into the lap of the forever from out the Bellemare's lighted halls, are surely dragging painfully and slowly, for the weary watcher of death-beds, for the poor and shivering, for the deserted wife, for the orphan child, for the chained prisoner. This is the mystery of life, this is the many-sided picture of existence, and yet, this strange world is a masterpiece of a just and merciful Creator.

CHAPTER XX

If all the year were playing holiday,
To sport would he as tedious as to work;
But when they seldom come they wish'd-for come.
—*Shakespeare*

From the moment the Canadian Pacific R'y train leaves Ottawa in the early morning, the interested traveller can easily feast his eyes on the modest little villages and rival towns, a whole succession of which greet him from the capital to Montreal and thence to Quebec city. These juvenile country towns at once thrust the idea of repose upon the city folks who may chance to visit them. The best of these boast of, at most, a dozen wealthy, respectable residents, a village street of antagonistic merchants, a post office, an established inn, a mayor, a doctor, the minister, and the priest, bad roads and spare sidewalks. One would never suspect any of these villages to be guilty of any romance whatever, everybody seems to have attained the summit of human ambition, and life flows on in an uninterrupted serenity that is fatal to the nervous system of our enterprising city geniuses. Yet, there have been wonderful things done among these rural scenes. There are volumes whose title pages unfold nothing of the mysterious tales that are hidden and bound up within them.

We must cross the broad green fields and enter the old-fashioned houses, we must repair to the white-washed church on Sunday and kneel in the high-backed pews, we must talk over our tumblers to the fat proprietor of the solitary hotel, if we want to gather the interesting details that characterize the village. They are the same "yesterday, and to-day and forever." Nothing new happens, and the old traditions never grow stale.

Between the cities of Montreal and Quebec, on the south shore of the River St. Lawrence, among what are familiarly known as the "townships," sleeps a little French village of the stamp I have just described. Rows of white-washed houses of the same pattern are to be seen here and there in the only street it boasts of, and scattered through the broad open fields are other residences of more or less importance. All the long summer days the sun glares down so hotly upon the dried straggling fences and the dusty village road, that scarcely a living creature animates the scene. The residents close their doors, and leave down the folds of green paper that deck each small window of their houses, and abandon the world to sundry pedestrians, who are forced by cruel necessity into the scorched street an occasional bare-footed urchin on his way to the grocery shop with a deformed pitcher to be filled with molasses, or a spare woman or two gabbling at the counters or doors of the miserable shops that follow one another in dingy succession through the street. But one is not to judge the place from this cheerless picture, by no means, for, apart from the neighborhood I have described, this is one of the prettiest villages in the Townships. It loses its charms only on the spot where man has interfered with Nature's plans, in trying to provide accommodations for the settlers. The trees have been cut down, and the fresh, green forest converted into a dry, dusty street, cheered all through the hot afternoon by the dreary chirp of a grasshopper, or the buzz of countless millions of healthy flies that swarm around the very doors and surroundings of provision depots. Outside of this, in any direction one chooses to go, the scenery is attractive and beautiful; the trees are tall and thick and abundant, meeting overhead, and enclosing cool, shady avenues, which seem to wind in an endless stretch through the forest shades. Birds twitter and carol sweetly as they flit unseen from twig to twig of the tall waving elms, and one would be apt to forget the existence of human beings, were it not for an occasional interruption of this peaceful monotony, in the way of a cozy cottage, whose gables peep through the foliage, the lowing of cattle, or the sweet, clear song of some village maid, as she saunters through the broad rich fields, with her pail held towards the impatient cows, and her large plaited straw bonnet thrown recklessly on the back of her head, or being twisted by its safe strings on the fingers of the idle hand. Amidst such enchanting scenery one forgets the dusty village, one loses the hum and buzz in the comforting notes that Nature warbles to herself. Everything is so cool and refreshing and quiet. The weariest heart sighs from actual relief when transported to a paradise like this—and no wonder.

Many, many miles from the village, by the "Elm Road," is one of the prettiest and most delightful and loneliest spots that nestle on the bosom of the earth. An almost oppressive silence reigns in the woods, and nothing seems to stir visibly. You can hear the wind playing its softest melody through the tops of the great trees, but the leaves farther down only sway noiselessly in a graceful silence. It might be too lonely, only for the variety and perfection that Nature displays at every step and turn ferns and mosses, and little woodland flowers which never bud outside the shady forest, greet one at every instant, and a feeling so peaceful and composed steals over the soul that the place becomes hallowed to those who have yielded to its powerful influence. All at once, one can perceive traces of habitation, a neat enclosure of rustic boughs borders the avenue, and the grass on either side is even and trim, then comes a large rustic gate leading into a gravel walk, having here and there, under some shady oak, a garden chair or lounge, and a little table all of the same picturesque rustic wood, then comes a gorgeous *parterre* of flowers, which load the air with their rich and heavy perfumes, and directly behind this is a low broad stone dwelling that one might have expected to turn upon from the very first. Great thick vines of Virginia creepers climb the sides and front of the house. Green and yellow canaries in cages hanging from the verandah, send the octaves of their warblings far back into the woods. It is as fair a picture as ever an artist longed to produce on canvas, one of those dwelling-places which seem to us suggestive of and consistent with nothing else but exquisite peace, comfort and happiness, and though we have no reason for imagining it to be a depository of perfect contentment, we yet repel any idea that might suggest itself to us of empty cupboards inside those walls, of a scolding wife in those cozy rooms, or of washing days in that picturesque little kitchen.

The mind naturally harbors only ideas of that lazy sort of comfort that of necessity comes from such surroundings as these. This is "Sleepy Cottage," of which all the villagers spoke in enthusiastic terms, and indeed, it must be said, "Sleepy Cottage" would have done credit to towns and cities of more popular fame than the humble little village of the Eastern Townships. Were it anywhere else it could open its beautiful gates to an appreciative public, while here it slept quietly away almost without interruption. At present its only occupants were an aged gentleman and a girl of about nineteen summers, a maid servant and the old gardener, "Carlo," the Maltese cat, and the birds.

The story, as well as it is known, was that Monsieur and Madame de Maistre had come from old France fifteen years ago and settled at "Sleepy Cottage", that Josephine, their little four-year-old daughter, had been kept in almost total seclusion all her life under the tuition of a French governess whom they got no one knew where, and that the first glance the villagers had of her was at the funeral of Madame de Maistre, which took place when Josephine was in her sixteenth year. Her extraordinary beauty and dignity had so impressed the simple villagers at that time that they never forgot it, and though they had seen her but very seldom in the three subsequent years, the memory of her sweet face never left them yet.

One cool summer evening, a number of the old male residents of the village had gathered around the broad steps of the "Traveller's Inn," and were disposing of themselves on the inverted soap boxes and low wooden stools that adorned the front of the public door, as best they could, one or two paring, with studied attention, ends of thick sticks, with which they had provided themselves before sitting down, others resting their elbows on their knees, and holding the capacious bowls of their black stumpy pipes in their big brawny hands, others again drawing figures in the light dust that covered the space between the impromptu seats and the sidewalk, and all chatting in a friendly sort of way, alike on the latest and the oldest items of interest. Just now, they were discussing the mystery of the young girl's seclusion at Sleepy Cottage when they were suddenly interrupted by a crowd of five young fellows who had crossed, unperceived, the fields leading from the depot, and now sought admission to the "Traveller's Inn."

The men near the door, as they rose in silence to make the passage free, looked at each other in mute wonder, and threw enquiring glances after the figures of the strangers as they crossed the threshold of the inn. They were five tall, well built, good looking young men, with all the traits of city life about them. Had a whole army of soldiers invaded the "Traveller's Inn" at this moment it could scarcely surprise the spectators more than did the appearance of these young fellows.

They enquired of the thunderstruck proprietor whether he had rooms to accommodate them for a few days, and he had just nerve enough to tell them that if they could manage with three rooms, that many were at their service.

Appearing quite satisfied with this arrangement, they had supper ordered.

It was not in immediate readiness, so while the life was being hurried out of the maid in the kitchen, the new-comers went outside and fell in with the crowd at the door step.

One of the new arrivals, the most striking looking of all, and with whom we will have to deal more particularly afterwards, addressed the reserved sages on behalf of all the rest.

"I suppose we surprised you this evening," said he, laughing, and throwing one leg over a vacant soap box, just as any of the natives would have done, "but our being here surprises ourselves as much as it does you. We come from the McGill College in Montreal, and we are going far into the depths of your forest here to look for a few week's sport."

The group of listeners appeared a little more reconciled to the intrusion by this explanation of it, and after a few moments of awkward silence, old Joe Bentley, who was near the speaker, said:

"Welcome, gentlemen! Ye're welcome to the village, and good sport ye can promise yerselves if ye'll go the right way about it."

"Then we must hope," put in a second of the students, "that some of you who know will not be above giving us a word of advice."

"The Lord forbid," ejaculated old Bentley in a most serious tone. "And the very best spot in the country is the spot we were talkin' of as ye came along. It's out by the 'Sleepy Cottage.' If ye can get that strange Frenchman to leave you through his grounds, ye never had such shooton' an' fishin as there is a couple of miles up on the other side of them."

"Who is the strange Frenchman?" asked the first speaker, as he felt in his vest pocket for a match to light his cigar.

"He'm. Give us an easier one than that to answer," said Martin Doyle, a crude, suspecting farmer, who smoked sullenly on the end of a bench. "How is dacent people, who lived here all their lives, to know who them invaders is that comes in on people with their quare notions and ways, never showing the daylight to the child God gave 'em till she's a fine young woman on their hands, and never spakin' a word to other folk, as if honest men wasn't their betters any day."

The new-comers smiled from one to another. It is so consistent with the character of these country people to guard against and suspect, rather than trust unknown people who come among them wrapped in a mystery of any sort.

"This is strange," said another student in a tone calculated to elicit all the information about the "invader," that the rustics were willing to give.

"Well," said Joe Bentley, in a more christian-like tone, "people has no business talkin' only of what they know, but we all know that some fourteen or fifteeen years ago, this man that lives in Sleepy Cottage now, kem here with his wife and baby, and took up living in the country. Off and on since that day we've seen the old man himself around the village, but Madame kept close enough from that day till the day of her death which happened about three years ago, when she was buried in the graveyard over, and that was when we first saw the girl ever since the day they brought her a tiny thing in their arms from off the cars. Dan Sloan, and some more of the fellows that goes shooting and fishin' through the grounds, says they saw her a little girl growing up, with a pinched-nosed, starved looking mamselle for a governess, hawking her around them grounds an snatchin' her off if they came within a mile of her."

Here the farmer removed his pipe and gave a long whiff of smoke, then replacing it in his mouth, he continued "We were all jest talkin' of him as ye came along, an' if ye wan't sport ye'll have to ask the old fellow, to let ye through his grounds, and then mebbe ye'll know more about him than we do ourselves."

The young city fellows did not at all dislike the idea of the adventure that was in store for them. They were summoned to supper shortly after old Joe Bentley had finished his narrative, and resolving to enlist the good wishes of the villagers at any cost they deposited a round sum of money on the battered counter of the humble "bar," to "treat the crowd," they said as they passed under the low doorway into the dining-room.

It was rather a noisy meal, and Sarah's best attempt at ham and eggs, vanished in the most practical appreciation, that five young college students can show when hungry. They discussed the recent topic of Sleepy Cottage over their cold apple pie and strawberries and cream, and they all decided that it was the most romantic thing in the world, that they should be just brought to the gates of the prison wherein pined a maiden fair, through the cruelty of an unmerciful father. They manufactured quite a novel out of the details, and laid themselves out with a will to unravel the plot, or die in the attempt.

"I'd bet my bottom dollar," said one student, as he drained his glass of lager beer, "that ye Prince of Hearts," will be the one to see this, "Lady fair," the first.

"We don't dispute it," joined in the rest, "he's the devil for working his way into the favor of women."

Here they all looked at him who had addressed the villagers first, and accused him of outdoing their grandest attempts in the siege of hearts. They called him "*Bijou*" and whether it was his name or not, he appeared quite satisfied with it. He seemed to be a little superior to the rest, judging by the deference and courtesy they showed him above what existed among themselves, and he, amiable and pleasant always, laughed good-naturedly at their words of praise, and little insinuations of assumed jealousy. They had come down to this quiet village on a "jamboree," and we all know more or less what students mean by that. It would be both unnecessary and uninteresting however to give an account in detail of these young fellows' adventures during their sojourn in the country; that part alone which affects the rest of our story, is the one we will dwell upon.

CHAPTER XXI

"Full many a flower is born to blush unseen
And waste its sweetness on the desert air."
—*Gray*

It was a hot, sultry afternoon, and even in the woods of Sleepy Cottage the breezes that ruffled the thick foliage were not so refreshing as usual. The door of the house was open, and on two large easy chairs on the vine-covered verandah were seated Alphonse de Maistre and his pretty daughter.

The old man wore large green glasses over his eyes, and his hands were folded as he sat quietly there, listening to the birds and inhaling the fragrance of the rich flowers which adorned the pretty garden.

Josephine lay with her head resting on the cushioned back of her chair, her fingers inserted between the pages of a volume she had just been reading. Both were silent for a considerable time. At length the old man spoke.

"*Es-tu là Fifine, tu ne parles pas?*"

"I am here in body," answered the girl in French, "but not in mind, not in heart."

"Always the same," the old man replied, with a tinge of sadness in his tone. "I thought you would learn wisdom before this, but you do not. What do you want that I have not given you, except company?"

"And what is all you have given me, beside that? I want what the beggars in my books have—liberty. You are not young, you are no longer sanguine and hopeful, while my poor heart is bursting with the fullness you will not let me spend. A living death like mine's a cruelty, a tyranny that God and man must condemn."

"Must I tell you again," asked her father passionately, "that you are differently situated from other girls? Do you not know that at your birth a woman who had been your mother's enemy cursed you and wished you trouble, and shame, and anxiety, and that I in my boundless love for you, will protect you in spite of fate, from such a destiny. The fear of such a thing being realized has sent your mother to a premature grave. You are now entering upon the age that is capable of framing your whole life, and why not reconcile yourself to the belief, that the world, which is dazzling you with its gaudy show, is false and delusive. It is a tinsel glitter, Josephine, the wreck of the innocent and good, turn your back on it for my sake if not for your precious own."

There was a pathos in the old man's voice that would have moved any young heart but the rebellious one of the girl he addressed. There was a feeling nigh to despair in his words when he spoke to her of herself.

The real case was, that she was betrothed already to a man of whom she knew nothing whatever. It was a contract as any other, and though every discretion was used before forming it, yet Josephine would not become reconciled to the idea.

This man, chosen by her father, was a distant relative of her own, and had been reserved for her in order that certain possessions might remain in the family. She had grown up with this idea, but it was extremely repulsive to her. She detested and despised in anticipation this man, whom she had been taught to think of as her future husband, and over and over she bemoaned the tyranny and cruelty of those who had kept her a prisoner all her young life.

There are in France, women who betray supernatural power in foreseeing the future as well as in performing sundry inexplicable feats. They are looked upon as magicians and are invariably associated with the influence of the evil one. It had been the fate of Alphonse de Maistre's wife to incur the inveterate displeasure of one of these persons, and on the day on which her first and only child was born, Dame Feu-Rouge, obtaining admission in disguise to the bed-side of Madame de Maistre, pronounced a fearful malediction on the sleeping form of the infant Josephine, to be realized in later years, when, to use her own words, "she would have grown up in beauty, like a fair, ripened fruit that is rotten at the core."

This cast a heavy gloom over the household of the de Maistres, and though not an over susceptible, nor superstitious family, they could not shake off the presentiment, that hung like a pall over their lives. They decided to leave France, and to seek out seclusion in the backwoods of the new world, where the preservation of their child would be to them, an easy matter. It was before they left their native country, that the marriage contract was signed between Josephine de Maistre and Horace Lefevre, the children being then four and six years of age, respectively.

Up to this time, nothing had disturbed the peaceful monotony of their new home, but, all day as Alphonse de Maistre prematurely aged and gray, sat nursing the grief that had lately visited him in the death of his wife, this girl, for whom he had sacrificed all, grumbled and sighed for the dangers, from which, it had cost him so much to rescue her.

To add to the heavy burden of sorrow that afflicted him, Alphonse de Maistre had to sacrifice, that which contributed most towards making his present home endurable, his eye-sight. It had been failing rapidly for years, and finally became totally extinguished after the death of his faithful, broken-hearted wife.

Even this appealing condition of his, failed to reconcile the wayward girl, to the life he had chosen her to lead; the great pity was, that proper care had not been taken to screen those pleasures altogether from the eyes that had been forbidden to feast upon them. Through volumes of romances, and love-songs, Fifine had gathered a knowledge of what it is to live unfettered, in that world of privileges which she could see only through iron bars. Her governess too, had abused the confidence placed in her by the parents of the girl, and had sung the praises of that world outside, until Fifine yearned to cast aside her fetters, and mix in with the lively throng. She had all the qualities of a worldly girl latent within her and a strong feeling of vanity about her personal attractions, and though she resigned herself to never being able to be seen by any one, she was just as fastidious about the fit of a costume she would wear as any Parisian lady of *haut ton.*

It always irritated Josephine de Maistre, to hear her father allude to the unfortunate cloud that darkened her young life, she always raged and cried and said it was *"bêtises"* and on this occasion she listened no more patiently than on any other; she sprung nervously from the chair, and clasping her hands behind her back, raised her shapely head to address a large green parrot, that was whistling in his great iron cage, on the verandah beside her, —"Poor Poll, Pretty Poll" —came from the thin, pretty coral lips. Poll, thrust his head on one side, and looked almost calculatingly upon the *svelte* figure of his mistress, and said in a meaning croak, "come to dinner—the guest is hungry."

"Greedy Poll," said Fifine, stepping in through the open French window, into the dining-room; she emerged a second later, holding a tempting cracker, between her dainty fingers, she opened the cage door and then lay back again in her cosy chair, having placed the cracker between her own lips. Poll, was quite used to being thus trusted, and stepping majestically out, he perched himself on the shapely shoulder of the young girl, and picked the cracker from its dainty resting place.

A few quiet moments ensued, disturbed only by the crunching noise of Poll's beak in the much relished biscuit, when suddenly Fifine gave a great exclamation of surprise, and darted off her seat. Poll, had abused the trust he had so long respected, and had flown off to quite a little distance from the house.

"What is the matter?" the old man asked, leaning forward anxiously in his chair.

"The naughty Poll has flown away," Fifine answered, "but he cannot go far, Preston clipped his lordship's wings a very short time ago—I will get my hat and follow him."

In another instant, Josephine, in the daintiest of garden-hats tied under her pretty chin, was chasing her truant bird through the wood. She had soon reached the limit of the house-grounds, for, though Poll was unable to fly far at the time, he skipped ahead most provokingly, just as Fifine neared him, and called out in his lustiest croaks, "poor Poll, poor Fifine, Poll wants a cracker, Fifine wants a beau—beau, oh dear, ha, ha, ha." The color had risen to the brunettes pretty cheeks, and her eyes had grown a little wild-looking, from the chase, her hat had fallen back on her shoulders, and the breeze played teazingly with the dark waves of her hair that bordered her perfect brow, she was looking up at a twig above her head, whereon was perched the provoking bird, and as she ran heedlessly towards it, her foot became entangled in a net-work of withered branches that lay in the long grass, and with a cry of pain she fell foremost, on the ragged edge of an old tree stump that stood between her and the soft harmless ground.

Had it been the most imaginative chapter of a dime novel, things could not have happened more opportunely than they did. Just as the echo of the girls cry of distress died in the distance, there was a crackling noise of the branches near by, and a man, young and handsome, with sporting tackle wound around him, stood beside the prostrate form of Fifine de Maistre.

"The d—l? this is a surprise," said the handsome stranger kneeling down on one knee, and untying the ribbons of the large-leafed hat, from the throat of the girl. She was turned from him, but he could see a tiny stream of crimson blood oozing from beneath the hidden face, and slinging aside his sporting regalia he raised the unconscious form in his arms, and looked enquiringly on the still features.

We can forgive the wasted moments of speechless admiration that followed, before he tried to restore consciousness to the inanimate girl, for her beauty had struck him into silent wonder, and being a man, what could he do but stare and admire. There is no appeal so eloquent to the heart of a man as that of a female face of perfect beauty, and when that face is clouded by pain or sorrow, or distress of any kind, a man can no longer control himself.

In this instance our hero had hit upon a nest of temptations—first, he moistened the corner of his silk handkerchief from a flask of water he carried with him, to bathe the throbbing temples, and to wipe away the blood that had disfigured the pretty face. The wound was fortunately a very slight one, and a little treatment sufficed. Having done this, he hesitated a moment and gazed lovingly on the still, motionless features and form of the strange girl, and then, weak, susceptible, unworthy mortal that he was, he bowed his handsome face over her, until two pairs of handsome, well curved lips had met in a—stolen kiss.

After this, he balanced a flask of brandy tenderly and carefully over the pale, set mouth, the even features puckered into an ugly grimace as the spirits moistened the tongue, then her bosom heaved with a great fretful sigh, and she raised the closed lids, slowly and tremblingly displaying to the expectant gaze of her attendant the loveliest pair of dark eyes he had ever seen.

There was a great, vacant stare of stupid wonder for the first instant of returning consciousness, then Fifine, starting up as if from a nightmare, looked bewilderingly around her in a puzzled, dazed sort of way.

"Are you better?" asked the deep, musical voice of the stranger so eagerly that Fifine realized at once that something must have gone wrong. She raised herself up with a great effort, and looked around in blank wonder.

It is not hard to understand how she felt, she, who had never in all her life known what it is to receive the simplest act of courtesy from anyone, now opening her eyes in a lonely wood to find the strong arms of a handsome man supporting her carefully, and holding her head tenderly against his breast for repose. Unschooled though she was in the general items of conventionality, she yet had enough womanly instinct in her to form a perfectly correct calculation of her own, on the strange things that had just transpired.

She felt, while she viewed her handsome hero with that first enquiring glance, that already they were something more than mere strangers to one another. What is there in a little stolen kiss to work such a wonderful change in one? How is it that, though perhaps unable to define everything clearly, a woman can always feel, always know when a man has tried his influence over her thus far?—for influence it certainly is, when a woman has given to the man she is capable of loving, permission to touch his lips to hers, she has at the same time bowed in voluntary slavery under his yoke forever. It is an experience that is never a past, and yet all that has happened before it becomes a blank in the heart, life dates anew from this circumstance, and "is never the same again." This was the nature of the sudden change that had come over our little heroine—the strange romanticism and novelty of the whole scene impressed her visibly.

"Better?" she queried, "Oh, yes. Polly!" and she looked up towards the fated tree that had caused her fall, then realizing her position, she turned to her deliverer, and in a slightly embarrassed tone, said, "I suppose I owe my thanks to Monsieur for aiding me to recover. I was hunting my parrot who escaped from his cage, and met this misfortune while chasing him through this untidy wood."

As she spoke, she raised her tiny, jewelled hand to her face, complaining of a pain in the vicinity of the wound that had been so lovingly dressed, and in trying to advance towards her hat, that hung on the projecting twig of a tree a faint little cry of suffering escaped her. She had injured her ankle too, and was unable to stand on one foot in consequence.

During all this time our young hero was being consumed by admiration for the lovely young girl. Such eyes! Such a whole face! Such a figure! She was fit to clasp in his strong arms and be borne home in a few strides— such a precious little burden she looked. But this he scarcely dared to do just now. Fifine realized her situation as quickly as if she had planned it all beforehand. In spite of the pain and injuries received, she could not help feeling intensely gratified at the romantic turn things had taken. What was the dearest parrot on earth beside a real live young man, handsome and *chic*, and with eyes and bearing just like the heroes in her French novels? Whatever way she might have reached home under ordinary circumstances, these were too promising to have her rely on her own capacity, and to make this understood, she made another attempt to walk, but apparently with less success than at first. Her silent admirer drew a step nearer, and held his arm towards her.

"Do let me assist you," he pleaded, "those little feet were never intended for the branches and boughs of a rough wood like this."

Fifine had never learned how to judge a man by his smallest words and lightest actions. She knew nothing of the thousand little deeds that are done by the counterfeit gentleman, which the real one would spurn with contempt, hence it did not seem at all like taking an advantage of her to hear this one address her with such an open compliment.

The effect was to his benefit. He saw immediately that this was a young girl, hopelessly unschooled in the rules I and regulations of the modern art of coquetry, and so his smile, half hidden, looked as though he meant to repay himself for this amusing trouble.

"Do you live far from here?" was his next question to Fifine who had become quite resigned to her happy misfortune by now.

"Not far, if I was alone and well, but," she added almost coquettishly, "having to trouble you to escort me will make the distance seem twice as long."

Her companion looked amused, he tucked her arm still more firmly within his, and drew her quite close to him. She had put on her hat again and looked sweeter than ever as they began the return home. He took up the conversation at her last words and said in a sorry tone.

"It is a pity we show so soon that our tastes are so entirely different. However, you will excuse me if I say it is your fault. Now, I prize this walk back just for the reason you assign for disliking it. You find it long because I am with you, and I will find it short just because you are with me."

Such words as these went straight to Fifine's susceptible heart; her most exaggerated dreams had never led her this far. She looked at him doubtfully, but it was no dream, she was actually leaning on the strong arm of a live man, listening to words, such as the most devoted Romeo might address to his idolized Juliet.

"But if I must agree with you," she said, "I must still disagree with myself, remembering that while I may never see you again, I must live all my life with myself. Besides I wonder if I could enjoy anything; that word was surely not made for me, I have never known it yet."

She was skilled as any adventuress in the art of captivating. If confidence and a recital of petty woes, from the tempting lips of a fatally beautiful girl, do not appeal most strongly to a man's heart, nothing will. Besides, consider the influence of circumstances. When that pretty girl and you are wholly isolated from every other man and pretty girl in creation, and she is making you realize by her dependence on you, how easily wrongs are righted, and how much strength there is in that strong arm of yours, who is to answer for the consequences? Men are such one sided creatures, they either lean all over on the heart side or altogether on the other. If their extravagance is the former, you can do anything you like with them, if you only go the right way about it, whilst if the other prevail, it is a hopeless case of barrenness against all your best endeavors. Fortunately most young men of our day lose balance on the *left* side and give all up to their intense emotions. They have never learned the A B C of self-denial, and they make an act of resignation first and then plunge into trouble.

Fifine's enthusiastic admirer felt at this moment like opening his heart, and closing her up in its safe fetters forevermore, and I fancy Fifine would as soon have had it as any other nook at the present moment, but neither spoke of it. They were making slow progress along their homeward path, and the suggestive surroundings and interesting circumstances were too much for the unsuspecting girl. She burst into a lively strain of confidence extracted by the answer her companion made to her last despairing remark about enjoying herself.

"My dear young lady, what has Fortune, so very partial to you in all things, left undone in your enviable life?"

There was so much of seeming pathos in his voice that Fifine could not doubt the implied sincerity of his tone, so she unsealed the secrets of her life, telling him all, except the unhappy cause which forced her father to bring her into such entire seclusion.

Many of my readers must have guessed, by now, that he whom the students at the Travellers' Inn called "Bijou," and he who is now making desperate love to Fifine de Maistre, are identical.

Just as the "boys" had said, "the Prince" was sure to break the spell, that fettered the life of the beautiful recluse. He had been on his way to her father, to seek his permission for himself and his fellow students to pass through his grounds, when all at once a new experience presented itself and he found himself talking all sorts of nice nonsense, to a "deuced pretty girl."

It is needless to dwell on the details of the first meeting between those two. Fifine had thought it wiser to leave her charming escort at the rustic gate, insinuating that he might come at any other time to visit her father, and that there was no necessity to speak of what had transpired in the wood.

"But, Mademoiselle," said "Bijou" as he leaned languidly over the gate that stood between them, "are you going to dismiss me like this, as soon as I have discovered the charm of your presence? If your father objects why could you not visit this spot unknown to him; I must see you again, at any cost."

He grasped the tiny, white hand that drooped over the gate, and looked her pleadingly in the eyes.

Fifine was dreaming. All the wild fanciful illusions with which she had brightened the dark days of her young life, seemed to be realizing themselves in a bright procession before her eyes. Here was that ideal lover with whom she had so often rambled through those solitary grounds in fancy—here he was in reality telling his tale of love into her ready ear. Here was the voice she had heard in her dreams, and there were the deep dark eyes that had haunted her out of the page of Eugène Sue's novel, through the long, long days of her loneliness. Compensation seemed within easy grasp. She looked up, into the face of the man before her, and the die was cast. She recognized there a power from which she could never fly. She shivered slightly as she realised that he was master of her will, in spite of herself almost. He saw his advantage, he knew before this how such an ascendancy profits the owner, and his eyes sparkled anew with a light which to other eyes than Fifine's would not have been wholly attractive.

The world is full of such people and their victims. We look upon a face under whose steady gaze we stagger; there are eyes we cannot encounter in a full unflinching look; there are hands whose touch thrills and weakens us, there are voices which sink into our souls, and mesmerize us at their will. Let the circumstances be what they may, we cannot forget the influence that thus haunts our lives.

Poor Fifine had not learned life's lesson wisely. She thought that after the first love came the "wedding ring," and then days, and weeks, and years of highest joy. What did this unsophisticated child know of clubs and bar-rooms and gambling houses, of city lamp-posts, and midnight serenades. What business has any woman knowing it for that matter? so long as she can render an account of every dollar and hour she spends in the day, what is it to her whether her "lawful wedded husband" chooses to watch the stars all night or not. But after all it is time woman learned better sense, it is her privilege to accept or reject this life of uncertainty, and yet, like Fifine, she looks lovingly, admiringly on the pictures bright side only, and fancies "Life's enchanted cup sparkling" all the way down.

The words of consent had passed the threshold of Josephine de Maistre's lips. She felt her hands pressed warmly as she uttered them, and the next instant she was limping alone up the garden walk, her sweet face beaming with unsuppressed smiles, and her hat hanging carelessly over her shapely shoulders.

There was no one in view when she reached the house, but perched on the little iron swing in his pretty cage was Poll, swaying himself complacently to and fro, and looking at his mistress first with one eye and then the other. Fifine spoke not a word, but gathering all the dainties out of the well-supplied cage, passed into the house, leaving the famished bird without a morsel wherewith to gratify himself.

CHAPTER XXII

"Oh what a tangled web we weave
When first we practise to deceive."

Are you feeling well enough to entertain the old man to-night?" said the plaintive voice of Alphonse de Maistre, as father and daughter resumed their seats on the verandah, after the simple evening meal was over.

"Oh yes," Fifine answered quickly, "my foot scarcely pains at all now, it will be nothing serious, I think, after all." Then in her sweet low voice she commenced to read to her blind old parent who sat in a listening attitude with his hands folded in his lap.

Suddenly the firm voice of the young girl wavered, she stammered and grew distracted. There were footsteps in the distance that made her heart beat violently. It was three days since her accident in the wood, and she was anxiously looking forward to a second interview with her lover. A moment after, her face was suffused with blushes as she found herself confronted by the handsome stranger.

"Pardon, Monsieur," he said addressing the old man, "I have taken the liberty to call on you, to solicit permission for myself and some friends to pass through your grounds on our way to the upper woods."

The voice startled the old man. The words were few and to the point; the speaker had evidently not sought a pretext for familiar intercourse, but his voice had too much of the city cultivation about it to please him entirely. His first thought was of Fifine.

"Are you there, daughter?" he asked stretching forth his hand, to make assurance doubly sure.

Fifine caught it in her gentle grasp and drew nearer to him.

"Tell this stranger in his native tongue," he said slowly, "that your father is blind and cannot see him, but that he will trust him and grant the permission he asks, if he will leave immediately, Preston can show them the road."

"I will spare mademoiselle the painful recital," interrupted the young man, now speaking in French, "for I have understood Monsieur her father."

"Who is this man, Fifine?" De Maistre asked nervously. "Is he from the village?"

"I know not, *mon pére*," she answered, trying to be calm, and then to the surprise of all, a loud laugh echoed in the evening air, and the voice of the truant parrot called out from the cage above their heads.

"Ha, ha, ha! he kissed her in the wood, Fifine, give Poll his cracker, polly wants a cracker." The girl's face was dyed with scarlet—and the young man's eyes looked daggers at the mischievous bird. There was an awkward silence for a moment and then "Bijou" with characteristic diplomacy exclaimed:

"What an amusing bird, he speaks uncommonly well, though his words are not very appropriate, certainly."

A shadow passed over the face of the blind listener, a momentary pang shot through his breast, he clasped his hands convulsively, then turning to the stranger he said in a steady voice:

"Never mind the bird, he says queer things at times. Sir, I grant you the permission you come to seek, my gardener, Preston, will await you at whatever time you appoint, and conduct you through. Good-evening, Sir."

Taking this for dismissal, "Bijou" raised his hat, slightly pressed the hand of the beautiful Fifine, and the next moment he was gone.

A strange and awkward silence followed his departure. Much might have been said on such an unusual occurrence as this, yet neither chose to speak.

At last the evening sun as though weary of the quiet scene, gathered all his truant rays out of the tree tops and from the purple mountain summit, and sunk to rest behind the sombre clouds that twilight spread across the sky. Then Fifine who longed to be alone, kissed her father good-night and retired to her own little room, after telling the servant to light a lamp and take her father to his chamber.

The story of Fifine de Maistre's life, from the time of her adventure in the wood, until six months after, would be to the unsympathetic, the most monotonous series of details imaginable. There is no bore like a man or woman who is in love, to those whose precious privilege it never can be, to be guilty of such a natural offence. A man never tires of any one so quickly as he does of some fellow who is "mashed," and girls who are not engaged never count her who is, as strictly one of themselves.

This therefore may be constituted as a plea for refraining to dwell upon the time so laden with exquisite joy to Josephine de Maistre, the time that made up the days and nights of this period of her life at Sleepy Cottage.

She had worked out such fallacious reasonings as justified her in the end, in holding clandestine meetings with her romantic lover, and so, each night when she had finished reading to her father, she stole quietly away to the rustic gate, at the end of the shrubbery, there to lend a willing ear to protestations of love and devotion, from the lips upon whose threshhold she knew, hung the words of her future destiny.

Things had gone thus far, when one night, Fifine in her old humor, was grumbling against the loneliness of her existence, and giving expression to her discontent in most touching terms. Her chivalrous adorer looked the picture of intense sympathy, as he lay stretched in the long grass at her feet.

"Fifine," said he, and something in his voice and eyes thrilled her to the very heart, "my darling, your words are loaded with pain for me; why do you grumble who should be happy amidst these surroundings. If your life were as blank and prospectless as mine, you might have good reason indeed to sigh and complain. You see, a man has to rough it with body and soul. It's not so hard to keep our bodies up, but the task is for the heart. Men should have no hearts, or else some one to love them always and well. I could gather so much courage in a worthy love."

The girl, poor simple child, was touched. She drew nearer to Bijou whose handsome head lay nestling against the rustic bench where she was sitting. He was watching the quick, nervous heaving of her breast, and he could see a slight tremor in the well-curved lip. She fell upon her knees before him, and as she spoke, two large round tears flowed over her pretty checks.

"But Bijou, do you not know that I love you as worthily as I know how, that life with you is all the world to me, and without you it is a miserable blank."

Then she laid her bowed head on his shoulder, and sobbed convulsively.

There was a curious expression in the man's face, as he raised the girl and made her sit beside him. Then taking both her hands in his, he said, in a low tone—

"Fifine, I was only waiting those words from your lips. They fill my vacant life with sweet and pleasant dreams, but in our case, as in all others, 'the course of love can not run smoothly.' You see I gave up my college course after I had met you, and since that time I have been thrown on the world's mercy, almost a penniless waif. I have no wealth to offer you, no luxury of any kind, no abundance, but love and devotion, and that cannot satisfy you."

"O Bijou!" the girl cried out in a passionate tone, "you wrong me, you do indeed. Give me your full heart and your empty hands. I am rich in the world's wealth, let me share it with you; give me that abundance of love you speak of, and I will be—Oh! so satisfied!"

A sinister smile passed over the averted face of the stranger, but the next moment, his arm stole around the slender waist, and raising the tear-stained face to his own, he pressed a long lingering kiss on the warm lips.

"If you will have it so," he said, "my love makes me selfish enough to comply, we can make each other happy by following such a course, is that not enough? If I had sufficient means at my disposal, I could complete all arrangements immediately, and there would be no further suspense for either of us."

"But, Bijou, see how fortune has favored us. Last Tuesday was my birthday, and papa, to reconcile me to my fate, gave me a cheque for my whole dowry, which I was not to have had for two years more. You can see how circumstances favor our attachment."

"It looks like it darling; I hope we are doing the right thing," and his voice implied a painful sense of conscientiousness.

Before parting they agreed to meet once more. Fifine persisted in offering her wealth, and Bijou did not decline. She might bring him the cheque at their next meeting and trust to his fond affection for the rest. He then bade her a tender farewell, and as she watched his departing footsteps, she was delighted when he turned a last time, sajing gayly, "*Au revoir, ma petite, à demain.*" Then he disappeared in a bend of the road, and she walked slowly back to the house, lost in the delicious labyrinths of loves young dream.

CHAPTER XXIII

"Oh, Love' before thy glowing shrine
　My early vows were paid—
My hopes, my dreams, my heart was thine
　But these are now decayed."
　　　—*Byron*

It was a dark, heavy evening in midsummer. Great volumes of leaden gray clouds were piling one over the other in the sulky sky, the air was laden with an unshed moisture, and a threatening breeze rustled through the dry, dusty leaves of the crowded elms. There was an unnatural stillness in Nature—everything looked drowsy and tired, the boughs swayed and nodded, and the flowers hung their sleepy heads like worn-out midnight watchers.

Fifine had hoped madly for the storm to keep off, and now as her fleet steps brought her nearer the rendezvous at the end of the avenue, her heart misgave her, and an indescribable feeling of awe, that had something of a dread presentiment in it, filled her very soul. She pressed the cherished gift for her lover close against her heaving breast, and when she reached the shady nook where they were accustomed to meet, her breath was coming in wild gasps, and her eyes were dilated far beyond their natural size. She was a little too soon, but in her anxiety, watchmg the clouds, the moments sped quickly by, until the arrival of the man she so madly adored.

He could not restrain a look of admiration as his eyes rested on her dark beauty. She had put on her daintiest bonnet, with cardinal ribbons tied under her chin, and a bunch of crushed camellias of the same becoming hue nestled against her shell-like ear. A light cashmere overdress surmounted a petticoat of crimson velvet, and tiny jewels were fastened at her ears and throat. The flush of excitement that mantled her fair young face, lent an additional charm to her countenance, as she looked into her lover's face with all the eagei joy and confidence that filled her heart.

Bijou looked a little more serious than usual, as he knocked the ashes from the end of his cigar.

"*Ma foi*, you are enchanting to-night, Josephine," said he by way of greeting, "but as it looks like a storm, we must make business brisk. I have come to-night, Fifine," he said, taking her hand, "to ask a proof of the words you I uttered last night. I want you to show me bravely that you do think a little of me."

"Only say the word, Bijou. Anything that is in my power. I will do it—anything that is not her voice faltered.

"Is not what?" he asked very tenderly, bending over her, and then she regretted having doubted him. How could *he* ask her anything that was not right? Poor Fifine.

"Never mind," she stammered, "I will do anything I can to prove the truth of last nights words."

"Darling" was the muttered answer "Come here, Fifine, nearer to me, I have something to show to your eyes alone—something that has no real worth at present, but I which will be a sacred thing in a little while."

Fifine, her eyes open wide, and a curious expression of wonder in her face, bent over his broad shoulder. She saw nestling in its bed of ruby velvet, a plain gold band, tiny as her slender finger, but rich and heavy.

She was slow to understand this silent surprise, and only said in a girlish way,

"How lovely it is."

Then Bijou looked earnestly at her, and his voice was almost mournful as he said.

"If it is beautiful as it lies there in its folds of velvet, meaningless and comparatively useless, what would it be, do you think, were it a bond of union between two kindred souls—if it laid the duties of love, honor and submission on one, those of love, respect and kindness on the other, if it were the outward sign of a man's intense devotion and the safeguard of a woman's honor, if it was a love that bound two creatures to each other first, and then to their Creator—what then, Fifine?"

"Oh, Bijou '" she cried, "you excite me with such grave speeches. If it were all these things it would indeed be sacred."

"Come, Fifine, you have said you will do my wish; let me place this golden band upon your ringer, and insure you to me for the days to come."

What sensational story she had ever read could equal this? Was ever any thing so purely romantic or exalted? In that moment all the dreary days of her lonely life seemed blotted out by the exquisite realization of a new happiness that was stealing over her. But still, there was an inward struggle in her soul. Thoughts of her father's wrath thrust themselves between her and her gratification. She lifted up her hands in fear, and said in a hushed voice.

"Bijou, I do indeed love you, but *this* I dare not do, *this* is too much. It is all so sudden, so soon." She recoiled a little as she spoke, and his face darkened ominously.

"Then your words were false!" he said in a cold, cruel voice, "and since you have deceived me I will ask nothing more. I did not deserve this from you, but we part in time."

He stood proudly up and prepared to leave. There was a struggle in the breast of his victim—that he could see. In another moment she was close beside him.

"Do not go, Bijou," she said piteously, "after you have taught me to love you as I do, oh! do not leave Fifine. Tell me what you wish, my Bijou I am ready to do your will."

There was an unpleasant smile of triumph stealing over his handsome mouth. He stretched forth his hand, and took her trembling one in his.

"You must wear this golden band," he said, "as a token of my earnestness, this will bind us one to another Let me see it on your dainty hand."

But she shrank again from his grasp. She was frightfully agitated. The low angry rumble of distant thunder was in her ears, the trees were swaying to and fro, and the leaves were turned upon their stems—the storm was drawing nearer!

At last she spoke again.

"You cannot mean, that I must become your wife in this strange way, Bijou," her voice was husky and trembling, "you have not the power."

He smothered a curse, and his brow contracted. "Power? why have I not power as well as another? are the cold words of a ceremony more binding than the outpourings of a burning heart? Of what avail are cold formalities to souls that are blended already in devotion and love?"

"Hush Bijou," she interposed, frightened at his vehemence, "such words are a profanation. A marriage ceremony could not increase our love, but it is indispensable all the same."

He saw she was firm and that the concession must come from him.

"I see you are a slave to public opinion and church authority," he said, "but this need not be an obstacle between us and our cherished plans. It is growing late now, but if we make good speed, we could reach the village before, dark, and secure the indispensable"—he laid a peculiar stress on the word, "though unnecessary services of the curate".

"But my father—the hour," cried the distracted girl.

"They of course are of more consequence than your love and your promise," he answered coldly, "decide Fifine, for I am impatient. Your home or your love, separation or your promise."

There was a moment of irresolution, but only one, ere the deluded girl yielded everything to the object of her insane devotion. A satisfied look stole over his face as he drew her arm within his, and prepared to leave the place.

Fifine knew very little of the village roads. Bijou though not residing in the place more than three months, led through the thickest and most unfrequented paths. It was growing dark. A yellowish sort of twilight, a forerunner of the storm, was now giving place to a heavy pall of black, that was stealing a descent, noiseless and quiet as a snowflake over the earth. The stillness was doubly oppressive to the unfortunate girl, who leaning on the arm of the handsome Bijou, passed out through the quiet rustic gate, leaving her home and her father amid such rich surroundings, to brave the world with a man of whom she knew nothing, save that she loved him madly, and that his name was Bijou.

Outside the garden gate, at a little distance, stood a small covered buggy, and a horse, the latter tied to a tree and pawing the ground with irritation. Fifine was a little surprised.

"I provided for the best or worst," Bijou said untying the restless animal, and helping Josephine to enter the carriage. Then silence fell on them again. They drove very fast, for the darkness was thickening and Bijou required all his tact, to engineer his horse safely through the path. Fifine at times would forget the rashness of the step she had just taken, and would fancy herself back under the old trees that, each moment, were being left farther and farther behind, until some short words from Bijou, broke the spell of her reverie and hurled her back into the strange reality.

They drove for a very long time, and at last Fifine could discern little lights twinkling in the distance, through the dark surroundings.

"How long it is!" she said once, a little wearily.

"Patience," Bijou answered, "we are near enough now," and then silence fell again, which was unbroken until the horse; steaming and panting, stopped before the door of a small house. The room into which he led her was low and scantily furnished, and only the dim light of a tallow candle, helped to make things discernible through the awful blackness that had settled down. Great leaping shadows danced over the low-ceiling and dingy walls, looking like mocking fiends to the despairing girl, whose heart was filled with a nameless terror at the consequences of her own rashness. But Bijou held her hand firmly within his own, and spoke reassuring words all the while. The clergyman advanced from a corner of the room—a tall spare man whose features being entirely new to Josephine, were scarcely discernible in the dim, unsteady light of the candle. He seemed not surprised at their coming, which in itself surprised Fifine very much. He coolly and systematically proceeded to "tie the marriage knot." His voice was terribly monotonous, and the words sounded more like a "*Dies irae*" in a *requiem* service, than those whose mission it was to crown the happiness of two young hearts.

They had scarce begun the solemn service, when a great flash of lightning filled the small close room, followed by a roar of thunder that drowned for a time the sepulchral voice of the clergyman. Fifine drew nearer to her lover and looked pleadingly into his face. But something in his eyes chilled and repelled her, she knew not why.

The storm increased, great peals of boisterous thunder rolled over their heads, the rain so long pent up, came pattering down m fury around them. The ceremony however was progressing, the binding words were sounding through the dingy little room, the ring was nestling now on Fifine's trembling finger, the closing sentence was being uttered, when a wild flash of greenish lightning crossed the little window near them, filling the room with its lurid glare, lending a most unearthly appearance to the pallid faces of the two men before her. A horrible feeling came over her, but it did not last long. As the flash disappeared, a gush of wind entered a broken pane, the candle went blank out before her stupid gaze, and she forgot everything in that one instant, for a merciful Providence took away her consciousness, and with a shriek she fell, a motionless heap on the floor.

CHAPTER XXIV

My curdling blood, my madd'ning brain,
In silent anguish I sustain
And still thy heart, without partaking
One pang, exults—while mine is breaking
        —Byron.

She turned on her side and woke, at least she opened her eyes in a wide stare, but could see nothing. All was black, opaque darkness around her. She raised herself on her elbow, her back ached, her head ached, every joint was stiffened. What could it mean? Had she fallen out of bed, she wondered? She tried to move but could not. She called "Anna! Papa!" but her voice sent back a mocking echo from the black stillness, no maid, no parent, hearkened to her cry. She looked all around. A colorless emptiness surrounded her. She stretched out her feeble hand, but nothing answered to her eager search. Was she alone in a creation from which the sun had been cancelled? Where was her memory? What had she done last? She tried to think. She had been painting—oh yes! but it grew so dark she had to give it up. She must have fallen asleep after it, she began to think consolingly, but no! she had gone into her own little room and put on her daintiest apparel; she remembered pinning the bunch of camellias in her bonnet. But even this was no clue, she forgot after that. Was she in the open air or indoors? She could feel no breath or breeze, nor was there anything within reach to reassure her. She was too puzzled just now to feel much frightened. She only wanted to think. Instinctively she raised her hand to her head, and then—memory came back with one full swoop as she felt the heavy golden band on her finger. A painful rehearsal of all she had done passed before her eyes, and when she remembered the fatal flash of lightning and the darkness that followed, she fell shrieking back on the hard floor. She knew now that she was alone in the dark dingy little house, that had terrified her so much at first. She raised herself again, tremblingly, and supported her reclining form on her hand, her arm resting on the cold boards. "But I am not alone," she said reassuringly; "Bijou is here," then raising her voice a little, she called "Bijou! Bijou!" but the silent chamber only sent back a dismal echo of her own voice. Then louder still she cried "Bijou! Bijou! Bijou!" her voice gathering courage as the maddening truth forced itself on her bewildered brain. Still no answer. She grew terrified at having broken the awful stillness. She strained her eyes to peer through the cruel darkness that enveloped her. No use—it was only looking through one blackness into another. She covered her weeping face with her little trembling hands, moaning and wailing as she rocked herself to and fro on the hard floor. Poor girl! She was only one of the million victims of that folly which rules universal girl-hood to-day. She had not been taught the lesson of life as every girl should know it. Like others of her age, all over the wide world, here in our own flourishing city as well, she had been given the elements of a valuable knowledge to play with, and fool with, and yawn over to her heart's content. This was all.

According to popular ideas, there are so many other things to be instilled into young girl's heads of primary importance, that education takes its own course, and enthusiastic mothers stay up half the night curling the flaxen hair, or paring the promising eyelashes of their pretty babies, but what becomes of the little heart that is growing wild for want of a tender solicitous hand to cultivate its helpless soil? What is the use? A handful of caramels goes a far longer way towards calming a fit of juvenile temper than a word of effective remonstrance, that will only spoil the pretty face, on mama's reception day too, or just before some liliputian tea-party. True it is that it is far more universal a practice than in former years to send one's children to school. But where does the advantage come in? The embryo woman is packed off to the most stylish boarding-school, she must be allowed a thousand deviations from the rules, on account of weak nerves or some equally imaginary disorder. She picks up in her hours of good humor a smattering of French and German, music or elocution, painting and fancy-work, but these painful superficialities only ruin the girl, who, had she been left without those oppressive appendages, would be an honest whole- hearted woman. Instead of this, our drawing-rooms are crowded with affected, insipid girls, who, being girls, are fair enough to view, but whose minds and hearts are prudently closed to inspection. These are the perfections of lollipop misses who left home for boarding-school, five, six or eight years ago, and come back conceited ninnies, who imagine every good-looking man must be appropriated, whether he will or not, as their slavish adorer.

These are no untrue assertions. Ask anyone of sound, natural judgment, how many sensible, edifying, worthy women are found at once in a ball-room or concert-room, or any other rendezvous of fashionable society. The answer, if not convincing, would at least be surprising. And yet, every year, numbers of these golden-haired, blue eyed girls leave the altar on the arm of some well-to-do young fellow, his, until death, and no one in the admiring throng of spectators doubts that the sequel of this bright day's doings will be one of endless felicity. But they are deceived. It is the wife's lack of sympathy in the hour of distress, her incapacity to solace the troubled mind and heart of the man who has loved her, that drives the young husband from his home, to seek distraction in the bottomless wine-cup. It is a repulsive picture, but a true one, and those who have not seen it yet for themselves will meet the stern reality some day, perhaps, before very long.

These deviatory details may enable the readers to understand more fully, and to condemn less readily the actions of Josephine de Maistre. She had placed unbounded confidence in the man who had come to her with his well-learned tales of love. She was young, susceptible and inexperienced, and had not thought that night should close in upon her bright, beautiful, cloudless day. But it was different now. The impulsive, generous, confiding nature was slowly being moulded by the hand of a bitter experience, into a skeptical mistrust of humanity, dreadful to see in a woman. All the careless years of her girlhood passed in mockery before her eyes to-night, until her poor heart was nigh bursting with pent-up sorrow and grief. She dropped her cold clammy hands into her lap and sat upright in the darkness. How long had she been here? Was it an hour, a day, or a week? How long must she remain here now? She felt in her breast for her pocket-book, and a look of undying scorn stole into her eyes when she found it was gone. She was penniless, alone, helpless; would this darkness ever dissipate. If she could only die, or go mad, or sleep again, she thought, as she threw herself passionately on the floor moaning and sobbing most piteously. Suddenly she sprang up again, maddened by pain, suspense and fear. Holding out her trembling arms in the darkness, she screamed despairingly, appealingly, "Bijou, my lover, my traitor, where are you? Come back and free me from this awful terror, rescue me, or kill me, anything—oh anything but this frightful solitude."

Still no sound answered her despairing accents as she dashed herself recklessly back on the floor, weeping and sobbing afresh. Then there was a moment or two of heavy silence, for it is in silence the heart breaks. After that the girl sat up again, with her feet tucked under her skirts. She brushed back her matted hair from her swollen face and clasping her hands over her knees, she filled the small dark room with a sharp ringing laugh. It was something horrible to hear—a voice once so soft and plaintive, now grating out shrill accents in a hard mocking tone.

"Ha, ha, ha," she sneered, "the brave monsieur Bijou, how he played with *la folle Fifine*. Was he not too sure perhaps? Fifine can love, but oh! more delicious, Fifine can hate! yes hate!! hate!!!" she repeated with a malicious pleasure, emphasizing the word, "and she can curse *le beau Bijou*."

"Oh!" she cried joining her hands in an iron grip, "may sickness and poverty and misfortune waylay him! may he love one who will break his heart! may this life be to him a temporary hell, to prepare for the eternal one in the next! Ha, ha, that is good Fifine, *pourtant, le beau Bijou* would be vexed to hear that, he would be shocked. We'll tell a secret to this brave young man. The world is big, Bijou, and Fifine is only a small weak child, but she loves to hate, and she loves revenge. She will walk till her feet are blistered, and her body worn and tired, but she will find Bijou, she owes him a little debt and she must pay it. She gives the devil his due, ha, ha, ha," and the wild unearthly laugh resounded once more through the dismal darkened chamber. In this horrible strain she continued chattering to herself and menacing Bijou, until suddenly she stopped short and bent over in a listening attitude. A sound had caught her ear. Something had broken the frightful silence besides her rambling maniacal chatter. Some other animate thing was within her hearing. She was breathless for many moments as she glared, eyes and mouth open, in the direction from which the sound had proceeded. She listened devouringly and could now distinctly hear a slow regular breathing, somewhere near, but which way she could not tell. Her flesh crept with a new fear. She dreaded being alone, and yet she preferred solitude to the knowledge that some one was coming to her in the darkness. She crawled on her knees a few paces forward, but as the sound decreased she crept silently back in the opposite direction. Still she could not hear more distinctly.

She therefore made a great stride towards another point, and now she could hear very plainly the regular breaths coming and going as of one in deep sleep. This suspense was worse than any. She laid herself out on the floor, rested her elbows on the boards and buried her chin in her palms. Wild thoughts of hatred and revenge chased one another through her unsteady mind, but still she could discern nothing but this tranquil respiration. She was weakening now. It must have been three hours from the time she awoke first, and yet there was no sign of light or life, nothing but this strange breathing, wherever it was. She was growing drowsy and threw herself back on the floor, with one fair white arm thrown over her head. She had advanced considerably to the left of the room, though the impenetrable darkness did not allow her to know it. Her breast heaved in great irregular sighs, and her long lashes drooped wearily over her tired eyes. Another moment and sleep would have come in its precious mercy to solace the poor afflicted soul, the wild staring eyes had been subdued into drowsiness, and the angel of balm was coaxing the tired limbs into repose, when a loud sigh broke upon the sleep- inducing silence, and disturbed the unfortunate Fifine. She opened her eyes suddenly again and waited for a repetition. This time she heard several queer sounds, like scratching and eating. Overcome at last by suspense, she started up, but in doing so, she knocked her head violently against some object that stood close by her. In her madness she never heeded the pain, but stretched out her hands for something to lean against, when fortunately she laid one of them on a stumpy candlestick, in the saucer of which she found a couple of greasy matches. A cry of joy escaped her as she struck a light, as quickly as her nervous fingers and glad excitement allowed her. At least now the horrible spell of darkness and uncertainty was broken. The candle hardly took at first, but as she watched it eagerly, with both hands around the timid spark, it spluttered and flared up into a tall lanky flame that made her surroundings look visible, if not bright.

It was the same little room to which Bijou had brought her for her wedding, she did not know how long ago. Now that she looked at it in a calm, keen scrutiny, she noticed that these stray pieces of homely, furniture had been thrown around, merely to give the place the appearance of being inhabited. No one had lived there for a long time, anyone could see. Great tangled cobwebs hung all over the wall and celling, and one corner of the miserable apartment was a perfect pool, from rain that had dropped through the defective roof. When Fifine had taken in these surroundings in her quick, searching glance, she tried to discern the source of the noises she had heard. This was an easy matter. Very near to where she stood, was a long dingy door that closed with a latch, and from behind this Fifine heard the sounds still issuing. Prepared for the worst, she got down on her knees and holding the candle a little way above her head, she raised the latch and pushed the door violently in. The next instant a great shaggy dog was bounding around her, lashing his paws on the floor and attempting to lick her hands and face. She smiled a little first when she remembered her fear, but her next feeling was one of joy, at the new and strange companionship, which might yet prove of service to her. Laying the candle down upon the floor, she drew the animal towards her and began to examine him. He was a large, well-built, glossy-haired fellow, with earnest eyes and a long, loose tongue, that hung a great way out of his mouth. Around his shaggy neck was a silver collar, on which was engraved "Sailor," and the two large initials, "N.B.," and after further scrutiny, she deciphered on the margin of the band, "I. Kennedy, Engraver, St. Paul St, Montreal." She threw her arms wildly about the animal and hugged him affectionately. At least she had a clue. In her new joy she quite forgone very precaution she had planned before, but now she was brought back from her ecstasy by remarking that her candle was almost burnt out. She had no other, and she must be content to sit there and await day break, or escape while there was yet a spark of light. She seized this last hope, for taking the dog by the collar, she dragged him towards the door of exit, and as she tried to undo the fastenings, she talked wildly to herself and to him. The door was fastened on the outside, proof positive, that she had been knowingly and heartlessly bound within those wretched walls. This excited all her latent hatred again, and with the mad strength of defiance and revenge, she tried to tear the fastenings apart with her naked fingers. She toiled bravely and fast. The light of the candle was leaping up and down, threatening to expire. Only once or twice did she pause to fling back the dishevelled hair that blinded her eyes, but at last she was rewarded, for with one supreme effort she succeeded in dragging in the door, and opening for herself a passage into the outside world.

"Not, bad Fifine," she laughed, as the night air swept in on her feverish head, "we'll get *le beau Bijou* yet. He'll say Fifine is mad, but we'll see—Fifine is not mad—she hates him though, and she will kill him, ha! ha!"

She walked about chattering wildly, holding Sailor by his collar, and saying senseless things to him every now and then. At last, when she had gone a long way without being able to discern a path, she sank down to rest near a clump of trees. Twining her arms round Sailor's shaggy neck, she laid her head on his warm body and soon fell into a heavy dreamless slumber.

CHAPTER XXV

Yes! there are real mourners—I have seen
A fair, sad girl, mild-suffering; and serene.
—Crabbe.

The gray of the morning was stealing out from behind the tree-tops, filling the woodland with a dim uncertain light. The tall spectral forms and great crouching figures of the darkness, now proved to be the limbs and broken trunks of gigantic trees. With the misty light of the morning all the ghouls and goblins of the night left the lonely forest and retreated to their secret abodes until dusk would come again.

A cold cheerless change was coming over the earth and two equestrians trotting silently through the wood, at this early hour, shivered and shook in the raw air of the morning. They spoke very little. The elder one was smoking, the other was looking moodily on before him. Presently the former stretched himself far on one side of his horse and thrust his head enquiringly forward. He took his pipe from his mouth and looked again.

"Philip, my son, what do you see there?"

"Where?" the other asked indifferently.

"Inside those twisted trees."

Philip glanced in the direction indicated, and in an instant was dismounted. He gave the reins to his companion and walked briskly to the spot that had excited their attention. When he reached the place he halted suddenly and looked aghast. An exclamation of horror escaped his lips. He bent over the object and beheld the figure of a human being, clad in female attire, sleeping on the crouched body of a great Newfoundland dog. But the arms and fingers that encircled and clutched the faithful animal were daubed with blood, and here and there on the fretful face of the sleeper were dried patches of crimson. The matted hair fell loosely round the regular features, but the picture on the whole was at once the strangest and most touching one it was possible to see. Philip turned silently and beckoned his companion to approach. Then both of them bent curiously over the form of the girl to ascertain whether she slept a temporary or an eternal sleep, and when her distinct breathing convinced them that life was not extinct, they called her and tried to awaken her. For a long time their efforts were vain. Nothing seemed capable of dispelling the stupor that had settled over her. She only tossed her head wearily from one side to the other when they spoke, and frowned peevishly, as though their words annoyed her. Once she raised her blood-stained hand and the two men saw with renewed surprise that she wore a wedding ring on her slender finger. This touched them anew, and they resolved to move her between them to the village, where a doctor could be consulted and her wants be carefully attended to.

But when they laid their hands upon her the dog showed his teeth threateningly, growling angrily in their faces. At the sound of her defender's voice, the girl lifted her eyelids and glared wildy at the two figures standing above her. She tightened her greedy hold around the animal's neck and screamed:

"Don't touch him, don't dare—he—and my revenge—all that's left—revenge! Ha, ha, ha.—"

Her voice died out and her eyes closed drowsily again. The two men stared at one another in mute surprise. Then the younger of the two, making a last effort, bent over her and said coaxingly:

"Let me take you off the damp ground, you'll have your death of cold,"

She started and looked strangely at him.

"Not death," she said in a tone of defiance, "not death until I have done my work."

"Tell us your name, good woman," the older man put in, not heeding her last remark.

"Name? I have no name now—outcast—*jolle*-if you like. But I will win my name back, I will—"

"Of course you will," sad one consolingly, looking at his companion and tapping his forehead knowingly.

"Come, we will begin right away; let us go now," and he raised himself up to start.

With a little coaxing and reassurance, they persuaded her to lean on them and rise up, but the poor little face became distorted and the eyes closed languidly as if she suffered intensely. She stood bravely up however, but in a moment she tottered and sank back again. Her companions saw that their efforts were useless in her present condition, so it was decided that while the elder man remained to watch her, the younger one should gallop to the village and secure the assistance necessary to transport her from this lonely spot.

Unfortunately the path chosen by Bijou on the night of her elopement with him, led to a succession of roads which wound almost interminably through woods and fields adjoining another village, situated some miles distant from the one they had left. This settlement was called "The Lower Farms." It was to this place that Philip Campbell and his uncle Douglas were travelling on that morning when they found Fifine in the wood. Bijou had made a very round-about trip, bringing the girl at least twenty miles from her own neighborhood, and leaving her in a spot where, if found, she would be looked upon as a resident of the Lower Farms.

With all possible speed, Philip Campbell rode into the village, going straight to the doctor of the place, to whom he confided their strange *rencontre*. Half an hour later, the zealous man of medicine with his attendant and Phil, were journeying back to the spot where Douglas Campbell kept kindly watch over the unfortunate female.

CHAPTER XXVI

"Jukes and earls, and diamonds and pearls
And pretty girls was spoorting there.
And some beside (the rogues) I spied,
Behind the winches coorting there."
— Thackeray.

"This is our waltz, Miss Edgeworth, are you prepared?" asked Vivian Standish, as he bowed before the girl in black satin, who was conversing gayly with a fine-looking elderly gentleman.

"So soon," Honor said, somewhat surprised, "why, I thought—"

"Yes, I know you did," he interrupted gayly, "but do listen to that music."

Honor rose, thus appealed to, and smiling an adieu to her first companion, she thrust her round white arm into Vivian's, as he led her triumphantly into the ball-room, where many couples were already on the floor.

"See, we have lost some of it already," he exclaimed, putting his arm around her slender waist. They had to wait another minute thus, to allow more formidable couples to move past them, recruits in "the terpsichorean art" who were ploughing their ways agonizingly through the crowd, leading their warm fat partners on the laces and frills of other ladies' dresses. As Honor and Vivian joined the moving mass, they attracted many admiring glances. They were well matched in size, both good-looking, and remarkably fine dancers, and as they glided here and there many criticizing whispers followed them.

Little Miss McCable, who has the reputation of being one of Ottawa's best dancers, bites her lower lips sarcastically, as an admirer of Miss Edgeworth's asks her, "does she not find her dancing faultless," and declares she "kaunt see what there is so striking about her."

But heedless of those who surround them, Vivian leads his fair partner through the crowd, as the strains of waltzes picked from "Olivette" and "Patience," flood the ball-room. Any girl may boast of being free from susceptibilities of a disastrous kind, but few girls *à la mode* to-day can overcome the resistless fascination of a dreamy waltz, and Honor Edgeworth who was the very poetry of motion in herself, was lost to everything else but her waltz at this moment—how well Vivian Standish guided, she thought—how well he held himself! how *distingué* he looked!

He had begun to puzzle her a little, and though she certainly did not like him, there was a sort of strange attraction for her in his voice, appearance and manner. I wonder if men can know what there is in a voice?

It is a precious talisman that serves at all times, and the one infallible means a man has to find his way to a woman's heart, for a woman never forgets the pathos, and sweetness of a voice that has called her "his own."

Vivian Standish had a voice to covet and to envy, he said the most matter-of-fact thing in a way that captivated the most careless listener, and the girls declared that when he spoke to them they were "perfectly distracted." Ottawa is the most interesting spot on earth for a person of any extraordinary ability to gain notoriety. If it is a girl the male element is effervescing all at once, men fall in love with her in turns, she is almost devoured with attention at evening parties, and visits all the suggestive nooks, and sits on the stairs with the handsomest and toniest of Ottawa's "big boys;" even married men get the craze, for Ottawa boasts of quite a little circle of benedicts, who are not slaves to petty prejudices inflicted as a rule on the married, and though not open advocates of "Free Love," they take all the privileges that hang around the border limit, for they do not doubt, but that any one might know when they are seen escorting pretty flirts, riding, driving, or walking through such delightful walks as "Beechwood," or "Richmond Road," that the topic of conversation is painfully appropriate to their vocations, and as a proof if any one were to join them, at the moment, they would be either admiring nature or art, or anything in fact but each other.

It makes as much difference in Ottawa as well as elsewhere, whether a young lady be only an instructress of music, but exceedingly pretty, or the daughter of a cabinet minister with a homely face and awkward gait. A man is a man in spite of society's most binding laws; but circumstances are so delightfully blended when a girl is rich, good-looking, clever—and disengaged, it is the chance of a lifetime, and were it not that such "chances" as these, usurp the opportunites of Ottawa's patient and less endowed girls, there would be fewer of these old young ladies, who haunt the drawing rooms and public balls of our city, year after year with the same result. Two or three years ought to satisfy any girl of ordinary ambition, and yet there are tireless maidens who only remain in their ninth or tenth winter, because of some petty constitutional ailing, that makes a better excuse than saying, "there's no use trying any more, I'm a year older this year and have less chance," and so they begin to settle into a sound resignation, and snub the more presentable daughters of social inferiors; they either turn into first-class Sunday school teachers, and denounce the pomps of a world whose excess has brought them to solitary womanhood, or they make unrivalled depositaries and disseminators of the local news of their little sphere, but they are as admirable an invention as any other, as they have many hours of leisure to engage in charitable and other occupations. There are plenty of these amiable "everlastings" at Mr. Bellemare's to-night, some of them apparently much appreciated, for while their homely, ungainly figures are whirled around the room on the arm of some calculating youth, fresh blooming girls must bite the ends of their feathery fans in a passion of disappointment, as they stand against the wall, or admire the pictures or statuary, or it does not matter what, so long as they need not look straight into the fun they cannot share. What a glorious epoch of womanly dignity, independence and worthiness! It is a picture one likes to draw for the contemplative admirers of the age.

A girl who makes up her mind to "go out" after leaving school, is I think, the most foolish and wretched girl under the sun, unless her parents or other relations have either a political, social or money influence to strengthen her, for many a daughter looks regretfully back upon the foolish steps which led her by contact into a world of fashion and flummery.

The exquisite ball-dress came home one night with the little paper from "Cheapside," or the "Argyle House," bearing its value represented in high numbers; a big account was opened in those dangerous books, a necessary affliction nevertheless, where the daughters will be "fashionable" and persist in having the same indulgences as the daughters of those who have less manners by far, but who can substitute good breeding easily by an abundance of "filthy lucre." In a ball-room, she is alone in a multitude, most often wishing heartily she were rolled comfortably in the blankets of her cosy bed, she may be a nice girl, men admire her as a rule, but men are too dependent in Ottawa to declare their opinions openly, when they thereby tread upon society's corns.

Although this is naturally a democratic country, social ostracism is not unknown amongst us. The daughter of any one who "keeps a window," or is at all engaged in trade, is as effectually excluded from society as if she were a moral leper, and although her attainments, intellectually and otherwise, be far superior to those of her more favored sister, (who is very frequently both stupid and uninteresting), her chances of an invitation are small indeed, until her father is in a position to head a subscription list or an election fund, and then, presto! all the insuperable difficulties that previously existed, magically disappear.

The brainless families of representative men, must of course monopolise attention, if all the rest went to eternal perdition, and what does it matter how vexedly a fellow tugs his moustache over the insipid drawl of some "powerful" man's daughter, while he eyes most enviously the form of her less safely established sister, and wishes to—he was some other fellow, and not himself.

Honor Edgeworth, strange to say, beautiful, and courted though she was in Ottawa, failed to catch any sweetness therein. While such a thing was new, it amused her, but already the shallow novelty had worn off, and it had become monotonous. Perhaps, if things were different, she could have entered with more relish into her world of gay distractions, but she knew, beforehand, that there are voids and vacancies in the heart, that can never be filled by the trivial pleasures of high life. When the eye has begun to scan the world for a particular face and form that it loves to look upon, it instinctively shuns both crowded rooms and festive halls.

This was why Honor looked so indifferent to the sensation she created this evening at the Bellemare's, gliding through the ball-room on the arm of the handsomest man present, but for all that her mind was not lazy, she was thinking deeply enough the while, leaning on the stalwart shoulder of Vivian Standish, drinking in the suggestive strains of the music to which they danced. Honor was also yielding to the influence of memory that had been awakened within her, that memory that pensively turned backwards the unforgotten pages of her past, filling her with a sad discontent, that soon betrayed itself in the wearied expression of impatience which stole into her eyes and over her whole face, and while so many girls around her, could have hated her for her luck, she sighed heavily under her rich brocades, and whispered to herself, "others look so completely happy, why need things be so different with me?"

Presently the arm that encircled her slender waist released its pressure, and a sad earnest voice, said in a half anxious tone, into the pretty pink ear:

"Why do you look so worried and fretful, are you tired?"

"No—yes—a little," she answered wearily.

"Let me get you some refreshment," was the solicitous rejoinder. "Come in here, Miss Edgeworth, see how cosy and appropriate it looks."

Mechanically she yielded, and on the arm of her admirer passed into a spot which was a veritable artificial summer. It may not seem consistent with the rest of Honor Edgeworth's character, to say that, though defiant and independent, with regard to every other influence in life, she found herself unable to battle against the strange and unpleasant feeling, that invariably filled her in the company of this man.

She had read and heard of "will power," and of the strength of the moral character asserting itself, despite the most gigantic efforts on the part of the victim, and though she was not inclined to raise this petty instance to the dignity of such wonderful manifestations, it yet savored of mystery to her, and thrust a repulsive consciousness of her own moral weakness upon her.

She was a "good girl," in the broadest sense; there was no nest of social vices inside that fair, honest face; the diplomacy and duplicity of fashion were unknown to her guileless heart, she was solid worth in every way, even while she sat under the broad leaves of rare branches, toying with her silver spoon, and listening to the earnest voice beside her. The wavy, chestnut braids that bound her shapely head, were natures own great gift to her, and had never been stowed away in idleness during the hours of her *deshabille*: the little tide of pink that ebbed and flowed over her fair face had never lain condensed within box or bottle upon her dressing-table, her face and form in all their loveliness were genuine, the double row of white even teeth, that gave a great charm to her pretty mouth, had never dreamed their early days away in dental show-cases, nor bathed all night by a toothless maiden's bed-side in a glass of water; much less did she ever tempt herself to encourage the authors of those wonderful advertisements that grace our daily papers, and which introduce to the world, renowned dimple makers, nose refiners, and other improvers of personal deficiencies.

It was perhaps the freshness of her beauty and the originally of her manner, that attracted her many satellites around her.

Lady Fullerton asks, "Is not beauty power?" and should I undertake to interpret the answer of the multitude I could but say—"it is."

There was not one in creation who knew better how to wield his weapons than did Vivian Standish. Many a time he had smiled inwardly at seeing the fruitless struggles of his victims to appear unmoved by his winning ways, but now, for once, he was balancing his precious judgment on a doubt. He was not too sure, but that this frank, clear, virtuous girl could read him through. Sometimes he felt uncomfortable. Just now, he felt as dogged as any ambitious school-boy ever did over an obstinate theorem in Euclid— here was a problem—there were all the rules for its clear solution, yet the answer never would come right. Perhaps he was preparing for another attempt, as he drew his chair closer to her and looked into her face, while they sat in the spot of all spots, the most flattering to his designs.

She greeted this new movement with a look of sudden surprise, but, unheeding, he bent over her slightly and said in his same provokingly sweet way:

"Why did you wear that cruel little rose-bud to-night, Miss Edgeworth?"

This is the sort of pleasant thing that Honor dislikes: whose memory or anticipation is always sweeter than the actual experience. She did not look at him this time, but still, toying with her spoon and glass, she answered slowly:

"Because—I like it best of all the flowers—"

"On account of its—" interrupted Vivian, and then paused, looked at her, and waited,

"Yes, exactly," Honor said, looking straight into his deep eyes, this time. "It is on that very account."

"I was going to say—'meaning'—" he almost whispered back.

"Well—?" Honor drawled indifferently.

"Take it off then—it is the only unbecoming thing about you."

"I infer," returned Honor, slightly arching her brows, "that you expect me to obey your word of command?"

"Which I spoke without the meanest right to do so, I suppose?" Vivian said humbly, "in that case, I cancel it and apologize."

"That is still, almost another command," she retorted provokingly.

"How so?" asked her listener, becoming interested.

"For pardon," Honor said, "I never knew a man who did not flatter himself that his apology satisfied for the grossest indiscretion."

He stood aimlessly up, and knocked a withered leaf of oleander from a tall branch that scented the spot where they were sitting, but instead of returning to his seat, he leaned his crossed arms on the back of her broad chair, and looking down on her, answered:

"Why are you a little less generous to us, poor unfortunates than you are to every one else?"

He was so gentle to her, he could not reproach her with a fault, and he had therefore called this a less degree of generosity.

Honor began to feel the effects of playing with dangerous tools, but without knowing that such an experience, is the greatest danger that can beset an untried life.

"How rashly you do presume, Mr. Standish," said Honor, "as if you could tell, positively, what I thought of 'you poor unfortunates.'"

"As if you could help showing us, your lack of appreciation in every possible way," he returned, still leaning on the cushioned back of the chair, where she rested her head languidly.

"Then, let it be so, for if you judge me by my action only, without bringing any of your own calculations to bear, I will be satisfied with the result."

"Miss Edgeworth," began he, changing his tone to one of curious interest and earnestness, "have you a bosom friend?"

Honor looked suddenly up at him, and grew serious.

"I have acquaintances who presume to question me, as though they had the rights of one," she said, sinking lazily back in her chair.

"Then, they usurp *somebody's* privileges, by so doing—do they not?"

The girl looked indignantly at him, and only withdrew her powerful glance slowly, as she said:

"Mr. Standish, I find it strange, that you should think me utterly different from other girls; pray, undeceive yourself I have my friends, and loves, and follies, and caprices like the rest and will have all my life. I expect to to be just as foolish in my love affairs some day, as you men generally consider most girls to be."

"I hope so," he answered meaningly, and as she rose to leave the conservatory, for another dance, she heard him mutter: "for my sake."

CHAPTER XXVII

"He whom thou fearest will, to ease its pain,
Lay his cold hand upon thy aching heart,
Soothe the terrors of thy troubled brain,
And bid the shadows of earth's griefs depart."
—A Proctor

"You had better watch him closely, Mrs. Pratt, his condition is precarious, and as he has been thrown on your hands, do not treat him shabbily—"

"You ken bet I'll not," said the matronly female, who stood half hidden in the humble doorway, from which Dr. Belford had just made his exit. "Lawks, doctor dear, I'll have an eye to him, jest as if he was my very own. It'ud not be me 'at would neglec' any Christian that fate had thrown on me hands."

"I thought so," said the doctor, half apologetically. "I'll call again shortly," and then, gathering in the fringe of his carriage apron, Dr. Belford bade Mrs. Pratt a temporary farewell, and was off.

The small shabby brown door closed gently enough, and separated Mrs. Pratt from the whole moving mass of animate confusion that reigned in the streets outside. As she stopped, on her way through the narrow passage within, to straighten the rag mat at the door of the front room, she sighed perplexedly and soliloquized resignedly:

"Fever! above all things else—bless the sickness—likely as not it could be the death o' me, and yet, how could I send the lad away or go back on him now."

A hissing noise from the kitchen, transported the meditative Mrs. Pratt in a wonderful hurry from her philanthropic reasoning to a saucepan of potatoes that were bubbling furiously in the water, over a good fire in her cracked cooking stove; but though she busied herself with her daily duties for the next hour, her face was unusually serious, and her mind agitated. She was reflecting earnestly on the new charge that had been thrust upon her, and wondering whether a tough old woman who had never had the measles could escape the contagion of typhoid fever,

Mrs. Pratt had a small faded cottage all to herself, the substantial token of the late John Pratt's esteem, before he left for his long journey to the better land; and though the locality was a poor one, and the neighbors noisy and rough, this particular dwelling impressed one strongly with in idea of the "shabby genteel" in all its painful gentility, and also filled the heart with a ready sympathy for the "old decency" that yet survived within those paintless, sunburnt shutters, and those faded, pitted walls.

But inside this uncomfortable appearance of washed-out brick and well-ripened wood, there was comfort and cleanliness and quiet. The front room, with its stiff cane rocker and chairs, its round table and well-adorned mantelpiece, its cretonne-covered lounge and tapestry carpet, was not a bad sample at all, of a drawing-room in a third-rate boarding house.

Upstairs, on the first and highest story, were three small, but scrupulously neat rooms, two of which looked out into the street, and the other into the common yard of some dozen neighbors. In the largest apartment of all, which was the aristocratic bedroom, was a narrow, iron bedstead, a little square, antique bureau, an open wash-stand, with a prim white basin set into a hole in it to fit, and a clean diaper towel, folded respectably across the pitcher that did not match the bowl. The boards, though bare, were yellow as gold. The faded shutters were closed, and failing hooks were fastened to a nail in the shabby sill by a piece of aged pink tape. On a small table by the bed-side, were bottles and tumblers and remnants of rough delicacies, that bespoke sickness.

The loud, heavy breathing of an invalid, was all that disturbed the quiet of Mrs. Pratt's best room, and this came irregularly, but oppressed and labored, from the prostrate form on the little iron bed behind the door.

Over the spotless linen of the warm bed, two hot, washed hands were lying, and buried in the small, soft pillows, was the flashed, feverish face of a young man. His brow was contracted and every feature bore the impress of the foul disease that had made him its victim. The dry, parched lips moved eagerly at intervals, and the thin fingers clutched one another in feverish excitement; the drowsy lids were only half closed, and great drops of perspiration were standing out on the poor flushed face.

Care and intense anxiety were legibly traced on the well carved features. The mouth was drawn in at its corners, the brow was furrowed by deep lines, and the black hair was well sprinkled with the grey dust of a hard and a bitter experience acquired on the road of life's fatiguing duties.

This sad, silent young man was well known in the neighborhood as "Mrs. Pratt's boarder," and when, after defying a serious indisposition for days, he came home one night to his little room, a helpless victim to its ravages, everyone said they were truly sorry, and counselled Mrs. Pratt to treat him "decent." Here he lay through long, sleepy, sultry days, dozing and raving, and tossing in the madness and delirium of fever, and suffering terribly, through endless nights of suffocation and torment.

Poor Mrs. Pratt had done her best, nobly and well, she had called in the doctor of best repute, and had advanced the "coppers" herself, such trust had she placed in the young fellow, wherewith to provide him with the necessary remedies and delicacies. When he was "real" bad she sat up herself to watch, and invited the widow Brady or some other interesting neighbor to keep her company.

Dr. Belford was a man of unrivalled skill in his profession, and to say the best of him was a true friend to the needy and the poor. No hour of the night was too late for him to answer their pleading cry, and hence it was that he became the very idol of the destitute of a great city.

He had come into Chapel Alley, at Mrs. Pratt's anxious request, and had pronounced her lodger, to be in the height of "typhoid fever." The case was even more dangerous than he cared to pretend, and the circumstances that had driven a respectable young fellow, such as his patient looked, to seek lodgings in a dilapidated quarter like Chapel Alley were such as engaged his sympathies at once.

The days were stretching into weeks, and still the poor suffering victim, raved and tossed in mad fever on his narrow bed. Dr. Belford was looking serious as he left the sickroom one afternoon, after watching his patient attentively for nearly an hour: he cautioned Mrs. Pratt, in an earnest voice to attend carefully to the invalid, impressing on her how serious a crisis was approaching.

He left the house a little troubled, telling Mrs. Pratt to leave her door unlocked, for he intended to return as often as possible through the night, to the bed-side of the patient.

Noiselessly, almost breathlessly, the good woman stole around her little house in stocking feet, as she journeyed with fresh or re-made delicacies and medicines from the little kitchen below to the close sick-room above.

She was faithful in moistening the parched lips, and in administering the remedies, with an edifying punctuality, and in fact, all the major and minor duties of a nurse were admirably attended to, by the whole-souled creature, who had taken this heavy responsibility upon herself.

It was close on ten o'clock of the night of this critical day on which Dr. Belford had left Mrs. Pratt's house with such a troubled look, and this charitable matron having completed all her arrangements for the night, deposited a small lamp with a heavy green shade of paper, on the bureau in the sick-room, and drawing a tall straight wooden rocker close to the window, settled herself, stocking and needles in hand to "knit out" the hours of her lonesome vigil.

On the heavily carved door of a square house on one of the most stylish avenues of New York City, was a silver plate, bearing the familiar name of "Dr. Belford." There was magnificence on all sides of this, his splendid home, and yet this good man spent all his days, and most of his nights in the squalid and repulsive quarters of the great city. He was a man of untold wealth and cared but little, whether his profession yielded him additional wealth or not, he had understood the great misfortunes of life, and had toiled with an iron will, to benefit those to whom an unfortunate fate had taught the bitter lessons of poverty and destitution.

The mansion which bore his name on its elegant door, was now a blaze of gas-light; the heavy curtains, shaded the grandeur of the spacious drawing-room, but the apartment opposite had its tall windows thrown open to the evening breeze. This was Dr. Belford's office, splendidly furnished, and comfortably situated, countless rows of ponderous volumes lined the walls, and over the rest of the spacious room were scattered heavy pieces of office furniture, that lay around in solemn imposing neatness.

Standing before a succession of bound volumes was a young man, with his hands folded behind his back and his head raised enquiringly to the books above him, he was passing over their titles in a quick review, and had just laid his hand in evident gratification on one of them, when a long shrill, silvery tinkle, made him start: "No use, I suppose," he muttered to himself, "I must be on the 'go.'"

A tall, thin man, like an icicle in livery, appeared in the doorway at this moment, and delivered a note into his expectant hand. The young fellow tore it open and read.

MY DEAR BOY,— The case I have been summoned to attend here is a matter of life or death, I cannot possibly leave the house before morning. Will you, therefore, attend to the "typhoid fever" case, I spoke to you of, in Chapel Alley, for to-night, and oblige,

J. D. BELFORD

"Humph!" said he, as he finished the last words, "I need to smarten up a little, it is now after ten: something serious must be up," he soliloquized, "or Doctor would never neglect that 'fever' patient, he is so interested in."

Slipping his feet, clad in their red silk hose, from the daintiest of velvet slippers, the young doctor drew on his fine walking-shoes, turned down the gas a little, closed the office window, and taking his hat from the rack behind the door, hurried out.

In a moment, the carriage was around, and stepping in he ordered Barnes to drive him quickly to Mrs. Pratt's humble abode in Chapel Alley.

The dark, close by-ways and lanes impressed the young doctor forcibly, after leaving the broad, paved thoroughfares flooded with electric light, and used, though he was, to those sights, the repetition caused him invariably to shrink within himself and close his eyes upon their repulsiveness.

At length they drew in towards the solitary house; from whose small upper window came the faint glimmer, cast through the slits in the shutter, by the dim light of the lonely watcher.

As the young doctor stood at the door, he could hear the loud talk and wild cries of the invalid above, he laid his hand on the shabby handle, when yielding to his touch, the door opened with a little creaking noise—Mrs. Pratt, leaning over the rickety balustrade above, whispered:

"Come straight up, doctor, he's awful bad!"

The lively young doctor took all of Mrs. Prate's stairway in two moderate leaps and was at her side instantly. A moment of explanation consoled the troubled looking woman for the appearance of a stranger in Dr. Belford's stead, and then on tip toe they turned into the sick room.

"He's been a fright altogether doctor," said Mrs. Pratt, raising her withered hands in an attitude of wonder "sich ravin' an' shoutin' and kerryings on I never see before—and I thought you'd ha' never come."

When the door of the sick-room was opened an expression of extreme pity crossed the young man's face: that anyone should burn with a merciless fever in the close confines of this narrow little space, touched him deeply. He turned and looked at the restless invalid, but the light of the small hand lamp was dim and he could not see very distinctly.

"Hold the lamp nearer, my good woman," he said in the most earnest professional manner, and as obedient Mrs. Pratt raised it high above her frilled cap, the doctor turned his eager glance on the prostrate figure before him.

The light now fell upon the flushed features of the sick man. His agitation had all ceased, and there lingered but a little expression of peevishness and anxiety, but his whole condition bespoke sickness and suffering.

A change, sudden and wonderful, flashed over the stern features of the doctor, he staggered just a step, and then bent lower over the face of the invalid—there—within the close narrow limits of a poor sick-room, in a squalid locality, one stricken down by a loathsome disease, the other there to alleviate his pain, did two fellow students meet for the first time since the long years ago when they had crossed the threshold of their school-room as boyish "chums" each to take his road in the great thoroughfare of life— yes—there was no mistaking it—those were the well remembered features of Nicholas Bencroft and no other. The doctor was lost in reflections when Mrs. Pratt impatiently interrupted him with—

"Well doctor—he ain't much worse, I hope?"

"He is no better," the doctor answered seriously, "he is at the crisis of his disease now. I will wait and watch with you to-night," he added, "go down like a good woman and tell my driver he can leave, I will watch until morning."

Mrs. Pratt was a very scrupulous woman, for a widow, and thought it quite hazardous enough to watch a sick man all alone, besides encumbering her mind with one that was very alive and well—and so she took upon herself to insinuate something of her alarm to the young doctor. But a little persuasion went a long way with susceptible Mrs. Pratt, and when the doctor had told her that he recognized an old friend in her sick lodger, she begged a thousand pardons and became very submissive.

While they watched by the bed-side of the unfortunate man, Mrs. Pratt grew communicative, and told the doctor how this sad young man came to her one hot Saturday evening and asked her for lodgings—how she had thought him "sort o' nice" and "took to him" and had had him now for near a twelve-month—that he had paid "reglar" and gave no trouble until the night the fever "struck him down"—his name was Bencroft, she knew, and his linen was well marked with a N. an' a B. in "real good writin"—and finally, how she hoped he'd soon get better, for his own sake and other peoples, "so she did."

When they looked at the sleeper again, he was peaceful and unoppressed, his breathing was feebler and less labored, and while they stood whispering at the foot of his bed, he gave a great sigh and opened his heavy lids languidly.

The doctor hastened to his side: the wild delirium had passed away, leaving the worried face of the sufferer calmer and quieter, he opened up his large lustrous eyes and said in a plaintive tone.—

"Thirsty—so thirsty!"

Mrs. Pratt raised the glass to his parched lips, and clutching her hands in his own feverish grasp, he pressed the goblet to his mouth and drank a devouring draught.

It was true that his wanderings and delirium had ceased. Mrs. Pratt looked meaningly at the doctor and whispered hopefully: "he is better?" but, professional-like, the doctor remained silent, and only looked very seriously on. The invalid dropped back again among his pillows, and fell into a deep sleep.

The night was now well nigh spent: outside in the leaden dawn, an odd, faint, sleepy twitter disturbed the silence, and an odd pedestrian's footsteps echoed, through the still street.

When this natural sleep stole over the weak and wornout invalid, the doctor bade Mrs. Pratt a "good morning" for a while, telling her she might expect him back in four or five hour's time.

"If your patient should wake," he added, "question him a little to ascertain whether he is entirely free from the illusions of his delirium or not—" and then with a puzzled wondering look upon his handsome face, the young doctor passed out of Mrs. Pratt's close, shabby house into the deserted street.

Thoughts and memories of the past, he had stowed so resignedly away, flooded his mind as he strode onward, he had dreamed until last night that the ghost of his by-gone days would haunt him no more, and when he had learned to live without his memories on the associations of the frequent past, he was brought forward again to meet, face to face, a forcible reminder of his yesterdays. "Poor Nicholas!" he soliloquized, "what can have befallen him, that this should be his end? I thought there was nothing left in life that could surprise me, and yet here is something that really does."

The days and scenes of his college life passed in a sorrowful panorama before the misty eyes of the young man as he strode along the silent street in the gray of the early morning, and as the beginning and the close of this happy period were reviewed before him, they passed into another phase of his life and clouded the frank young, face with a shadow of regret and pain—"at least"—he muttered to himself—"I might have spared myself this, after I had taught myself that it was madness to remember and wisdom to forget."

A trio of midnight revelers, deserting their haunt of debauchery on a dilapidated street corner, here interrupted the strain of his meditation, and as he raised his eyes to look upon the ragged figures, and bloated, forbidden countenances of these men, there passed over his pensive features, a look of contentment and resignation which said—"At least, if my life has been a bitter and an unfortunate one, I have been spared these rags and this degradation. And yet," he continued, as he walked rapidly along the by-ways and thoroughfares of the great city, "it is a wonder that I escaped it, for in my time we were just as degraded, only we disguised our hideousness under the garb of respectability." Then a look of bitter, almost hopeless disappointment came over his face, as he told himself secretly, "And I struggled against all these propensities, fought with and overcame all these follies for the sake of *her*, who has cast me so easily, so willingly out of her life." He was turning the broad paved corner that led to Dr Belford's house, and quickening his step he reached the door just as the old doctor himself was passing out into the hall.

"Hallo!" said the old gentleman in genuine surprise, "where have you been carousing until such an hour?"

There was evidently a familiarity between these two that spoke of strong regard on the part of the younger, and of a fatherly fondness and interest in that of the elder doctor. An explanation followed which gratified Dr. Belford immensely.

"Since the danger looks less, my boy," he said, "and that you wish to attend him, I see no reason why you shouldn't. I've trusted you with as serious cases already."

With this they parted, each tired and weary with his midnight vigils, repaired to rest until the full stir of the morning that was just breaking.

CHAPTER XXVIII

"I have a bitter thought—a snake
   That used to string my life to pain;
I strove to cast it far away,
   But every night and every day
   It crawled back to my heart again."

"You are unusually early this morning," said a pale, handsome woman crossing the threshold of the elegant dining-room, where the silver and crystal and tempting viands stood in inviting array on the massive table.

The lady wore a loose dark wrapper, girdled at the waist, and her thick hair, prematurely grey, was drawn back from her large, intelligent brow, and secured in graceful coils at the back of her shapely neck.

"I have a case of unusual interest, dear Mrs. Belford—that explains it; at least I have stolen one from Dr. Belford, and with his ordinary kindness, he does not insist on reclaiming it."

"Well, I don't object," Mrs. Belford replied gayly, "only I hope you can manage to get through quickly, for I have an engagement for you early this afternoon, and I would not relish a disappointment in the least."

The young doctor looked proudly at the handsome woman as she spoke, then drawing himself up to his full height, as he surveyed himself in the mirror, "You may rely on me," he said with his most courteous bow, as he took his hat and left the room, with a last "good morning" to Mrs. Belford.

"Deary me, but I'm glad you're well again," said good Mrs. Pratt, as she leaned over the now restored patient. "I thought ye were a goner sure, till comin' on mornin'. An' how do ye feel now, there's a good boy?"

The pained look on the sufferer's face passed into something of a smile, as he answered in a low, weak voice,

"Much better, I thank you," then the old, troubled shade returned to his flushed features, as he asked anxiously, "Will the doctor come soon again? I want him particularly this time."

The pleading words were scarcely uttered when the rickety door creaked once more on its hinges. The stairs were taken in a jump, and the doctor stood at the door of his patient's room.

Mrs Pratt thrust out her anxious head, and whispered,

"He's alright, an' wants ye very bad this very minnit."

Laying his hat and cane on the "ottoman," (an old soap box costumed in faded chinz), the doctor entered the room and approached the bed of the sick man.

Taking advantage of the occasion, Mrs. Pratt now fairly "tired out," escorted herself to the adjoining room and laid her weary bones on the uninviting "settee," that was the hallowed source of all the pleasant dreams, that haunted her daily siestas for many a year.

The bright vivid glare of the mid-summer sun, was condensed into a subdued light, as it stole through the little scorched shutters, that adorned Mrs. Pratt's front windows. The doctor drew an old-fashioned chair, close to the bed side and addressed his patient cheerily:

"Well, you are much better, this morning, I think?"

The restless head turned with a quick movement towards the speaker. The bright feverishly lustrous eyes dwelt in dilated wonder on the face before them, there was a nervous twitching about the dry lips. Then the tired eyes closed languidly and the plaintive voice said:

"My mind is wandering; I am not a school-boy now."

The doctor knew there was a recognition, and taking the burning hand in his, he said tenderly:

"Yes, Nicholas Bencroft, we will be school-boys again if you like. Those were happy days; let us go over them together once more."

A strange, sad expression flitted across the invalid's face. He turned completely round and peered into the face of his companion. Then stretching out both feverish white hands, he cried out:

"Yes, thank God! Elersley, it's you; you have come just in time."

"Open the window and let me have a breath of fresh air," said the sick man after their greetings were over. "I have something to tell you that is weighing me down with grief, and promise me, dear old fellow, that you will leave no stone unturned to do the right things, that I will point out to you presently."

"If it is in human power, Bencroft, how can you doubt the eagerness of one old chum to serve another?"

"But I have done an awful wrong and you may loathe me and desert me when you see me self-condemned."

The despairing tones of the weak voice touched every sympathetic chord in the heart of his listener.

"I don't care what you may have done," he cried, enthusiastically, "let me help you all I can, you will not ask an impossibility I know."

The invalid heaved a labored sigh, and began his story.

"If I knew I had yet a year of health and life before me, I would not trouble any one to undo the black and dishonorable knot, that these guilty hands have tied, but I know too well that but little strength is left me. To begin at the beginning, Guy," he said, looking eagerly into the kind face of his listener, "boys make foolish attachments at school, that they sometimes regret all their lives. This, as you know, was my misfortune. Whatever diabolical attraction there was in that one man for me, I never could tell. All you fellows ridiculed me for it, but some evil fascination, though I did not so qualify it at that time, held me to him in spite of myself. The rest of you, wiser than I, learned to look upon his handsome face and polished manners as a clever mask, but I was blinded and could not see like the rest. You know how many foolish acts I did during those college years to serve him. Oh! if I had only known then that I was laying the foundation of my future misery with my own willing hands," and the speaker's large eyes flashed with a hatred and defiance that made his plain face look grand and handsome.

"I left school a year before my father died, and I had just become initiated in his business at the time of his demise. I admit it was rather a heavy undertaking for one so young as I was then, to continue the extensive business my father had so successfully carried on for years.

"But I was encouraged by hopeful relatives and did not myself dread any untoward consequences. Things went on quite smoothly, and I was making money fast, when one day I was nearly stunned to death, on seeing my old college chum walk in the office door. He looked handsomer than ever and greeted me very cordially, with just a touch of the old condescension in his manner. I was, of course, delighted to see him. We talked over old days freely and familiarly. Finally I saw the drift of his visit. He represented to me that he had invested largely, at the advice of some friends, in the lands of the great North-West, but had lost a great deal by the speculation. In his despair, the first friend he thought of was myself. He got around me in his old way, and before he left my office that morning I had loaned him, madman that I was, the sum of five thousand dollars, without any question whatever of security. He swore to me that I might rely on him to deal honestly with me, and, blinded by the old infatuation, I gave him a cheque for the amount and sent him away contented. Give me a drink, Guy, and fix up my pillows, please." The young doctor did these things as gently as a woman, and without interrupting the strain of confidence, sat down patiently again and resumed his listening attitude.

"Months glided by," continued the invalid, "and no one was any the wiser of the rash act I had committed, but now that I had leisure to repent, it worried me greatly, and I could not shake off the depression it caused. The time was approaching when a heavy payment would fall due and I was in daily agony, waiting for the remittance of my loan, but, needless to say, it never came. I wrote to the address he had left me, but no answer was forthcoming.

"Within a few days of the date on which I had to meet this heavy payment, the load of anxiety that pressed upon me was suddenly lightened by the sudden re-appearance of my friend in my office. His smiles succeeded in reassuring me once more, and in breathless suspense, I drank in every word he uttered. He spoke of a great many unnecessary things first, and then concluded by saying in the coolest manner possible:

"'I fear you will be a little disappointed about your money, but I will not be able to pay you for some time yet.'

"I stood petrified at his audacity. My first impulse was to seize him by the throat and pay myself in blood, but when I looked at his handsome face my determination vanished. He looked curiously at me in return, and asked in a tone like one who is feeling his way:

"'Are you safe in your business?'

"'Good God!' I cried, exasperated, 'I was until I saw your face. You will be my ruin.'

"He seemed to look sorry all at once, then brightening a little he said:

"'There is only one way in which I can help you, but you must lend a hand yourself.'

"'What is it?' I cried, eagerly, hopefully.

"'I am going to be married,' he answered gravely, 'to a wealthy heiress, and as soon as her money is in my possession, I will pay you back your own.'

"There was nothing repulsive to me in this prospect. I was awake only to the vital interests of the welfare of my mother and family, that depended on my faithful discharge of the duties of my responsible position.

"Seizing him eagerly by the arm, I asked him, 'When will she marry you?'

"'There's the rub,' he answered perplexedly. 'When do you want the money?'

"'I must choose between my money and absolute ruin on Thursday,' I said, 'and this is Tuesday; I leave the rest to your honor and your heart.'

"'Well, the case is this,' he said, looking at me fixedly, 'she will not marry me in her own town; we will therefore take a trip elsewhere, but the difficulty is, I don't know yet where to go. If, however'—and he leaned on the railing of my desk and looked at me with a searching glance,—'if you want your money badly you can have it in this way: There is a small vacant house, distant some miles from her residence, and thither we could drive at any time. Why could'nt you, robed as a curate, perform the marriage ceremony, and secure your money? We could be properly married at any other time, though you are as good a one to tie the knot as any other.'

"The villain looked at me steadily. He was turning his old power of fascination to account. What was the whole blighted life of this unfortunate heiress to the ruin and disgrace that my failure would bring down on myself, my mother and sisters. I did not hesitate, with this thought uppermost in my mind.

"'I will do this thing,' I said determinedly, 'whatever it costs me.'

"He directed me accordingly to leave Montreal, the seat of my business, in the morning and reach the little village in the townships, where his other victim lived, before noon. We would meet there, he would drive me out to the parsonage, *pro tem*, and give it a look of habitation before bringing his bride there. We purchased a few dilapidated pieces of furniture from neighboring farmers and laid our little plot successfully. It surprised me to think of him as capable of doing such a villainous thing, and looking so calm and collected all the time. He smoked inveterately, and occasionally sang or whistled some careless tune, as though his heart felt not a feather-weight of care or sin. In the evening I was installed in the vacant house, with no living creature near but the great black dog I had brought with me from home, and who had always followed me for years, everywhere I went. However, I stowed even him into a dark recess, that was guarded by a little rickety door that fastened with a rusty lock. It was a black awful night, nature gave vent to her just indignation in every way I sat there, feeling already guilty and remorseful, until near nine o'clock. Then hearing the roll of a distant carriage, I tried to busy myself around, and look as domesticated as possible under the circumstances. I thought I should give up and lose all at the sight of the pretty, innocent, trustful child for whom he had planned this hideous deception. But I was as pitiable a victim myself as she, and the thought of my impending ruin drove every feeling of humanity out of my heart. We began the mock ceremony, slowly and solemnly. We had just reached the most critical part when a great flash of lightning leaped in at the broken window, stunning both of us and prostrating the girl. The candle went black out, leaving us in total darkness. When I recovered from the shock, the noise and elemental din were such that I could distinguish nothing. I waited a moment or two and then spoke. I received no answer. Half maddened, I got up and struck a fresh light, and looked around me. The traitor, the doubly-dyed villain had gone, he had taken the horse, and there was not a trace of him left. He had secured the unfortunate girl's money through the instrumentality of one who had violated every principle of honor and justice, to save the name and social standing of those who were dependent on him. I suppose I did not deserve to die then. I was given days and nights of endless duration in which to live over and over again, the agony and despair of that bitter experience. What was I to do? I had not secured my money, but I had this additional misfortune on my conscience: I had wrecked the life of a fair young girl, and had the hitherto spotless page of my dealings with my fellow-creatures, stamped with a foul indelible stain, that cried shame and retribution on my whole generation. I fled—of course—when the hasty realization of my misdeeds forced itself into my mind. I was frantic and desperate as I tried to make my way through the thicket, and at last on arriving at the village, I took the midnight train and travelled to a town in the State of Maine. From this place I wrote to my creditors, confessing my financial difficulties, and begging of them not to seek me out, nor take any further interest in me, as I had resolved to begin my blighted life over again, in a strange land among strange people. I tried O, Elersley! God knows how hard, to earn honest bread, but I did not deserve success, and so God refused to bless my labor. I left Maine, and came here to New York, two years ago. I turned my hand to everything, but the bitter sting of misfortune was at the bottom of all. I tried my pen, recently, for my limbs seemed incompetent for any active service, but sitting here in this little narrow room, through the long night, trying to invent some gay little snatch of fiction out of the store of a mind so crushed and oppressed, was too bitter a mockery to last very long. My fair fashionable heroines looked at me in my dreams with eyes blood-shot and revengeful, saying, 'This is what you have brought me to.' For I suppose, Elersley, that girl never did a day's good since. Her fate has been constantly preying on my mind. I have spent a life of wretched expiation already in this world, God only knows what awaits me in the next. I have studiously avoided the sex I have outraged by this deed, feeling myself an outcast and a traitor in their presence. I have turned my back on the few haunts of pleasure that were open to me, for the sound of my own voice in gaiety, frightened and reproached me. As for *him* Elersley, though I have not seen him, nor heard of him, since, yet I know he is revelling in the luxury of his ill-gotten wealth."

The sick man stopped a moment, and let the tired lids droop languidly over the dark eyes, then opening them again, he looked full into Guy's pale face. When he resumed his voice was nervous and weak.

"You have now the truthful story of my woe," he said, brokenly, "are you still willing to help me?"

The question brought Elersley back from his wanderings.

"Do you tell me truthfully that this is the villany of the boy we pampered so at school?"

"That is the story of Vivian Standish's cowardly conduct," said Bencroft, in a tone of deep resentment.

"Good Heavens!" muttered Guy, "who can tell what more he has been able to do? Give me your hand Bencroft. As you have been the dupe of a blackguard who disguised his villany under the mask of friendship, I will stand to you. Will you allow me to write down this confession over your own signature, lest a nuncupative testimony be not sufficient to condemn him. We will call in Mrs. Pratt to witness the signing of the paper." Guy's suggestion was immediately followed out. The invalid grasped the pen with wonderful strength, and signed his name in a firm legible hand to the document. Mrs. Pratt, looking as dignified as the occasion required, affixed her mark, and so did the widow Brady, who just happened to "drop in." Guy rose and looked at his watch. It was past eleven now, and he had still other duties to attend to before keeping his word with Mrs. Belford.

"Are you going," the invalid asked impatiently, making an effort to rise in his narrow bed. "Look here Elersley," he cried, "I want to thank you, to praise you, if I could, but my poor voice is shattered and weak. If I could only crawl on my knees before you in gratitude, how gladly I would do it, but I will never leave this poor little home of mine alive; my heart is broken and my spirit is worn out. Only tell me you will search the world for the pretty French girl he called 'Fifine,' and tell her the story of my life, my grief and remorse. Punish her deceiver as he deserves and come to my lonely grave at the last and whisper to me that retribution has come. Until then I cannot rest. Oh Guy! there is no misery like the misery of a life whose dark shadows haunt it's victim perpetually. Look at her!—there she is now—oh! so angry and sullen; ugh!—she is cursing me—threatening me—tell her, for God's sake, Guy, tell her to spare the sick, wasted man—see—she is coming nearer to me—save me—save me—" and in wild shrieks and tossings, Nicholas Bencroft plunged back again into the mad delirium of the fever.

CHAPTER XXIX

"Love is a great transformer." —*Shakespeare.*

The reader must understand what it is to experience sensations such as flitted through Guy Elersley's breast at this period of his life's *dénouement.* Any of us who have fallen in with the tide of the great living world, know that the draughts of gall and the drops of nectar reach our lips from the same chalice: our noblest love has often been the parent of our most sinful hatred, and we have cursed in despairing tones the very scenes, days, persons and associations that once constituted the fondest memories of our hearts.

We have a great antithetical existence before us, but the beauty of experience can only be seen by the backward glance, 'tis when we turn our sad and tear-dimmed eyes to look over our bended shoulders at the thorny way that bears the impress of our weary feet, that we can feel what a grand and salutary prayer our lips might make by substituting the murmur and the cry of pain by a holy accent which should be a "fiat."

The strain of mournful confidence that had passed between these reunited friends brought its own bitterness to Guy Elersley's heart. How unfortunate it was that on the eve of his departure from his former home, Vivian Standish should have been the one of all others he had trusted with his little message of love!

Guy passed over in silent, painful review, the details of his recent career. How well he remembered the pain and disappointment that had driven him away from Ottawa city.

He had thought once that such a conflict of emotions would kill a stronger man than he, but

"Nothing in the world beside,
Is stronger than the heart when tried."

To begin a new life on the wreck of an old one is a very hard and painful task, and one that Guy Elersley, above every other living creature, would never have attempted unless when influenced by so strong and pushing and stimulating a power as the love of a good woman—this alone, it was that worked reformation in Guy Elersley: from contemplating her pure and noble soul, he had been seized with an ambition to grow like her, her word and example sickened him of his old pursuits until he wondered and wept over the sacrifice he had so heedlessly made of his youth and character.

He left the scene of his temptations, and in close, quiet study in the great, stirring city of New York, he slowly, but surely and steadily rebuilt the wreck and ruin of his younger days. He had devoted himself once before to the study of medicine, but had given it up in a moment of foolish frivolity for an occupation far less worthy, but now he returned to his volumes of science with a vow of perseverance on his lips and a dogged determination in his heart.

He had been fortunate enough to form the acquaintance of Dr. Belford, who, taking a fancy to the studious boy, offered to receive him under his special charge and instruct him more fully in the profession he had adopted.

Guy attributed each new phase of luck that overtook him now to the same unseen power which seemed to sway his life of late. Under Dr. Belford he worked diligently and well and finished the career in medicine he had so recklessly interrupted before for other pursuits.

Through all the trials and difficulties of his new life, Guy felt himself sustained by a lingering hope that seemed to buoy him up against every depression, and thus for many long months he toiled assiduously under the influence of that shallow hope until each day seemed to prove to him more clearly than another, that all the best endeavors of a lifetime cannot restore a trust once broken, or a confidence once shattered.

Even this bitter realization he strove to gather into his resignation; he had grown prematurely wise and learned, and had taught himself to accept in submission the apparently unjust decree of destiny.

But sometimes when he came home tired and weary at nightfall and laid his head, full of aching thoughts, on his pillow to rest, capricious fate released him from his skeptic views of life; the hard lines faded from around his handsome mouth, and a slow smile, as of old, crept back there from its exile, for when he was tired or sad, a fair vision invariably stood beside him and smoothed away the traces of care from his face. He could feel the velvety touch of her dainty hands, and see the beauty of her consoling smile whenever he closed his eyes in a weary doze on the reality of his present life, but when he raised his lids the spell broke suddenly, and New York and Ottawa were a hopeless distance of cruel miles apart.

He had never once doubted that Vivian Standish would deliver his parting message, and the only bitterness of his better life had been her silence, cold and cruel, after that appeal his heart had made, before leaving.

But now the thought struck him all at once: may be she had never received this little messenger of his devotion. Could any man so base as Vivian Standish had proved himself to be, commit, by the merest chance, an honest or a just action? He doubted it; at least he gave himself the benefit of the new uncertainty, and resolved to work out this intricate problem to its bitter end or die in the attempt.

"Because I love you," said the low sweet voice of Vivian Standish, as he paced very slowly, with Honor Edgeworth, by his side, up and down through the crowd that had assembled on Carder's Square, to enjoy the excellent music of the Governor-General's Foot Guards' Band which was filling the evening air with its dreamy strains.

These two, were like every other couple present, in a crowd and yet isolated: the "band night" is one, so full of generous encouragement, to the growing sentiment of our young city, that one is forced into an appreciation of its benefits, whether one is inclined or not.

Long before the appointed hour for playing, animated couples form a solemn procession, along the streets and grounds which surround our dignified "Drill Shed," but it is just as the twilight begins to draw itself into the corners of the far-off sky, and over the half distinct gables, and chimney tops of the imposing buildings that rear up their solemn spires, against the sky, that the suggestive strains of a "Blue Alsatian," or "Loved and Lost" act, powerfully as a third agent of affinity, in bringing the hitherto shy and reticent couples nearer than ever, and in linking the obstinate little hands of a moment before, firmly in that of the love-sick adorer.

Every one goes to hear the band, big and little, men and women, young, and old, though, what old people, and little brothers or sisters want there, is more than half the "grown up" sons and daughters can tell.

It is all well enough to coax your uninteresting little brother of fifteen, with a double supply of sponge cake at tea, if you have no one else in view to escort you to the "band," but why in the name of all that is provoking, does he not know, that his duty is done, when he is supplanted by some one's bigger brother, who has a moustache and smokes cigars.

Honor Edgeworth had no unsophisticated youthful kin, to try their clinging propensities on her, her "aunt Jean" brought her everywhere, and everywhere they went, they found Vivian Standish. It gratified the old lady immensely to see how Honor "took" among her friends, it gratified her, in proportion, as it stung, a great many mature young ladies, who rather disliked, in any emphatic way, to see a new source of attraction deposited in their midst.

Ottawa has come to a deplorable state of depression, with regard to "matrimonial transactions;" it is now of vital importance to young ladies, who have an ambition to distinguish themselves at the altar of Hymen, that they take "masculine tastes," as the axis around which is to revolve, in graceful motion, the actions of their daily lives; but for this no one need think of censuring Ottawa's noble women, their conduct is not so servile or dependent as the unfair critic would like to paint it. We must not forget, the truth of the little by-word, that "circumstances alter cases," what is perfectly justifiable in Ottawa would be "abominably atrocious" in many other Canadian cities.

Every one knows, that in the capital of our splendid Dominion, there is the finest collection of young men, that creation can afford—they are numerous, handsome, wealthy, sensible, specimens of what youth should be, (in their own opinion), and with the knowledge of all their qualities combined, these precious creatures, are just conceited enough, to make sure, that there will always be, at least one for each in the whole city, who will appreciate such a display of accomplishments and qualities, as they monopolize.

One can easily understand therefore, how flattered a girl must feel, even, though she is the daughter of a wealthy father, and enjoys a comfortable home, when one of these distinguished beings comes to invade her heart, with his abundance of personal charms and scarcity of personal wealth; some girls never survive it; they die of ecstatic emotion in a week, and are consigned to a premature grave; others outlive it into the practical phases of wedded life, to the intense mortification of their husbands.

We will now return to the groups of unfettered maidens, from Upper Town, Centre Town, Sandy Hill and Lower Town, that are enlivening the band scene to-night, many have given Honor Edgeworth, a pardonable word of very reserved criticism, of course they know her numerous advantages, men spoke of them right to their faces, but that never made them feel badly; who ever met a girl yet who felt the least put out, if one rival of hers, had a dozen admirers or more to her none?

But Honor was most undeserving of all the attention she received, for she neither appreciated the gallant endeavors of her male admirers to make themselves agreeable to her, nor cared an iota for the jealousies or slighting remarks that passed the lips of her girl contemporaries.

It was Jean d'Alberg who saw it all, and feasted maliciously on the "sour grapes" looks and words of Honor's less fortunate acquaintances. Honor had hoped that Vivian Standish would not join them that evening, for she amused herself as well with a great many others, and even found him uninteresting at times, but Aunt Jean would not support her at all here. She had assured herself long ago that Vivian and Honor were well made and mated, and that nothing could be more harmonious than their union. With this idea uppermost, she did everything in her power (which was a great deal) to throw them together, and she had not made any mistake, as far as her calculations of the man's character went—she was perfectly right in imagining that he was one who knew thoroughly how to "improve an opportunity."

Honor had to acknowledge that in no way did Vivian Standish offend or displease her, but still his manner fatigued and worried her—everyone else admired and appreciated him more than she did, and yet he faithfully and persistently thrust himself upon her, always polished, amiable and pleasant, but still, painfully eccentric in some way she could not fully define nor analyze.

To-night, as usual, just as an old friend had coaxed Jean d'Alberg into a lively conversation, Vivian Standish came quietly through the crowd, scenting the air with his fine cigar, which he smoked with a sleepy sort of relish, and stood beside Honor.

She knew perfectly well he was beside her, she felt him before he advanced at all, but when she turned suddenly to look at him, her face wore as blank an expression of astonishment as if he had been a ghost.

"You?" she exclaimed; "how is it that we seem to be travelling invariably towards the same point?" she asked then, in the strangest tone possible—but he was equal to her. He removed his cigar from between his handsome lips, and with a lazy sort of determination in his action and words, he slid his arm into hers, and bending down close to her ear, asked—

"Do you really ask me why I am constantly travelling to the spot where you are?"

"That is something like what I did ask, if I remember well," the girl answered with provoking indifference.

"Then it is—because—I love you!" he whispered, almost huskily.

The band continued to fill the balmy air with its sweet, suggestive strains. Sounds of laughter and mirth reached them from all sides; Vivian was less of his well-controlled self than ever to-night, but Honor was just as cold and indifferent as if the handsomest and most popular young man in Ottawa had slighted her instead of avowing his unsought love for her.

"Do you hear?" he asked, on seeing her remain persistently indifferent.

"I am not at all hard of hearing, Mr Standish, I assure you," was the cruel answer.

"And is that all the word you have to say in return?" he asked in a tone of wretched surprise.

"You are toying with very serious words," she answered earnestly, "and this is neither time nor place for it. Let us speak of something else."

"May I continue smoking?" he then asked, as coolly as if they had been his first words to her. "If you object, Honor, don't mind saying so. May I at least call you Honor?"

"You overpower me and yourself with such a multitude of questions," the girl answered languidly, "but since you ask me permissions which I grant a great many others, I will not refuse you.."

"Thank you," he said almost sarcastically, "when we are hungry we take the crust that is flung to us, though the dainty morsel served on a crystal plate satisfies us best. What *is* the matter to-night, Honor, you seem worried and peevish?"

The sudden change of tone, from the moralizing to that of anxious enquiry, amused Honor.

"I generally seem in that way until I have been in your company for a while," she answered with such a careless, meaningless tone, that he pronounced her a hopeless little *sans coeur* with a sigh, and dropped the subject.

Vivian Standish was plainly courting Mr. Rayne's *protégée*, and a great deal had to be said in consequence. With his carefully learned manners, Standish had worked a successful conspiracy against retribution. He had coolly stowed away any disagreeable souvenirs of his past life, and troubled no more about them. He veneered his whole character with such an engaging mansuetude as served to deceive the most penetrative of those he met, and not even the most suspicious of his Ottawa acquaintances had ever insinuated that a surface so calm and unruffled as his could ever cover a phase of character which could be nocent or even objectionable in the least degree. Some disliked him for reasons they could not define, and had in consequence to refrain from expressing their antipathy. Many were jealous of him, and the majority admired him freely.

He was one of those "clever" men who had taken the trouble to analyze and solve the intricate though simple problem of existence, and to adapt this precious knowledge wisely and carefully to his own especial selfish benefit.

It takes a rogue to understand a rogue, and the reason of Vivian Standish's complete success in playing off his counterfeit manners, was because he had chosen to display them within a circle where shrewd or suspecting observation never found its way. He saw clearly what a field lay open to him in the drawing-room, and the delightful company of Ottawa's *élite*. All he had to do was to introduce himself to this "tony" little city fashionably dressed, and with that self-sufficient reserve that characterizes the "high toned." He registered at the "Russell," and walked Sparks street every afternoon with a haughty step, looking as conceited and interesting as possible. He drank in the local chat with eyes and ears open, before making any uncertain move; then he sought the acquaintance of the fashionable young men of the city — they are easily traced. One has but to run over the list of their aristocratic names on the pages of the visitors' register at Government House, or they are the noted presidents, patrons or members of some "awfully nice" club, "you know!" or they are very well represented in the business books of certain well known tailoring establishments; and if none of these are sufficient, the Court register has a voice now and then whose suasory accents could convince anyone.

But nothing in these discoveries would surprise Vivian Standish, for there was little left savouring of "hard experience" that he had not passed through at one time or other of his agitated career. He was no stranger to the secrets of a little city like Ottawa. They are good enough to frighten small boys and women. He, who had plunged into the very heart of the mysteries of life as they are found in the grand metropolises of the whole world, rather interested the comparatively innocent and unsophisticated youth of the Canadian capital, who recognized in him a graduate of that school of experience whose dangerous knowledge was being tasted, as a novelty, yet by them. Inwardly he smiled at the susceptibilities of the youths he came across; he saw mirrored in them the youth of every other corner and nationality of the globe. Worldling though he was, he was capable of very wise reflections, and was given to moralizing in a sort of way. He never made it a premeditated point to draw any unschooled youth into wrong; he did not seek to make any innocent one the victim of an evil influence, as many do who seem to be very active agents of the Author of Evil himself, — young people who cannot gloat over their own spiritual ruin until they have dragged the foolish, weak souls of unsuspecting victims into the wreck they covet for themselves. He was satisfied to be virtuously discreet among the unsuspecting, and be highly companionable among those who were wiser in folly. He was glad to recognize Elersley in a strange city, and Guy, friendly and hospitable ever, took him into his charge until he had him thoroughly initiated into the ways of his adopted life.

Guy's room was the scene of many a jovial merry-making for successive nights after Vivian's arrival, and if cigar stumps and empty bottles were ever indicative of rollicking bachelor hospitality, they surely told the tale emphatically of Guy, for a very respectable heap of such *restants* generally made one conspicuous feature of next morning's "cleaning up"

Standish was a jolly fellow, and the others took to him readily; he smoked, drank, jested, or indulged in any other imaginable pastime that was proposed, thus showing himself a complete sympathizer with his new-made friends.

When he stepped into the "feminine" circle, he was equally well received, he was so entirely different in his attractions from the stale *beaux* that had introduced him to their lady friends. His first words invariably made impression, and everything he said or did was stamped with the quietest, most languid, and yet most thoroughly fascinating style, that victims were ready to fall unsought before him. There was a resistless power in the deep, dreamy look his beautiful eyes constantly affected, and in the unsteady strength of his shapely hand, as it happened, no matter how inadvertently, to touch the dainty fingers of some susceptible belle; and even if his personal advantages failed him completely, there yet remained his most powerful attraction—his voice. Ottawa girls had never heard such original and such pleasant little nothings as Vivian Standish told them at every moment of his conversation, and the perfect cultivation of the voice that thrilled their blessed little hearts with its resistless accents, induced many a fair and blushing maiden to hand him over her conquered heart, as a pitiable trophy that he had so fairly and yet so mercilessly won.

But Vivian Standish, in coming among the Ottawaites, had not been attracted for the purpose of making such havoc among feminine hearts. Any man can do that, in any place, and under any circumstances, if he has a mind to. A woman to him, was a useless and troublesome appendage, after he had kissed the dainty hand that had emptied its substantial treasure into his roomy pockets. Courtesy, like every other quality he had taken the trouble to acquire, had its matter-of-fact mission to perform, towards accomplishing a great part of his mercenary purposes, and hence the sacrifices he so often made cheerfully and admirably for the gratification of some idolized daughter who was sole heiress to a comfortable dozen of thousands.

His lucky genius had not driven him on to Ottawa for nothing, of this he assured himself emphatically when he found out that Honor Edgeworth was likely to substitute Guy Elersley in his uncle's favor, and find herself, some day, rolling in wealth that had been scraped together by the hands of those who had not owed her a single debt of gratitude; to his reason such unfair freaks of destiny called loudly for resentment; he claimed a right of monopoly as well as this more fortunate girl, and he meant to exercise it too, though as quietly and noiselessly as possible, he flattered himself, and encouraged his project with the universal male belief, that a few little wild words of sentiment, and marked attentions, suffice to level the trivial fortifications of any woman's heart; his study was to make the right impression on the responsible guardians of his choice, that his appeal, when made, should be encouraged by these all-important voices. In this he attained a splendid success, but his plots and plans were too clever for his own management, and entrapped him in that very place, where he considered himself most strongly fortified.

Henry Rayne, now growing weaker and older, had been as easily influenced by the assumed manners of this adventurer as was any indiscreet woman; the glitter, to his eyes, now dimmed and obscured by age, was that of the solid metal, and the well-studied phrases and words that came so blandly from the deceptive lips duped the old man pitifully.

Jean d'Alberg herself had caught the contagion, and smiled pleasant greetings to him when he visited at Mr. Rayne's house; there was only Honor who evaded the cunning trap, but even she was blinded a good deal. Although the eternal fitness of things made it impossible that such antithetical natures should ever blend in a harmony of any sort, he was still fortunate enough not to produce the discord that would seem to arise very naturally from such an unsympathetic contact.

Honor, without liking Vivian Standish, endured him well enough, and enjoyed his clever conversations very well; she could not guess the fierceness of the moral struggle that was taking place, as he calmly and calculatingly planned her doom. She only felt a little of that repulsion that purity and innocence naturally feel when brought into contact with vice and guilt, for our moral natures have a special instinct of their own, which attracts or repels characters whose influence upon them may be beneficial or injurious, thus often causing us to dislike or distrust persons without any apparent cause.

There was only one extra reason why Honor Edgeworth, above so many others, failed to yield herself a ready victim to the wiles of this fascinating man, and that was because her heart, unlike the generality of those tiresome appendages, was closed to petition. She had learned to love once, truly and warmly, and the gay, young, reckless hero whom she had silently but devotedly honored at the secret shrine of her unsullied heart, had suddenly passed out of her life, without a sign, or a token, or a word, leaving her to weep over the wasted treasure of sentiment she had so greedily hoarded up for him alone; not that this caused her to lose her faith in man or vow to live a life of solitary sceptic amendment for having indulged a foolish passion in her early days, but because she firmly believed the object of her fond regard to be at heart a worthy one, and because she felt that her happy lively sentiment, becoming spent and weary, had only laid itself obscurely away, to taste the hopeful sweetness of a "love's young dream," —by and bye, she promised herself, when her "fairy prince" came back, and woke up the sleeping cupid from his bed of sighs, the world would be happier and brighter, and full of pleasure unalloyed forevermore. So in the lonely meanwhile, little words of kind regard, and little deeds of gallant courtesy, seemed to her as only forerunners or harbingers of what was coming to her out of the "to be" from the lips and hands of her absent lover.

Such a way of viewing things naturally influenced this girl's character and brought her back to that distracted existence, that contact with practical life had almost annihilated. Her old meditative propensities stole upon her again, it was nothing new now to see her with folded hands and dreamy eyes that looked vacantly into the space before them.

A wonderful change was also coming over Henry Rayne; he who had spent a good fifty years of his life in active service for society, now began to feel, like countless others who had gone before him, that after all, the most he could claim as the wages of honest fame and honor, were the cushioned depths of an invalid chair, the first grade, to the narrow bed where he would sleep his eternal sleep.

The old man was growing daily weaker and more childish, having never known any of those influences through life, which become identical with the very existence of those who have tasted them in wedded life, Henry Rayne found himself in the sunset of his years with scarcely a tie to bind him to the world for which he had done so much. There was only Honor, who stood out in relief from the monotonous experience of his life, and invited him to tarry a little longer on the border-line of time; every moment that passed into eternity now seemed to bring this girl nearer and nearer to his heart, for it was necessary, that at least in death, he should learn the lesson of sacrifice, that had been so well-spared him through life.

With the first warnings of his decline, Henry Rayne had learned to realize how cold and bitter and cruel a world this world would be to his little *protégée* when he had left her, and for that reason he occupied himself altogether, in the latter years of his life, in studying and promoting a welfare for this precious charge, that would survive himself for, may be long years of a lonesome life.

With this intimate knowledge of the old man's heart, one can perhaps understand the partiality with which Vivian Standish was received into the home of Henry Rayne, as a constant visitor.

CHAPTER XXX

Oh, to be idle one spring day!
To muse in wood or meadow;
Glide down the river 'twixt the play
Of sun and trembling shadow.
I'd see all wonders neath the stream,
The pebbles and vex'd grasses;
I'd lean across the boat and dream,
As each scene slowly passes.
—A. L. B

The bright, golden summer days were growing scarcer and scarcer; band nights experiences were fast becoming items of the past—that past which had realized itself so strangely to poor Honor. She had hoped sanguinely, trustingly, and now it seemed that fate would bring her defiant proofs of its iron will in spite of herself.

She had not taken it as a sign of inconstancy, that Guy had never sent the smallest message of encouragement to her, but rather tried to weave it in as a sprig of the laurel crown she daily wove in silent sadness, for her truant lover, when he would return, full of happy explanations, to claim her all his own.

Vivian was as constant and devoted when the leaves began to turn, as when the leaves began to bud. This was perhaps the most intricate plot of his scheming life, but he was proving himself equal to it: he was probing his way slowly and quietly into the well guarded sanctum of Honor Edgeworth's heart, trying to accumulate every energy of his soul into one eloquent appeal to her obstinate nature.

The gorgeous colors of the western sky were fading dimly one evening, behind the misty mountain tops. It was towards the end of August, a lovely evening, such as comes back to us before the autumn, as a reminder of the closing season.

Vivian Standish, pausing suddenly, rested his oars on the placid water, and contemplated in silence, the figure of Honor Edgeworth, reclining on the cushioned seat of his handsome boat. They had rowed a long way up the canal, and any sentimental readers who have been there, either alone, with only the memory of some dearer one, or still better, in the actual company of some strangely loved acquaintance, will not hesitate, in pronouncing this still, cool, shady retreat, one of the most suggestive spots on earth. If anyone's untiring devotion and wildest appeals have not, up to this, made any impression upon the being one loves, the very best remedy is to launch a cosy boat into this very canal, and pull with a mighty strength for four or five miles up from the "deep cut." Soon a sequestered paradise is reached, where the bended boughs interlacing, whisper, in caressing, rustling to each other, over the narrow stream of rippling water below, here pause and wait. There is a hush whose voice is more eloquent than any human appeal. The low gurgling music of the little waves that creep techily over and under the hanging boughs that teaze and obstruct them in their onward passage, the crowded leaves, rubbing their swaying heads affectionately together; the gentle wind resting in sighs of relief upon the graceful tree tops, and sending its messages of love from bough to bough, until it spends itself upon the quiet bosom of the waters below; the love-sick birds that woo our beauteous nature in this, her bewitching costume, with their rich and rarest warblings, vie with one another in chanting from their ruffled throats their little tales of ecstasy and love, all teach us clearly, that out in the busy world there is no witchery like this.

In the open sunlight, nature dons her every day attire, but in the shady retreat of these, her chosen spots, she coquettishly arrays herself in most resistless costumes.

While one pauses, leaning on his oars amid such scenes as this, one cannot but feel like flirting very earnestly with nature; the surrounding beauty cannot help reflecting some of its liveliness upon the admirers, and the stray, "tangled" sunbeams that lose one another in the thick foliage cannot but give a new love-light to the eyes that linger thoughtfully upon them. So that the first impulse to admire nature being gratified, each finds a consequent impulse towards natural admiration, creeping into the heart. *She* looks questioningly into *his* eyes, and if *he* knows anything he will respond appropriately, and after that, each finds out that the other is one of the most enhancing elements of the beautiful that they have been contemplating all the while.

To Honor Edgeworth, it was the most delightful treat possible, to drink in the beauty and elegance of such surroundings, to this at least, her heart was never closed—it was easy enough to battle against the hoarse voice of temptation in the busy world, but here, all was different, this was a spot created, not for the art and acceptations of conventionality, but for the freedom ahd expansion of the heart and soul.

To lie in a recumbent attitude and feel the gentle breath of the breeze, playing among her yielding curls, or listen to it, whispering its effective lullaby into her ears, to drink such a long draught of nature's own narcotic, as would steal her away from the world of reality, closing her drowsy lids upon the actual, and unfolding to her in tempting dreams, the realizations of all her exaggerated, but cherished ideals, this was the luxury of living, this made life worth prizing, worth striving for in Honor Edgeworth's eyes.

There are many beside her, who are fond of being nursed into this drowsy state by some such delightful influence. People, there are, who without ever acknowledging their weakness, for such a thing, are often seized with the strangest moods and cravings, a longing for sweet words, or tender caresses, or something correspondingly emotional in the abstract fills them up, they would like to lie lazily by some smouldering fire, on an easy couch, and have some gentle hand to smoothe away the wrinkles from their brows, or some loving voice to whisper suggestive little trifles, into their willing ears: when they see a flood of moonlight filling the earth with its soft stillness, they immediately long to animate the scene by their own presence, but, with some treasured beauty, leaning on one arm, and looking bewitchingly into their love-lit eyes, every emotional sight, sound or feeling, brings to them the possible intensity of a gratified love, the fruits, they *might* gather from their own sentiment, if they had power to indulge it. This is why we meet so many dreamy, romantic girls, who are ever on the *qui vive*, expecting the hero, with deep eyes and heavy moustaches, that never comes. Girls who see more beauty, and poetry, and romance, in the distant "red light of a cigar" twinkling through the darkness, on some quiet night, than in all the stars of heaven combined; girls who expect that every silent, handsome man, who gives them a passing glance (of aimless curiosity) is a wonderful character, just stepped over the threshold of some of Ouida's or The Duchess' volumes, ready to seize them in his steady arms, if they sprain an ankle, or faint over some fright; ready to rescue them from some terrible accident, and then fall violently in love, marry them, but, unlike the book, in reality, "live in miserable wretchedness for ever after."

Such also are those *yearning* men, who are ever taking flights into the delightful world of the ideal—men, who try, with a pair of plentiful eyes, to conquer "female heartdom," who think to find the "open sesame" to that valuable depository, by knocking the practical element out of life, and by grasping at chance, in the dim, soulful, dreamy, intense, abstract world of thought. Men, who the punster would say in the dewy twilight or still moonlight, are _pie_ously all for *soul*, but who in the raw early afternoon are _sole_ly all for *pie*.

But from a suspicion of an inclination to such influence, I must surely except Vivian Standish, he could neither see, hear or feel any fascination in those things, and yet, he was not without knowing, that herein lay the weak point of souls more susceptible than his own; he was cunning enough to know, that a young lady is at the limit of all her reason and control, when ushered into such a spot, as that which he had chosen as a resting-place during their row, on this eventful evening.

But with all his precious knowledge, there were a few very simple things, which Vivian Standish had never learned; he understood other people perfectly, it is true, human nature, was as legible to him, as the plainest book, as a rule, he read faces, as he would the morning- paper, and yet, strange to say, he knew less of his own self than he did of any one—he was clever enough to veneer his character well, that others might not know him, but apart from that he was a mystery to himself—he had certain instinctive ideas of his own bias and inclinations; he knew every positive quality or defect he had, and in that same he had plenty to remember, but he never asked himself, whether he was proof against every passing circumstance or not; he met them generally, with an admirable collectedness and *sang-froid*, but, depending on the spur of the moment is not the safest thing in a person of his pursuits. The cleverest diplomatists and adventurers have been betrayed by themselves and so was he.

While he sat, watching the contemplative features of the girl in the boat before him, something, in the clear depths of the admiring eyes, struck him; there was an expression of infinite longing over her face, her mouth was drawn into a sad smile, and her hands were folded listlessly on her lap: a few withering daisies and butter-cups, that she had snatched an hour before as they skimmed along the shore, lay carelessly between her fingers, and the loose ties of her broad hat were fluttering on the breeze, under her pretty, upturned chin. If ever repentance could have worked its influence over a guilty soul, it could not have found a moment more propitious than this, wherein to accomplish its task, the very last susceptibility of a heart, hardened and inured to sin was struggling to assert itself, a long, unheeded impulse, was trying to shake away the fetters of vice and crime, and free itself to noble action.

The fierce combat between his good and evil spirits waged for an instant, he must either fall before this commanding angel, or crush with a mighty blow, and forever, the already weak agent of good, whose "wee small voice" tantalized him strangely at this moment.

But while he hesitated, his destiny decided itself; a new phase suddenly substituted his calculating indifference, he felt a strong, jealous passion flooding his whole soul, he saw the beauty of Honor Edgeworth's face by an entirely new light, he scorned the suspicion—but the truth was terribly bare, he had been caught in his own meshes—he loved this girl. It did not steal upon him, nor come by slow degrees, but rushed in a crushing torrent of realization, into his heart. All the words of devotedness and admiration, that he had spoken to her of late, were only a mockery, to what his passion suggested now.

Love, to so many others an enviable blessing, threatened to be a miserable portion for him, for naturally enough, coming to him as it did through the channels of the soul, it had to partake of the unholy nature of these unhealthy and corrupt by-ways; and hence instead of the pure, buoyant emotion that fills the honest breast, in the redeeming passion of its first exalted love, there rushed into the heart of Vivian Standish, a poisonous torrent of insuperable desire, that held him like an iron-bound victim, foaming and struggling in his own chains. A look of devouring admiration flashed from his fiery eyes over the face of the girl. She was thinking; thinking something pleasant, something fascinating, thinking of someone agreeable to her thought—who was not *he*, this he knew, and a crushing feeling of envy, worse than the worst hatred, filled him. Whose memory did he, by his own voluntary action, awake within her by bringing her to this spot? who was it, conjured by her, sat between them, or perhaps substituted him altogether? "Egad," he stifled, between his teeth, "I must know the worst of this." With a voice that bespoke a terrible power of self-command, Vivian, blandly broke this heavy silence—

"I need not ask if you enjoy yourself, Honor, I can see that?"

The girl turned her head slowly towards him, as if loth to raise her eyes from the visionary world, that fascinated her, and smiling, as if in sad remembrance, answered abstractedly,

"Yes, I am easily influenced by such surroundings as these," and as she spoke she waved her hand with a graceful gesture that took in her picturesque environs.

"That *movement*, included me, I wonder if the *words* did as well," he said quickly, and so huskily, that Honor looked up a little startled.

"Well—yes, you too," she said laughingly, though a little stiffly, "you must suppose that you have your share of influence over me as well as every other thing and person associated with my life."

"Only as well, as every other thing, eh?" he interrupted sneeringly, "only as well, as a terrier dog—or a dutiful servant—or a well-cooked dinner, I suppose, is that it?" and leaning over on his oars, he looked savagely into the trembling girl's face.

Honor straightened herself into a stiff, sitting posture, and looking indignantly into his eyes, answered haughtily —

"Mr. Standish, you have rather a strange way of jesting to-day, might I trouble you to resume your old self, at least while I am obliged to be with you?" but his eyes only rivetted themselves still more greedily upon her, and his hands trembled still more nervously, as he clutched the oars.

"Jesting?" he said in a mocking tone, "jesting, did you say? No Honor, I have jested all my life, but I swear to you, that now I am in terrible earnest, do not provoke me at this moment, for I can scarcely hold myself responsible, hereafter, for what I may do—it is your work that I am in such a state, not mine—come now—tell me, of whom were you thinking when I spoke to you a moment ago? I must know it or you regret it—tell me?"

A slow withering smile of sublime contempt, crept into the handsome face of the threatened girl—

"Spare your *brutem fulmen*, Mr. Standish, I pray you," she said in pitiful sarcasm, "you will not terrify me—I must say, that I did not require this emphatic proof to convince me of how thorough a gentleman you are, I could have believed without it, but I think if your intention was to take advantage of respectable circumstances and gain a noble victory for yourself, you might possibly find easier terms yet than those which oppose you now, get some one who defies you infinitely less than I do; you need not then trouble to bray so loud." And as she finished speaking, she turned her head, in languid disgust away from the peering face of her companion, and carelessly paddled the tips of three dainty fingers in the quiet water, at the same time humming a gay little selection to herself. Her perfect ease and composure disconcerted him, not a little, it certainly was the most efficacious way of bringing him back to his polished senses again.

But though the first madness of his attack, was gradually subsiding, he still sat silently gazing into her face, until becoming somewhat concerned, Honor looked coldly back into his searching face and said with the most provoking supineness, in her tone.

"When you have gratified your eyes sufficiently with their insolent occupation, will you be kind enough to either row me yourself, or allow me to row myself back to the boat-house, or anywhere convenient to the shore?"

This awoke him to the actual state of things; he straightened his oars, and made sundry other preparations to start, but as he leaned forward to take the first backward stroke, he looked steadily into her face and said in a husky, almost defiant tone,

"Dust, like this, can never blind my eyes, but resign yourself, for Guy Elersley and you will never meet again." In spite of herself, Honor was startled a little; a greyish shadow flitted across her face, her lips trembled for an instant, and a wincing expression shot from her eyes, the words sounded so much like a prophecy of evil, how could he say them so emphatically unless he knew something, could it be possible that Guy was dead? Oh no, she would not yield to such a gloomy idea of the possible, this man was only trying to frighten her—but frightened she would not be, she suddenly recollected herself, and in a splendid manner answered him,—

"Indeed, Mr. Standish! Although you introduce a strangely inappropriate subject, I must say your intelligence grieves me, for I like Guy Elersley exceedingly well, and should be heartily sorry were I given to credit your statements with the slightest suspicion of truth."

He had begun to congratulate himself that, at last, he had secured her unawares, but the last remark confounded him altogether—baffled in every attempt he gave up trying to threaten her, and resolved to come back now, if he could, at least to her former favor.

Carefully smothering all his latent passion of jealousy and rage, he addressed his next words in tones of such humiliation and regret as took Honor by the greatest surprise.

"Honor, what have I done?" he said seriously and sorrowfully, "have I forgotten your dignity in the intensity of my emotion?"

"It was your own you forgot," she interrupted, "or you could never have forgotten mine, but then one can't be too hard on a person for forgetting such mere trifles, I don't blame you, yours is so insignificant, that I often forget it myself."

"I deserve it all, Honor, go on—I have been a brute I see—but it was not I, it was the demon of jealousy within me, will you not say that you absolve me Honor, for believe me I knew not what I did?"

Something of actual despair rung from his voice, he bowed his face with its pained expression, and Honor believed him sincere, perhaps, after all the man was beside himself she thought, he who had never before made the most pardonable breach of etiquette or courtesy.

The jealousy that was the evident cause of his strongest utterance, was perhaps, what any woman can forgive her lover's rival most easily, for it gives a spice to love, so with a little appeal to her womanly sympathies,

Honor thawed out, and answered his miserable self-condemnations in forgiving but reserved terms.

"Do not trouble yourself so," she said half consolingly. "I assure you, your words have had no effect in the world on me; if I thought differently of you, they would have meant more, but as it is, console yourself that you have injured no one half so much, as you have yourself."

The ambiguous words deceived him—he looked gladly up and exclaimed—

"You are an angel, Honor!" but he had not understood the deep meaning of her thought, he did not know, that, when we love, truly and devotedly, or even cherish and esteem some one, an unkind word or a cruel retort, from those lips to us, makes a breach, which no forgiving phrases can ever right again. When the heart that loves has been wounded by the hand it adores, no remedy can ever fully heal the rankled spot, where the poisoned arrow has lodged. We can forgive the injury of one, whom we have never cherished nor loved, we can treat with indifference the slights of those we care little about, but it takes an angel's mercy, an infinite fortitude, a supernatural test of our moral strength to raise up again the golden idol that one word of cruel unkindness, has shattered within our hearts.

It was nearly dusk when Honor and Vivian Standish landed at Mr. Rayne's boat-house, near the bridge. The night air was growing cooler, and the stars were breaking through the cloudless sky in quiet succession.

With the tenderest of solicitude, Vivian carefully placed Honor's wrap around her shoulders, and gently assisting her up the steep ascent of the boat-house stairs, he stole his hand under the knotted fringe of the warm shawl, and thrust it within her arm.

Honor, for a great many reasons, chose to sign a treaty of peace with Vivian Standish. She suspected that he knew, perhaps more than he cared to show, of her attachment for Guy, and if a word of unmeaning forgiveness, could serve to buy him over, she did not hesitate in purchasing discretion with such counterfeit coins, for she cared little, if she were exalted or not in such opinions as his.

Thus, they proceeded, quite amicably on their homeward way, both in an unusually good humor. There is a auspicious feature about such suddenly assumed gaiety, that cannot but amuse the disinterested participator; when either in such a case as that of Vivian Standish we wish thereby to drown the memory of a recent mistake or blunder, by indulging in loud mirth, that distracts the mind from the unpleasantness just experienced, or when we are under the painful influence of some personal trouble, be it a substantial loss of any sort, or the more unfortunate burden, cast upon us by any social stigma, then, when the whole world, learning of our misfortune extends its hand in stinging sympathy, and looks with painful enquiry of curious compassion, to see "how we take it," what a piercing spur we thrust into our pride, to drive into it that forced merriment and happy resignation, which we blindly hope will stand for indifference in the eyes of a criticising society, at all times, it is neccessarily a short-lived effort, and so it was in the case of those two young people. When they reached Mr. Rayne's house, and separated at the gate, the masks fell immediately, and each went his way laughing at the absurd mockeries of life, by which, we cheat one another face to face, at those ridiculous attempts at veneering, through which it is as easy to see, as through a pane of polished glass, and yet, to which we have constant recourse, as though the human heart were more presentable in its mean disguises of truth and honesty, than when laid bare, in the actual existing state, of diplomacy, selfishness, and deceit.

CHAPTER XXXI

"But all was false and hollow, though his tongue
Dropt manna; and could make the worse appear
The better reason."
—*Milton.*

"I will surely be recognized by some one, if I stay here this evening," Guy said, as he brushed his hair and readjusted his cravat, before a neat mirror in one of the prim bed-rooms of a Sparks street boarding- house. "I had better seek some way of keeping myself ahide for awhile, until I find out, how love-matters are progressing in a certain quarter," and as he soliloquized, he turned to the open window that faced the busy street, just in time to catch a glimpse of the "street car," as it hurried by. There was a placard in conspicuous letters on either side announcing to the public that a "moonlight excursion would take place, that night *per* steamer '*Peerless.*'"

This suggested itself to Guy as one way of spending his dull evening in tolerable comfort. He looked at his watch, and found it wanted yet a quarter to half-past seven. He looked out at the dull gray sky, "I don't think fair Luna under whose patronage they give their excursion, will favor them with her presence to-night," he muttered in a satisfied voice, "and for that I thank her profusely."

He opened his large valise, that lay beside the bed and took from its respectable inside, a handful of good cigars, these he deposited in his coat-pocket, he then thrust his head into a large rimmed felt hat, that partially covered his features, and otherwise gave him an appearance of disguise, and having carefully closed both window and door of his tidy room, went quietly out.

Down through the familiar streets, where he had so often strolled a few little years ago, he strolled again to-night, but how different a man! The usual processions of the working-class were thickening as the "after tea," leisure hours advanced: the "loafers" of the old type with soft slouched hats bent over their eyes, and with mouths full of very strong tobacco and language were posed artistically here and there in classic- looking groups, at the corners of Sparks and its intersecting streets. Cabmen lounged around the vicinity of Dufferin Bridge, as it were in the very postures he had seen them take, when last he strolled along that path, a dissipated, reckless, love-sick youth. But it gratified him to-night beyond anything, as he looked in critical survey from corner to corner of the "Russell," to recognize among that never failing gathering which haunts the thresholds of this flourishing hotel, the "friends of his youth" without *him*. He had not realized the step he had taken, until these scenes brought back the past so forcibly, to lay it beside the prosperous present. How many times had he stood idly before those doors, reckoning it worthy sport indeed, to pass unscrupulous remarks on passers-by behind his half-smoked cheroot: he cast a sympathetic look, as he thought, at a couple of unsuspecting girls, who just then were making their way along that thoroughfare, and his face said very plainly, "Well, you hardly know poor creatures, what noble jests your tiny feet, and tiny waists, and faces and figures, your gait and your dress, are causing for that high-minded audience across the way."

Sussex street had its same quaint, deserted, look, except that the different stocks in the melancholy business establishments looked a little more fly-stained, and time-worn, the sausages and meat-pies in the restaurant windows were a trifle staler looking, and more suggestive of sea-sickness; the thriving hotels, and boarding-houses were a degree dingier, time having laid his dusty finger unmolested, on their muslin-screened windows, telling a woeful tale of laziness and neglect.

At last the bright broad "Ottawa," came in view, sparkling and rippling in the red sunset, like a mass of liquid gems.

The majestic "Peerless," was at her old post near the wharf looking as comfortable and as inviting as ever: the same Notice stood out in all its faulty spelling, where pleasure-boats were for hire, and all the bright yellow sawdust which of late years has so deeply wounded the delicate enthusiasm of the aesthete, traced in golden letters its story of industry and honest labor, on one of nature's unwritten pages. The decks of the favorite "Peerless" were already well-filled with excursionists, who looked over the firm balustrades at the numbers of eager pleasure-seekers who still poured down the steps leading to the boat. Pulling his broad brimmed hat more definitely over his face, Guy fell in behind a group of descending people, and reached the boat barely in time, for as he stepped on board, the captain followed, the men hauled in the gang-way, the last shrill whistle deafened the ears of the passengers, those on the shore who watched the pleasant proceedings, now waved their handkerchiefs and hats, there was a great paddling and splashing until the steamer turned out into the broad river, then quietly, gracefully and lightly, she skipped along the clear calm water, just as the evening shadows were veiling the turrets and spires of surrounding edifices in their heavy mist.

Soon the wharf and its anxious spectators faded from view, then by degrees the towers and gables of the Parliament Buildings dropped into the shadowy distance, the tall pine trees along the shore receded within clouds of dark, smoky, blue, little twinkling lights sprung from the gathering darkness along the water's edge; the twilight was growing into black night, and the tame pleasures on board were developing into wild merriment.

There was no moon, but this is not necessarily a great disappointment, provided her absence does not foretell rain. A very dark night on deck, with strains of dreamy music echoing from the lighted apartment within, does not seem to the young couples seated by the railing outside, looking into the blue-black waves, as the most tiresome and unsuggestive circumstance in life.

Fully protected by this impenetrable darkness, Guy made his way to a secluded corner of the deck, where, besides being isolated and free from observation, he could both hear and see the merriment that was now at its height within. A soft, sleepy sort of breeze was blowing from the water, and now and then heated participators of the dance drew near the little windows to catch the cool breath of heaven as it stole in.

Guy sat silently and pensively smoking his expensive cigars, planning and plotting all sorts of things to the accompaniment of bewitching strains of twittering waltz music and peals of merry laughter from within. He became distracted now and then in spite of himself, wandering away from his important mental problems to yield to the influence of association and remembrance which stole over him in a sad sort of pleasant way. Here was just the kind of evening he had *once* enjoyed immensely, and might possibly enjoy again; there were all the same faces he had seen countless times upon countless occasions before laughing and chatting merrily. One or two couples out of the crowd who had been in the first grade of love-sickness when he last saw them, now seemed to belong more emphatically to one-another than before, and the sadder but wiser looking fellows who followed some of these developed ladies about gallantly, were loaded with satchels and shawls and other feminine tackle which strangely became them in Guy's eyes; they danced less, flirted less than they used in Guy's days, but then matrimony has its martyrs and its sacrifices, like every other institution, and the thorns and roses grow on the one branch. Some are unfortunate enough indeed in culling the matrimonial nosegay, for very soon the over-mature rose falls in withered beauty to the ground, leaf by leaf, and the disconsolate admirer stands open-mouthed and sorry, with a bare stalk of healthy thorns between his finger and thumb, but it is mostly his own doing, for even if his fair enchantress has spared him the disagreeable necessity of "popping the question," she had left him the power to decline.

Guy learned more of practical life from his nook in the dark on this festive night, than a year's ordinary observation could ever have taught him. He shook his head in amused pity once or twice as he recognized some of his "old friends" among the gay crowd; how well he knew of old that some of those civil servants had likely made the tour of whole departments that afternoon to borrow the half-dollar admission fee that granted them all this pleasure to-night, fellows who had been rollicking all their lives, who had not hesitated over anything, who would as soon fall in love with a troupe of bouncing actresses, and follow them around from city to city, as they would eat their dinner, and yet he could see the gratification of unsuspecting girls as these destitute enthusiasts sought and enjoyed their company. It amused Guy to see some of them actually looking serious, as they led some fair creature on their arm through the moving circle of the dance; or bent suspiciously over the chair of some golden-haired beauty on the deck. Guy tried to improvise a consistent sequel to these little love-signs, but it grew ridiculous naturally enough, he gathered all these interesting little circumstances within the limits of "a plain gold ring," but these are "deuced" narrow limits for two healthy people and one small income to thrive in.

He tried to imagine the placid pretty faces of the patient pampered blondes and brunettes, if these same devoted ones, now so interesting as lovers, were to come home some luckless evening as prosy husbands and say "Eva," or "Bee," or "Ada, it's all up with us now, the bailiff will be here in the morning, I knew this sort of high life couldn't last—" and then to fling himself down in democratic contempt on the parlor sofa, with its dainty tidies and cushions of "appliqué" or pale-blue satin, and use its rosewood or mahogany framework as the commonest bootjack. Of course a fellow is always sure that these ornamental little wives have no other consolation for themselves or any one else, but in the copious tears that swell up into their pretty eyes, they must sit down and sob to break their dear little hearts with every now and then a hysterical sentence from behind the dainty lawn handkerchief, saying "what will everyone think? What will Lady Featherly say? We wont be asked to any more 'at homes' now, and the ball at 'Rideau' is next week, oh dear—boo—hoo—hoo!" Of course the merciless husband gets mad because his poor little helpless wife sees fit to weep over a fate that must disgrace her in the eyes of the social world. She wouldn't mind being refused everywhere for "credit" as long as they had enough to eat and "kept up appearances," and she knows very well that no one will believe her when she says she and "Percy" gave up house-keeping as a "nuisance." Then there are those who will be delighted over her reverse, the ones she never would invite to her five o'clock teas or evening parties, will chuckle now over her misfortune, she tells herself bitterly. How can she do without servants, she who has never brushed her own hair all her single life. She can only cry and be sorry she ever married. She is so unequal to such awful responsibilities. Asking herself what she *could* do to assist "Percy" in this catastrophe, only gives her another fresh grief to realize. She sees that lawn-tennis is a useless accomplishment before the bailiffs threat, dancing or singing, or good looks are equally worthless in such a dilemma, high-toned friends are of no avail, they drop the acquaintance generally, under such circumstances.

The helpless little beauties must then break their hearts in grief, they cannot do what less accomplished or less fashionable girls would be able to do in such a moment, how could anyone expect them to say, "Let us dismiss the servant, I know my household duties as well as she, henceforth *I* will make your shirts and knit your stockings, leave off these expensive places of amusement, I have not been accustomed to them and can live without them." How can they do this who have lived a single life so inconsistent with the acquirement of such rude accomplishments as characterize the daughters of respectable but far less fashionable citizens than their fathers. A sudden stop in the dreamy waltz hurled Guy back from the mysteries of the future he had undertaken to unravel, he laughed inwardly as he re-settled himself comfortably on his chair, at the vagaries his fancy had indulged in at the sad expense of these unconscious couples, who were as happy in their present state of mutual appreciation as though no cloud however dark and heavy in the coming future could dim the brightness of this hour.

'T'were hard to tell what other extravagant freaks Guy may not have indulged in after this, for the orchestra had ceased grating its instruments into accord, and was inviting the dancers to join in a gay "Rush Polka," but the sound of voices near him caught his ear suddenly and he started up in a listening attitude. There was no mistaking—he leaned farther away from the little window from whence streamed a flood of lamplight, and holding his breath, he listened eagerly for the next words.

"I was inclined to call for Honor," said one, "but I felt so certain of meeting her here that I deemed it unnecessary."

The words came plainly, not loudly, but distinctly to Guy's hearing as they crossed Vivian Standish's lips; he recognized the bland deceptive voice and set his teeth in contempt; he had come to Ottawa, for the sole purpose of hunting up this gallant hero and a kind fortune had placed him within his very hands. Another voice broke the ensuing silence, one that had a great effect on Guy, for he could only remember the familiar strains of his uncle's voice by its ruins, it was weak and tremulous and uncertain, its saddened tones touched Guy considerably.

"You see," the old man was saying "you never can rely much on girls, Honor was taken with such a bad headache to-night that she preferred we would leave her behind, Madame d'Alberg insisted on my coming, since I was well enough for the first time in a long while."

"Certainly, you should not have missed the trip," Vivian answered, "but I am sorry that Honor should be indisposed, I wanted her particularly to-night."

So—thought Guy, it has come to this—"Honor"—how pat it came from his vicious lips. He made up his mind at this juncture to listen to every word, feeling sure to find some valuable clue before this night was over. The voice of assumed anxiety broke from Vivian's lips and interrupted Guy's thought.

"I hope you are on the way to complete recovery at last Mr. Rayne," he said, "really I begin to feel anxious about you."

Guy fancied the old man shaking his head in the usual contemplative way as the words came—

"Oh no, my dear boy, my system has completely broken up now, my decline is a matter of months only, now."

Vivian was about to protest, when Mr. Rayne continued:

"And I don't mind much, time was when I felt life full of responsibilities that cheered me on, but now—my old age is almost a blank—"

Guy understood this illusion and winced, the unsteady voice still continued:

"Since Honor's welfare in the dim future, when I shall be dead and gone, promises to be safe, I have had no reluctance to die. I lived for her."

At these words Guy strained every nerve in his body and listened devouringly. Vivian spoke next,

"What surprises me," he said "is that Honor has not been snatched away long before this."

"She's a strange girl," Mr. Rayne answered pensively, "she does not take fancies easily, she has treated open admirers with such provoking coldness since she has 'come out' that I wonder at her having a friend left."

"That is what weakens my hope," said Vivian Standish, in a splendid mockery of despair. "I fear that she might meet my proposal with the same indifference, and thus make my life a miserable blank."

The color rushed to Guy's face, and then faded as suddenly away. "Infernal villain!" he muttered, and it was only by an extraordinary effort he conquered the impulse to spring upon the person of this vile adventurer, and strangle him then and there. What providential influence had brought him back to Ottawa at such a crisis, he asked himself.

"Well," he heard his uncle say distractedly, "I have not broached the subject to her yet. She is a strange disposition and cannot be treated like others of her age and sex. I think the better plan would be, for you to deserve her love first, and from what we have all seen of you, I reckon that will not be the hardest of tasks. This is September—if you wish, after three months longer, I will speak to her, and tell her my opinion of you."

"How can I ever thank you or repay you sufficiently, dear Mr. Rayne," was the answer Guy heard to this painful speech of his uncle's. "I have no fear," continued the hypocrite, anxiously, "except," and he hesitated—"that she may have loved already—that is the only obstacle I dread."

"I don't think it," said Henry Rayne. "I'm sure she has not—who could she have loved?"

"You ought to know," continued Standish "whether at any time of her life she has met with some-one she preferred to any other. Do you think for instance," and his voice lowered so that Guy could scarcely catch its accents "that there was anything between her and—your nephew, Guy Elersley?"

Guy's face wore the strangest expression of contempt and pain, as he leaned nearer still to the side from whence the voices came. He could see them now—dark shadows only on the misty outline of the night. They were leaning with their backs against the small green railing, each smoking a cigar. Guy crouched nearer the protecting wall, and waited patiently for the issue of this strange *rencontre*. His uncle was silent for a second, and the uncertain voice with which he answered Vivian's last remark, pained him severely.

"Why do you think that?" he asked, almost huskily, "That never struck my mind, and if it had, I assure you, Standish, much as I esteem you, I would have kept that boy by me. If I suspected that Honor would ever love him, my life's happiness would have been complete."

Guy's eyes were growing moist.

"It is only natural," said the smooth, bland voice of Vivian Standish "that you should like to encourage the welfare of your own, but I must say, that Guy Elersley did not make a proper use of the advantages fortune threw in his way." Guy agreed sadly here "I think he was a little ungrateful besides, in return for your kindness, for I had always understood from him, that in his eyes, you were worth only the wealth you would leave him at your death. I don't want to run down the absent ones, but all the same, I must say, that Elersley had his faults."

Guy ground his teeth in smothered hatred.

"Spare me this, Standish," said the old man pleadingly, "for in spite of all that has happened, I cannot teach myself to forget how I loved this boy all his life, fondly and foolishly, and if he were within my arm's grasp at this moment, I doubt whether I would not take him back to me again as warmly as ever, for I never cease to reproach myself for having treated him so severely for so small an offence."

"It is your excessive mercy and goodness that cause you this regret," Vivian said, "for you surely were lenient to him in your justice after all."

"Let us drop his name," interrupted the old man, "it has not crossed my lips for years, but now that your suggestion brings back the past to me, I am puzzled and surprised a little. I remember now, how Honor carefully collected every little trifling belonging of Guy's that had been left at our house, and carried them to her own room, where they have laid since. I thought at the time, it was to spare me the pain of coming across them, as she had heard something of our dispute; but now, I recognize the possibility of there having been a more pitiful motive. She never utters his name either. I wonder have I done them both the awful wrong of thrusting myself between their young hearts, and spoiling the happy ambition of their lives—may God help me to repair it if I have!"

Guy's head fell wearily on his folded arms that rested on the back of a vacant chair in front of him. This was such a painful scene to witness in silence that he felt himself almost overcome. He never cherished Honor so wildly or devotedly as he did at this moment. The details that fell from the lips of his uncle were items of a sad, sweet tale for him—he no longer doubted of her faithful love for him now.

Lest Mr. Rayne should become too remorseful for the injustice he had done these young people, Vivian hastened to speak in a reassuring voice.

"But it is plain, Mr. Rayne, if your nephew thought anything of this girl, he would have sent her some word or token of regard at parting, in spite of you or anyone else, that might encourage or sustain her love during their separation. This he did not think it worth his while to do, which is almost proof positive that he cared very little for her."

"Heaven help me to bear this!" was Guy's inarticulate prayer as those last words reached his ears. "Of all the infamous blackguards and disreputable scoundrels I ever met"—here he stopped, and listened again. They had resumed the topic of Vivian's proposal.

"I tell you," said Mr. Rayne wearily, "to visit and court her for three months longer, anyway. At the end of that time you can propose if you will, and I will give my consent readily. I am glad to hear you say you have means enough to hold you independent of my little girl's fortune. I would not like to see her wedded for her dowry."

"The wealth of character and beauty is her real dowry, Mr. Rayne," the hypocrite replied, "Any other is worthless before that."

"Aye, aye! you are right there, my boy," added Mr. Rayne, shaking his head pensively. Then changing his tone suddenly said, "I feel a little chilly here, Vivian, my boy; let us go inside."

"Take my arm, Mr. Rayne, and let me feel that in even so little a thing I can make myself useful to you."

They passed in silently where the lamp light and music and merry sounds flooded the gay rooms. Guy bent forward as they closed the little glass door behind them, and caught a glimpse of the changed, wasted, melancholy old man he loved so well, leaning on the traitorous arm of a tall, straight, handsome one, who was associated with the bitterest feelings of hatred and revenge within his breast.

How he longed to be away from this merry-making crowd, where he could lay his wearied head to rest, and where the mockery of life might cease to taunt him for a little while. Only one thought saved him and encouraged him through all—the thought that *she* had not forgotten him, in spite of the base treachery practised by the man he had trusted. Through all his painful realizations, this angelic face of his beloved, soothed and comforted and cheered him until he felt a new strength in his arm and a new fire in his heart, urging him on to retributive action.

Out of all that crowd of merry-makers that landed back on the Queen's Wharf, close on to midnight of that night, not one had noticed the solitary figure under the broad felt hat, though his very friends jostled and elbowed past him in the throng.

Stepping ashore, he hired a carriage and drove rapidly away. He had spent an evening with all the old faces after an absence of years, and not one of his many friends and acquaintances suspected Guy Elersley any nearer than the possible distance of the unknown.

CHAPTER XXXII

"Was I deceived or did a sable cloud
Turn forth her silver lining on the night?"
—*Milton*

"Three months! three months!" Guy said in a low, puzzled voice, as he lay wide awake on his bed, turning and twisting all the circumstances of his recent discoveries over and over in his head. "I can never stay here all that time. Besides, I have a good deal to do." He thought over it a little while longer, and then looking quite satisfied, he turned himself comfortably on the other side and went deliberately off into a peaceful sleep.

Three months never appear to us to contain half of their real length when we have much to consider and much to do in a given time of that duration. One month had already elapsed, during whose flight Guy had made some important discoveries.

He had traced up the bogus parsonage, and had even found, by some lucky accident, the residence of Philip Campbell, the rescuer of Fifine de Maistre. The "Lower Farms" is, of all secluded spots, about the most secluded, and people went there just as Guy did—through curiosity. It tempted Guy in his search as being the most direct route from the house where the extraordinary wedding had taken place. He had been sitting in the small public room of the village inn a few hours after his arrival, hiding his anxious face behind the folds of the country weekly newspaper, when the conversation of a group of men at the counter in the corner interested him.

"Take somethin', doctor," said one burly, good-natured fellow to an aged person of apparent dignity and respectability, "you must feel all out o' sorts after this day's work."

"Not a bit," said the man addressed, "we doctors grow quite accustomed to such sights when we have reached my age in the profession."

"I dare say, indeed, doctor," said a credulous looking youth, who was rubbing his unshaved chin and lips with the broad back of a sunburnt hand, "ye must have interestin' sights now and then doctor, though wan 'ud think there wudd'nt be much fuss in a place like this, barrin' it comes from folks' own contrariness, like Michael Doyle's daughter to-day—the world knows if they'd stuck to the old style, like their dacenter neighbors, and burnt their safe tallow candles, Maggie Doyle wuddn't be shrivelled up to a crisp to-night from coal ile 'splosions. We all told 'em so!" —wound up this matter-of-fact youth, after reviewing in a few words the sad fate of one of the village girls, who had, the night previous, met her death through a lamp explosion that had set fire to her clothes.

"'Tis sad to see a young woman the victim of death," the doctor said reflectively. "I get quite overcome myself when I see them suffer. I have never forgotten the pitiful sight of the young woman we picked up in the bush leading from the 'Grey House' one morning about three years ago."

This familiar allusion of the old doctor's to his experience of that eventful day was as well understood by every one there as it was by himself, but somehow such persons of eminence as doctors or curates of small villages always find the rustic inhabitants ready to appreciate their tales, were it their hundredth repetition. Fortunately for Guy, some rough sycophant expressed himself interested in the allusion, and asked a question or two, which succeeded in bringing out for about the sixtieth time from the doctor's lips the whole story of Josephine de Maistre's rescue. Guy strained his ears as he leaned sideways to hear the interesting details. He could scarcely conceal his agitation as each precious item dropped from the aged doctor's lips. Finally, Guy laid down his paper and approached the listening group.

"I have overheard your strange story," he said, addressing the venerable man of medicine, "and being of your profession myself, I naturally interest myself in your experience. Did your unfortunate patient die?" he tried to ask in the most careless curiosity.

The village doctor looked condescendingly on the intruder, and the others in dumb courtesy moved aside to let the new comer through.

"No, she did not die," the doctor answered, rubbing his hands, "but though she recovered her bodily health, her mind was terribly deranged. None of us could glean anything of importance from her wild answers, she was foolishly inconsistent in everything, but when she spoke of her 'revenge' and of 'Bijou,' whoever that was."

Guy felt as if his heart had bounded into his mouth, and had to muster all the moral courage he could to prevent his betraying himself, his tone was a masterpiece of affected indifference when he asked,—

"Do you know what became of this poor victim after she left here?"

"Oh, we did not lose sight of her," said the doctor, in a tone which insinuated that a suspicion of such neglect insulted the dignity of his profession, "by no means. When she had recovered her physical health under our treatment, we had her transferred to 'Beauport,' where she was sure to be well treated—It was as sad a case on the whole, I think, as was ever recorded," mused the would-be wise and experienced physician, and as Guy agreed with him, he strolled lazily towards the door, and in another moment had quitted the inn.

Guy felt himself now to be the direct depository of a great mission, which his conscience bade him fulfil right away. Just as hurriedly and as anxiously as if he were hastening to the death-bed of his nearest relative, Guy took the very next train down to Quebec, resolving silently to spend every exertion he was capable of in this precious duty, or die.

In the fiercest battles of our daily lives, there are only two incitants which can never fail to give our heart a hope, our hope a courage, our courage a strength, and our strength whatever possible success can be wrung from fate under such circumstances; these are, the two great influences of hatred— and of love. There is no strength so fierce, so terrible as the hater's, just as there is no strength so steady, so hopeful, so ambitious, as that which guides the lover's hand. We would do a great many hard and trying things for our love's sake, but those things which the righteous could never do—even for their love—are the better sweets of an active hatred. Love has its limits, but hatred—its only sweetness is its infinity, its boundless freedom, and its endless resources.

There was something of both these stimulants pressing Guy Elersley onward to determined action. All the mighty strength of years of subdued love and sincerest devotion spurred him hopefully on, and all the crushing power of a few days' hatred goaded him on to merciless action. He stowed away that other every-day life of his, and assumed this new phase of his existence dutifully and well. The reward stood in the distance, smiling and beckoning, though 'tis true that his eyes could only discover the familiar outlines of his heart's idol through the doubtful mists of the "possible", but it were as well to spend his pent-up emotions in this way as have them crushed from his heart by a merciless blow of fate, in bitter disappointment.

It would scarcely interest the reader to follow Guy Elersley in his rambles, from the time he passed out of the dingy doorway of the village public-house until he drew up, after a long drive, before the imposing entrance of "Beauport Asylum." The bracing air of the country road that leads to this establishment had had a most beneficial effect on Guy's temperament, and therefore as he alighted from his *calèche*, his step had resumed something of its old lightness, and his face had lost some of its serious expression.

Guy cogitated sadly as he sauntered quietly up the gravel walks that lead to the main entrance of the edifice. With its air of quiet and peaceful dignity, its beautiful paths, and *parterres* of blooming flowers, its fountains and grottoes, none could suspect that its melancholy mission was to shelter the noblest work of an Infinite hand in a wrecked and shattered state. There are collected the precious, priceless ruins of the masterpieces of the Artist of Life; an assemblage of ruins over which the most hardened cannot refrain from weeping, were it their very last tear.

Before making any inquiries, Guy passed silently as any ordinary visitor through the different apartments of the "women's ward," carefully studying and scrutinizing any young or beautiful faces that might answer the purpose, he was there to serve: but a pained expression of growing disappointment like despair was settling on his face, as he scanned the last group of quiet, staring countenances that remained to be seen. There was nothing in all that mass of wrecked humanity which satisfied him.

Quiet, reserved women, looked up into his face with a meaningless gaze as he passed from one to another in his eager search, turning their heads stupidly in his direction, as they knitted their well-shaped stockings diligently; other dishevelled, drivelling imbeciles, gathered up in the corners of benches or on the floors, raised their empty eyes to look carelessly out through masses of tumbled hair at him, and then with some half articulate chuckle to clasp their hands tightly around their knees again, and drop their heads into their laps.

From these harmless, foolish victims, Guy passed eagerly on to the more thrilling presence of the maniacs, but even here, though wild shrieks and dark threatening looks greeted him on all sides, he could not find a clue to assist in unravelling his secret plot. There were loud toned viragos who screached and roared in fearful imprecations and appealed to unknown people, victims of the demon alcohol—there were the dark, sullen, silent ones, brooding over their imaginary or real wrongs, and weeping and moaning piteously—there were the dangerous, careless and happy victims, who filled the dismal cells with their heart-rending peals of wild laughter, that fall upon the heart like the loneliest knell—there were the apparently quiet, religious ones who addressed their Creator in ceaseless, meaningless prayer, crying for forgiveness and mercy, but there was no bright, pretty French child, who called for "Bijou" or her "revenge," and this discouraged Guy very much. Presently addressing the guide, who escorted him through these apartments of living death, Guy said:

"Have you no cases of love mania, one younger than these?" waving his hand, as he spoke, in the direction of the rooms he had just visited.

The middle-aged guide shook her head sadly and said:

"Not at present, Sir, the last one of that sort, died a few months after admission.

Guy's heart sank as heavily as a lump of lead within his breast.

"Died?" he reiterated in a tone which bespoke a faint hope that the other had made some mistake.

"Yes, Sir, poor thing," said the pensive-looking woman addressed, "she was a beautiful sight to look upon too, such a pretty face, and such slender little hands, she was very melancholy for three or four months, and then died."

"Do you know the circumstances that brought about her derangement?" asked Guy, almost in despair of ever solving the tangled problem now.

"I think, if I don't mistake," quietly answered his informant, twirling her thumbs, "that her husband had deserted her, and then committed suicide, although they had been married but a year."

Guy grasped this as the straw to which he might yet cling, and looking hurriedly up at the demure woman who stood watching him silently, he interrupted:

"Pardon my inquisitiveness, madam, but I am in search of a friend, who, I was told, was sent here nearly three years ago, being at that time the unfortunate victim of a love episode."

Guy fancied the reserved matron was casting covert glances at himself, and he fairly staggered as she said in a long breath—

"The pity is, you young gentleman don't repent in time. Where's the use o' looking for the girl, now, she's mad; why didn't ye leave her her senses when she had 'em?"

"My dear woman," Guy gasped, with dilated eyes, "I am not the party to blame, I am only a friend of the young lady's, I am sorry you should consider me guilty of such a serious crime!"

"Oh, beg your pardon, sir," the woman interrupted coolly, "but its not such a great mistake of mine, I'll be bound the young gentleman as has had his finger in the pie, is just as sleek and fine to look at outside as yourself," then meditatively "there's no trusting young men by their looks now-a-days."

Guy could not shirk the truth of this, for Vivian Standish's "outside" was far more polished than his own, and he therefore accepted the woman's tame apology and calmed down.

"I would give anything I own, that would assist me in recovering her," he said, so earnestly, that his matter-of-fact guide rested her lean chin in her hollow palm, and agreed to "think" for his benefit.

After a second or two fraught with extreme anxiety for Guy, the woman asked:

"Do you know of anything particular to trace her by?"

Guy recalled the village doctor's account and quickly told her, that, the circumstances connected with her mania had so impressed her, that she continually talked of revenge, frequently using the name "Bijou," "she had also," he continued, a little less hopefully, and more reluctantly, "a large Newfoundland dog with her, when she left the doctor's house on the 'Lower Farms'"

"Ah, now I know!" the quiet matron exclaimed in subdued surprise, "the young lady with the dog, sure enough—sure enough, but we don't count her somehow," said the woman, interrupting her exclamation of surprise.

"I am so glad that you remember at last," said Guy, whose heart was throbbing with anxiety while she spoke, "do tell me all you remember of her, like a good woman."

"Well, you see," the provokingly slow woman began, "I was just serving my first year, and I was full of pity and sympathy for the poor souls I saw in trouble—though I become quite used to 'em now—and this young creature in particular went straight to my heart. I was good to her, and she took to me, and we became fast friends; she never would give up the great big dog, and he clung to her in return for all he was worth, but one day this sweet creature called me, and says she, 'don't be uneasy about me Mrs. Hammond, there is nothing very wrong with my brain,' says she, 'I've had a very bad attack of brain fever,' says she, 'and I feel its effects sometimes yet, but that will soon pass away,' says she, 'and I'll be as right as ever again,' I did not mind this," continued the narrator addressing Guy confidentially, "for the worst of them sometimes talk as sensible as you or me, but, for all that, I hoped in my heart 'twas the truth, and I kept on coming to see her, and talking common sense to her, like I would to you or any other sensible folk, and by and bye, I found out that her own predictions was true, and that she had quite recovered her senses. We reported this, and the attending physician agreed with us, and we were all mighty glad, sir," the woman said kindly "for the sweet girl's own sake."

"And what became of her then?" asked Guy, impatiently, unable to await the woman's pleasure to hear the happy sequel.

"Well sir," continued she, "the young lady said she had neither money nor friends, and expressed a wish to retire to some place, where she could practice acts of gratitude to the Almighty, for having saved her from the threatened fate of madness. She did not tell us quite as plain as that what her intentions were, but we soon found out, so unless anything unusual happened, you will find her yet, cloistered voluntarily in the home of some pious ladies who dwell on the outskirts of the city. Anyone will drive you there; you are on the road now; it is far enough on the outskirts of the town, but a pleasant drive for all that, and sure, sir, I, for one, wish you the best of success in your undertaking."

"Thank you, my good woman, a thousand times I thank you. You have lightened a great burden from my heart, and I will not forget it either," and as he showered his protestations of gratitude on the head of the gratified matron, he bowed himself out, and beat a hasty retreat back to his carriage.

CHAPTER XXXIII

"Then gently scan your brother man,
Still gentler sister woman.
Tho' they may gang a kennin' wrang,
To step aside is human."
—*Burns.*

"Is it the little home on the hill?" said the half-indignant *calèche* driver, "well, to be sure I know it as well as I do the nose on my face; step in sur, and: you'll soon see if I do or not."

Jumping hastily up, Guy settled himself for, as he hoped, the last drive to the first part of the success he strove so hard to win.

Quebec, as every tourist has acknowledged, is a "fine old place," and now that his heart was somewhat lighter, Guy allowed himself to realize, like the others, that he had indeed come to a "fine old place," and one whose memory threatened to cling around his heart for the remaining years of his life. Many thoughts filled his busy brain as he rattled along in his two-wheeled conveyance over the country roads, drinking in the freshness and beauty of his rural surroundings, and yielding gladly to the bracing currents of country air that swept past his troubled face, cooling and refreshing him considerably.

By and by, growing a little curious about the nature of the place to which he had ordered this man to drive him, he leaned forward a little and asked the broad-faced Irishman, who was lilting a merry tune to himself as they jaunted along.

"What sort of a place is this we are driving to, Pat."

"Och, faith yer honor, mebbe 'tis dhrivin' to the divil we are, for all Pat knows. G'long there, Sally."

"But I mean the convent, Pat, surely his devilship does not intrude there?"

"Oh thin, the Lord forbid," Pat answered as he, turned the contents of his battered felt hat towards Guy; this characteristic piece of head-wear was just completing that interesting transformation that is the inevitable fate of all long-lived black felts, viz. to develop themselves into a promising green, which is quite in its place on the head of an Irish hackman.

Guy thought it worth his while to interest himself in the fellow, and asked rather curiously—

"You are a Catholic Pat, are you not?"

"Faith I niver was anything else since I was anything at all," was the contented reply. "I got my honest name in a Catholic chapel in th' ould sod, an' I'll take it as honest as I got it, to a Catholic churchyard when I die."

"That's right," said Guy, half seriously, though slightly amused at the strange way the fellow spoke his determination.

"Have you ever been to this place, we are going to, Pat?"

"Troth there isn't an inch nor a fut o' ground in all Quaybec that this ould nag and meself didn't explore some time or other."

"Who runs the institution?" Guy queried next.

"The divil a run it iver got as long as I know it," said Pat, as he gathered up his shabby whip, to the accompaniment of some snack of his oily tongue, which succeeded miserably in inducing his languid old mare to stretch her angular supports over more space at a time, "tis allays bin standin in the wan spot since me father was a lad, and that's longer ago nor I can remember, seein' that they put off rearing me up 'till the rest was all grown up an' out o' the way."

Guy could not refrain from smiling at the droll way in which his companion handled a subject, he had learned before, and therefore to-day's experience was nothing new to him, that direct questions will never get direct answers from an illiterate Irishman, and so he resigned himself beforehand to the ordeal he was passing through at present.

By and by however, Pat drew forth from a depository of doubtful cleanliness and respectability, a short, black pipe, that fitted becomingly between his plentiful lips. Then after a moment's hesitation, he said doubtfully, over the sea-green shoulder of his ancient broad-cloth.

"I suppose, sir, you're something of a smoker?"

Taking this as one way of asking a permission to indulge, Guy answered readily. "Indeed I am, Mr. Crowley, that precious weed and myself are not strangers, at all."

"So then, ye carry it about with you, as well as meself?" he said, with a timid chuckle. Guy agreed that he did, just to satisfy him; the next moment the forefinger and thumb of the amusing Pat Crowley, in all their innocence of toilet attentions, were thrust into the depths of his waistcoat pocket, from whence they unearthed a solitary match; instinctively he flourished this on

Honor Edgeworth | 229

the leg of his baggy trousers, and applied the flame to the empty briar-root, that protruded on its short stem from his substantial mouth; but after a vain puff or two, he flung it impatiently away and replaced the time worn pipe within the flavored precincts of his waistcoat pocket.

Guy, who watched these interesting proceedings in silent amusement, could not subdue the curiosity which prompted him to say.

"I thought you were going to have a smoke for yourself, Mr. Crowley?"

"H'm, so did I, meself," returned Pat.

"And why don't you? I don't object."

"Och divil a thing but smoke was in the insthrument, bad luck to it,— however sir, as ye say ye carry the tabakky about wid ye, take a loan o' the pipe an' welcome, for 'twould never be Pat Crowley, 'ud sit down with that in his pocket, that could make another man happy, and him not wantin' it nayther."

The hint had the desired affect. Guy's face broke into a broad smile, as the true meaning of the words showed itself.

"I have the tobacco he said, and no pipe as you suspect, and your moral is mine, too Crowley, so here's the tobacco and use your pipe to the best of its advantages old fellow."

As Crowley's gratified smile wrinkled over his face and rested in emphatic creases around his eyes, he readjusted the dwarfed pipe between his sallow teeth, and Guy heard him mutter, as he leaned forward to rest the lines, while he rubbed the little shavings between his brawny hands. "Ye're a dacent mother's son, ivery inch o'you, so ye are."

When the curling clouds of smoke, piled upwards over Crowley's head from Guy's good tobacco, the "nag" was touched up, with a multiplied emphasis on the technical snack, and was kept trotting to the utmost limit of her lazy agility during the remainder of the drive. Crowley must have repented his own surliness in the stingy information he gave, respecting the place they were driving to, for, settling himself in a safe heap on the leather cushion of his semi-respectable conveyance, he began:

"This house, yer honor, that we're dhrivin to, mebbe, you'd like to know, now that I do remember that I know somethin' of it, 'tis the natest little hole in Quaybec, though I don't think many knows much about it, ye see, it doesn't belong to any reg'lar nuns, them allays does good, and so does these, although they remind me more of the 'old maid,' they live in what they call 'volunthry sayclusion,' an faith it don't matther a hang to the world what they live in, I belave there's no love lost between 'em an' the world, leastways no one knows where they came from, an' there's not manny as tries to find out, they do be singin' an' prayin' an' carryin' on wid all sorts o' religis capers, and in troth, I think meself, that Pat Crowley's battered ould sowl 'ud look as fine in Heaven any day, that is, if it ever gets there."

"I daresay, Pat," Guy answered, "you are a very good man no doubt."

"I'm not good, bad luck to me," the old fellow returned half gruffly, "but faith if I do the 'ould boy' a turn now and thin, it's sore agin me grain, an' I'm not without tellin' him so, but shure he's the very divil for plaguing the best natured man in creation, unto doin' mischief."

Guy laughed outright at this original declaration and said teasingly:—

"You should run away from the devil, Crowley, like the ladies in this little retreat, and wisely shun temptation in such seclusion."

"Troth, the deuce a temptation 'ud iver bother thim, while there was anyone else to be had, divil a one o' them 'ud be there at all, if they iver got the temptation to marry, och I know all about 'volunthry sayclusion,' I'd do it meself rather than be an ould maid."

"I think," Guy said, laughing, "that you are in as much danger of one of these, as the other, but you should be a little more partial to these virtuous ladies than you are. I'll not speak any more of them, lest you should condemn them altogether."

"Well, sir," said the old cabman, rising from his seat, "ye may go in now and judge for yerself, here's the blessed saintly spot itself and a dale more snug and genteel it looks than my little house. Now, I'd bet me Sunday brogues, 'tis yerself'll be sorry such fine young women 'ud believe in volunthary sayclusion. When you get inside them walls ye'll see that 'tis jokin' I was, an' that there's fine specimins of beauty and gentility there that 'ud make quare havic among your own kind, if they remained outside," he said laughing broadly, and poking the end of his whip into Guy.

"I dare say, Crowley, but my mission here is strictly a charitable one, and I don't intend to let anything else distract me from it," said Guy, good humoredly, and as Crowley knotted the cracked leather lines around a trimly painted post that stood by the entrance, Guy closed the modest little gate and walked steadily up the gravel path, to the long low square building that stood before him. There were even rows of small windows, tastily but simply decked in muslin screens and showing dainty bows of spotless ribbons; a few pots of blooming plants standing outside on the broad flat sills lent a charm to the quiet beauty of the shining panes and the muslin screens. Neat beds in the front of the house were covered with the richest flowers, and well trimmed lawns sloping away at either side of the spacious building, thrust the idea of primness on the intruder. As a limit to the grounds were groves of tall thick trees encircling all the well-kept *parterre* within.

There was a low, broad verandah in front of the house whose steps Guy had just mounted, and when about to drop the shining knocker he held in his hand, the saddest, sweetest strains of a human voice he had ever heard, arrested the movement. He laid the heavy "dog's head" quietly back and walked a couple of steps towards the end of the platform, which commanded a view of the rear lawn, with its summer-houses, and vines, and rockeries, and all such lovely elements, which contributed towards making the rustic nook a veritable paradise.

Glancing stealthily through the green lattice-work that separated him from the grounds, Guy saw, with intense admiration and wonder, the figure of a young and lovely girl, seated on a low rustic bench, with a great, shaggy dog crouched at her feet. She held within her dainty hands, a small book covered in black cloth, and swinging from the end of which was a long silk tape and a medal, with which her delicate fingers were toying carelessly. Presently she closed the little volume, bound the long tape around it, securing it with the tiny medal, then folding her hands, she raised her eyes, and in the saddest, sweetest and clearest tones, her musical voice warbled the words,—

> "Mother pure and mother mild
> Hear the wailing of thy child.
> Listen to my pleading cry,
> Hearken to my heart's deep sigh—"
> *Ora pro me*

The dreamy, dark eyes rested for a moment in their upturned attitude, the slender hands remained clasped tightly together, but only while the echo lingered of the sweet, sad voice, which had stolen from her lips as a breathing anthem from on high. Guy was mesmerized—lost to everything but the one vision which fascinated his gaze; he had ever been susceptible to beauty's influence—with some people, the silent contemplation of breathing beauty becomes a wild passion, and in Guy Elersley, appreciation of such eloquent loveliness was bordering on this superlative limit—and yet there was so little art about the being he was devouring with such greedy eyes. She wore a plain, neat costume of drab serge, a deep linen collar fastened high at her throat, and deep bands of the same at her wrists; her rich, dark hair was short and crept in large negligent waves over her shapely head, her face was very pale, which contrasted favorably with the dark hair and eyes, and the deep rich color of her well-curved lips. The close-fitting spencer jacket was gathered in with a very broad belt at her small waist, and the neat, heavy skirt fell in uninterrupted, plain folds to her ankles. Suddenly, while Guy watched her, she started as if waking from a lethargy, and turning to the animal that crouched lovingly beside her, she said, —

"Come Sailor dear, we are late for study hour."

Instinctively the brute roused and shook his shaggy fur at the sound of her voice, looking up trustfully into the kind face of his mistress. With a light and fleet step, Fifine turned towards the side entrance of the building, wherein she and her faithful companion vanished in a moment, leaving Guy petrified with silent wonder and admiration on the other side of the lattice work.

It would be impossible to describe the conflict of emotions that passed through Guy Elersley's breast at this moment; the bitter indignation he had felt up to this for Vivian Standish was nothing when compared with the inveterate contempt and hatred that substituted it at sight of this lovely wrecked flower, which he saw pining and withering in beautiful decline, far away from the world she could so easily have dazzled. It was with a dangerous light in his eyes, and a threatening vow in his heart, that Guy knocked this time at the broad hall door. His call was answered by an elderly woman of quiet, reserved appearance, who neither seemed surprised nor concerned by his visit. In as respectful and business-like a manner as possible, Guy asked for the lady directress of the institution, and was immediately shown by this silent noiseless woman into an apartment at the right, where she left him to wait alone in his wonder for a few moments.

The room was scrupulously neat, and tolerably well-furnished, but there was a painful simplicity and provoking fitness and quaintness about the things he saw, that upset his nerves uncomfortably. Every element of furniture was so intensely appropriate, and consistent with all the surroundings; the silence was so settled and sacred, and the noiseless tread of the inmates, as they glided here and there through the passages, almost irritated him. He was soon distracted from these trying observations, however, by the entrance of a dignified haughty-looking woman of about forty years; she was attired in the same simple costume which he had just admired on the young girl in the garden, except that her hair, sprinkled here and there with silver threads, was tucked neatly under an old-fashioned head-dress of muslin that strangely became her handsome face. Still standing a little inside the door-way, this cold, reserved woman looked enquiringly, and waited for Guy to speak his errand, whatever it might be.

"I have intruded here," Guy began with not too much confidence in his colloquial powers, "to enquire for a young girl named Josephine de Maistre, who, I am told was admitted here some time ago. I do not know the young lady personally," Guy frankly avowed, "nor have I ever spoken to her; but I have been entrusted with a very serious duty to discharge relative to her, and if it be not encroaching on your rules, I would be glad to interview the young lady."

An answer came in cold words, from an unmoved face:

"It is not our custom," the stately woman began, "to admit young male visitors to our home without urgent cause for so doing. Show me that you are justified in seeking a deviation from our custom, and I will grant it."

Guy fidgeted with his watch chain, and with a little hesitation which shewed how much he dreaded any indiscretion on his part, he asked,

"Are you acquainted with any details of Miss de Maistre's life before her coming here?"

With the same placid face, his companion answered,

"I know everything—she has had no secret from me."

"Then I am safe in broaching the subject to you," Guy answered more freely, and accordingly, in as brief terms as possible, he confided his mission to this haughty woman, leaving her then to judge for herself whether the responsibility bequeathed him by dying lips justified or not his intrusion within this quiet home. When he had finished, the set brow of his listener relaxed a little, into an almost involuntary expression of interest.

"You may see her presently," said the stern lady, "I am glad you have come so soon. It was very hard to persuade her at first that God's retribution would come time enough, she was so eager to avenge her wrongs with her own hand, but now that she has fully conquered her sinful desire for vengeance, God thinks fit to act. I will send her to you directly," and with these words she swept noiselessly out through the shadowy doorway, leaving Guy tangled up in the strangest sensations.

There was a moment of suspense before the dignified woman re-appeared, leading the beautiful heroine of his vision in the grounds into Guy's presence. There was a melancholy beauty in that face, whose memory never after ceased to haunt his heart. Something so appealingly sorrowful, and yet so coldly sad, that one pitied and admired and loved in the one glance. The long, dark lashes that fringed the white lids, and rested languidly on the pallid cheeks, every now and then shaded the deepest, dreamiest and most mournful eyes Guy had ever seen, and the subdued passion and smothered emotion that the keen glance might detect trembling on her full, red lips, was grander to Guy than anything else human he could conceive. Then the large, creeping waves of the dry, dark hair that encircled her intelligent brow, and nestled around her well-formed ears to her shapely neck behind, capped the climax of Guy's rapturous admiration.

The childish simplicity with which she stood before him coupled so strangely with a mien of reserve and independence, put Guy greatly at a loss to know how he was to take this strange creature. There was no conceit, no vanity, no empty pride accompanying all that dazzling beauty. Guy allowed that at one time this face must have worn becomingly the expression of coquetry—may be there was once a pleasure in showing this face to its best advantage, with the assistance of studied apparel, but now! all that was a buried past. There was now a look of wild, natural beauty that had not been fettered by rules of fashion or style; no attempt at effect in the plain, simple costume that clung so becomingly to her *svelte* figure. No artful use was made of those perfect features; she looked like a child-woman—so sweet, so innocent, so simple, and yet so grand, so sad, so serious.

Guy stretched forth his hand in a friendly way, as she entered, saying,

"We are strangers in one way, Mademoiselle de Maistre, but in a thousand ways we are very good friends, at least, such is my disposition towards you."

She placed her small, tender hand in his, and scanned his face a little doubtingly.

The majestic lady "directress" encircling the girl in her arms, said earnestly,

"I will leave you with this gentleman; trust him, my dear, he is your friend," and then she very considerately left the room.

Guy, on finding himself alone with the object of his search, entered into business immediately.

His voice was touchingly respectful and sympathetic as he addressed Fifine.

"I hope," he began, "that you will not object to my recalling certain events of your past life, mademoiselle. I have been commissioned to bear you a message, relative to a detail of your unusually sad experience, but I would first like to know that it does not pain you too much to hear your past repeated."

"Oh, sir!" she said, clasping her hands and looking devoutly up, "don't spare me on that account. When we have been able to do wrong, we should be able to bear the consequences, whatever they be. Besides, my past has never been a past to me—all is as vivid to-day as it was in the first hours of my experience. I have only memory left me from that frightful past."

"Then we may as well proceed to the point immediately," added Guy, who was feeling slightly uncomfortable over the task.

"I am a doctor by profession, mademoiselle, and have, for the last few years, been practising in the city of New York. Some months ago I was summoned to the bed-side of a man in typhoid fever, in whom I recognized an old school friend. He was evidently delighted at the freak of good fortune that brought us together, for, as he told me, there was a secret gnawing at his heart, that he longed to disclose. I sat down beside him and heard, mademoiselle, from his fevered lips, the shameful account of a wedding ceremony, of which you were such an unfortunate victim."

Fifine was clutching her fingers convulsively, and there was a look of suppression in her sad face that touched Guy, he was, however, anxious to get through with his disagreeable tale, and hurried on.

"He bade me seek you out, mademoiselle, only to tell you that since that eventful night, he has wandered through life, dogged and shadowed by a cruel remorse, which ultimately laid him on the bed where I found him. One thing he craved with his dying lips, mademoiselle, that the message be borne you from him, of your freedom; that you be told how that ceremony was a mockery, null and void, and after this disclosure, if pardon were possible, that you might try to forgive him his blind share in the disgraceful deed. The person I allude to, mademoiselle, was the pretended clergyman who married you that night." He looked now into the struggling face beside him, he knew the conflict that was raging in that soul. The trembling lips parted while he watched, and he heard the low murmur of a sanctified soul, as it breathed. "As we forgive them that trespass against us," she answered back the look of anxious enquiry he cast upon her face for a moment, and then cried:

"Do you say I am free? Not bound to anyone? Untrammelled all this time that I have lived in imaginary slavery, oh, how much I have suf—" but she checked the impulse that bade her murmur, and said instead, "because I have done wrong myself, I can forgive. *I* know how the guilty heart craves for pardon, how the loaded conscience aches for relief, and therefore, you can take my entire forgiveness back to the penitent who asks it. After all," she continued, in a sort of soliloquy, "forgiveness *is* easier than revenge."

"You are a noble little soul," said Guy, touched by the piety and fervor of this blighted little heart.

"Ah, sir! it is not that," Fifine said regretfully, "I might have been that, if I had lived contentedly among the comforts, where God had so generously placed me, and not sighed to adopt a world of sin and shame, rather than sacrifice it. I can never be that now. I have killed my poor loving father: I have blighted my life—there is only penance and atonement now to bid me hope," then passing her hand wearily over her eyes, she exclaimed in a long sigh, "So strange, all this! I thought that ugly chapter was over and done with, for everyone but me. And this man that sent you, who is he?" queried she.

In words as brief and clear as possible, Guy told her the story of his night by Nicholas Bencroft's bed-side, dwelling emphatically upon the pitiful effects that remorse and reverses had left, where innocence and prosperity had once been. The girl's face clouded at intervals, as she listened to the strange, touching recital, and she felt a sympathy in the end, for this other poor victim, who, like herself, had been led into evil, blindfolded.

After a long, long interval, Guy rose to depart, not however, without having made every arrangement with Fifine that was necessary to render her justice, and give Vivian Standish his due. Even towards this latter, she would not now indulge feelings of her old hatred. She asked that he be dealt with as leniently as possible, "for, sir," she argued, "the wicked are wicked only because of their weakness. They are *so* much weaker than the good; and just as the man of physical strength is merciful with one who is physically weak, so should the rule apply to moral strength, and let him who can brave temptation deal gently with the poor, weak sinner." And then they parted to the time, Fifine having agreed to seek permission to enable her to take any active steps that should be deemed necessary for the rendering of calm, quiet justice to Vivian Standish's victims.

CHAPTER XXXIV

When Peace and Mercy, banish'd from the plain,
Sprung on the viewless winds to heaven again
All, all forsook the friendless, guilty mind,
But Hope the charmer, hunger'd still behind.
  —*Campbell.*

The gold and amber leaves, turned their withered edges inward, and fell, in sear, crisp decay, from the half-naked trees. The flowers were all dead. The songs of the summer birds were entirely hushed, and thus stripped of all its rustic beauty, Ottawa stood, in mid-autumn, awaiting the pleasure of winter.

It was the season, which of all others, appealed most eloquently to Honor Edgeworth's heart, to her, the season of "falling leaves" and "moaning winds," was nature's most sympathetic response, gratifying, as it did, the melancholy tendency in her nature.

The dear, dead summer, had fled into that vast eternity. Little, trifling experiences, that at one time meant almost nothing, looked precious and eloquent, now that her eyes viewed them, with that backward glance, which one casts so sorrowfully on the things that are receding from them forever. Little words she had heard, little kindnesses she had felt, little songs she had sung, aye, and even little tears she had shed! all were wafted back for one delightful moment of sweet regret. She stood by the window again, as she did a year ago, two and three years ago, as she would, likely, in years to come, sunk in a reverie, watching the leaves fall, as they fell a twelve-month since; the leaves were just the same, the sky seemed still unchanged, the wind chanted the same weird, lonely lamentation, only *she* was different, something had come into her life in that interval of years, and had gone out of it again, leaving it so desolate, so aimless, so blank! She had had a good draught from the cup of life, since that other autumn evening, when she stood at this very window, moralising on the transient nature of all mortal things. She had drunk deeply enough to know, that for souls like hers, happiness, is scattered among briars and thorns; she was a wiser, a sadder, perhaps even a better girl, this autumn day, but she was not happier, oh no!

In a slow, solemn procession, the items of her years' experience, passed before her eyes, between the dead leaves and the closed window pane, she saw a panorama of memory. She was looking back with a sorrowful gratification upon the work of a couple of twelve-months, sighing now and then, smiling now and then, but never very happy over the suggestive souvenirs.

Altogether, Honor Edgeworth, had nothing of the superficialities, which characterize the majority of Ottawa young ladies, who have the "splendid advantages," and "glorious times" that she enjoyed. One was easily convinced, on knowing her, that riches and light pleasures, such as delight the average society girl, could not constitute her happiness, she shared these things out of a sense of duty, because it was customary for girls in her position to do so, but principally because Mr. Rayne had expressed a wish to that effect. She had been, and not unknowingly, the subject of sublime envy for a whole season in Ottawa, and had created no little *furore* in a succession of stylish watering-places during the summer spell, and yet, here she was, after all that, in the face of another winter of gaiety and excitement, with the same cold indifference in her heart, and the same reserve and dignity in her manner.

Henry Rayne, was fast declining in health. The exertions of an active life were beginning to tell seriously on him, his heart troubled him, and his head troubled him, and Honor's future troubled him more than either. He continually worried and thought over the time, when he would not be nigh to protect her, or guide her: her welfare was about the only mental problem he tried to solve, as he sat through the long hours of the day wrapped up in a cushioned *fauteuil.*

Vivian Standish, still flickered around the flame awaiting his doom; there was hope for him, while Henry Rayne regarded him, in the favorable light he did. His past career, seemed to have become a blank to him now, he could not understand how retribution had not caught up to him in the race, and so dropped trying to: he did not fear Bencroft, for his share of the guilt was about equal, but the magnanimity, or idiocy, of the "little one" if she had survived, he thought to be very convenient; of course, if through his instrumentality, she had passed into a fairer and a better land, why so much the better for all parties concerned. He had held himself on the "look out" for months after his vile commission, ready, for the first insinuation of his guilt, that went abroad, but now that the period had lengthened into years, and he had pretty nearly exhausted the wages of his deed, he felt a sort of protection, and blotted out all uncomfortable reminiscenses from his memory. He had laid himself out, now, to play another little game, but this game, in its *dénouement* had surprised him more than he expected.

Being a conceited fellow, he did not relish indifference, much less, marked coldness, nearly so well, as the pronounced admiration, with which he was wont to be received, but with all his attractions and efforts, he could only extract the most rigid politeness from Honor Edgeworth. "Bad beginning," he thought, as he tugged his long moustaches, and smiled superciliously with his handsome lips and dreamy eyes. Vivian Standish, for so many years, by profession a deceiver, had at length, made a false step which compromised himself seriously, as quietly and neatly, and securely as he had ever entrapped any victim, he was now entrapping himself in his own very meshes. Very coldly and mechanically indeed, he had planned his courtship with Honor Edgeworth, a thing, in his intentions to be a pure calculating process, a speculation, and now unknown to himself, almost unfelt by himself, his low ambition had led him into a snare; he began to grow uncomfortable under the calm, steady gaze of this dignified girl, he measured his words, and restricted himself generally, which in itself, was the strangest possible thing for him to do. He began to feel, that to lose her now, would make something more than a pecuniary difference to him, he had transferred the object of his craving from her dowry to herself, and to feel that he really wanted something which in any way could add to his material comfort, was, in itself the most powerful stimulus, that Vivian Standish had ever known. The fact that he worked out his own gratification sustained him through many a discouragement; may be it will cause no one to wonder either, for when one has gone through fire and water for someone else, one's heart clings almost involuntarily to him ever after, one's interest never dies out where his welfare is at stake.

It had been thus, with Vivian Standish, but the object of his daring deeds had been his own other self; that never satisfied nature of humanity, which, continually cries for more, that unreasonable element of our existence, that is not content, when we have dipped our trembling hands in the sluggish, sullied waters of sin and shame, to gather the little bright deceptive flower they craved to hold, something that looks so tempting and precious on the dangerous water's edge, but which when gathered becomes offensive, and is cast so recklessly aside. How many of us there are, that sit in moody silence, grieving and wondering over our own ingratitude to ourselves; peevishly grumbling at our moral poverty, scanning with pitying disgust the persistent weakness of our natures, sighing with a hopeless resignation over a miserable destiny of broken resolutions and vain attempts, and wondering when it will all end, and relieve our burdened souls.

Vivian Standish, had become a moral wreck, more by accident than by nature. Phrenologists would scarcely have defined his handsome features as indicative of wickedness in the soul, but the victim of a mistaken vocation, has always been known to carry his propensities to the very worst limit; ending generally when all hope is vain, and amendment an impossibility. Sometimes one does hear of the evil-doer being overtaken in his dark course by the voice of conscience; a warning whisper, from some spirit-like voice, has occasionally stayed the hand of the murderer, the self-destroyer, the robber, or the drunkard; but I fear, it is a more familiar thing, to every one of us, to know, that when a man has once determinedly begun his downward course, it is rarely, he stops at the precipice; if he has risked great things on one occasion, he will hazard greater dangers on many occasions, never waiting, never halting, to think or to regret until he reach the final hazard which is life itself, consequently death itself, and then the awful sequel which is hushed, or whispered in a trembling breath, like a horrible ghost story, the consequences of eternal darkness, and agony, and despair.

The winter set in at Ottawa, the cold north-east winds blew over the bare streets and through the naked trees for days and weeks, and then, the soft, white, noiseless snowflakes stole over the desolate city, making it suddenly as bright and lively and cheerful, as it had been dreary and melancholy before.

December, with snow and cold, and icicles and sleighbells, substituted the lovely "fall," and turned the wearisome scenes of summer remnants, into the gay, sparkling picture of lively winter.

It was December, and Honor Edgeworth's lover had not proposed yet. Henry Rayne had still serious misgivings relative to Honor's real sentiments, which prevented him from encouraging Standish to take the final step. All through the summer and autumn months, Honor and he had been thrown a great deal together, he had given up his occupations elsewhere, and was now permanently established at Ottawa; in the mornings, when Honor drove or walked up town, to do her shopping, she often met him, either lunching at the confectioners, or coming out of the Post Office, or standing aimlessly at the Russell House entrance: invariably, he joined her, carrying all her small parcels, if she walked, or helping her in and out of her tiny phaeton if she drove. Every eye, any way trained in matrimonial calculations had given its knowing wink, at these two, which translated from eye-language means, "they're going it," or "that's a match:" other girls who did their shopping all by themselves, sighed wearily at "some people's luck," and turned their heads purposely aside, to admire some grand display of millinery, or jewellery, or whatever distraction was at hand.

In the evenings, Love's "at home" hour, these two were always together, and if it was not to escort her to some place of entertainment, Vivian whiled the delicious hours away strolling leisurely around the grounds of Mr.

Rayne's house by Honor's side—thrown sleepily on some rustic bench beside her, with his well-flavored cigar between his handsome lips, and the dreamiest sort of love looks floating between his half-closed, deeply-fringed lids, muttering half audibly those thrilling little nothings that seem so consistent with pretty ears, and a half-averted, blushing face in the autumn twilight. When the evenings grew too chilly, even with a provokingly becoming wrap and tiny skull cap, perched on the back of her head, Honor and her devoted admirer spent their time within doors, playing, singing, or chatting suspiciously with their feet on the fender. Honor had never thought it necessary to question the propriety of encouraging this intimacy with a man whom she would never love, it seemed quite pleasant to her to have some one who could talk intelligently and make himself generally interesting, always by her—satisfying herself that she might safely measure his sentiments of regard by her own, and, therefore, never dreaming of any serious result from their amusing pastimes.

There are so many girls in Ottawa that like very much having an admirer, an ardent lover even, if he suits their fancy enough to make other girls jealous, or even worthier-minded girls can comfortably endure an intelligent, accomplished young fellow to pay them these snug little attentions for a whole season. There is something in a certain species of the genus girl which quite overcomes her at times, when she feels so lonely and so blue that nothing in all sublime creation can restore her but the soothing odor of a cigar, the deep, earnest accents of a certain smoker of that cigar, and the clasp of the strong, firm hand that has placed that delightful weed between those suggestive lips,—when on a winter evening she steals alone into the drawing room and lowers the vulgar glare of the gas until everything is misty and undefined as her own heart, and then throwing herself on the spacious *fauteuil* before the grate fire, soars into the world of her imagination, and is happy with her heart's idol for a few dreamy hours, or depositing herself carelessly on a cosy sofa, she throws her arms over her shapely head, and spins away at the cobwebs of her thoughts and wishes, and regrets, but always on the *qui vive*, listening for *a* step, *a* voice, and wondering now and then, with a start, whether it was the very material door-gong that she heard, or only the dim, intangible echo of a wild wish in her agitated heart. Oh! you little group of "teens," there is a day coming! Brush away those filmy cobwebs of your pleasant dreams; they are hiding your reality. Shut out that mass of "tangled sunbeams" that interrupts your future; there is a pall over the heart, now bounding in its untold delight. There are tears in the dreamy, wistful eyes; there is suffering portrayed on the pretty face; the spirit of anguish keeps its steady guard at the threshold of those smiling lips—but—what have I done? Oh! forgive me, youth now tangled in those golden meshes. I unsay the words, mine must not be the tyrant hand to tear away the screen a merciful Father has placed between you and what is to come. No! no! smile and dream and hope and wait on.

One evening, as Henry Rayne lay reclining among his cushions before the glowing coals, Honor and Jean d'Alberg burst in upon him in his solitude, full of fresh, blooming spirits, laughing and feeling numb with cold.

"Here? you selfish old pet," Honor said, running towards him, "toasting your limbs by the fire, so cosily, when your little girl is freezing on the streets, starved and numb!"

The old man leaned back his white head on the velvet upholstering, and looked lovingly into the bright, happy, blushing face of the girl standing behind him, then taking both her little "frozen" hands in his dry, warm ones, he squeezed them tenderly, saying—

"To be sure, you are numb, you lovely little witch. Have you been firing snow-balls, or shovelling snow or what?"

"Most likely," Honor answered with mock dignity, "a young lady aspiring to the wisdom of her twenties is sure to spend her time firing snow-balls against the fence."

"Oh, no of-*fence* to you, frozen queen," Henry Rayne interrupted, looking shyly up to see how his pun was appreciated.

"Not a bad attempt for a dull mind at all," the girl said laughingly, "don't forget it, and I'll give you a chance to use it again, when there's more appreciation in the room than there is just now."

"Come, come, you little humbug, take off that gigantic sacque, and sit down here; *upun* my word I won't make any more of those nasty *jeu de mots*."

"Oh, I see you are a hopeless case," Honor said, sighing heavily, at the same time undoing lazily the great seal fastenings of her seal coat, as he bade her. She then drew out the long pins from her velvet "poke" and removed that becoming article from her head.

"Give them to Jean," Mr. Rayne said, motioning backward, "she will be going up directly."

"It is well she has transferred herself to that place already," Honor replied, "or she would not be too flattered to think that her presence had made such a little impression all the while."

As she delivered this little speech, she touched her dainty fingers to the bell beside her, and when Nanette appeared in the doorway, she gave her

her costly bundle of street wear to carry away upstairs, and as the faithful attendant piled them respectfully on her arm, Honor prepared to seat herself beside her guardian, for a "little chat."

"Well, I hope you're ready at last, dear knows it does take a time for you females to get out of your finery," Henry Rayne said in assumed impatience.

"There now, don't grumble out in 'sour grapes' style," Honor replied, playfully, "you can't blame anyone if you did not happen to be a nice young girl, to wear poke bonnets and jerseys, and becoming little nothings— we know you poor unfortunate males are half dead with envy, when you contrast your clumsy suits, every one's the same to look at, with the endless variety of our costumes, but all the same you can't say it's anyone's particular fault that you have all been great grizzly men."

"Well, upon my word," Henry Rayne laughed in astonishment, "I hope you have an idea of your sex—come, stop that silly babble about men pining for a transformation, and sit you down here near me; I want to talk of something more reasonable than that. Surely you're ready now?"

"Yes, quite—oh! but wait one minute—Nanette," she called, balancing herself on her dainty toes, towards the door, "I'll take my handkerchief from my muff, please,—there," as she shook out the dainty scented folds of a lawn handkerchief, "I am quite, quite, quite ready—begin when *you* like, and end when I like."

She drew over a tiny footstool and sat upon it, and nestled her head on the arm of Henry Rayne's chair. Lovingly he stole his trembling hand over it, and as he toyed with her graceful curls, he began to tell her his little secrets—

"Honor, you've been going out a great deal of late," he began,

"Oh, don't lecture me for always being out late," she interrupted, provokingly.

"Now don't you say another word, little puss, until your elders consent."

"Very well then, cross elder, go on," said she, taking his hand in hers and rubbing it gently up and down her velvet cheek.

"But perhaps you feel like prattling a little, after coming in," he interrupted, half regretfully, "so, let you begin, tell me where you've been this afternoon, and what you saw, and all about it, and when I've shown you by example what a patient listener is, I shall expect a return of courtesy when my turn comes."

"Well, if it isn't just dreadful to have to yield to the caprices of some people," murmured Honor, with pretended resignation, and then glancing reassuringly up at the kind old face above her, she began—

"This afternoon, didn't you know, we went to the matinee—Miss Reid, Mr. Apley, Aunt Jean, Vivian and the *charming* Miss Edgeworth, all together.

"To the matinee, eh little one? And did you like it?"

"Well, I love the theatre, any way," argued Honor, "and so I liked the performance to-day, it was rather—exalted."

"Exalted, was it?" Henry Rayne said in a listening sort of repetition, "how exalted?"

"Oh, first a love match—vows of fidelity—a wedding—a neglected wife—a husband that flirts—then quarrels, and tears, and rage, and despair, and the other party that is always a handsome man, to sympathize with the afflicted wife, then jealousy, threats and a duel, and the love match all over again."

"Well, well," laughed Mr. Rayne, "that is as well as if I saw it all. I think you take to 'exalted' phases of the drama—don't you, little one?"

"Well, you see," she said, shaking her head wisely, "other people's miseries and misfortunes, seem so romantic and exalted to us—there's the secret; I'm sure there's nothing we girls relish more than the story of some newly-wedded pair that disagree, of a wife who pines in sentimental solitude, or revenges herself in tragic retribution—that is great excitement for us—but amiable as any of us are, I don't think we'd consent to make romance for our girl friends at such a cost as that, do you?"

"Well, I rather hope you would not," Mr. Rayne answered, with a smile.

"How true it is though," Honor continued, "that we are all so much better adapted to bear one another's burdens of life than we are our own, we are always ready to say 'If we were they, we should never have done such and such things in such and such circumstances,' and after all, I do not think that in our own emergencies, we do one whit better, do you?"

"You are right there, child," her guardian answered, reflectively, "under our trying circumstances we always want to do our best, and yet our neighbors cannot help fancying that in our places they could have exercised so much more discretion than we—that is the way we make mistakes in life, attributing force and virtue to ourselves, which could only make themselves manifest were we in other people's shoes."

"Now, you think just like I do, I am so glad, because Vivian didn't, he said he thought other people, at least *some* other people, always did things infinitely better than he could do them."

"Did he?" queried Mr. Rayne, with a mischievous chuckle, "well, I suppose that those *'some other people'* actually can, in his eyes. I wonder who he meant?"

"I am sure I don't know," said Honor, tapping her foot nervously on the shining fender, "but we both agreed that if such a thing happened in real life as was represented on the stage to-day, the man who thus slighted and neglected any woman he had promised to cherish and love, should be punished just as far as justice and humanity could go in punishing him."

"That is certainly true," said Mr, Rayne, "the punishment, in my eyes, should equal the crime, and the crime, I think, is unpardonable—but come now, we've talked enough about these awful things; I want my turn—you see—Honor, this is the fifth of December."

"Yes."

"And Christmas will be in three weeks more."

"I guess I know that," Honor said meaningly.

"Well, I want you to do me a big favor this Christmas."

"Really?" said Honor, in surprise, "What big favor can I do for you?"

"I want you and Jean to organize—"

"What?"

"A splendid, big, grand—"

"Christmas pudding?"

"Not quite—but a 'stunning' ball, a real stylish ball; ask everyone you know; throw the doors wide open and give an entertainment with great *éclat*. You must empty the drawing-room quite out, have the orchestra engaged, and a *menu* that will outrival everything. I want a jolly, rattling Christmas merriment that everyone will remember ..."

Honor looked quickly up, and said in a tone of astonishment:

"Well, dear old baby, I hope you have a queer notion at last—why, that would be no end of fuss and worry and trouble."

"No matter," he answered, "get help everywhere for everything. I told you first, because you can coax aunt Jean better than I can, don't 'go back on me' now, after I've confided my little plan to you. I expect a great deal of help from you."

"All right then," said Honor, striking one tightly clenched little hand down on the open palm of the other, "if it costs so much that we will all have to sell out and beg for New Year's, you need not blame me; I'll give you all the help you want, don't fear, but when the fun is over, I hope you won't have too much trouble to help yourself."

"Never mind the consequences," her guardian answered good-humoredly.

And so it was settled that there would be a grand ball at Mr. Rayne's house during Christmas week; the invitations were issued and busy preparations begun by all hands. The long drawing room and library were opened into one, and all their furniture conveyed into other apartments. The dining room and comfortable morning room, or family *boudoir*, were also opened into one large refreshment room. The little study under the balcony (down which Guy had climbed on the eventful night of his escapade) was fitted up for a *tête-a-tête* corner, with comfortable arm-chairs, bird cages and sweet smelling plants. Then there were decorations made of palm and flags, and millions of sundry other things to crowd into a little space of time.

Vivian saw little of Honor during these days of endless fuss and bustle, but he appeared satisfied to sit and chat quietly with Henry Rayne, who was unable to share in the general riot and confusion. There seemed to have sprung a strange intimacy between these two men, and this link was no other than Honor Edgeworth, in fact, she was so dear to the heart of her kind guardian that it warmed to anyone who showed an interest in her. One evening as Vivian and Mr. Rayne chatted together in the latter's study, Honor broke in upon them, holding between her dainty hands a steaming bowl of broth, which she commanded Mr. Rayne to "devour there and then." Obediently as a child, he supped the wholesome draught, and when he had drained the last spoonful, she kissed him hurriedly on the brow and bustled out again, smiling pleasantly, and telling her guardian he was "a real good boy."

When the door had closed upon her, Henry Rayne, turning to Vivian, said half sadly.

"She is the sweetest girl under the sun, I think my heart would break without her."

"Then I think you might sympathise more ardently with me," the young man answered, half doggedly, "I am nearly tired of waiting for that opportunity that never comes."

"Don't blame me, boy, before you know," was the serious retort, "I am trying my skill in your cause all this while. It is solely in your interest that I have planned this Christmas festivity. I can imagine no moment more propitious for the pleading of your cause, than one snatched from the confusion and excitement of such an hour, when the heart is made suggestive by strains of music and peals of laughter and sounds of gaiety and gladness everywhere."

"You are right," Vivian said, smiling. "I did not give you credit though, for so much sentimentality."

"It is not that," the old man answered sadly. "No, my dear boy, but, no matter how capricious and fickle time is, it cannot alter the heart. What is love to-day, was love in my day, and for ages before, and will be to the end of time. It is a very universal passion, and is easily aroused. A note of music, a breath, a sigh or a little pressure of the hand may be enough to call it out from its hidden nook within the heart. You can't tell me what it is to love, my boy, nor can I tell you, though we've both passed through the experience, the explicable part is a prominent part, I admit, if we analyse the little creeping sensations of gladness, that a touch of her hand, no matter how inadvertent, or the steady gaze of her deep eyes, could cause us to feel. Why, my dear boy, I am an old man now, but my memory is young yet, and I dwell on this dear page of my past, with the same feelings of gratification that animate you on your first experience. I don't know now, any more than I did then, though I'm an older and a wiser man, what there is in a woman's clear eye, a woman's voice or a woman's hand, to make us shiver and creep, and unman us the way they do; but perhaps 'tis the mystery makes the charm, if so, may it never be unravelled, for a fellow's love days are about the only things which can compensate him for the misery of the rest of his life."

This, contrary to appearances, fell as gall on the heart of Vivian Standish, he who had never loved with a pure, unsullied devotion, grieved to hear of the joys of one who had. It is bad enough, that certain luxuries of life have been denied us, either through our own folly or the still less bitter interference of others. How much worse it becomes when we are forced to listen to the story of their worth, from those who have gained what we have so recklessly lost! Such words as those addressed by Henry Rayne, were perhaps the only ones that could impress the hardened heart of Vivian Standish with a hatred for the crimes and follies of his life.

CHAPTER XXXV

My latest found—
Heaven's last, best gift.
My ever new delight
    —*Milton*

Christmas Eve of 188-, with all its soft, fleecy snow, its merry sleigh bells, its decorations, its plenty and its poverty, its rejoicings and its wailings, its hopes and its fears—the day of huge, warm fires and smouldering faggots, of sumptuous dinners and scanty crusts, the night of all others, that the satisfied thanksgiving of the rich, and the heart-rending craving of the pauper, meet at the throne of God.

At noon of this bright, merry Christmas Eve, among the many passengers on board the mid-day train that rushed into the Union Depot, was one who interests us more than all the business fathers, school girls, or college students, or other absent members of Ottawa families, returning to spend Christmas with their friends. He is a young, good-looking man, in a long sealskin coat and cap. As the bell ceases its clanging on reaching the platform, he seems to pull his cap down purposely, and otherwise to gather himself into the plushy depths of his warm furs, he hires the first cabman that accosts him, shoves in his heavy valise, which is all the baggage he has, and in a gruff sort of voice, orders to be driven to the "Albion Hotel." There is nothing surprising in it at all, the gentleman certainly looks like a "Russell House" patronizer, but then the "Albion" is quiet and secluded, and perhaps this gentleman prefers it to the endless noises of greater hotels. The gratified cabman, happy over his hasty bargain, which delivered him from a half hour's stamping of feet and clapping of his fur covered hands, never cares to wonder whether the occupant of his sleigh is a disguised swindler or an Earl *in-cog*, but jingles his sleigh bells hurriedly in the direction of Nicholas street.

Christmas Eve, with a pale, clear moon, shining placidly down on the still, white features of nature; the tall, bare boughs, sprinkled with the afternoon's flakes, are showing out brightly in the silver light of the Christmas moon, great soft feathery masses of white clouds chase fair Luna through the deep ethereal blue of the heaven's vault.

From every respectable direction in the city, sleighs are speeding merrily along with their dainty bundles of woollen wraps and tucked-up skirts. Prim young gentlemen, in their shiny swallow-tails, with their creaseless white cravats and little scarlet buds in their buttonholes, work their way into top coats and fur jackets, and dropping their latch-keys into their breast pockets, start off, all going in the same direction, towards the grand dwelling on Sandy Hill, that everyone knows to be Henry Rayne's.

Apart from Rideau Hall, which is the grand centre of all festivities and pleasures, for those who sojourn in Ottawa during the winter months, there are a few other places whose very names are pleasant to the ear, on account of the warm hospitality they suggest, but were Ottawa in general, far more sociable and hospitable a city than it is, we would scarcely consider that it merited any special eulogy on that account, for, if it were willing to profit by the great advantages it enjoys over other cities, of learning how to render itself agreeable, generous and worthy, in its social relationship with its people, it could not follow a more admirable example than is set by its much esteemed, much beloved ruler.

The pity is, that the old enthusiasts, and the early promoters of Bytown's prosperity, could not have lived to see the day, on which their little town became an important city, the capital of a grand Dominion, and the home of Royalty. That His Excellency the Marquis of Lorne, and his Royal Consort, the Princess Louise, should come amongst us to take up their abode, is in itself a proud boast, not alone for Ottawa, but for Canada at large, but that in their amiable condescension, they should throw open the portals of their home, and receive with such gracious and unaffected courtesy, their humble inferiors, overflows the heart of Canadian society with intense gratification.

What a suasory example it is for those, who through some freak of fortune, being enabled to shake off the dust of honest toil and industry, are very ready to look downward with contempt upon the rank they have just left. What must they think of our noble, hospitable Governor, and Her Royal Highness Princess Louise, who so amiably and courteously receive social inferiors within their home? How can *they* feed themselves with a shallow pride, and affect a ridiculous superiority, when the daughter of Her Most Gracious Majesty, Queen Victoria, will condescend to assemble under her own roof, persons of a social grade so far removed from her own.

But in profiting by this lavish display of hospitality, Canada contracts a debt, and incurs an obligation, which she will not hesitate to pay generously and willingly, with profoundest love, admiration and loyalty. Such names as those of our Governor-General and of his Royal Consort, become engraven upon the heart of the country, for future generations to revere, honor and admire.

We will now return to the remote cause of these just reflections, to the residence of Henry Rayne, who is indeed one of Ottawa's distinguished entertainers.

Floods of brilliant gas-light stream out through the windows, illuminating the shaded avenue and blending with the modest light of the full moon outside. Inside the air is heavy with the perfumes of decorations and blooming flowers. Exquisitely made adornings greet one at every turning. In a room opposite to the drawing room, are Jean d'Alberg and Honor Edgeworth, ready to receive their guests: the former looks very imposing in a dress of myrtle green plush and pale blue, brocaded satin, which is most becomingly made, and which, with a pair of diamond earrings and a matronly little head dress, comprises her whole *toilette*.

Honor is a marvel of feminine loveliness, her brow as white as marble, and her hair creeping over it in its chestnut waves, has a beautiful effect; there is an enhancing flush of excitement on her cheeks, and her eyes sparkle with unusual brilliancy. Attired in a long flowing dress of white waterplush and satin, from which hang on all sides, little trembling fringes of delicate white pearls, Honor is more like a vision of the supernatural than anything real. Where her costly robe falls in graceful folds to her dainty shoes and sweeps over the floor for yards behind, it is literally covered with natural rosebuds and sprigs of heliotrope that rival with the loveliness of her whom they adorn. Her bare white neck is encircled by strings of tiny pearls, coils of pearls are also twisted in her dark brown hair, making her a breathing goddess of loveliness and wonder, as she stands awaiting her guests' arrivals.

"I will have time to run and say a word to dear Mr. Rayne," Honor says, gathering up her handsome skirt and skipping out of the room, she races up the stairs with the recklessness of a child in its morning wrapper and knocks timidly at the door of the temporary sitting-room above. At the faint sound of "come in" she pushes open the door and stands in all her splendid array before Mr. Rayne.

"Do you know, I wish so much you could come down stairs," she said techily, "I am lonesome every second for you," and kneeling on one knee beside him, the lovely girl encircled the old man's neck with her bare white arms, caressing him childishly.

"Oh, ho!—come now, don't begin to play your little frauds on me, how lonely you are to be sure, looking like a queen in a vision, and ready to break a hundred hearts, be off, you are a dear little humbug, ha ha ha."

There was something of the old humor of long ago in the laugh that Mr. Rayne directed into Honor's pretty pink and white ear.

"What a voice!" Honor exclaimed in mock horror, "truly, you've quite deafened me with that terrible shout," and she frowned pettishly, putting her little gloved hands sympathisingly to her ears.

"Well, that will hold for a while," he answered mischievously, "you need not trouble yourself coming up to hear me again for a while."

"You mean old darling," the girl returned playfully, "I'll go down stairs and not think of you once more all night," and in another instant she was re-established below in all her dignity, while the pressure of her lips yet lingered in a sweet impression on Henry Rayne's cheek.

In an hour from that time the quiet, vacant apartments of Mr. Rayne's house were crowded with a fashionable and merry throng. Young faces beamed with gladness as they glided under the "mistletoe" with their partners, to the strains of dreamy waltzes. The programmes were all filled by now, and the evening's pleasures fully started. Everyone raved about Honor, and with reason, it was quite amusing to see how demonstrative the majority of the young ladies present tried to be with her, intending that this lavish display should be interpreted by the rest as a mark of the familarity which existed between them and Henry Rayne's handsome *protégée*.

Miss Sadie Reid, Miss Dash and Miss Mountainhead, and all last season's heroines were there, it is the best and worst feature of Ottawa society, that, like a circus, if you attend one fashionable entertainment, you have attended them all, the *belles* of one ball are the *belles* of another, and the wall-flowers of one are the wall-flowers of another.

"Honor, whose waltz is this?" said Vivian Standish, pausing before her and looking admiringly into her eyes.

"Oh dear, I don't know," said Honor in assumed despair, "I've lost my programme and am thrown quite on the mercy and veracity of my gentlemen friends. I regret to say—if you say this is yours—I cant refuse it, for I've neither programme nor memory to prove the contrary."

"I hope you may regain neither to-night, for I think, I must make you remember, you've promised me, all the other waltzes, to-night."

"Indeed, I doubt, if even this is yours," retorted she, "I've given you one already."

"It is a wonder you remember," he said, a little sadly. "Surely you do not regret it—any way this one is mine, and we are losing golden moments, all this while—come—" encircling her waist, and as the music made an appropriate *crescendo*, she heard him add in muffled enthusiasm, "My darling."

After waltzing a delightful, ten minutes or so, Vivian very artfully stopped, at the exit which led to the suggestive little *boudoir* outside, and stole away, with Honor on his arm, into a quiet recess, near the tall French window, from whence the moon-lit, snow-covered gardens were plainly visible, the gas-light inside was burning ever so low, a sweet sleepy sort of perfume filled the room, strains of a German waltz were creeping in twittering echoes into the little corner where this handsome couple had seated themselves, the critical moment had come. It was now, or never.

CHAPTER XXXVI

But happy they, the happiest of their kind
Whom gentle stars unite, and in one fate
Their hearts, their fortunes, and their beings blend

—*Thomson*

Guy Elersley, had long ago abandoned the noctivagent tendencies, that had only saddened and distracted his life, but to-night, as the clock struck nine, he deliberately closed the book he had been reading, with a heavy sigh, lit a cigar, and getting himself into his furs, he strolled noiselessly out, the great doorway of the quiet hotel and commenced an onward journey at a brisk pace. He heeded neither the flood of subdued light, that hung like a veil of hallowed glory over the earth, on this bright Christmas Eve, nor the busy pedestrians, who hurried to and fro, with well-filled baskets for to-morrow's celebrations. He did heed an odd beggar-child who stopped, to hold towards him a Christmas number of the "*Free Press,*" for a penny, or who still more appealingly extended a little bare frozen hand for charity. He had not far to go on this nights' ramble, but he walked thoughtfully along, like one, on a serious errand, the old familiar sights of other days distracted him somewhat, his eyes wandered mechanically over the walls of the little church of St. Alban, the martyr, whose angular spire, stood prominently out in the clear moonlight. A corner away from this, and the glittering roof of St Joseph's Church attracted his gaze, he was passing close by it now, and a strange instinct directed his steps towards it; he pushed open the yielding door, and stood in the streaming moonlight, among vacant pews, and holy stillness. The Christmas decorations were just discernible by the flickering light of the sanctuary lamp, and from the windows and altars of the quiet little church, the faces of hallowed saints looked down in their venerable simplicity, making the moonlight that made visible their holy smiles, sanctified and imposing. Guy Elersley had many qualities, both good and evil, but he was as innocent of church- going, as he was of murder; of that, at least no one had ever yet accused him, nevertheless there was a dormant religious enthusiasm in that young breast, which needed but the touch of the right hand on the yielding chords of a full heart, to call forth the melodious strains of an impromptu chant of praise from the creature to his Creator. The soul of our youth of to-day, resembles in many cases a musical instrument, which stands in its grandeur and magnificence, unopened and untouched, the cobwebs of neglect grow over the elegant framework, the dust of ages cloud its wonderful beauty, because there are no hands to touch its magic strings, and call forth the hidden melody it contains, some day, the silence is broken by hazard, a note has been touched, which repeats and echoes its sweet melancholy, with such an eager pathos, that one regrets the many years of wasted ecstacies, which time has consumed, and which might have brightened a lonely life, if the secret had but been known. To-night, for the first time in his life, the chords of Elersley's heart, almost rusted, from their wearisome rest gave out such a soul-stirring melody, that he wondered himself at his susceptibility, he crept into one of the pews near him, and bowing down his head upon his trembling hands, he burst forth in a series of mental prayer, when he raised his eyes again, it seemed to him that an angel had come, and stolen away every burden of his life a calm, peaceful feeling had crept into his soul, banishing all the fears and anxieties of a moment before, he felt as if in the darkness, a bright star had broken forth, showing him the way to a better and a happier life, and as he pondered, he suddenly remembered that this was Christmas Eve, that in truth to-night a glorious star had risen, which would shed its hallowed light over all Christendom, and bring "Peace on earth to men of good-will."

He walked out of the holy edifice, feeling as he had never felt before in all his life—telling himself how much of life's sweetness he had thrown away in miserable exchange for its bitterness and gall. But though no word of determination or promise formed itself upon his lips, he felt a resolution filling him of future amendment, a desire to seek after the strange sweetness he had experienced to-night, and in this mood he pursued his way.

He too was attracted to-night towards the light and the music and the merry-making of Mr. Rayne's house.

A host of overwhelming recollections swam before his eyes as he neared the place; there, from the gate, he could see the fated balcony which had tempted and facilitated his stealthy exit on that wretched night when he had broken his uncle's stern command.

"It looks festive," he murmurs sadly, opening the gate noiselessly and striding up the frozen pathway, "but why need it pain me so?" he said, as if finishing a soliloquy, which would reproach his relations for so easily renouncing his memory.

Slowly and noiselessly he stole up the crusty walk until he found himself outside the tall French window in the recess under the moonlit balcony. He could hear the strains of music and the peals of merry laughter—bitter mockery at such a moment! He knew that while he suffered in suspense outside, *she* was the object of much admiration within, that the words of false flatterers charmed her ear, and the smile of pretended devotion gratified her heart. A man can bear much, but as it is in his love that he shows himself strongest, it is also— alas!—in his love that he is weakest. A true woman, then, must never encourage a passion in the heart of a man which she will not share with him to the very end. There are some things in life we can jest about and make trifles of, but we must spare the human heart. There is no jest, no levity appropriate where that is concerned. Not but that hundreds of heart-less beauties have toyed laughingly with such playthings all their lives—they have always done it, they do it still, and will likely continue to do it so long as the world remains what it is; but, all the same, we can never cease to regret that a woman should ever make such a vile mistake, she, whose mission in this life is one of heart, should never stoop to misapply the advantages that a wise Creator has confided to her, and whereby she finds her way directly to people's susceptibilities, to conquer them for a good cause for their sakes, her own sake, and God's.

Guy was sadder than ever to-night, for besides the customary melancholy of his life, he was under the painful influence, and in the very presence of pregnant associations, gone-by days were doubly visible and clear to him under the shadow of this dear old home that he had so recklessly sacrificed.

The snow was carefully swept away from the low, broad steps, and the thick covering of matting was comfortably visible in the moonlight. Guy stood to scan the brilliantly illuminated windows: There were figures gliding here and there through the rooms and corridors, shadows flitted to and fro, little strains of far-off music crept into his ears—nothing definable, certainly, sometimes just one deep note of the bass violin, or a little shrill twittering of a noisy part, but it made his poor heart ache, and it filled him with those unshed tears of smothered emotion that are spilled like gall upon the heart that no one sees. He had been watching for only a few moments, when a grating noise startled him. He slid into the shadow of a broad pillar, which supported the portico, and there stood still and expectant. A little silvery laugh right inside the window went straight to his heart, then followed a word or two in a musical masculine voice, then a strong effort, and yielding to it, the long French window opened with a creak.

Up to this Guy had had some chance of escaping, but now as he narrowed himself into the limits of the shadow cast by the huge pillar, he saw two figures advance and lean against the opposite casements of the open doors. At the same moment the moon sailed out from behind a pile of snowy clouds, and Guy Elersley saw with his greedy eyes—in all her loveliness, in all her dignity, in all her feminine grace—Honor Edgeworth, his heart's long-cherished idol, but she was not alone. Beside her was the tall, stalwart figure of a man in evening dress, whose head was inclined towards her, whose eyes were seeking hers with a tender expression of sentiment in their depths. In a moment Guy had caught the outlines of that face, and instinctively he clutched his hand and bit his lip, for he had recognized Vivian Standish flirting with the girl *he* loved. Her hand was now in his, and he was drawing her closer to him. The impulse filled Guy to dart forward and level those guilty arms that dared to encircle the sacred form of one so good and pure as she, in their sinful embrace, but he quelled it, determining, at any cost, to hear the issue of this strange *rencontre*—it would be the verdict upon which hung the life or death of his dearest hopes.

"Honor," he heard Vivian say, "you will surely take cold here in this open window."

"Nonsense," Honor said indignantly, "a fine night like this? I am not so susceptible as you think, nor as fragile a piece as I look."

Still toying distractedly with her little jeweled hand, Vivian continued:

"You may not be susceptible to cold, but you should be to warmth, such as my heart offers you, the heat of love's immortal flame—Honor—can you give me no hope that will make the future worth living for?"

"Surely," she answered seriously, "you have not lived such a worthless life, all these years, as leaves the future a perfect blank for you."

Guy fancied how Standish must have winced uncomfortably at her words, he wondered at the provokingly composed way, in which he answered her.

"It is not that exactly," he said, "though I am not at all surprised that you should think it of me, but, somehow, all the ambitions that have hitherto stimulated me, seem now to have dwindled into a secondary importance, of course, it is nothing to you, that my life has become one long miserable suspense, since destiny has thrown us together, because our little happinesses are no sacrifice in your great eyes, you cannot feel the smallest sympathy for a victim such as I, if it were a little terrier, you had unconsciously wounded, you would take it caressingly in your arms, and make a gentle atonement for your fault, but there is a difference between little terrier pups and human hearts, like mine—"

"Is there?" Honor said with a cutting sarcasm, which delighted Guy's heart, "you really are giving me a piece of information which I should never have gained from my own personal conclusions. But, have we not had enough of this romantic nonsense, Mr Standish? I think they have begun another dance."

"I don't care if they have," the handsome lover cried huskily, clasping Honor's hands passionately, and looking into her face with a sort of hopeless defiance, "I have a word to say, that has been long enough hanging unsaid upon my lips—hear me now—you must—Honor—I love you—and I want you to become my wife."

There was a breathless pause of a second—Guy feared the beatings of his heart would betray him—hungrily he waited to catch the word that would fall from Honor Edgeworth's lips—his rage, his contempt, his indignation, had all subsided during this interval of terrible suspense—he had forgotten for that little moment the depravity of the man before him, he only knew, that in Honor's eyes, this was a dashing, handsome, fascinating young fellow, and that the great crisis of his own life as upon him—one other minute and over the vista of coming years, would have settled a pall of hopeless darkness or a flood of gorgeous sunshine—he listened in smothered breaths, the moon hid herself behind a dark, curling cloud, he could not see now, but he heard the voice, that had filled his heart for years, speak out m firm and clear, though gentle accents.

"Mr. Standish," Honor said, "will you kindly release my hands from your uncomfortable grasp," his hands immediately fell by his sides, "I will not say your precipitation surprises me," she continued coldly, "somehow, nothing, that *you could* do, would actually surprise me, but I must say it displeases me. One instant, suffices for me, to review my conduct towards you, since the hour of our first meeting, and I can find absolutely nothing therein, which could have encouraged or even sanctioned you, in such a wild plan as this—you cannot be quite yourself to-night—let us forget this unpleasant episode, and return to the ball-room. I regret having come here at all."

"And you think I suppose, that I will pocket my emotions with such a dismissal as this? Are you a tyrant altogether?" he asked in terrible anxiety—then suddenly changing his tone, he appealed, "Honor, you know it is not we who control our destinies, it is not we who create or guide our propensities, is it *my* fault that I have fallen in love with you? Is it your fault that you are beautiful and loveable and grand? I have striven with a mighty struggle to overcome my passion, but fate had another will. You are a woman—kind, good and true, you profess to understand the human heart; now mine is before you in all its blank misery—be merciful Honor—I will love you and cherish you all my life long—I will be your most devoted friend—I will sacrifice every evil for your sake, and learn from you how to do what is right and good—say you will consent to take me and let me not face the future with despair in my soul—do not raise my hand in temptation, for remember if the heart cannot grant life it can grant death," Honor gasped—

Guy opened his eyes, and tried to read the face of this mysterious man. Even Guy, schooled as he was in the catalogue of this unfortunate's crimes, almost pitied him now, and had she been an unsuspecting girl, would most certainly have yielded to his passionate request—he could scarcely expect that Honor would act otherwise, until her voice broke the awful silence and said,—

"No more of this, Mr Standish! You are speaking the language of the wicked, and it is offensive to me; if you value my regard at all, do not strive to lessen it—you have been plain and abrupt with me, let me be the same with you—I can never be more to you than I am at this moment— all the devotion and love you offer me is no temptation, I may tell you though, it most likely will yet flatter a worthier girl than I, your name may yet be gladly shared by a better deserving woman, this I earnestly wish you—but as I can never, positively never, be a degree nearer to you than I am to-night, let us drop this painful subject, and bury it with the other follies of our past."

Vivian Standish stood up straight and grand-looking before Honor, as she spoke the foregoing words. He was, evidently, not prepared for this, he hesitated for one instant, deliberating with himself, and as Guy saw his mortification and disappointment, he could not help feeling that in one of their successes depended the other's misfortune—he began to hope again; he could see the struggle in the face of the rejected suitor, he might have pitied him in the end but for the words of sneering retort that burst from the white lips at this same instant,—

"Well, it was not my luck to be the first—poor me! How could I have the audacity to seek a hand that is waiting for another's grasp? But though you scarcely deserve it, Miss Honor, I will tell you to give up cherishing the forbidden image that fills your heart—a man whom your kind guardian has turned—"

Guy winced, and Honor, raising her bare white arm in the moonlight, in an imposing gesture, cried,

"Stop, sir! How dare you address me thus? I have answered your questions, be kind enough to leave me now, your presence is growing distasteful."

"I knew that would hurt," was the jeering retort, "but bless your little heart, give him up, it is an empty ambition to pine over, he cares no more for you than that pillar there," pointing to the one which concealed Guy, "but then there is more romance about forbidden—"

"Leave me, I command you, before I am provoked to speak my mind as plainly as you deserve to hear it," then, pointing inward, she repeated emphatically, "Go!" and with a broad smile of mock courtesy he bowed before her, kissed his hand insolently to her, and saying,

"You dear little thing, I really half like you," he skipped towards the ball-room, leaving her alone in her excitement.

The noise and merriment had not ceased all this while though this little room was quiet and deserted, whether the guests had suspected who the occupants were, and in consequence kept at a respectable distance; or whether it was just as pleasant to deposit themselves around on the stairways and in the corridors, during the intervals of the dance, I can scarcely tell, but in any case the cosy *boudoir* was, left entirely to the young hostess and her admirer.

When Vivian had passed into the ball-room again, Honor turned in, and sank into a low chair by the window, she touched one opened half, peevishly with her tiny slipper, to shut out the night air that had begun to chill her; a loose white downy wrap that she had thrown over her shoulders hung negligently to one side, leaving one round white arm bare, her head rested languidly back on the crimson cushions of her chair, the little fringes of pearls that nestled at her bosom on her low bodice, shivered and trembled as she breathed. The gas burned very low within, and with its subdued light only helped to make Honor still more like a spectre than she was. Guy, standing quite close to the panes, could see the gray pallor that had come over her agitated face, her eyes wore that far-off look that is not of earth, as if she were peering through the impenetrable, into mysteries beyond, he leaned forward breathlessly, noiselessly, and looked into the room, she was alone—quite alone, looking pale, and ill, and tired—Oh, how he longed to comfort and protect her! how his heart ached for the right to do so!

"What are men made of, and what puzzling secret tendency is common to every human heart, that such situations as this totally overcome it? What is there in the smile of a woman, in the glance of her eye, in the sound of her voice, to speak so eloquently to man's susceptibilities; why does one woman never see this power in another, nor one man in his fellow-man? Is it a portion of ourselves that we recognize in those we love, that their loss is our wreck and their gain, our fortune? Oh mysterous mysteries of the human soul, ye taunt us and teaze us, but ye are our life, our happiness, and our hope, may we never solve your fascinating secrets, 'tis their obscurity is their charm."

Guy was a strong-minded, unromantic fellow, truly enough, but as he looked in upon the graceful reclining figure of the girl he loved, lying still and thoughtful among the cushions of her chair, his heart was just as inflamed as any victim's of sentiment, his passion filled him, welled up to his very lips so violent, so strong, that it burst its feeble limits and broke out in one resistless word, "Honor" the very sound of his own voice startled Guy, he could have rushed from the spot into oblivion forever, had not the still reclining figure grown suddenly animate, like a spark of electric fluid the word vibrated through her whole frame, she started suddenly up with an expression of blank dismay on her face.

"Honor," he repeated, more calmly this time, "do not be frightened, it is only I."

"You! Guy Elersley," she almost gasped, looking full into his eyes, with a half wistful gaze.

"Yes, Guy Elersley," he answered, a little sadly, "am I intruding?"

"It is not that," she said hesitatingly, "but your presence surprises me so, I thought you were—"

"Miles away, no doubt," he interrupted, "but now that I am really here, am I ever so little welcome?"

"You do not need to ask that," Honor said a little formally, "I think the name of the house is too well-known to necessitate such a question."

"Oh, Honor, you know I do not mean that, why don't you spare me a little?" Then looking anxiously around the room, he asked, "am I safe here, to speak to you without fear of being seen or interrupted?"

"May be not," she faltered. "We had better go outside."

She drew the thick heavy folds of her white wrap over her head and shoulders, and stepped out under the shelter of the portico. When they reached the farthest end she stood, and said in amused surprise—

"What business of terrible importance could have brought you here in this way?"

"I cannot tell you that immediately," he answered seriously, "but you will know it by and bye, Honor," taking her hands in his, and looking meaningly into the deep gray eyes, "will you be vexed if I tell you that I have just overheard your conversation with Vivian Standish?"

"Not half so much as he would be," she answered good-humoredly, "have you been playing eaves-dropping?"

"In a sort of a way, yes, I was startled by you both, while stealing an entrance, and I slid behind that pillar there for protection, and of course had to stop there then."

"If I remember now, Vivian's words compromised you sadly so, for he spoke rather deprecatingly of the regard that pillar had for me, he must have known you were there?"

Guy wondered if Honor was playing coquette with him now, he could not take his eyes off her, she looked so bewitching and lovely, wound up in her soft white wrappings.

"You are jesting now," he said with a sad earnestness, "Honor, if I had come to tell you, that after many months of suspense and sacrifice, I had sought my way back to you, to tell you that, all my hopes and aspirations were incapable of realization without you, that life would never be more than an empty dream, unless I had won you, would you pity me, and believe me, and relieve me?"

As he spoke, he pressed her slender little hands tightly, and looked hungrily, pleadingly into her large dreamy eyes. She looked suddenly up, and their glances met, may be for four or five seconds, their eyes remained in this fixed gaze, then, there were no words required, Guy Elersley had read his answer clearly, unmistakeably; gently, tenderly, lovingly he placed his arms around her, and gathered her into his close embrace, he felt her shiver in his strong arms, then suddenly remembering himself, he asked—

"Are you cold, Honor?"

"Cold! so near your heart as this, is it cold enough to freeze me?"

"Try it," he whispered, "Oh Honor, could it be possible that life holds so much enchantment for me yet, are you going to let yourself be won by such an unworthy admirer as I am, but at least, I can swear to you, that I have never yet loved any creature as I have you," then interrupting himself as it were, he asked teazingly—"By the way, who is this *other* fellow that Standish accused you of loving?—first, is it true that you did love him?"

Honor fidgeted for a second or so, and then looking shyly up into Guy's face, said—

"I hope you won't be vexed, but I am afraid it is a little true I assure you, I could not help loving him."

"Well, this interests me somewhat," Guy muttered in assumed jealousy. "Who is he, what is he like, what is his name?"

"Oh, he is not very nice," Honor retorted coquettishly, "quite plain, almost homely, I should say, but I can't give his name, he did not give it to *me*—yet."

"Oh, he didn't eh?" Guy said in a voice of gay enthusiasm, "well have you contemplated what you will do when he offers it to you?"

"Well, I suppose, it would be rude to refuse him, and it is one of those particular cases, where I would not like to make the slightest breach of etiquette."

"How considerate you are. Well, come now, tell me his name—you must?"

"If I must, I must, I suppose, but I am sure he would be vexed, if he knew that I told another man his name, on a moonlight night, in that other man's arms, his name is—," and while she hesitated, she looked mischievously up into his radiant face, and then hung her pretty head half shyly, saying, "Oh, *you* know—his name is—Jones!" She turned away her blushing face after this, and Guy, who never felt so happy in all his life before, laughed merrily over her little joke, then stooping to the pretty lips, yet sweet with their delicious confession, he stole the first long kiss of love! A very strong mark of his affection, if we believe, like Byron, that "a kisses strength, we think, should be reckoned by its length." Then the merriment died out of each passionate face, Honor's society gravity passed like a quick shadow over her radiant features; placing both her hands on Guy's strong heaving breast, she raised her wistful face to his, and said so seriously,

"Guy—what has passed between us to-night, has formed the crisis of our lives. We have told one another of our loves, and now we must remember, that whatever comes or goes, we belong by a sacred right, exclusively one to another. We have laid bare our lives' secrets, our confidence has been mutual, let us never forget the responsibilities that these avowals entail, I believe we are both happy to-night, and I hope it is only the beginning of a sequel of many such nights and days."

Guy held her beautiful face in his hands and said in loving earnest—

"You have spoken the very words of my own heart, Honor, not until my soul gives up the capacity to love on earth, will I for one instant prove faithless to the pledge I have spoken to-night." As they walked slowly back to the open window, Guy took occasion to ask Honor, whether she had cared in the least degree for Vivian Standish; Honor only looked up smilingly, and said—

"Don't be jealous of the regard I have bestowed upon him, poor fellow, he deserved it all, but after this, I fear, he may not get exactly his due, however, I have done with him for the rest of my life."

"I have a little dealing to do with him," Guy said meaningly, "and the only condition upon which I could have shown him any leniency, would be that you had ever cared for him; I am glad to know you have not."

"I would not say it, to bring him rigid justice at your hands," Honor interrupted, "but still I would rather declare, that I am entirely innocent of ever having had the slightest penchant in that direction."

"I will not prevent you from making that a boast," Guy answered, "but I might have known, that there could never exist any affinity between you two."

They had reached the doorway now, and Guy took the little hand Honor extended within his own—

"Good night," he said, and then rubbing her fingers caressingly between his warm palms, he said reproachfully:

"I have kept you too long, have I not, your hands are so cold?"

"Never mind that," she answered sadly, "that is not the coldness which makes us suffer most, if you never make me feel any other coldness than this, we will be good friends all our lives."

"Trust me," he answered earnestly, "that time will never come, Honor, when my coldness will chill you, the coldness of death will come upon me first."

Then their lips met again, and with a fond good-night, they parted.

Honor stole back to the little room within. She had not been an hour away altogether, and yet it seemed to her she was a dozen whole years older in experience. The night air had brought a ruddy glow into her pale face, and the happy tale of love just gathered from Guy's lips had kindled a light of dazzling beauty in her eyes.

When she returned to the ball room, leaning on the arm of a fussy old bachelor whom she had intercepted on the way, everyone noticed how bright and happy she looked, and the would-be sages shook their heads and envied Vivian Standish in their hearts for having captured such a prize of rare beauty and goodness.

It seemed quite *apropos* also that Vivian and Honor should evade one another for the rest of the night, this they did, though not in a remarkable way, for Honor was too worldly-wise to betray herself before a ball-room full of people. Their mutual separation gave other young enthusiasts ample chance to amuse themselves with each other.

Vivian Standish moved through the crowd with the same placid, self sufficient smile that he always wore, he was just as interesting and as gay as ever, and to the delight of all the young "fancy free" ladies, sought their society more generously during the rest of this evening at Mr. Rayne's than he had ever done since rumor linked him with Honor Edgeworth.

Miss Mountainhead, who had always had a wild enthusiasm for Vivian Standish without ever being able to form his acquaintance, followed his graceful figure greedily with her calculating eyes through the crowded room to-night. She felt that before this entertainment ended she would have met and spoken to him, and she was beginning to exult therein already. As she sat cogitating thus, a group of young men formed themselves a little in front of her: looking up, she saw Vivian Standish, who was amusing the rest, with some droll quotation. Little did she realize what she was contemplating in this deceptive face, what a perfect practitioner he was in the art of seeming and appearing, commanding his outside as he did, with an ease that did him credit! No one except Honor in all that gay coterie, had ever seen him disconcerted or in a dilemma, even at this very moment, who could tell? not even Miss Mountainhead, who studied him so closely, that he was racked by painful emotions while he was causing merriment to this little group of friends.

It was a splendid opportunity for Miss Gerty's introduction. Bob Apley, her cousin, stood very near her listening to the fun. He knew perfectly well how she longed for this gratification, and yet he would not give it to her now when he had such a golden opportunity. She had waited long enough for him to seek her out, but all in vain she resolved not to let this night pass without satisfying herself.

While she seemingly listened with all cold serenity of countenance to Madame d'Alberg's commonplace remarks, she quietly stretched out her blue satin slipper and proceeded to impress her negligent cousin with the fact that she wanted him to fulfil an old promise of his; not heeding her first gentle reminder, she turned her face with its eager listening expression, very pronouncedly to Madame d'Alberg and repeated the movement with an increased emphasis, resolved to make him notice her before she gave up.

With a curious, puzzled expression on his face, Vivian Standish turned to see who could be paying such marked attentions to his shining "pomps," but his surprise only augmented a hundred-fold on seeing the guilty slipper of a young lady with whom he was not acquainted. She was fanning herself violently as he turned, and without looking back she muttered behind her fan in his direction "can't you introduce me?"

The whole situation burst upon him in a moment, he knew her to be acquainted with every other one in the crowd but himself, and her satin slipper had mistaken him, in its errand, for her "cousin Bob," leaving the impression on his foot. It was too good a situation to forfeit, so taking Bob Apley by the shoulder, he turned him around and said—"Miss Mountainhead, allow me to introduce my friend Mr Apley." The poor girl looked aghast; her confusion left her speechless.

"Is this not the one?" Vivian queried provokingly, "you see I didn't understand from dainty slipper, which friend you could mean."

He had managed that no one heard the joke besides Apley and themselves, but she looked more to be pitied over it than any sea-sick maiden she blushed and stammered, and got confused by turns, until Vivian artfully shifted the topic and asked her for the pleasure of the next dance.

The night sped on, and the Christmas festivities at Mr. Rayne's came to a close. No one was any the wiser of the difference that it had caused between Honor and Vivian, each had succeeded well in deceiving curious eyes, and in puzzling the suspicious, jealous ones who surrounded them.

Amid many glad greetings of "merry Christmas," Honor's guests departed after having enjoyed a most glorious evening in the house of her hospitable guardian.

CHAPTER XXXVII

"The true
And steadfast love of years,
The kindly, that from childhood grew,
The faithful to our tears"

—*Mrs Heman*

The day after the ball, to the great grief of his devoted household, Henry Rayne was much weaker than usual. His tasty, tempting breakfast went back untouched to the kitchen. Although he had not gone down last night to the scene of gaiety below, his intimate and privileged friends had visited him in his own apartments above, and the reaction of this excitement had assumed alarming features to-day.

Honor hastened to his side the moment she had finished a hurried toilet. She got herself impatiently into a wrapper of dark red cashmere, which fastened at the waist with cords and heavy tassels. A little ruffle of lace bound her throat, and her feet were thrust into dainty slippers, her beautiful hair hung in two long braids down her back, making a perfect picture of her *en deshabille*. She walked stealthily to the door of the sick room, and seeing the dim eyes of her loved invalid looking at her, wide open, she ventured in. She advanced slowly to the large chair on which he sat, and half-seating herself on the cushioned arm, she threw her arms around his neck and asked in a melancholy voice, "how he felt this morning?"

"They tell me you are not so well, to-day, is that true, dear old pet, when I have come to wish you the brightest, happiest Christmas day that will be spent on earth?"

The dim eyes of the old man turned lovingly on her for a moment, his lips trembled and his voice was suspiciously shaky as he answered,

"Oh, 'tis nothing to dread, my darling; I am only a little weaker, that's all."

"Yes; but that's a great deal," Honor retorted, "and we must try all we can to restore you before to-morrow. You were getting on so nicely. I wonder what can have made the difference."

"Why, you'll quite spoil me," the gentle voice tried to say jestingly, but the eyes closed languidly and the head drooped helplessly back among the cushions. Two great, round tears stood in Honors eyes, she bowed her head over the suffering form, and kissed the clammy brow of the invalid—she tried to say something of encouragment, but great sobs of stifled anguish choked the passage in her throat.

A moment after, the sick man raised his lids wearily and looked on the girl's clouded face.

"My dear little one," he faltered, as he saw the wet lashes and the trembling lips, "I think, after all, you love your old friend a little bit."

Honor tried to smile through her tears—it was like a little rainbow bursting through the clouds. She knelt down beside him, and looking up earnestly into his face, said,

"You *must* get better, if 'twere only for my sake. I did not realize before as I do now how essential you are to my very existence. I shudder to imagine life without you, and yet if you do not eat and nourish yourself during these days, you cannot—" but she would not say the fearful word—her head fell on his shoulder, and she burst into tears.

"My darling!" muttered the unsteady voice of the invalid, "life was never so seductive to me as it is now, there was a time when I did not much mind whether I lived or died, but that was before I had you,—since you have begun to share my solitary life, turning it's dark, dreary nights into days of happy brightness, I have seen it with other eyes. I have resigned my days as they passed, one by one, with a greedy, unwilling resignation, because I had learned to prize them and to love them, after I had prized and loved you; but, now!—if I must give them up all at once and forever, I am not going to grumble." A low sob of suppressed pain escaped the girl's lips. "I have had more comfort in this world than I ever counted upon," he continued, "I have not known poverty or destitution, and since a merciful Creator has spared me from so many briars and thorns of life, I must be doubly resigned to leave the comforts I have so undeservedly enjoyed, and obey His call."

"Oh! dear Mr. Rayne!" sobbed the girl, "do not, pray do not speak like that, you are so low-spirited to-day. You will be quite well yet, you are strong enough to battle with a little illness. Don't say you are going to leave me so willingly—such a thing would break my heart," and bowing her head on her folded arms, she wept silently and bitterly.

After a moment of painful pause, Henry Rayne raised the drooped head and said in a tender, loving accent,

"We are distressing one another, my darling, run away now, and distract yourself elsewhere. I have much to think about." Honor turned to do as she was bid, but she had barely reached the door when she heard the feeble voice of her guardian calling her back. When she stood before him again, his eyes wore a pensive, distracted look, and his voice was wonderfully serious, as he asked,

"Honor, do you love me now, think you, just as you would have loved your own father, had he lived?"

Clasping her hands in an attitude of thoughtful attention, she answered,

"Have you had any reason to doubt it, my more than father?—have I, in word or deed, ever caused the slightest shade of disappointment to darken your brow, that you deem this question necessary?"

"Tis none of these, my little one," he answered tenderly, "but your words reassure me, and I like to hear you say them"—then changing his tone suddenly, to one of pleading enquiry, he asked. "If I were to wish you to do me a great favor, Honor, which involved the sacrifice of your own feelings, and the risk of your future happiness, but that, I did so, merely on account of my great love for you, do you think, you could be so unselfish, so grand, as to slight every other consideration for mine, and grant me my wild wish?"

With a little wistful, puzzled look on her face, she answered "There is no word of binding promise, that it is possible for my lips to utter, nor no deed bespoken before its committal, by your request or command, that you may not consider, as wholly yours beforehand, for the confidence that you have deserved I should place in you, assures me, that you will ask nothing of me, which is not thoroughly consistent with my welfare and happiness."

"What a noble creature you are!" the old man exclaimed faintly, then turning, and looking her tenderly in the face, he said "I understand, then, that very soon, when I make a request of you, you will not deny me the extreme gratification of giving my request due consideration?"

Impulsively, frankly, innocently, Honor thrust her little hands into those of her guardian, and smiling half sadly, said "A promise is a promise—there is mine."

CHAPTER XXXVIII

"Hark! the word by Christmas spoken,
Let the sword of wrath be broken,
Let the wrath of battle cease,
Christmas hath no word but—Peace"

Christmas day was unusually gloomy at Mr Rayne's this year, but it was quite a voluntary stillness, that reigned there; no one felt gay, or happy, while the loved master of the house was so low. Jean d'Alberg stole around in velvet slippers, and the others scarcely moved at all, as for Honor, she lived in the *boudoir* below stairs lying awake on the cosy lounge, dreaming all sorts of day dreams, while she awaited the end of this painful interruption in their domestic happiness.

The sky was slightly overcast with soft, gray clouds, but the day was fine, and Honor watched the happier passers-by, through the large window opposite, with a lazy, aimless interest.

Vivian did not come at all, as might have been expected, in fact the day was one of the most unusual, that had ever been passed within the walls of this cheerful home.

Circumstances mould our lives so strangely and capriciously, that we are ever doing things, which in after moments surprise ourselves those unplanned, unplotted, spontaneous deeds of ours that spring from the natural source of action, directly as it is influenced by some passing circumstance of moment! These are where the true character is betrayed, and the mind and heart laid bare, in their most genuine state. Afterwards, when everything is past and done, we can judge of ourselves at will, we can regret the golden opportunities, we so foolishly squandered, or we can wonder at the strength and magnanimity, that we had unconsciously displayed in the hour of trial. Only, we know, that such little moments of an existence have but one passage through time, and their foot-prints are indelible, on that well-trodden shore, be they, then pleasant or bitter, to think upon, they must hold their place in our memory, but once, and forever, there is no going back over the mistaken path; the weak steps that have faltered and staggered where they should have been firm and strong, may act as melancholy guides, for the future, but their own deformity is as immortal as the spirit.

This period of Honor Edgeworth's life, fully exemplified these strange theories, as she lay, during the long, dreary hours of these anxious days, peering, with the eyes of her soul, into the dark and mystic realms of the unrealized. There are moments when we seem to coax stern destiny, into a lively confidence, and in one passing glimpse, she shows us many closely-written pages of the "to be."

Experience comes to us in a reverie, or in a dream, and we raise ourselves up from that couch, in a stupid wonder, but our hair has turned white, hard lines mark the once smooth features, we are sadder, wiser, more cautious men, but I doubt if it has made us any better. The halo of golden sunlight that hope sheds over the future, has a holier influence over our present life, than the shadows of suspicion and distrust, with which anticipations of evil and darkness, cloud the vista of coming years.

For a young girl, the possible phases that life may assume is one long mystery and dread. She knows that while she sits in patience and quietude, her destiny is being surely and irrevocably woven by other hands. She will have no bread to earn, no battle to brave, no struggle to conquer, the thorns and briars on the path far ahead are trampled by other feet, and plucked by other hands, and when the miles have been cleared and trodden, the unknown laborer comes forth from his obscurity, and humbly asks her to arise from her quiet nook, to shake off the inactivity of her maidenhood, and to tread the beaten path with him.

After this, if a stray obstacle comes in the way, there are two pairs of hands to gather, two pair of feet to trample whatever obstructs the smoothness of their onward path, each growing stronger and more willing for the others sake, 'till they reach the tedious journey's end, content and happy.

All this Honor tried to see clearly and impartially. It had pleased destiny to send back him whom she loved more than all the world besides, and to send him back unaltered, except that he was handsomer, truer, and more devoted than ever.

The precious secret, that she had guarded for so long, and with such a jealous care, had been coaxed from its hiding-place over the threshold of her lips, and henceforth life meant something vastly different from what it had hitherto been. She had died, as it were, to her old self, she would be re-created to that life of holy mysteries, henceforth a double mission awaited her, double hopes, double fears, those little untried hands—and she raised them before her—must work two shares in the task of life, but there was no discouragement in the thought. Those who have loved as earnestly as she did, will understand why, for there is a secret courage, and a secret strength, for those who have learned to cherish the image of another, and to work out another's welfare.

There is a fortitude born on the altar-step, whereon the wedded pair has knelt, to speak the marriage vows, that none but the wedded can know, that none but souls bound together in a holy wedlock can understand, the fortitude that endures in the breast of a woman, through all the fierce struggles of her married life, that dies only with the last long sigh of relief at the hour of physical death, that is unquenched by the ashes of misery and woe that fall on its flickering flame, from time to time, the fortitude that thrives on sacrifice and endurance, and which if governed by christian motives, becomes a pass-port for the tried soul, before Heaven's far-off gate.

Honor felt beforehand, that the active life which lay untouched in the future for her, was to be sweeter, and happier far, than the passive existence of her girlhood. Matrimony, in her eyes, was a state of such sublime responsibilities, that she could spare her thoughts to no other consideration during these dreary hours of anxious solitude.

She spent her whole days in sketching the hereafter, just as she would have it. Already she was planning her wifely duties, and asking herself how she should learn to be always as interesting and as dear to her husband as she was to her lover. She invented modes of amusement and distraction, that would make home cheerful and fascinating for him, resolving within herself, that, if it lay in woman's power, to attract and bind a man's heart to his fireside, in preference to the old haunts of his pleasures, she would do it.

Two days of close, concentrated, uninterrupted thought, did not leave Honor unchanged. Her face grew serious in its beauty, her step was slower, her conversation less gay, and the distraction of visiting a sick-room, caused no happy re-action to her pensiveness.

It was now the twenty-seventh of December, a wet, rainy, raw day, fine, straight lines of persistent rain fell with a dreary drip on the snow's hard crust, pedestrians with their frozen umbrellas, slipped and slid along in ill-humor; shop-girls and others, who were out from sheer necessity, sped along with smileless faces, and frozen ulster-tails, sulking as they jerked from one icy elevation to another in the flooded slippery walk, and raising their upper lips in ungraceful curves, as their straightened curls stood out in painful stiffness, or fell in wet, clinging bits over their eyes.

Honor shuddered, and shrugged her shoulders as she turned away from the window, and threw herself into a large chair beside the lounge whereon was the sleeping form of her invalid guardian. The girls' face wore a look of dread and anxiety, something of painful impatience hovered around her mouth, and her eyes looked tired and sad, as she laid her head languidly back among the cushions.

"How long he sleeps!" she murmured anxiously, "I don't like this listlessness that has come over him lately; he dozes now all the time." Then springing quietly up, she stole over to the low couch, and stooped down beside the sleeping figure, she rested her chin thoughtfully in her hand and looked earnestly and lovingly into his face. The eyes were only half closed, the breathing was loud and labored, now and then the lips moved convulsively, as if in an effort to speak. Something so unnatural and so forboding dwelt on his kind, dear features, that a racking pain seized the girl's heart as she looked, her throat filled up, and hot, blinding tears welled into her eyes.

What is there sadder or more painful, than the quiet, tearful vigils that some dear one keeps by the sick bed of the unconscious invalid. With scalding tears in her eyes, and a burning misery in her heart, the sorrowful mother stoops over the doomed form of her sleeping child, gently chafing the fevered hands, tenderly cooling the flushed and fevered brow; softly pressing the trembling lips on the clammy cheek of her darling, driving back her agony with a heroic cruelty, lest a sob or a sigh, or a falling tear disturb the quiet slumber of the little one she loves. A mother and her child, a wife and her husband are never drawn so closely together, one never seems so truly a part of the other, as during a moment like this. It seems her baby has never looked so fair, so faultless in its mother's eyes, as when 'tis viewed through the blinding tears, that its sufferings and illness have brought into those searching eyes. A husband's follies and trifling neglects are never so generously forgiven and forgotten, as when, on bended knee, the wife he has loved peers greedily, devouringly into the shadowy face, when clouded by suffering and pain and so it is through all the grades of binding love we never know how dear our parent, brother, sister, friend or lover is, until we have watched the weakened forms struggling with some dread disease, the filmy eyes are then so full of mute appeal, the faint accents of the poor weak voice thrill our hearts with sympathy and love, the pressure of the feeble hand is most powerful in drawing us back, soul to soul, and heart to heart, as though neither of us had ever done such a very human thing, as to wrong one another. Honor tried to think, while she watched through her tears, what it would be to live, without this precious friend forever nigh, to guide and comfort her. In all the days of their happiness together, they had never spoken of the time when a separation must come the farthest flight her fancy ever took, into the distant future, still found her existence blended with Henry Rayne's. To her, he was now no older, no weaker than he was that day, long ago, when first she laid her eyes upon him; and now the horrible possibility of a cruel separation, thrust itself between her tears and the quiet unconscious face before her.

While she watched, sunk in a melancholy reverie, the bell of the hall door gave a great ring, which startled her suddenly, it also awoke the sleeper who looked vacantly into the tear-stained face, and smiled sadly. Honor got on her knees, and looked anxiously at the worn features "How do you feel, my dearest?" she said with an effort to be calm, "Any better?"

"I shall soon be better than I ever was before," he answered quietly, but so seriously that Honor suspected the terrible meaning of his words.

"Don't you feel at all livelier or stronger?" she asked in a despairing tone. "You know you were so down-hearted yesterday. Do say you feel a little relieved?" But before he could answer, Fitts appeared in the doorway, with the letters and packages of the morning delivery. Two were for Honor, and all the rest were Henry Rayne's. She had only given a careless glance at hers, but that sufficed to make her heart beat a great deal faster, and her eyes to sparkle suspiciously. Stooping over the figure of the invalid, she kissed the heated brow gently, and went out, leaving him with his important correspondence. She stole down to the library and gathered herself into a great easy chair, and then, drawing her letters deliberately from her pocket, she broke their seals and straightened out their creases. One was a delicate little note from a girl-friend, which, at any other time, would have been a pleasant distraction, but which was now refolded and replaced in its dainty envelope, unappreciated and uncared for. The other—oh, the other! with its dear familiar outlines, looking almost lovingly into her eyes—"My darling Honor," just as his voice pronounced it. Her hands trembled slightly while they held the quivering sheet, from which she read in silent rapture. When she had finished, and looked at it, and examined it over and over again, she dropped her hands carelessly in her lap and said half aloud.

"What *is* the mystery in all this? I must write and tell him when we expect Vivian again. This is queer! but then Guy knows best—oh yes! Guy surely knows best."

Towards five o'clock of this same afternoon Vivian Standish was announced by Fitts. To every ones surprise, Mr. Rayne admitted him to his presence, though he was feeling more debilitated and ill than usual, and what was more astonishing still, they remained for upwards of two hours closeted in close conversation. They never raised their voices nor made themselves heard during the whole interview, but talked steadily and quietly all the while. Finally Madame d'Alberg, thinking the exertion too much for her patient, bustled into the room and intimated as much to Vivian in the mildest possible terms.

As she expected, Henry Rayne was much weakened by the effort and refused to speak or take any nourishment for the rest of the afternoon. He dozed lazily and languidly until nine o'clock, and then waking somewhat refreshed, he turned towards Jean d'Alberg, who sat knitting by his side, and smiled pleasantly.

"I hope I see you in a better humor than before, you dear old bear," she said quizzingly. "I thought you would eat me up a while ago for bringing you a bowl of rich broth"

"I suppose I do bore you at times, Jean," he said penitently.

"Well, I should say you did," she sighed in mock heroism, "why, you are the crossest, and crankiest and sulkiest patient it was ever a woman's misfortune to nurse. Come now—I am going to dose you with this beef tea, just for refusing me awhile ago." Her quick blustering way always amused and aroused him, and he yielded more easily to her than to the others, but her hand was somewhat nervous to-day as she administered the nourishing liquid. She, too, saw the ominous shadows of a serious change in the pale, wasted face.

"Why, you are as feeble almost as myself!" he tried to exclaim, "see how your hand shakes."

"It is that knitting," she answered distractedly, "but I must finish those silk stockings for Honor's New Year's gift, so I hurry them up while I can sit in here alone."

"For Honor, eh!" he said so pathetically, that the words moved her. "I believe you love her too, Jean?"

"Indeed I do, Henry, she is half my life to me now."

"Thank God," he said, falling back on the pillows, "she will not be so utterly alone when I—" but he turned his face to the wall and stifled the terrible word.

Jean shuddered. Suddenly he turned back again, and looking very earnestly at the motherly woman beside him, he began:

"You will be good and generous to her all her life, will you not, Jean? Spare her all the pain and care and trouble you can, poor little one, she cannot bear much, cherish her always as you do to-day and she will not be ungrateful. Remember that she was all I had in life: property, riches and fame were as naught to me, except inasmuch as they were conducive to her welfare. And now that I must give them all up—"

"Whatever can you mean, Henry Rayne, talking such nonsense; it is a shame, you are the very one will bury us all yet."

He shook his head feebly. "No Jean, I will never see the spring-time," he said sadly. "Life is dear to me," he continued, "I would not now renounce it if I need not, but there is an Almighty will to whose power the mightiest mortal must yield without complaint. I have tasted life's bitter and sweet for three-score years and more, and I must not grumble now when I am called to leave down my weapons and tools. Other hands must tackle the unfinished task, my share is completed."

"You are depressed in spirits to-day," said Jean d'Alberg consolingly, "the sun has gone down, and the darkness always makes you feel blue, but to-morrow you will have abandoned these gloomy reflections."

"I will never abandon them now, until they be realised facts to me," he interrupted wearily—then in a low soliloquy he rambled on, "oh, Honor, Honor! it is only you who beckon me back from the road to eternity, and poor weak mortal that I am, I sigh for you, in preference to the bright promises of a land, where I can benefit you more than I ever could here;" then addressing Jean again, he said, "will you tell Honor that I will speak a few serious words with her in the morning—you can tell her too, for fear she would be surprised, that Vivian will be present at the time."

"I will Henry," Jean d'Alberg answered quietly, rising to prepare the invalid's drinks. As the darkness crept down over the cold, dark streets, Mr Rayne swallowed his evening remedies and retired for the night.

As soon as her charge was snugly gathered into bed, Jean d'Alberg, leaving Fitts in his dressing-room, went quietly in search of Honor. She found her sitting on a low stool, before the grate in the sitting-room, with her elbows resting on her knees and her head buried in both hands. stealing behind her she drew back the bowed head, and looked into the girl's eyes.

"Tears!" she said in amazement, "why are you in tears, my darling?"

"Don't think me weak and foolish, dear aunt Jean," Honor said, trying to laugh it off, "but I was thinking if Mr. Rayne, as I sat here alone, and with the thoughts, the tears came."

Jean looked more serious, than Honor had hoped to see her as she said.

"Well, my dear, trouble comes to the best of us, some time in life. If you hadn't it now, you would have it later, and it makes a less painful and durable impression on the heart while it is young."

"But, dear aunt Jean," faltered the girl, looking imploringly into the elder woman's face, "do you really think that Mr. Rayne is *seriously* ill, I mean—" and as the tears flooded her eyes, Jean d'Alberg kissed her fondly and answered,

"My dear little girl, he is in God's hands, could he be in better? Whatever is best for him, that kind Father will give to him, let us hope and pray—I have just come to you with a message from him—"

"Oh! what is it?" Honor interrupted eagerly.

"He merely said, that he wanted to speak a few words to you in the morning," she said unpretendingly, then going towards the door, she looked over her shoulder, and added, in such an artful, careless tone, "and Vivian Standish will be there too, I understand."

The light in the room was dim and subdued, or Jean d'Alberg would have noticed a strange expression flit across Honor's face at the mention of this news, but the turned down light protected her.

Jean d'Alberg had undergone a wonderful transformation since the day on which she took up her residence in Henry Rayne's house. A little susceptibility was yet flickering, at that time, in the heart that had grown so hardened and selfish, and she had brought it to a spot, where such lingering propensities were easily fanned by every passing circumstance, fanned and fed, until the broad flame was forced to burst out afresh, and consume the harshness and bitterness that had once dwelt with them. Her former virtues budded now anew into a second childhood, adorning her advancing years with gentle, lovable, womanly attributes, that endeared her to every one she knew, and rendered her indispensable to Honor who had learned to find in her all the qualities of a kind, good mother.

Thinking this message that she had just brought Honor needed consideration, Aunt Jean very properly made a trifling excuse to leave the room, much to the distracted girl's relief and satisfaction.

"So—the hour has come," she thought bitterly, when she was left alone, "he has appealed to the only one for whose sake he knows I would lay down my very life" and out of this bitter reflection, the meaning of the strange interview she had held with her guardian so shortly before rushed upon her in an entirely new light. *Now* she knew what Mr Rayne meant by the "favor," which involved the sacrifice of personal feeling and inclination. Yes, *now* she recognized herself the dupe of the man she had so proudly rejected still, in all the bitterness of her reflection she had not felt one reproach against Henry Rayne suggest itself within her. She knew him too well now, to suspect anything else than that in some way he too was tangled in deceptive webs. If a promise from her lips was spoken at his request, she knew that the motive within his heart was nothing, if not her personal happiness, her future welfare, or her gratification for the moment. Still, all that could not cancel the obstinate fact now so bare before her, that in giving her word to her guardian at the time it was sought, she had given the lie to her own heart, and had signed the death warrant of her own most sanguine hopes. Now she must leave her destiny to chance. She would keep her promise—aye, to the very letter—if nothing happened before this terrible to-morrow, she would lay her life at the feet of her benefactor, to dispose of it as he deemed best. Guy Elersley was the man she loved, the only being in the whole wide world that influenced her life, but if it were her fate to be the victim of deception then with the mightiest strength of a womans will will she would cast his image out of her heart forever. She would live for the man she loathed, a life of voluntary martyrdom. The struggle would benefit her in any case. If it were too violent an exertion for her moral nature, it would, in its pitiless mercy relieve her of her burden of life, and fold her weak hands over her broken heart forever. If, on the contrary, her moral and physical strength held bravely out to the painful end, the struggle would cease after the crisis, and leave her unburdened, unfettered, hardened, cynical, cold, selfish, but unsusceptible, and incapable of ever being influenced again by any sentiment or passion, and this terrible experience promised, in any case to visit her but once in her whole lifetime.

While she thought, she remembered the little note Guy had written her that morning, telling her to let him know when her next meeting with Vivian Standish should take place. Instinctively she rose up, as if to leave the room. What could it matter now to either her or Guy whether they had ever loved each other or not? Was it not the only misery of her life that her love had come between her and the will of her kind guardian? Duty is such a sober piece of heroism when one's affections, one's very heart-core are not its sacrifice. The conscientious can go bravely forth to the stern call of duty, the obedient follow out unhesitatingly its command, the virtuous seek it out to accomplish it, but when apart from these moral qualities the heart stands out, a weak victim of passion, that passion that clings to the things it loves, that lives because they live, when a heart thus circumstanced is assailed on both sides, when love and duty put forth their respective claims, who sneers because the noblest, grandest heart gives itself up vith a groan of wretched resignation to the fascination of its love? Men may talk, pens may write, bards may sing of magnanimous deeds in the abstract. In theory we are most of us saints, if we had been our neighbors, we would never have had a fault, but being each one our own miserable, unfortunate self, we must fling ourselves into the open arms of temptation, at the same moment that contrition fills our heart for the rash deed.

Of Honor Edgeworth the reader might expect wonderful moral courage. May be, he too has faith in the fallacious doctrine of worldlings—that he believes good souls have not their struggles. The world generally shrugs its shoulders in the face of the virtuous, and declares that in the hearts of the good there is no moral struggle equal to that which quakes the breast of the evil-doer, but to assure itself of its terrible error, it must play the part of the publican and learn to subdue its passions under a mask.

Honor had determined upon doing the right thing, but she was not perfect enough to stifle the burning sensations that were caused by such a determination. She turned from where she stood and walked mechanically towards the window. The ceaseless drip, drip of the rain on the frozen ground had nothing in it to comfort her, it was pitch dark, and with a shrug and a shiver, she turned wearily away with a long, sobbing sigh and left the room. She crossed the hall into the library, which was quite deserted, though the gas burned, and a bright fire cast shadows on the ceiling and walls around. Throwing herself into an arm-chair before Henry Rayne's handsome *ecritoire,* she drew from a tiny drawer a delicate sheet of note paper, upon which her trembling hand, traced nervously—

"My DEAR GUY—"

Then without waiting or thinking a moment, she hastily wrote on—

"I have just received the intelligence that I am to be interviewed to-morrow morning by Mr Rayne and Vivian Standish. It may be rather late to tell you now, but I did not hear of it until a few moments ago. Mr Rayne never leaves his room before eleven, when he sometimes comes down for lunch—that will probably be the hour of the interview.

"I see no earthly use in sending you this information, except that you have asked me to do so, and *you* know best.
Ever your devoted
HONOR."

She folded it, and sealed it in a dainty little envelope, then thrusting it into her pocket she went quietly into the kitchen and closed the door.

Mrs Potts, sitting artistically on the edge of a yellow-scoured kitchen table, opened her small eyes in blank astonishment at the unexpected visitor. She was surrounded by clippings and sheets of paper, which she scolloped quite tastily to fit the broad shelves of her tidy dresser. As soon, however, as Honor crossed the threshold of her *sanctum,* she skipped down with an agility that would have done credit to a woman twenty years her junior, and wiping the palms of her accommodating hands emphatically in her blue-check apron, she advanced to receive Honor's orders.

"Go upstairs like a good soul, Potts," said Honor, in a hushed voice, "and walk very quietly, and tell Fitts I want him in the library."

"I will, Miss," the old woman said respectfully, and as she stole up the back stairway on her errand, Honor returned as softly to the library, where she stood by the window awaiting Fitts.

In another moment, the door opened, and with his most respectful bow, the man-servant entered the room. Honor's face was serious, and her gaze searching as she asked:

"Fitts, will you do a little favor for me, without telling any one of it?"

"I'm sorry, ye'd think it needful to ask me, Miss Honor, I'd rather, ye'd kno right well, that I'm only too proud when you ordher me, let alone, axm' me, as if I as your equals," and the poor fellow, looking half sorry as he spoke, touched the girl's heart.

"Well, Fitts, I must first tell you a great secret, which I am sure you will be glad to hear," Honor said a little gaily Fitts scratched his ear and looked embarassed, "Mr. Elersley is back again in Ottawa."

"Och don't I hope, 'tis yerself is in airnist, Miss Honor," the old man answered between smiles and tears, "is this really the truth?"

"Without a doubt, Fitts, and to prove it for yourself, I am going to send you to him with this little note, he is staying at the 'Albion,' it is not far, see him yourself, it will please you both; I do not like to ask you to go out on such a dreadful night, but the message is important."

"It will be the powerful queer night, Miss Honor, when I'll not like to go out on your little errands, and more particular when it's to see Mr. Guy that I have loved since he was a lad."

"You are a good, devoted servant, Fitts," she answered, "go now, and don't be long, for you may be wanted."

The man looked proudly at himself as he thrust her dainty note carefully into his inside pocket, and without further ado left the room.

CHAPTER XXXIX

"But bitter hours come to all,
When even truths like these will pall,
Sick hearts for humbler comfort call,
The cry wrung from thy spirits' pain,
May echo on some far off plain,
And guide a wanderer home again."
—Proctor.

Next morning, it was a bright and cheerful sun that streamed mat Honor's window, the rain had all passed away, and the air was mild and refreshing. Hastily dressing herself, Honor hurried to Mr. Rayne's door to ascertain how he had passed the night, but as she reached it, she met Aunt Jean coming out, with her forefinger on her lip, and whispering "Sh—sh—" in such premature warning, that Honor looked bewildered as she enquired the cause.

"He is sleeping nicely now, run off, we must not disturb him, it is such a natural little sleep," Madame d'Alberg said in a low voice.

"Oh, is that it?" Honor exclaimed in great relief, as she turned willingly away and followed Aunt Jean down the broad stairway.

They took their silent little breakfast together, and then as Jean rose, to busy herself about the morning occupations, Honor bundled up a mass of pale blue wool, which she was resolving into a cloud, and went off to the library.

How long she sat there she could hardly say—every now and then she discovered herself, with her hands resting idly on her work, and her eyes gazing vacantly into the space before her; faces, figures, scenes, were passing backward and forward, as she watched, sensations of every kind racked her whole being—but it is not surprising at all, when one considers her in her true light.

People, like her, who have a tendency to intensity in all things have it most of all, in their loves, and hatreds, and no one can understand the nature of her emotions, but those who are themselves intense lovers or intense haters. He who has all his life, loved in a calm, cool, collected sort of way, has never known the acme of moral endurance.

Maybe, the love that I allude to, is not felt more than once in a score of years, by any individual of a community, now-a-days love has been transformed as much as it was in other days, a transformer, men have invaded that dark solemn forest of the soul, where certain passions roamed in hungry fury, wild, and unfettered, these have been secured, in our day, and have been tamed and domesticated; our children play with, and fondle, these monsters, that were so dreaded in earlier centuries by gray-haired mortals; let them beware, there is a hypocrisy in this, since hypocrisy is coexistent with life in any of its phases, and some day, the petted tiger or lion will not feel like play, his old nature will seek to assert itself, and then woe to the victim of this terrible caprice.

A sudden stamping in the hall outside, brought Honor quickly back to stern reality the footsteps vanished up the stairway, and she winced uncomfortably as she told herself it was Vivian Standish. Resolving to remain where she was until sent for, she re-applied herself vigorously to her work and avoided further distraction, but what was her amazement when, a few moments later, the door behind her opened, and Henry Rayne, leaning on the arm of Vivian Standish, entered the room. A cry of genuine surprise burst from her lips, as, scattering her mass of wool-work on the floor, she rushed to her guardian's side with joyful greetings.

"Oh, I am so glad," she cried, "to see you downstairs this morning, how much better you must feel?"

The feeble old man tried to smile cheerfully back as he said:

"I have made this effort for your sake, my dear, whether I go back up those stairs again with a light or a heavy heart, depends on you."

A shadow flitted over her face, then looking in supreme disgust on the man beside them, she answered,

"On *me*? Then you know very well that your heart will be as light as a feather, going back."

"Get me a chair, Vivian, boy," said the feeble voice of the invalid, turning toward Standish. He moved a step to do so, and had his hand on a low cushioned *fauteuil*, when Honor rushed before him and laid her hand on the other arm of the chair.

"How can you ask a stranger to serve you, when I am by," she asked, half choked with sobs, of Henry Rayne, "What have I done to merit this?"

As she clutched the opposite side of the chair, her eyes and Vivian's met, there was a flash of contempt and a look of defiant love, and then, with all her woman's strength, she wrestled the chair from his strong hold, and placed it behind her guardian. She refused to sit herself, the folding-doors leading to the drawing-room were partially closed and she stood against them, toying nervously with the massive handle near her. When quiet was restored, Henry Rayne began to speak. He seemed to pass, unnoticed, the confusion of a moment before, and said in the gentlest accents, addressing the girl.

"Honor, we have come here this morning for the purpose of deciding a question which, of late, has received very serious consideration from your friend here, and myself. I am now growing old and feeble, and have all the indications of an early decay in my constitution. Since the first moment that you were given me as a responsibility and a grave charge, my mind has been in a constant worry, lest, in the smallest degree, I would not render you your due as your own father would have done. In all matters, I have tried, as well as I knew how, to place myself in that very relationship to you, and if I have not succeeded I could never know from you, for you have always been a kind, grateful, considerate daughter. What I am about to discuss now, is the very last thing, relative to you, that will abide by my decision. I have, since my recent illness, considered everything that could assist me in securing your welfare, before I go, and as well as my eager, though maybe, not overwise judgment can direct me, I think I have adopted the best plan of all, it needs only your sanction to complete it and set my mind at rest. I will not remind you of your promise to me, because, on second thought, I have learned that to ask you to sacrifice your own heart for my sake, would be enough to taunt me in the other world, so I will merely appeal, showing you that with what discretion some sixty odd years of tough experience have given me, I presume I can direct you now."

The girl, standing motionless by the doorway, looked her guardian fully in the face; she struggled for a moment, a secret, hidden struggle, and then answered calmly: "My dear Mr Rayne, do you not know, that such an appeal as this, is unnecessary? If you have something to command of me, state it plainly, clearly, I will understand it better. You have, it is true, guided me with faultless judgment and discretion, you have been kind, and solicitous and careful from the first moment we lived together. What is it you now ask in return? What do I owe you for such devotion?"

There was a faint ring of reproach in the words, as she uttered them—something which sounded as if she had said "yes, 'tis true you have done all this for me, but was your motive no worthier than to trust to these influences, for a power over me in the future?"

A trifle sadder in his accent, Henry Rayne answered, "Do not put it like that Honor you pain me. It is not a debt—no, no! you have generously paid me, and overpaid the attention I lavished on you, but now, what I want to complete my earthly happiness is this." He beckoned to Vivian, and taking a hand of each, was about to join them, when Honor drew hers suddenly away, and turned pale with agitation.

"I understand," she said huskily, "you wish me to marry *that*" pointing in Vivian's face. "Well, as there is nothing which I could refuse you, I must not refuse you this. It is well you have not asked me to love him, or to respect him, for that is beyond me, but if he wishes to secure me, after what he has learned from my own lips, he deserves that I should wed him, and the consequences of such a harmonious union."

Vivian never moved a muscle; he sat silently, quietly listening to it all. Henry Rayne interrupted gently.

"You are excited, Honor, and hence it is you speak thus, you will think better of it later. Do you promise me, then, to accept Vivian Standish as your husband, showing your faith in my discretion, and proving yourself dutiful to the end?"

There was a pause of a second, the word was on the girl's lips; one other moment and her destiny was sealed: but suddenly a cry of "Villain!" broke through the doorway, and simultaneously, Guy Elersley appeared on the scene.

"Villain!" he cried, collaring Vivian Standish, "how can you stand there and hear this girl give up her name and her honor, into such vile keeping. You are a coward and a blackguard, and I will prove it."

Vivian Standish grasping the back of a chair, stared in furious amazement. Honor, with delighted surprise on her face, now stood defiantly up and looked proudly on, and Henry Rayne rubbed his misty eyes wonderingly, and peered into the face of the new-comer. An exclamation of great joy burst from Honor's lips.

"Guy!" she cried, "you are just in time."

"Guy!" repeated the old man, "did someone say Guy? Quick, tell me where is Guy? Guy! Guy!" and with the words the feeble head drooped upon his throbbing bosom, the eyelids closed wearily, he raised his wasted hands to his aching temples, and with a long, heavy sigh, fell backwards.

Everything else was forgotten, for the ten minutes it took to revive Mr. Rayne. Honor, trembling with fright, supported his head on her bosom, and spoke appealingly to him. After a little his eyelids quivered and opened, he breathed again and sat up.

"Are you better?" Honor asked, bending over him in great eagerness.

"Yes, my dear," he answered kindly, "I am all right now, but where is Guy?"

"Here I am," Guy said, advancing a step, "I hope you will pardon the manner in which I have entered your house, after years of absence, but I have come, and only just in time to vindicate the wrongs of poor, duped victims, and to rescue innocence from the foul grasp of corruption."

"What do you mean, Guy?" his uncle asked in curious consternation.

"I mean to tell my pain and my regret at knowing that while you have forbidden the shelter and comforts of your home to those of your own blood, who have committed deeds of harmless rashness, you have been welcoming and fostering with lavish generosity under your roof a vile man—a wolf in sheep's clothing!"

"May I, as seeming somewhat concerned, ask who this is?" Vivian interrupted in the blandest tones, laying his arm on Guy's shoulder.

"'Tis yourself" Guy cried, shaking him violently off, "you coward! villain! rogue!"

"Guy, you mystify me," Henry Rayne said in strange wonder, "pray explain. Whatever can you mean by such queer conduct?"

"'Tis a painful task, uncle, but I must do it. This man, in whom you have placed your trust, has foully wronged you. He thrust himself upon you with his deceiving manners, and you were content to take him thus. You never questioned him about the past, nor did he care to inform you of his swindling career."

Honor trembled and turned pale. Vivian's eyes flashed fire, and he ground his teeth, while Henry Rayne only gazed in a stupid sort of wonder, while Guy enumerated these dreadful things.

"He was not content," Guy continued, "to shake off that past, reeking with loathsome and dishonorable crimes, but he brought his knavery within these respectable walls—he dared to pay his attentions to your ward, and speak words of forbidden love into her ears, while the crime of having enticed as young and respectable a girl from her comfortable home, to swindle her out of thousands of dollars, which she owned, yet lay unexpiated on the black chapter of his heart."

Guy scarcely pronounced the words when Vivian Standish sprang in mad fury towards him, crying—

"Liar! slanderer!—your words are false!"

"Pardon me, sir," Guy said, in mock courtesy, "for contradicting you, but" (going towards the door) "if you will allow me, I will prove my *false* statements."

All eyes followed him, and to their blank amazement, there stepped into the library from the room outside, a beautiful and sad looking young girl, plainly but neatly clad, and who was followed by two professional looking men, who stood on either side of her.

Vivian Standish gave one quick, searching glance at the features of the young girl, and Honor saw in a moment how every tinge of color died out of his face, a grey, unearthly shadow crept over it, and his features assumed a set expression of misery which almost excited her to pity.

"Do you recognize this *gentleman*, mademoiselle?" Guy said, addressing the girl, and pointing in mock civility to Vivian.

"Oh! yes, sir—I do indeed," she answered in a sweet, melancholy voice, "it is Bijou—see! he recognizes me!"

All eyes were turned on Vivian Standish. He trembled violently. He looked up once, while they all stared him so suspiciously, and that look was directed towards Honor; he saw her clear grey eyes buried in his tell-tale face. He leaned against the tall back of a chair unsteadily, hesitated a moment, and then addressing Henry Rayne, said, in a husky and trembling voice,

"It would not avail me much to try my defence under these crushing circumstances, Mr Rayne, but at least I can have my say as well as the others. I admit that in years gone by, I was guilty of many things of which you did not suspect me, but a man is not supposed to disgrace himself for his whole life because he has at one time committed extravagant follies. I thought I had buried my past forever, or I should never have taken advantage of your hospitality as I have. Guilty as I was, I could not help being influenced by the fascination that bound me to your home—the resistless attractions of that girl," pointing to Honor. "I leave it now, disgraced, condemned, but at least, you, who are all so blameless, can consent not to crush me entirely. In administering justice, be a little kind, my misery is bitter enough—God knows!"

Then Fifine de Maistre stepped forward and laid her hand on the shoulder of the wretched man.

"Vivian Standish," she said, "you have wronged me, inasmuch as a man can wrong a woman; you have driven my good father to any early grave, and blighted every hope I had for the future, and though my heart lies shrivelled and dead where *you* have left it, *I* forgive you!"

At these words, the look of hard contempt in every eye, melted into one of glowing admiration; tears stood in Honor's eyes, though she had worn such a merciless expression before, and Vivian Standish as he raised his face from his trembling hands, looked calmer and more resigned, he turned his eyes on the slight figure standing beside him, and said in a nervous voice of emotion,

"May God bless you, Fifine, you can never regret these words."

Henry Rayne's feeble voice was the next to be heard.

"This strange, painful news," he said, "is a greater shock to me than anything else in the world that I could hear of. I have received you Standish, and treated you as an intimate friend of my family, and had you in return, confined your deceptions to myself, I might yet have forgiven you; but knowingly, to extend your treachery to that innocent and unsuspecting girl, aware, as you were that she was all in all to me, is a base ingratitude that living or dying, I will never forgive. What would she have become? blighted in hopes, ruined in prospects for life, and by my urgent request too, that, she would have been very soon, but for—you," he said, turning towards Guy, "you, my boy, have saved my heart from breaking, though I did not deserve it from you. I suppose it is too late to seek your forgiveness now after I have judged you so hastily, and punished you so severely, but God knows, I have repented of it many a time since."

His voice broke down, into a weak sob, and he bowed his head.

"You think too harshly of me, uncle dear," Guy said, advancing, "for I have long ago forgotten the past; the day I left your house I took my first step to good fortune, and I have never regretted your severity since, though it pained me much at the time. It has all blown happily over now, however, and I have tried in a measure to atone for the folly of my past, let us learn a lesson for the future from the misunderstanding, but in every other respect let us forget that it has ever occurred."

"Bless you, my noble boy," were the words his uncle answered, "you are a treasure, and I am proud to own you."

Meantime, the other two gentlemen, stood watching the strange proceeding, until Guy, remembering them, said—addressing all present—

"These gentlemen will explain their own presence."

Whereupon, one of them, the most respectable of the two, stated in brief, business like terms, that "he had been the family lawyer of the Bencroft's for many years, and that previous to his recent demise, Nicholas Bencroft had laid information with him, against one Vivian Standish, for swindling him out of a considerable sum of money, and that he had come there to see the man identified by the one who knew him best—it being unnecessary now, to tell him, he concluded, that the punishment of his crime awaited him," he then drew back to make clear the way for his companion, who, as he advanced said,

"And I sir, am the person engaged by the father of this young lady, previous to his death, to hunt up the mystery of his daughters' disappearance. The whole catalogue of her wrongs and misfortunes being attributed to you, you are my prisoner, until your trial has taken place."

"May God help me!" came in heart-rending tones from the bowed face of the accused man. "It has all come down upon me together," he moaned, raising his trembling hands to his throbbing temples, then with one pitiful, appealing, contrite look he scanned the faces of all those present, and gave himself voluntarily up, a guilty man, a culprit. He was escorted out of the house where he had shone as a star in the days of his freedom, out of the spot which held all that his poor miserable heart could care for now. Vivian Standish, the bright comet of Ottawa's gay season, seated in a corner of that covered sleigh, on that bright morning, was a hopeless, ruined man, outcast, dejected, wretched.

Fifine de Maistre, in her sad voice, spoke a touching farewell to Honor and Guy and Henry Rayne. The holy resignation of her words, and the Christian spirit in which she forgave her wrongs, had strangely edified her hearers. Mr. Rayne and Honor pressed her very hard to remain and share their hospitality longer, but this she gently declined to do, and with affectionate, grateful thanks to all, and to Guy in particular, she left the house in company with the serious looking elderly lady, who awaited her, the last but one of the interesting personages who had appeared in the closing scene of the strange drama of "a culprits life."

When quiet was restored, and the din of accusing voices had ceased, Henry Rayne looked proudly up at the manly young fellow who stood before him, and said,

"Guy, I can never thank God sufficiently for having sent you so fortunately, in time to interrupt the course of the terrible destiny that I was forcing on to my poor little girl. A little longer would have made all the difference of a lifetime—a young life shattered and crushed in its bloom, and some day *she* would be justified in cursing my memory and my name, after I had tried, in blind love, to secure her unalloyed happiness. I cannot live to return you, in deeds of active merit, compensation for the good you have done me—that I know and regret, but in some way I must find a means of acknowledging all I owe you, my dear boy." Here he hesitated a little, and looking from one to the other of the young people standing before him, resumed.

"I suppose I am more unworthy than ever, to express a wish or a hope now, but let me tell you, before I die, of the wild wish that animated my heart to the very end, the gratification of which, would be the summit of my earthly expectations."

"What is it?" and "speak it!" broke, simultaneously, from the young people's lips.

"'Tis this," he said, stretching out his feeble hands, and taking one of each in their nervous clasp, "'tis to join together both those little hands, by these, my old, trembling ones, that would so unconsciously have wronged them to knit them together in one holy link, that I might fasten, with the last remnant of my lifes strength—that is the old man's ambition now, the ambition of long ago, re-awakened and revived, the plan conceived before the clouds of dissension gathered over our happy home the plan re-conceived when the dark clouds have melted away into obscurity, and threaten us no more."

The hands thus joined, this time lay willingly clasped together. Honor did not seek to snatch hers from the light, warm grasp that held it a prisoner, while Guy gathered in the little trembling fingers into his strong palm, as the miser does the yellow gold he has long coveted. The lovers looked meaningly at one another and then Guy, whose eyes were brimful of unspoken emotion answered his uncle saying,

"You had said you could not live to compensate me for what I have just done. Now, let me tell you that twere worth a whole life-time of wrongs and misfortunes to me, if compensation meant *this*" and with these words he brought his other hand over the willing little captive he already held in one. "It has been the dream of my life too, uncle," he continued, "it has been the only hope that encouraged me through weary scenes of strife and disappointment, and if I can receive it from your own hand, and with your blessing, my cup of bliss vill indeed be filled to overflowing."

"And you, little one?" Henry Rayne faltered, looking up at Honor through his tearful eyes.

"I?" the girl answered with blushing, averted face, "It is the most I had over hoped for. Therein my happiness also dwells."

The old man bowed his head for an instant, and then raised his eyes and scanned the face of his *protégée* curiously.

"Do you mean to tell me," he asked in profound astonishment, "that you have loved Guy Elersley through all these years?"

"That I have," she answered firmly.

"But—" began he.

"I know what you would say," she interrupted quietly. "That a moment ago I was ready to sacrifice my love, to belie my heart, to crush my fondest hope—and that is true, indeed. I was a friendless, helpless, orphan child when you took me under your care, and watched me, and guided me, and gave me every comfort your happy home afforded, in everything you have proved yourself the most devoted friend in the world and knowing this, feeling, realizing this, as I did, could I on the mere account of natural prejudice, deny you the favor you asked of me so humbly? What was my love, my ambition, my hope, to my duty towards you, the representative of my dead father? Nothing at all. I did it miserably, badly, I know. I clung to my heart's inclination with the very last breath of freedom I drew, and then when I had trampled it, though so cowardly, I felt that I had done my very best to repay you your devotedness and kindness. If destiny has pleased to show us that she was only trying us, we at least have given proof to one another of our confidence and love—but I earnestly hope that never again will destiny play the same game with our hearts."

A low sob broke from the old man's lips. As she finished, he drew her gently towards him, and in a voice that shook with pain and emotion, he began:

"Oh, Honor! my dear little one. How could you have tortured your poor noble little heart like this? What terrible things I must have made you do unthinkingly? and I dreaming all the while it was my boundless love alone that influenced me. But believe me, child these feeble, wrinkled hands would burn heroically over the slowest fire before they could be raised in voluntary tyranny over you. I would rather far that these dim eyes became stone blind to the light of heaven than that they should cast one glance of undue reproach upon you. Aye, and my very heart would break within me rather than it should foster one sentiment that was not love for you, and yet, feeling thus, I was driving you to ruin and wreck. Instinct taught you the terrible truth, and you would blight your life rather than not suit the whims of a thoughtless old man. How can I ever look you in the face again? Oh! my dearest child, this indeed is too much—too much—too much" and sobbing violently, the bowed head, with its snow-white locks, fell on the shoulder of the tearful girl kneeling beside the old man's chair. In her gentlest, most childish and winning way, Honor, brightening up her countenance, said to her disconsolate guardian,

"Well, if you are really sorry, as you pretend, it is not a very good proof that you love me as much as you say."

At this the bowed head was raised, and a glance of hopeful enquiry cast on the girl's face.

"Well, it is this way," Honor continued, answering it: "you see, if Vivian Standish had never been encouraged by you, he would never have come here at all, and Guy would never have been alarmed about us, and would not have come back at all, and then, of course, we would never have all been reunited. I would be a gloomy, grumbling old maid, that could never be happy, and life would have been painfully glum for the future, whereas," — and here the old, care-worn face smiled, as it watched the good, kind features of the girl—"you brought everything to a beautiful crisis, by pretending to force another man on me, for I really don't believe now, you meant me to marry him at all," she said, laughing outright, and kissing away the remnants of the old man's grief from his sorrowful face.

"You are an angel of consolation, besides everything else," was all that Mr. Rayne could answer to her pretty speech, but he clasped again the hands of the two young people he loved, and in an earnest, pious tone, he said:

"I give you, one to another: may you live to gladden and comfort one another's hearts, through a long, prosperous and holy life; and remember, that each time you dwell upon the memory of the old man, who was foolish, only in his wild love for you both, that he has begged of God on this day, to sanction this humble blessing by one from on high, and that the desire for your future welfares, was the very last desire he had satisfied in this life and now, my children, I will leave you, I am tired and worn out, and would like to rest. Will you each lend me an arm, as though no estrangement had ever come between us? Come! forgive the old man. Come, Honor! come, Guy! 'tis the last time I will ask you to assist me up these stairs."

"Do not say such ugly, ominous words, dear Mr Rayne," Honor pleaded, sliding her arm in a fond way into his, and with Guy on the other side of him, the old man, smiling happily, was assisted back to his pillows, whence, it may as well be said, he never rose again.

The excitement of Vivian Standish's capture and arrest, with the unexpected circumstances of Guy's return, and Honor's great sacrifice, had only served to hasten the slow progress of a fatal illness. For days after, he weakened gradually, but hopelessly, yet filled with such a holy resignation and peaceful endurance, as could not help softening the terrible grief that would have been resistless, had he suffered without fortitude or hope.

CHAPTER XL

Man's uncertain life.
So like a ram-drop, hanging on the bough.
Amongst ten thousand of its sparkling kindred,
The remnants of some passing thunder shower,
Which have their moments dropping one by one,
And which shall soonest lose its perilous hold,
We cannot guess.
—J Baillie

The tired, spent moments of the old year's midnight, were crawling into eternity, the fierce December wind was sighing out its wearied farewell over the frozen streets; the thick white frosts were gathering on the window panes, in crystal shrubs and icy forests; December was howling, in a spectral voice, the ominous cry of the "Banshee," in anticipation of the old year's death. It was well nigh the hour of another day's dawn, but in the house of Henry Rayne everyone was astir. In the old, familiar home, where we have intruded so often upon happy inmates in their joy, we now steal an entrance, to witness the gloom, the stillness, the oppressive silence of an awful grief. There is a wasted hand lying over the neat counterpane: it is clammy and feeble, there is a feverish brow, tossing on a downy pillow, parched lips, dim eyes, shadowy features, are now what we recognise, instead of the good- natured, smiling face of Henry Rayne, there is labored breathing, causing the weak breast to heave and fall in heavy sobs, there is the sound of stifled weeping and half muttered prayers from those who kneel around his bed. Honor is kneeling at the head, with blanched face, clutching her clasped hands nervously, while her pale lips repeat a supplication for him who is dying before her. Guy, on the opposite side, stands peering eagerly into the face of the doomed one he loves, watching and waiting for the last terrible change that will ever come. Jean d'Alberg, kneeling at the foot, with her face buried in her hands, is stifling the tears and sobs that burst from her weary eyes and breast, and at a little distance away, the two faithful servants are weeping and praying over the last of him, whom they had learned to cherish and idolize.

Suddenly the dim eyes grow somewhat bright, a sweet smile hovers around the mouth of the dying man, he makes a feeble effort to take the hand of his little girl in his. Honor sees it, and quietly lays her cold hand in his, she is conscious of a weak pressure, which almost breaks the bounds of her heroic endurance. Then the dying glance is turned on Guy, and the same effort repeated, he too lays his trembling hand in that of the dying man, beside Honor's, with its last feeble effort they feel the hand of the man they had each loved as a parent attempt to link theirs together, when that is done he tries to move his lips, bending low over him. Honor can catch the words, "Love—one—another," and then the voice fails, after that, she hears stray, broken syllables, "happy," "memory," and "at last."

Guy, taking Honor's hands in both his, across the death-bed, pledges his love for life in a tone so clear and loud that the dying man can hear it, for he smiles, and looks at each, and with the half-stifled words of his blessing, he closes his weary, languid eyes, and his spirit passes away.

All the toil and worry of life have perished with that last long sigh, no more work awaits those weary hands, so Honor crosses them reverentially on the still breast. His dying smile lingered on his dear kind face, even in death, and people as they came and went wiped away a tear and said, "it was easily seen the old man had died with an unburdened conscience." Every one regretted the demise of such an estimable man, the daily papers came out next morning and evening with lengthy obituaries and tributes to the memory of one who was known to be such a valued citizen. The funeral was one of, if not the longest, that was ever seen in the streets of Ottawa, and every man who joined the solemn procession was a genuine mourner for the kind-hearted deceased.

People stared and wondered at seeing Guy returned, but they were also very glad, for he was a universal favorite with those who had known him before.

Through all her bitter grief Honor had shed no tear, though every tinge of color had faded out of her face, and her eyes grew wild and vacant in their gaze. When the bustle, and excitement had all subsided, immediately after the death of Mr. Rayne, Honor had stolen into the room where he lay, in the depths of a handsome coffin, sleeping his eternal sleep, and throwing herself on her knees beside him, she bowed down her head until her own fair, warm cheek rested against the icy cold face of the dead man she loved, here she neither wept nor moaned, but in silent, tearless anguish mourned over her departed friend. She gently chafed the stiff, cold hands with hers, and smoothed back the silver hair from his marble brow, there was a load of crushing weight and pain and care down deep in her poor heart, but still no tear would come to her burning eyes. By and bye, when she had spent nearly an hour beside the lifeless figure she loved so fondly, Guy missed her, and suspecting her whereabouts, came stealthily to the door of the room where their dead relative lay, it was closed, but yielded to his gentle pressure, and opened noiselessly,—sure enough, there she was, still lying beside the dead smiling face, but now she was speaking, in a low, murmuring tone, such heart-rending words as brought the tears to Guy's own eyes while he listened, unnoticed.

"Lonely?" she was saying, in a long sigh, "Oh, yes, poor Honor will often be very lonely for her dear friend and parent, she will look for him in all the dear, familiar nooks where once she loved to see him, but she will always be disappointed, he will never, never see her nor speak to her again. Oh, I might have known," she rambled on, "that this was too much happiness for me—but dear, dear Mr Rayne, open your beautiful eyes and look at me. Just once again, in the old way—we are alone now, will you not say a little word to poor Honor?—See how I kiss you right on your dear lips, like of old, but your lips are so cold, I do not believe you feel or care for my kiss—"

Guy could stand this no longer, he feared the girl's mind would become demented if allowed to continue in such a strain; he stole over, and putting his arms gently around her, he drew her away from the figure of the dead man—

"Honor," he whispered, "you must come away now, this will harm you—you look so tired and ill already, you must take great care of yourself darling,—for my sake, do." Very mechanically she obeyed, and turned away. Guy felt as if in this mutual sorrow, they had been drawn closer together than any other tie could bring them; he raised the pallid, serious face, and kissed it tenderly, saying—

"You must bear up, my darling, for you know what a great grief it would be to him, to know that you suffered so."

"Trust me, Guy," she answered softly, "I will brave it—but then you know, he was my father, and I loved him."

"Yes, that is all true, my love, but you must remember he is better off, and he has left his blessing with us, for all our lives."

"And we will merit it, Guy, will we not, he was so good, so kind, so true?"

"That we will, Honor, I swear it, I will never forget the pledge I spoke into his dying ears."

"Nor I," she answered, in a whisper.

They left the room together, and Honor stole away to her own quarters; she saw no more of her dear guardian after that, until the funeral day, when she pressed the last long kiss of eternal farewell on his cold, unfeeling lips, that was the scene which racked her poor tried heart with all the sharpest pangs that grief doth know she fancied, at that moment her endurance must yield, and her heart break, but she remembered dimly having been carried away to another room, and when she saw and felt again, all was over.

Two days after the interment of Henry Rayne, Guy and Honor sat chatting quietly together in the little sitting-room from whose window, Guy had caught the first glimpses of Honor, on that autumn evening long ago. In a close-fitting dress of heavy black, Honor looked more imposing and dignified than ever: her face was very pale, and there were deep, dark lines under her sad eyes. Guy too was serious, though handsome and careful as ever; their grief it is true, had thrown a heavy pall over the happiness of their new love, but still, each, felt, that it had served only to draw them still closer together, they were now all in all to one another.

"You are looking pale, and ill, my darling," Guy said, rising and throwing himself on the handsome fender-stool at her feet, "I hope you are going to try and regain your former health and spirits very soon."

"Oh, yes indeed, I intend to, Guy," she answered sweetly, "I can do that easily, for your sake."

"Don't forget that you are exclusively mine, now," he said looking straight up into her clear, gray eyes, "and very soon, I want to let every one know it too." Honor smiled sadly.

"Foolish boy," she said, half in soliloquy, "you will have enough of me all your life, take your time now," while she spoke thus, she was burying her gaze in a beautiful little ring, which she twisted thoughtfully around her finger, without lifting her eyes, she said in such a serious tone.

"Guy—I hope you have not forgotten, to balance well in your mind, all the consequences and penalties of the step you are in such a hurry to take— remember that all is not so smooth and tempting as one sees it through the illusionary eyes of a first love. After all, we women, are only human and as likely to err as any one else; let us not then deceive ourselves, that sometimes in our lives, little thorns will not cross our path, and little storm-clouds obscure our bright, warm sun—if you have not prepared yourself for this, it is not now too late—better give in at the brink of a precipice than risk a fall—"

"Honor—your words are strange—maybe true, but not appropriate here, it was your voice, your example, that recalled me from the downward path of recklessness I was pursuing when I met you, I was haunted by your look, and your words always stood between me and evil, at last I fled, I ran away from temptation, I sought a new field of action, I worked in it, ever in the presence of your dear face, looking into your deep eyes, listening to your sweet voice, success awaited me, I rose, higher and higher; prosperity lavished her favors on me, I worked hard to redeem the name I had tarnished, and thanks to you, my noble darling, I have succeeded!"

"You exaggerate a woman's influence, Guy, I admit that there are women who are grand enough for this, but they are very rare; woman, it is true, has much in her power, a great deal in her ambition, but to accomplish all that you say, one needs a loftier stimulant, a worthier motive, than a woman's love."

"Ah! 'tis not you who have tasted the experience," he answered, "'tis I, and now, I answer safely, when asked by a less fortunate man, the secret of my success, 'Go, seek the society of high-minded, noble women, you will learn your duty, from their lips, as none others can teach it,' and believe me, Honor, this I know to have been the rescue of many, and you are the indirect source of all this good. If then, I have learned so much as a stranger to you, is it likely I can ever regret the fortunate step that will bring me under the immediate guidance of your hand and heart? Ah no! Honor, I will never again know what regret is."

"So be it," she answered seriously, looking into the fire, "but why I spoke, is, because so many, in fact nearly every one, enters the marriage vocation now-a-days, as though twere a trifling risk, as though to a woman it were not fraught with the sublimest responsibilities it is possible for the noblest woman to assume, as though it were indeed, nothing more, than the gratification of having secured a husband, the fuss of an elaborate trousseau or the *éclat* of a wedding ceremony. Why are our cities so plentiful of sin and shame, and wrecked youth, if not, because of women who never considered the serious importance of their vocation as mothers, who were unworthy their title of wives, who tired of their self-assumed duties. If any of these destinies awaited me, Guy, I would rather die to-night, than risk them—the thought makes me shudder."

"You, Honor?" he said, viewing her with very evident admiration, "such a destiny as that for *you*, you are jesting, for since you can save, and reclaim others, you know, you are above every taint of evil yourself."

"You still persist in your obstinate view, eh?" she said, smiling. "Well, remember, I warned you in time. I hope there will never be cause for regret in the future."

It was growing late as they sat there talking quietly. The sun-streaks vanished from the window sill; the dark, grey shadows of twilight began to steal around them, but they scarcely heeded the change. They loved one another now with that pure and ardent love which finds all satisfaction, and all comfort in it's own existence. They had not shown their attachment in wild enthusiasm or showy demonstration, but it is not the largest flames that burn the most intensely. The love that lies quietly, unspoken in the heart, the love that endures in silence, that strengthens in solitude, that thrives in hope, is the truest and holiest, and most exalted love of which the human heart is susceptible. Such love never dies. As it has lived, so there comes a time, sooner or later, when the heart's dream may safely float on the surface of the deep, honest eyes, and the heart's desire flow in fitting terms over the unsullied lips. Such a love invariably brings its own reward.

The darkness had nearly spread its thickness from ceiling to floor, when Jean d'Alberg put her head in at the sitting room door, and exclaimed,

"Well, upon my word; such 'two spoons' I never did see in all my life!"

Both young people looked up and smiled.

"If you'll please to substitute two spoons for *tea*-spoons you may come to the dining-room now, for tea is quite ready," she said, disappearing out the doorway again. Hand-in-hand Guy and Honor rose, and went out to patronize Aunt Jean's comfortable table.

Three months after this, on a wild March morning, Guy Elersley and Honor Edgeworth became man and wife. It was a very quiet little wedding in the early, early morning, without any guests or spectators save the priest, who tied the marriage knot, Dr. and Mrs. Belford, of New York, Madame d'Alberg and Anne Palmer, or "Nanette."

There was a tempting breakfast for the little party after the ceremony, to prepare which, good Mrs. Potts had put the very best of her abilities to the test, and before noon of the same day, Honor and her husband, with Nanette and Aunt Jean, were rolling along to their new home.

Mrs. Potts and the faithful Fitts followed later in the season with the furniture and belongings, and all were established in a home full of pleasant distractions and promising happiness but under the same old management as ever, and bound by the same old ties of long ago.

Ottawa began to miss Henry Rayne and his household, and many a word of kind remembrance was uttered as a friendly tribute to their memory.

The wonderful story of Vivian Standish's disgrace never found its way in detail into the gossipping circles of the capital, although there were a few who shook their heads and winked their eyes and affected to know all about it.

Josephine de Maistre had gone back to the peace and comfort of her seclusion, after the critical interview, and no one of Mr. Raynes household had betrayed the secret. There were only a few little unavoidable words afloat, by which the curious public of Ottawa could surmise why Honor Edgeworth had so coldly rejected her handsome suitor at the last moment, and why Guy Elersley had come back in the nick of time, to be reinstated in his uncle's favor.

Honor was the recipient of many dainty notes of well-worded congratulations, and the sweetest sounding—like Miss Dash's and Miss Reid's—were those whose writers envied with a great bitterness the luck of Henry Rayne's *protégée*.

I need not follow the course of events farther than this, although strongly tempted to tell of certain stylish weddings that followed this one in busy succession. My pen would be kinder, if it might, than merciless. Fate to my other heroines, who are threatened to remain "fancy free" for a deplorable number of years to come, and after that—forever.

The married life of Honor Edgeworth could not but be consistent with her single life. In peace, happiness and prosperity, and in the enjoyment of health, wealth and mutual devotedness, we leave our worthy hero and his worthy wife.

May our destinies,—as they unroll themselves from the scroll of time, be as promising, as salutary, and as well deserved as theirs.